Thief
of
Sorrows

KRISTEN M. LONG

Thief
OF
Sorrows

KRISTEN M. LONG

First published in the United States of America in January 2023
by Kristen M. Long Books
www.kristenmlong.com

Thief of Sorrows
Book 1 of the Thief of Sorrows Series

ISBN Hardcover: 979-8-9868360-0-3
ISBN Paperback: 979-8-9868360-1-0
ISBN Ebook: 979-8-9868360-2-7

Cover illustrated by Alice Maria Power
Design and formatting by Whimsy Book Cover Graphics

CONTENT WARNING:

Please be aware that this book does contain scenes of emotional, physical, and sexual
abuse, physical abuse of a child, human trafficking, suicidal ideations, depression,
PTSD, sexual assault, and violence (including but not limited to scenes of torture and
death).

For Kamden,
The heart and soul of this story.
You are not forgotten.

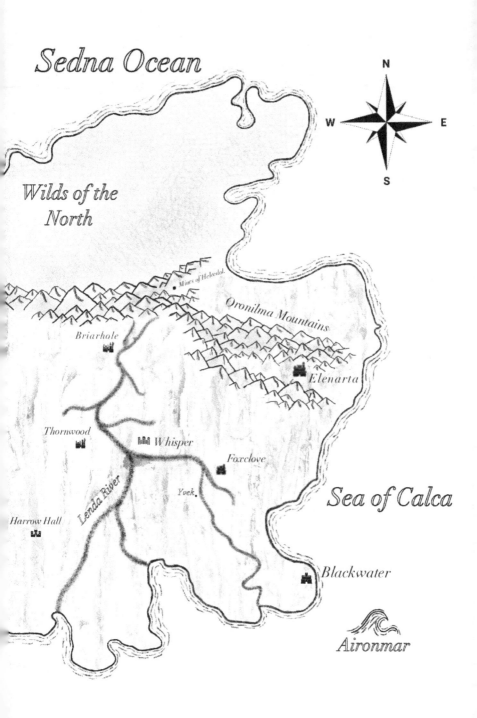

CHAPTER 1

"Well, that's unfortunate," Isolde Cotheran said, as she buried the blade into the hollow of the guard's neck. "We could have been friends."

The blade slid free as he fell to the forest floor, his eyes wide as if in surprise. Garbled words faded away as they escaped his now ruby-red lips. A pool of blood trickled into the dark tunic and dead leaves scattered about.

The usual, rejected thoughts invaded Isolde's mind.

Who was he? Did he have a family? What was his name?

And the worst one of all.

Did you have to kill him?

Shaking herself free, Isolde wiped the blade on the guard's pant leg and pushed it back into the scabbard at her hip. Killing wasn't something she enjoyed. Still, she couldn't risk the guard running back to his platoon and raising the alarm. Without a second glance, she hooked a gloved hand over a branch and began to climb.

Moron. All he had to do was tell me the count of guards on duty tonight. Isolde shook her head. *Hope you thought it was worth your life.* Although she wasn't quite sure even that would have saved him.

She stopped halfway up the massive oak, her steps sure and relaxed as she strolled along a wide branch. The presence of the others hiding amongst the leaves pressed against her skin like a warm assurance. Cries of agony streaming from Foxclove had long since ceased. The many tortured voices were now silent in the dead of night.

"You're quiet. Which is highly unlike you."

Isolde slid her gaze to the shadow lurking on the branch next to her as Fane descended from the canopy. The hawk, now resting on her shoulder, adjusted his footing. The sharp talons burrowed into the leather of her worn, black cloak.

"I just killed a man, Malaki. Do you expect me to be chatty?" she asked, turning her gaze forward once more, away from her second-in-command. "Besides, I figured you would enjoy the silence."

"For you, silence is never a good thing." Malaki paused, hazel eyes gazing out into the dark. His colossal shoulders rolled, the leather strap keeping the sharp, double-edged axe in place strained. "Especially not tonight."

"Why, because a lot of men might die?" Isolde asked, her eyebrow cocking. "By my hand? That's nothing new."

He shook his head. "It doesn't have to be that way."

"Yes, it does." A firm line formed on her mouth as her gaze fell. There was no avoiding it. Not this time. Only one particular question had yet to be answered.

"Do I let the bastard live?" she muttered, crossing her arms. Tiny puffs of breath leaked through the mesh cloth pulled tightly over the lower half of her face. A face that had not aged in thirty-five years. Since her twentieth birthday. Her sun-kissed skin had yet to hold a single wrinkle. Much to Isolde's vain satisfaction. Water slid down the black hood meant to hide her from the world onto the quiet forest below, which was now soaked in blood.

A familiar sigh ghosted from the shadows. His husky voice stirred her humanity, the one part of herself she wished to bury, at least for tonight. "It's a choice you can't take back," said Malaki. Her beacon of light in the storm of uncertainty.

"Obviously," she said. Her emerald eyes, laced with ribbons of silver, rolled in annoyance.

"You are the one who asked."

Her narrowed gaze, ignited by the power stirring beneath her skin, slid to where he lumbered. "Rhetorical questions do not demand obvious, obnoxious answers, Malaki." Irritation blossomed as a whisper of a chuckle filtered through the downpour between them.

"With you, there is no such thing as a rhetorical question, Isolde. Especially when the decision of ending a life is on the table."

"I shouldn't even have to make this damn decision," she said, turning back to the once beautiful territory. Rows of newly constructed barracks surrounded Foxclove manor. A handful of guards patrolled the muddy grounds snaking between the buildings. Light danced off the swords that hung at their sides and tips of the spears clutched in their grasp.

Fane, perched on her shoulder, nuzzled closer, nipping at the edges of her mask. He was white as snow, save for the spots of red that decorated the tips of his feathers that were tucked tightly into his sides. Stretching out the edge of the hood, Isolde created a small crevice for him to burrow into.

"Yet here we are," a light, sensual voice purred from above. Drops of water cascaded over the leather hoods drawn tightly around Isolde and Malaki's faces as the lethal creature stretched precariously. Her dark purple hood and cloak groaned in protest.

"You speak as if we have a choice in this situation, Blyana." Isolde's eyes shot up in annoyance as she ran a gloved finger down the bridge of Fane's beak.

"I'm not trying to change your mind," Blyana said, a sly smile creeping into her voice. "I never have."

Isolde chuckled. "You mostly encourage this kind of thing."

"Bad behavior is my specialty."

"No arguing with that," Blyana said.

"You two keep talking and they're bound to hear us," Malaki rumbled, a whisper of thunder in the night.

"Stop being such an old man, Papa Bear" Isolde said, pulling the lip of the hood further around Fane. "A little danger would be good for you."

His massive shadow shifted, his arms crossing. "I get plenty with you."

"This is true, Isolde," said her weapon's expert, Cillian. His lean shadow broke through the darkness on her left as he took careful steps forward. He kept a steady hand on the trunk of the tree. "Too much excitement will undoubtedly send the old man to an early grave."

A sharp snarl pierced the small space, causing Fane to bat his wings in agitation. A faint light shined in Malaki's gaze as his eyes narrowed. "You'll think old, Cillian, when I throw you from this tree."

"Don't overexert yourself now. I hear that's ill-advised in the elderly." Cillian's voice was filled with humor but Isolde knew better.

While he possessed an air of ease, Isolde could see the stiffness that ran along Cillian's defined arms and the strain at the corners of his dark eyes. His gloved fingers pressed into the bark of the oak. A contact for something steady and immovable. Heights had always been his enemy. An adversary, created in childhood, that had never been defeated.

His obsidian gaze swept up to Blyana where she perched on the limb above. Worry shined in his eyes as they ran over the open air beneath her.

Isolde fought the urge to roll her eyes at his fussing. It was an unnecessary worry. Isolde knew Blyana's abilities and heights were more of an asset to her, than a hindrance.

"Enough, Cill," Isolde said, the hint of a smile coating her words. "I don't need my cover blown with Malaki beating your ass senseless before the mission even starts." Cillian merely nodded, his face fighting a grin as his muscles relaxed a fraction. She felt Malaki's irritated gaze fall to her, but he kept his tongue in check.

"Children," Blyana murmured as she stretched out on the limb, an arm and leg dangling.

"You all remember your positions?" Malaki asked, ignoring her completely.

A beat of silence followed. The only sound was the steady rhythm of the rain. Isolde knew this was coming. Changing the plan, especially now…It would be a problem; she had known it would be. Apprehension prickled at the back of her neck as the heavy silence continued.

They had gone over the plan countless times. Picking apart Foxclove like it was a roasted chicken until nothing was left. They knew every angle, every possibility of failure until Malaki was satisfied and on board. Still, she had known springing this change on him wasn't going to be pleasant either way.

"Answer me," Malaki growled.

"There's been a slight change of plans," Isolde said, the words forcing their way around the ball of apprehension stuck in her throat.

Malaki's head whipped around. "We don't have changes in plans, Isolde."

"Well," Cillian said, as he dusted a piece of bark from the dark green, leather coat hugging his chest, "tonight we do."

"What changes?" Malaki asked. Tension rolled off him in palpable, blazing waves.

"The gold is not the only thing leaving with us tonight," said Isolde.

Malaki froze. Fury planted his limbs firmly in place. The steady stream of power bled through the cracks of his self-control that was ignited in his eyes. "Explain yourself...*now*."

"We received word from our point of contact in Yvek," Isolde said, her voice even and cold. "They found bodies floating down the river just north of the outpost. Tortured...mutilated."

"And?" Malaki demanded. "What does this have to do with us?"

Cillian's words, low and lethal, broke the silence. "It wasn't just the older ones, Malaki. Dagan ordered children to be put to death as well. To prevent the mingling of virya and human blood. Two of which were his own. He couldn't stand the idea of his precious viryian lineage linked to a human."

That particular prejudice had existed since the time of the gods and the War of Kings. Butchering of human children was not an uncommon practice for their kind.

The virya.

Beings blessed with extraordinary abilities that ranged from morphing into terrifying beasts, controlling the elements, and everything in between.

"All because they weren't born monsters," Blyana spat. A spark of power brushed against Isolde's mind. She could feel the spotted leopard lurking just beneath Blyana's skin. A small movement caught Isolde's eye.

Blyana's forefinger scrubbed against her left thumb. The rough, jagged scrapes, Isolde knew, were a nervous tick. A small tattoo of a serpent was etched into the skin, just below the first knuckle of Blyana's thumb. It was symbol, a brand that had marked her as property once upon a time.

Cillian followed Isolde's gaze and quickly wrapped Blyana's twitching fingers in his own, his fear of heights momentarily forgotten. Carefully, he pulled the mask free from his face. His rich, caramel skin, sprinkled with bits of black scruff, glowed in the few rays of moonlight that managed to break through the clouds. Leaning forward, he gently kissed her leather-clad knuckle. A soft purr echoed through the air, the edges of Blyana's face crinkling with a shy smile. Isolde saw the fire die a little in her eyes, but not fully.

She could see the struggle, the anger that guided Blyana. Much like her own, Isolde could sense it crackling through the humid canopy. It caused her own power to stir in response. The irrevocable force pushed forward to meet the potential threat head-on. The rush of chaotic violence strained against her resolve. Fane shifted his weight nervously on her shoulder.

Teeth grinding, Malaki said, "Who did you promise, Isolde?"

Swallowing back the malice, Isolde replied, "A mother of one of the children they found dead." She had seen sorrow before, but not such wretched despair. It was as if the woman wished for nothing more than to slip into oblivion. As if she never existed. With the dead child still clutched to her chest, she begged Isolde, disguised as the Hood, to help those who remained at Foxclove.

"Taking the humans was not part of the plan," said Malaki.

"Since when do we ever stick to the plan?" she asked.

"You shouldn't have made that kind of promise! It puts us all at too big of a risk." He rose from his crouch, the tree limb shaking under his weight. "We're scrubbing this job." He turned on his heel, drops of rain dancing across his hooded head.

"You didn't see what they did to them," Isolde said. Visions of the bodies played in her mind. "Even the infants." She pushed back against the memory before it could consume her completely and swallowed the heavy lump in her throat.

Malaki's hand tightened around a tree limb keeping him rooted. The wood groaned under his unforgiving grip. Rumors had spread throughout Arnoria of the treatment of slaves at Foxclove...but never about the babies.

"It's true," Cillian said, taking a few careful steps to rest a hand on Malaki's shoulder. "I know this isn't ideal, but those people don't have time. They can't wait for us to form another plan before the same thing happens to them. Would you leave them to that fate?"

Malaki shrugged away from Cillian's grip as his hands balled into fists at his side. Isolde wanted the remorse, the guilt for changing the plans at the last possible moment. But none found its way to her heart. *It was necessary*, she told herself. *He wouldn't have agreed if I'd told him before.*

Turning back, Malaki scanned the barracks. They stood like tombs, windowless and devoid of life and hope. With a heavy sigh, he met her gaze and she knew Malaki understood one simple fact. She would go whether he went or not. Without a moment's hesitation, she would throw herself into the pits of hell. It wouldn't be the first time. But leaving her side was not an option. Isolde knew it never was for him.

"How many?"

"What?" Isolde asked.

"How many did you promise to save?" Malaki rasped.

She licked her lips as the answer stuck to the back of throat. "As many as time would allow."

A string of swears whispered through the dark as Malaki's gloved fingers gripped the back of his hood. "We can't save them all," he growled.

"I'm aware of that," she bit back. "There's a small group in the dungeons just to the east, closest to the river. My point of contact told me they were in the worst condition. The ones that probably wouldn't make it much longer."

"The ones that will be the most trouble to get out you mean," said Malaki. The words hung in the air between them.

"The ones that need our help the most." Her voice was hollow, as if she couldn't believe what he was saying.

He took a deep breath, his eyes squeezing shut. "I assume there's more than one boat lurking about downstream."

"You even asking is an insult," Cillian muttered. His fingers toyed with the blades at his side. Isolde looked up to Blyana, who stared down, her cat-like eyes reflecting in the dark. Isolde knew she would follow her lead, no matter where the path led. Along with Cillian. It was Malaki she looked to now.

The hazel eyes she had known her whole life were hard and full of worry. As if he was trying to mentally will her into turning back. She wanted to be angry with him. Angry for not listening, for constantly questioning her judgment. *Even after fifty-five years of being by my side, he still doesn't trust me.*

"The first sign of danger," Malaki said through grinding teeth, "we leave. Whether we get them out or not." His eyes darted to each of them in turn. "We make it home."

Cillian nodded, his eyes shooting up to Blyana, who merely waved her hand through the air in dismissal. Isolde stroked Fane's head, her eyes purposely forward.

"Isolde?"

"Fine," she said under her breath.

"Fine," Malaki bit back. "You and Bly will extract those in the dungeons. Cillian and I will find others that are able to move easier, ones that can help paddle."

"And in small groups," Isolde added. "Few are easier to hide if necessary."

Malaki sighed heavily and turned his attention back to the manor. She could practically see his mind wrapping around the series of new problems that could and would meet them head-on.

Foxclove, while the smallest of the seven territories in Arnoria, stretched out in all directions. It had been the desire of Lord Theort, the previous ruler of Foxclove, to see from all angles. "Nowhere for the enemy to sneak up on me," he had said to her, playfully tugging at her dark brown curls when she was a child. Of course, he had been anticipating an army...not a small cadre of thieves and assassins.

Now, row after row of dirty metal barracks wrapped around the perimeter in tight, uniform rings. Replacing the once lush fields Isolde played in as a girl.

Like a giant, glistening serpent, the Lenda River stood between them and the first row of barracks. It served as the main means of transportation for the coveted goods of many territories. Little rivers sprung from its body, creating small communities and perfect hiding places for those who wished to remain hidden.

Torches perched along the stone wall that bordered the manor fought against the storm. Their flames flickered precariously on their posts, providing little light to what lay below.

"It's smaller than I remember," Isolde said. Memories of running through the lovely wooden halls flashed in her mind. She saw the Lord of Foxclove, his warm, fatherly smile beaming down as she ran past.

"Hmm," Malaki said. "It doesn't even look the same. Not with the barracks." His finger extended toward the manor. "Or whipping posts."

Isolde looked to where he pointed. A small stage, hardly big enough to hold five men, stood before the main gate leading into the stronghold. A platform had been erected, set with a single overhanging arch. In the center was a rope, its end fashioned into a noose. An iron ring was driven into the wood of the four posts used to keep the platform aloft. Streaks of red stained the beams.

Isolde inhaled sharply, her teeth setting beneath the mask. She could feel Malaki's gaze on her. The familiar look of pity she hated was undoubtedly there.

"I see Dagan has been remodeling," Blyana said.

"Lord Theort would not have tolerated such things in his territory," said Isolde. A sick aching filled her chest, squeezing as the words lifted from her lips.

"No, he wouldn't," Cillian said, his mask now secured around his face. "Seems that Dagan didn't heed your warning, Isolde. Must not have made a big impression." A small air of amusement ghosted on the edges of his voice. "Losing your touch are you, Hood?"

Isolde growled, the sound mingling with the light chuckle from Blyana. Fane chirped in irritation, his beak nibbling at her mask. "My warning had the same sting as it always does." Her instructions were easy enough: change the treatment of humans and half-bloods, or die.

Dagan had clearly squandered that warning. Not a hint of change could be seen; if anything,...things were far worse. "It would appear Dagan likes to play games. Even ones that involve the abrupt end to his life."

Along the ridge of the wall, guards walked the perimeter. The tips of their spears shined in the light of the torches. Arrows nestled in the quivers on their backs. Isolde gently stroked Fane's chest, her words bleeding into the air. "If we are going to get them out, the guards need to be taken care of first."

"With pleasure," Cillian said, his voice chipped and ice cold. Blyana's tiny chest rumbled, her eyes igniting as the monster just beneath the surface prowled.

"Easy," Isolde said, her own instincts flaring. "It would be ill-advised for you to transform so soon." She knew Blyana's limits, what triggered her power to come forward and seize control. Anger, revenge, and bloodlust. Much the same as her own. It was a natural reaction for a virya. An instinct that was as much a part of them as their powers were.

Blyana scoffed. "Isn't it my job to tell you that?"

Isolde rolled her eyes. "Fur ball."

"Bossy bird brain," retorted Blyana.

Isolde grinned, her eyes shining with the power coursing beneath her skin, saturating her blood. "If you are going to transform, at least wait for the action. We can't have you burning out in the first few minutes."

"I don't know," Blyana mused. "It might be worth turning into a bloodthirsty monster, deprived of all thought and humanity, to tear apart Dagan and his men one by one."

"Remember the last time you changed?" Isolde asked. "It didn't go so well." They had nearly lost her. The power snuffed out all of who Blyana was, with only the vicious animal remaining. Isolde shuddered from the memory. At how close she had come to being forced to kill her.

"I seem to recall a certain *pigeon* nearly tearing us apart the last time they transformed," Blyana shot back.

"It wasn't intentional." The words felt hollow, wooden in Isolde's mouth, as violent flashes of that day resurfaced. "And I believe you mean a fierce *falcon*. In the end, I didn't hurt anyone…permanently."

"Foxclove could use some permanent damage tonight," Blyana said.

"You know I can't risk it," Isolde said. "Only if I can't shoot a bow or hold a blade would I even entertain the idea. It's not worth it." Some virya rarely transformed for fear of losing themselves to the power that lurked beneath. Their power was simply too chaotic, too unpredictable.

Isolde was one of them.

"It won't come to that tonight," Cillian said. "Not if we stick to the plan." She hoped he was right. The pain still echoed in her bones. A constant reminder of what it felt like to be completely undone.

"Malaki…Cill…start making your way around the outer ring of barracks," Isolde said, her voice firm. "Then move more inward."

Malaki sighed. She could all but see his eyes roll and jaw flex.

"No worries," Cillian said, shifting next to Malaki, who growled. "I'll make sure he remembers." Tiny daggers shined along his belt like a row of teeth in what little light penetrated the canopy as Malaki shoved him back. Cillian gripped the tree's trunk, his fingers leaving small indentions in the wood.

"You are forbidden from killing him, Malaki," said Blyana.

"No promises," he said, his massive battle-axe gleaming from his back. "See you at the river." Limbs found their way to Malaki's feet, as his power created intricate steps that circled the trunk leading to the ground. Cillian followed behind, keeping his hand trailing along the trunk with each step.

"Lazy." Blyana scoffed.

Isolde slowly turned, Fane with her. "Is that the pot I hear calling the kettle black?"

Blyana rolled her eyes. "I'm not lazy. I don't make the plants and creatures around me do my bidding. Where's the fun in that? If I want out of a tree, I jump. Simple as that."

"I'm sure that doesn't bode well for Cillian's anxiety," said Isolde. "What about Malaki's healing abilities? I'll be sure to mention your lack of fascination the next time you need patching up."

"Please," Blyana said, her eyes rolling. "You're the one who cares about scars. You're the vain one, not me."

"I'm not vain, am I Fane?" Isolde cooed, her fingertips scratching his chin. The hawk chirped happily, his eyes closing against her touch.

From the forest below, a chorus of vulgarity filtered through the branches, followed by a growl and the scurrying of feet. "They might actually kill each other," Blyana said, after a moment.

Isolde sighed, a grin tugging at her lips, "Well, it's not like the place is crawling with guards to see them anyway."

Only a handful of uniform-clad guards patrolled the upper lip of the stone wall near the dungeons. One to the east and the other surveying the western border. A thankful smile played on Isolde's lips. At least that part of the plan had been accurate.

"Imbeciles," Blyana mumbled, tucking in a strand of blonde hair and securing the hood around her face and head. "Dagan has become far more lenient in his security since his father's untimely passing. It's almost unfair."

As nimble as the cat lurking within, Blyana leapt down onto a branch beside Isolde. The dark purple of her hood twinkled faintly. A sea of stars danced on her head as she stepped out into the open air.

"He'll regret that decision." Each word sounded odd, distorted as it spilled through Isolde's mask.

A bow and quiver were draped across her back along with a pair of silver-handled swords adorned with intricate carvings of mountain peaks on one and roaring waves on the other. Small, intricate rivers of metal ran along the broad side of the blades. They held a faint, green sheen. A sight that made her blood run cold. Isolde had always thought the blades looking like living metal. A monstrous creation meant to destroy her kind. Various blades were hidden along the linings of her clothes. These too held the same eerie glow. They were the many tools she used to shelve out vengeance.

Confidently, she strode to the edge of the limb and extended her hand. Flapping his wings, Fane jumped forward, his talons fastening around her fingers. He cocked his head to the side, his amber eyes piercing into hers. She could never be sure if he understood her words but a feeling, she didn't quite understand, told her he did.

"Don't come unless it's necessary." His sharp eyes merely blinked back before he flew off, disappearing into the canopy.

She took a deep breath and tugged at the edges of her hood, pleased to find her dark brown hair laced with strands of fiery red was tucked away securely. The familiar tide of adrenaline barreled through her veins. It ebbed and flowed with the power, the life force humming beneath her skin. Her own monster...was awake.

"I do not bow to fear," she said, taking a step out into the darkness. "It bows to me."

CHAPTER 2

Death filled Malaki's nose as he and Cillian raced through the rows of silent barracks. At 256 years old, the smell never grew easier to bear. He fought back the nausea and blinding rage, drawing on his centuries of training to stay focused. Not a soul dared peer out into the night for fear of attracting unwanted attention from the guards.

A trail of dead guards and streams of blood lined the pathways he and Cillian left behind. Throats lay open and lungs were punctured by blades, preventing even a hint of a scream as the guards fell.

"This one," Cillian said, his expert hands roving the shiny new lock at the first barrack door. "Damn it. Dagan's replaced the old locks with elithrium infused ones. This may take a bit."

Malaki remained quiet, his fingers clutching at the handle of his elithrium laced battle-axe. Isolde's twin blades possessed the same material. The deadly metal always made him feel off, on edge. As if his power was being pulled from him little by little. *That's its purpose, I suppose.*

"I wonder how he managed to get some," Cillian pondered.

"Who knows," Malaki murmured. "As long as you keep those gloves on, you'll be fine." In its rawest form, elithrium was lethal to the virya. Its potency, if held in contact with their skin long enough, would pull flesh from bone. But once it was mixed with another metal, it lost much of its power. Depending on the amount of metal and elithrium used, it would only rob a virya of their strength and powers rather than their life. Still, Malaki knew the importance of keeping a barrier.

If a virya was struck by a weapon laced with elithrium, a poison would leak into their blood, preventing healing. Even his magic had its limits when it came to mending a wound caused by an elithrium blade—without the help of the antidote, that is. Still, depending on where the wound was and how much elithrium was in the weapon…it could mean death.

Unease filled him as his gaze swept over the quiet yard. It landed on the farthest building, the one he knew Isolde and Blyana were lurking near. He didn't like her being out of his line of sight. It was a habit he had brought with him from her childhood. A habit that infuriated her to no end.

"She'll be fine," Cillian whispered, clinks of metal pinging off the metallic walls. The sound was far louder in the eerie silence. "You know that."

"Shut up and open it," he ordered.

"Not chatty tonight, I see." Cillian continued to work, his fingers poking, prodding, and turning. Malaki had no doubt in Cillian's skill as a lock pick. It was a talent he had brought with him to Thornwood years ago. A skill he had graciously…and annoyingly taught to Isolde.

"Not when the plan changed," Malaki growled. "Not when she didn't see the need to fill me in."

Cillian looked up from his crouch, his black eyes shining between the slit of his mask. "Why should she?" he asked. "Would you have listened?"

Before he could respond, Cillian plucked the lock from its hinges, gently pushed, and slipped inside. With his back to the door, Malaki followed into the belly of foulness, the darkness swallowing him whole.

"Good evening," Cillian said, his voice echoing against the walls lined with crudely made wooden slabs and broken bodies.

Malaki at last turned to those who now sat straight up in their beds. Their eyes were far too wide for their sunken, dirty faces. He forced himself to relax, the axe hiding behind the broad planes of his back. Chains of iron draped from bed to bed, cutting into skin-covered bone, leaving little room for the captured limbs to move.

"Who are you?" A man whose age Malaki could not begin to guess, rose as much as possible. His unshaven face was hollow and covered in filth.

"We," Cillian said, his gloved finger flicking between himself and Malaki, "are here under orders from the Hood."

"The Hood?" A small girl asked. Her eyes, Malaki noted, were a striking shade of brown...Familiar...far too familiar. Her face...a face he had tried to forget for decades flashed in his mind. Shoving the memory away, he forced himself back into the miserable present.

"Indeed, my lady," Cillian said with a bow, his arm brushing the ground. "At your service. I know these are remarkable accommodations Lord Dagan has so graciously bestowed upon you, but if you wish, we can take you away from this place."

"To be slaves somewhere else?" a woman asked, leaning forward, the chains rattling in a way that set Malaki's teeth on edge. In her arms was a child whose eyes shined with painful understanding. Yet from the lack of food, he wouldn't have guessed him to be older than four years of age.

"Not slaves," Malaki said, meeting every pair of eyes in turn. "But free people. Away from the king and Dagan's reach."

"How can you guarantee this?" she pressed. Her eyes were hard-not with anger but with yearning.

"Have you ever heard of the Hood failing?" Cillian asked, his arms crossing as he leaned against the filthy wall. "I was once a slave on the run. The Hood freed me as well. You can be free...if you choose to be."

Murmurs echoed through the small crowd. Their eyes turned to those they loved for guidance, some for approval. The woman looked only at her child, thinking of a future that was not her own.

"Anything is better than this," she said, her voice cracking. "Even if it is a risk."

Cillian nodded, his deft hands slipping the lock pick back into his pocket. "We need to keep absolutely quiet. No talking, no touching anything. Is that understood?" They nodded in agreement. Their fingers worked quickly on the locks until all were free of their bondage and standing. Or attempting to.

Malaki scanned the children clinging to their mothers' skirts. "You will need to carry them," he said, gesturing to the little ones who shied away from his pointed stare.

The women turned and scooped their terrified children up into their arms. "My arm," one of them said, her eyes full of tears. "I can't lift it." A large dirty bandage ran down the length of her arm, ending at her wrist bone.

"Very well," he said, beginning to strap the axe over his back.

"I'll carry him," Cillian offered, stepping forward, his knives sheathed and hidden from sight. "Wouldn't want you to throw your back out now, would we?"

Fury coated Malaki's tongue like hot lava, his hands balling into fists at his sides. Cillian was already squatting before the child, whose eyes widened in uncertainty. For someone who'd barely reached his forty-fifth year, Cillian was awfully cocky. *He'll pay for that later.* After a few words of coaxing, the little boy left his mother's side and sidled into Cillian's leather-clad arms.

"Quietly," Malaki said. His eyes met all of theirs, ensuring they understood the importance of their silence. They followed him through the doorway. Their steps were a rhythmic beat any virya would have a hard time deciphering from the rain that had begun to fall harder.

He took five at a time, not daring to take the group as a whole. Once through the door, he pointed to the two long boats waiting at the end of the bend.

"Stay here and get the boats ready," Cillian instructed two of the healthier looking men. Their eyes scanned the others, and a look Malaki did not care for crossed their faces. As they turned with the oars in tow, he snatched the ends and held them in place.

"These ships stay here," he ordered, a hint of power bleeding through, igniting his eyes. They stared back at him in terror, their mouths agape. "Remember, we are not like you, humans. A virya, is far stronger, faster...You won't make it far."

They nodded vigorously, their hands shaking around the handles.

With a grunt, he released them to their work. "Make sure they and anyone else we send makes it on board."

"Yes," they said, their hands already busy with the lines.

He ignored the cutting glance Cillian shot him as they ran back through the barracks.

"Why don't you just threaten to take off their heads next time?" Cillian whispered, banking right. "I'm sure that will have the same effect."

"Those cowards would have left them to die." They stopped before another barrack, this one far newer, the lock much shinier than the rest.

Cillian dug for his tools. "You don't know that." He bent down and began his work on the lock. Faint rays of green danced across his gloves.

"Yes, I do," said Malaki. "I know that look."

Metal clinked beneath Cillian's fingers. One of the picks twisted in his grip. "What look?"

"The one that gives away someone's intent to betray. It's the same one I've seen you give me before."

Cillian chuckled, the lock finally giving way. "Only in sparring, my dear Malaki."

"You keep running that mouth of yours," Malaki bit, his temper flaring, "and we'll see if it's just sparring next time."

"I don't know if you could handle me if it became more than a friendly competition. I might accidently kill you." His eyes crinkled, the only hint of a smile hiding beneath the mask.

"There are plenty of reasons for you to keep me alive," Malaki said.

"It certainly isn't for your charming personality," Cillian retorted. "Or to see you sulk around because of the choices Isolde's making."

"What's that supposed to mean?" Malaki demanded.

Cillian sighed, his fingers stilling. "I see that you don't approve. It's written all over your face. With any decision she makes, there is resistance from you. It makes her second-guess herself." He turned back to his work, the dark hood shaking slightly. "Every decision she makes, she thinks it's the wrong one. No matter what she does, she will be wrong in your eyes."

Malaki looked down on him, his eyes wide with incredulity. "Do you agree with her? Changing the plan last minute, leaving me in the dark?"

"Partly," he admitted with a sigh. "I understand changing the plan right before it's about to begin is not the way to go about it. That robbing Dagan of every last coin in Foxclove was the goal…But what choice did you leave her, Malaki? You can't seriously expect her to leave them here like this."

"I've known her since she was born," he hissed, his teeth grinding. "I think I know her a little better than you."

"Then you're a fool if you didn't see this coming," said Cillian, an edge carved into his words. "You can't expect a flower to grow in the shade of a towering oak."

Malaki growled, his eyes igniting.

"All I know," Cillian said, "is that I see someone wanting to do good in a world that hates her for it. That wants to kill her for it. Good people get tired of being good to ungrateful people, Malaki. Eventually, she will too."

The lock fell away but neither of them moved to open the door. Instead, Cillian stood, his fingers slipping the pick back into his pocket. "I'm trying to stave that off as long as possible. It's very difficult to fight upstream your whole life. She will find her way, but she doesn't need someone constantly second guessing her…especially you."

Malaki squeezed his hands into fists as a heavy sigh broke through the mask. "I know she cares. She's lost so much, more than any one person deserves to." He refused to meet Cillian's probing, observant gaze. Rain pelted his hood, hiding his face even more. "It is her biggest fear. Losing those she loves. What loved ones remain, anyway."

"She cares about them." Cillian's arm waved around the compound. "All of them. You can tell by the risks she takes for them…she cares." While Cillian's eyes were those of someone no older than twenty-five, Malaki could see years of anger shining in their depths.

Twenty years had passed since Isolde caught Cillian sneaking into Thornwood, pilfering the pantry of what scraps he could find. He wasn't sure if it was their shared love of blades or sweets that captured Isolde's heart and led her to offer him a place in their cadre. Either way, Cillian had become a whetting stone for not only Isolde's skills…but Blyana's as well when she too joined the fold ten years later. And a pain in Malaki's ass.

"Again," Malaki said, shoving his shoulders back, his eyes cold. "Something you don't need to tell me."

Sarcasm etched into the lines of what little Malaki could see of Cillian's rich, caramel skin. "Of course. I just had to make sure you weren't forgetting anything, old man."

The groan from the door masked the growl seeping through Malaki's teeth. A small whimper greeted them, the sound ghosting through the damp, putrid air. Mud licked at the soles of their boots as they walked soundlessly through the barrack.

These beds were smaller, Malaki realized. Tiny bundles lay under dirty sheets of burlap that rose and fell in rapid procession. Carefully lifting a corner, he stifled a hiss of fury. A child, no older than four, was clutching a newborn. Around them was a woman, or what remained of her. No muscle was left on her bones, just a thin sheet of pale, bruised skin. His eyes, roving over them, determining how best to move the small family, halted when they found hers staring.

They were wide and a stunning shade of deep blue. Like early day break. "Hello," he said as gently as possible, dropping to one knee beside her.

"Hello," she said in return. "Have you come to take me from my children? Have the gods called me home at last?" Her voice was so calm, so serene, Malaki knew it meant only one thing. She was preparing to die.

"No," he said, his voice soft and warm as an afternoon breeze. "I'm here to take you all somewhere safe. You and your children."

She shook her head, a dampness spilling over her eyes, making them impossibly bluer. "I can't."

"Why not?" he asked.

Removing one thin arm from around her children, she threw back the sheet to reveal what once used to be her legs. Anger like Malaki had not felt in so long surged forward, his eyes shining. He gripped the frame of the too-small bed, needing something to ground himself, to slake the fury.

"I tried to escape with them," she explained, fingers rubbing the deformed, constricted legs as if willing them to move again. Not a single bone was straight. "I was given a choice. My legs...or my children."

"I can carry you," Malaki said, his voice a hollow plea.

She shook her head. "I will not put myself before them." She smoothed out the pale, blonde curls from the little one's face.

"We can get you help," he pushed, knowing exactly what she was about to ask of him.

"There is nothing else in the world I can give them besides this," she cried softly. A stream of tears formed a clean path down her dirt-covered face. "A chance to live."

Malaki could not stand to look at her anymore. He dropped his head, the lip of his hood hiding his eyes. He said a silent prayer of thanks for being the one to find her and not Isolde. But that relief was short-lived as she said, "Do not pity me. The ones in the dungeons have suffered far greater than me."

A slight shuffle to his left drew Malaki's attention. Cillian stood before him. A child was in each arm and one clinging around his neck. Three women stood behind him, their arms full with more children. All were mangled or injured in some way. He looked past them to the bodies that remained in their barracks.

To bodies that did not move...and never would again.

He turned back to the woman. Her face was now smooth as she looked at her children still asleep beside her. "They will hurt you," Malaki rasped.

"Not in any way they haven't already." Her fingers grazed her baby's face, her touch feather soft.

"They will kill you," he pressed.

She chuckled softly, her lips brushing the infant's warm, sunken cheek for the last time. "If only they would be so kind."

CHAPTER 3

Isolde and Blyana crept along the river's edge. Their forms were nothing more than shadows in the night; ghosts of death lurking in the depths. Arrow after arrow flew, cutting through the rain as easily as it did the flesh of those unlucky enough to be in their path.

"We need the silence," Isolde said, her hand holding tightly to Blyana's tiny wrist as she gripped the handle of one of her throwing knives.

"Kill joy." Blyana slipped the blade back into the holster and took off along the river bank. Following closely behind, Isolde made sure to retrieve every arrow if possible, so as not to waste the elithrium tips.

Stopping just outside one of the watchtowers attached to the dungeon, Isolde slung the flesh from an arrow's tip. It landed in a mess of skin, muscle, and blood at Blyana's feet.

"I do hope you clean those," she said in distaste.

In response, Isolde plunged the arrow's bloody head into the puddles at her feet and swished vigorously. "Happy?"

Blyana merely rolled her eyes as Isolde shoved the clean arrow back into the quiver. "Animal."

"Again," said Isolde, pulling out her climbing knives, "pot calling the kettle black." She thrust them into the side of the wall and began to climb. Blyana followed a moment later, staying within the path Isolde set, keeping to the shadows.

Breaching the lip of the wall, they worked their way south. Isolde had an arrow raised and ready. "I am *not* an animal," Blyana said, seething, her eyes narrowing.

Isolde chuckled. "Really? Then why stay in the hayloft?"

"If you must know it gives Cillian and me some...privacy."

Isolde stopped, her head turning to look back, a mischievous grin on her face. "You do have a room. Both of you do, as a matter of fact. With wide, comfortable...*durable* beds. Ones that aren't suspended twenty feet in the air."

A pause in the rain opened a window for Isolde to see the wicked grin shining from Blyana's eyes. "Rooms with very thin walls," Blyana said. "As for the height...well, let's just say a little bit of danger does wonders for Cillian in bed." Footsteps cut their words short. Just around the corner, Isolde heard the distinct sound of a button coming undone and a steady stream of urine splashing against the stone surface.

Keeping away from the puddles, Isolde rounded the corner and gripped the back of the man's greasy, unkempt hair and shoved. His face collided with the stone wall in a sickening crack. He fell in a heap of urine and grime at her feet. Small specks of blood dripped down the side of the wall.

Blyana peeked around the edge, her head tilting sideways. "So rude. You could have at least let the man finish."

"Patience is not one of my virtues," Isolde said, her lip curling.

"That's an understatement."

"Lucky for us," Isolde said, "they left the dungeon doors unguarded." They perched along the outer most wall to the south. It was the one barrier to the river and boats that waited to take them to freedom. A small opening set with rusted bars gave a view of the massive, heavy doors leading down to the belly of the hell below.

"Probably afraid of a little water," Blyana said, securing the final bonds around the guard's wrists.

"This coming from the fur ball who hates to swim. I'm sure you'd sooner see someone drown than set one toe in water."

"I suppose that would depend on who is drowning," she hissed. "Although I can't think of anyone worth the effort."

Isolde grinned, her eyes searching the still grounds below. Foxclove was as familiar to her as Thornwood. She knew it all nearly by memory. Her many trips with her uncle, Alaric, the Lord of Thornwood, to discuss trade deals with the late lord had been worth it.

They left the unconscious guard tied and gaged just inside one of the nearest watchtowers, his pants still down. Neither Isolde nor Blyana deemed his privacy something worth wasting their time on.

The tower's inner staircase led to the lowest level without another interruption. Heavy rain continued to fall in sheets, creating large puddles in the center of the courtyard.

Isolde motioned a finger forward, and they crept along the wall behind discarded whiskey and wine barrels. Each step was silent, not even the water's broken surface betrayed their presence.

Staying out of the dying torches' traitorous rings of light, they slid along the wall. A single guard passed by, his eyes red and unfocused, the stench of ale coating the air around him.

Isolde notched an arrow and took aim, her arm locked. But just before the arrow released to find its mark, the man turned back to the doors. The look in his eyes stilled Isolde's hand. She knew that look. It was one of shame and self-loathing.

His stubble-covered jaw clenched and unclenched as if he couldn't decide which path to take. A war raged in his gaze, his bare hands balling into fists only to fall slack again at his waist. With a heavy sigh, he turned on the spot and continued on his way. A slight slump of his shoulders forced her arm down and the string to relax.

"What burden are you carrying?" she asked. They watched until he disappeared from sight, allowing them to slip through the doors to the dungeon unseen and unheard.

"Awfully generous of you," Blyana said looking back out into the night.

"I have been known to be quite generous on occasion."

"Not that generous." Blyana snorted. "Why spare him?"

Isolde shook her head as she turned the corner. "I don't know. There was something in his eyes…Regret perhaps? Maybe I wanted one less death on my mind."

A foul stench of body odor, blood, and waste that began at the door only grew until Isolde's eyes were watering. The mask helped a little, but not enough to completely block out the smell. Blyana held the back of her hand to her mouth as she gagged.

Torches lit the spiral staircase leading down into the belly of the fortress. Sniffles and cries echoed off the cold, stone walls before the landing appeared. On the last step, Isolde peeked around the corner.

Each wall was lined with cages. Their height was barely adequate for a full-grown man to stand up straight and not nearly long enough for them to lie down comfortably. At the far wall hung a pair of shackles, rusted and jagged. They were connected to a chain, fastened to a wheel, allowing the torturer to raise a victim as high as they desired.

A pool of fresh blood painted the straw and stone beneath. Next to the shackles, hung a whip with three tips of sharp elithrium iron. Their ends dripped with a faint sheen of blood and flesh.

Forcing herself to focus, Isolde slung the bow over her back and crept forward. Each cell was equipped with a pair of shackles anchored to the wall and a cot just below them. Isolde pushed forward, refusing to let her thoughts wander.

Mercifully, not all of the cells were occupied. Only three at the far end, closest to the whipping stage. *They must have wanted an audience.*

On the right, nestled in the back of the cages, sat a small child and an elderly woman. Not wanting to scare them and draw the guards back down, Isolde gently tapped her knuckle on the bars. They were newly installed, free of blemish and wear. Dagan had done some remodeling here as well.

They both jumped but remained quiet, a scream clogged in their throats. The woman looked at Isolde in disbelief but the child merely said, "It's you, isn't it? You're the Hood!"

"At your service," Isolde said, her arm sweeping widely across the ground as she sunk into a deep bow. "Where are the others?"

"They were punished, then sent back to the barracks," he said. His rich brown eyes were far too knowing for one so young. They dropped to his blood-crusted hands. "Or the men took them back to their quarters."

Isolde's gaze flickered to Blyana who's hands slowly drifted to the handles of her daggers. A coldness had crept into her eyes, one Isolde rarely saw anymore. It was as if death itself stood beside her. They had been too late. There was no chance of getting the others out of here now.

Fury licked at Isolde's veins, burning through every ounce of resolve to remain calm. But she knew the danger she posed to the child, to them all if she lost control.

"What do they call you?" Isolde forced herself to asked.

"Cadoc."

"Well, Master Cadoc, who is that over there?" Isolde asked, squatting down next to the little boy who now clung desperately to the bars separating them.

"Mama," he whispered, darkness sweeping into his gaze. "The others were first. The ones that had minor offenses. They were lucky." His voice was so small and hollow. "They made her watch as they whipped us…then Mama was punished."

Tilting her head, Isolde could see the harsh red lines that decorated Cadoc's back. Trails of blood streamed between the cuts that ran down his tiny form.

"I tried to fight them, tried to get to her." Tears fell down his face as pure malice shined in his eyes. "Then I was punished again...and they...they." Cadoc's teeth ground, his eyes squeezing shut. He fisted his hands into his hair, his fingers pulling. "They hurt her."

"It's over now," said Isolde. She knew his pain, knew it all too well. And it was a pain no one could erase. The pain of not being able to save someone you love.

"Why hasn't she woken up?" he demanded, mercifully interrupting her thoughts.

"You let us worry about that," Blyana said, her voice like a soft purr. Cadoc looked to her, suspicion darkening his brow. "We'll help her," she continued, seeing the distrust. "Let's get these locks off first."

The elithrium-plated locks clattered the ground at Blyana's expert touch—a skill she learned from Cillian. Isolde forced herself into the tiny space, her knees digging into the blood-soaked hay. Blyana moved on to the cage to the right.

"You aren't what I expected," Cadoc said as she began working on the shackles around his ankles. "The rumors...the stories..."

Her deft fingers froze around the picks. "Really? Has my reputation preceded me?" she asked forcing her words to be light. "Tell me, what do they say about the Hood these days?"

"They have called you many names—"

"That's not surprising," Blyana said, scoffing.

"Don't interrupt," Isolde said. "Go on."

"Some people," Cadoc continued, his gaze dancing to Blyana, "call you the blade that pierces the night, the gods' vengeance...death's shadow."

"Oh, my," Isolde said, forcing her fingers to return to their work. "I do sound rather terrifying."

"No," he said. "You're none of those things."

"You make me sound almost noble, Cadoc." Isolde smiled sadly to herself. "Like I still have a heart."

"If you didn't have a heart, Hood, then why would you be here now?" he asked.

The bonds fell through her fingers in a loud clatter. She could feel Blyana's concerned gaze on her back from the next cell.

"Well," said Isolde, "don't make it a habit of telling others. I have a reputation to maintain." She forced the words from her throat, shoving down the nearly overwhelming sense of unease.

"I wish I was that brave...that I was strong like you." His head dipped forward, strands of dirty blond hair falling into his face. "Maybe if I was, I could have stopped—"

"You are not to blame," Isolde said, cutting his words off. She held his gaze, willing the words to make sense to him. This was a familiar path, one she had taken before. Many, many times. It was one she knew he would take as well. However, this was not the time or place for him to start the particularly dark journey of self-hatred.

The old woman, whom Isolde could only assume was his grandmother, stood as far as she could and crossed over to him. "The gods are the ones to blame." Anger laced her words as a lifelong hatred burned in her eyes. "They chose to grant only a few with your *abilities* and leave the rest of us to be slaughtered, defenseless. To live and die as property in the service of your kind."

"I do believe that was over five thousand years ago. No one today was alive to see such things come to pass." Isolde stilled her temper, her teeth gritting at the woman's ungrateful, cutting tone. "Would you rather I leave you to your fate until someone not of my kind comes to your aid?"

The woman scowled, the endless wrinkles of her cheeks and forehead deepening. Her arms knitted across her impossibly small chest.

"I didn't think so," Isolde said, her eyes rolling.

Tiny fingers gripped Isolde's gloved hand. "They say you can control the winds, earth, and tides. That you can transform into any animal at will," said Cadoc.

"That would indeed be a feat now wouldn't it?" Isolde said, her lips tugging into an amused smile.

"They say…you can't be killed."

A chuckled flittered through her mask, the sound deep and menacing. "How they flatter me."

"Is it true?" he pushed.

"No," said Isolde. "Anyone can be killed. Even me. It is highly unlikely though. I am, after all, the best thief in Arnoria."

"And assassin," Blyana said, her fingers working against the lock of the opposite cell. "Let's not forget that little asset as well."

Cadoc shook his head. "I think you're more than that."

"Do you?"

"Yes," he said, his tone suddenly serious.

Isolde's eyes slid to his. "And what do you think I am, little one?"

"Something…special."

"Special indeed," said Blyana, her eyes light with amusement.

"I'm nothing special," Isolde said, ignoring her. "I am merely someone who cares enough to act."

"Lord Theort was special too," Cadoc said, his gaze falling to his hands. "He was kind."

"He was a good man," the old woman said. "We were no more slaves to him than his son was. He only claimed us as such because of the king's law. We were his family." A sadness crept into her face. "That all changed when his son took his place after he died. His son is a heartless man raised by an evil, vile woman. We know what danger is, Hood. We live it every day."

A heavy sigh broke through Isolde's lips. "I can see that."

"How can a son be so different from his father?" There was accusation and betrayal in her voice and gaze. They demanded an answer, but it was not one Isolde could give.

"I don't know," she said, pushing up. "Nor do I presume to. Right now, my concern is to get you out of here in one piece."

Without having to ask, Blyana was there, her hand extended and eyes smiling. "Would you mind escorting me out, sir?" she asked.

"Where will you take us?" he asked.

"Somewhere far more comfortable than your current lodgings, Master Cadoc. Now come along. The Hood has other errands to run tonight." The boy smiled and gripped the gloved hand not much bigger than his own. Looking back, he held up his other to the old woman who took it earnestly.

Isolde moved on to the cell on the opposite side. The woman within did not stir at the sound of the door opening or the crunch of hay beneath Isolde's boots. Her chest rose and fell in rapid, irregular jerks.

A pool of blood, black as ink in the limited light, stretched beneath her back. She was naked from head to toe, the remnants of her clothes discarded carelessly in the corner.

Bruises, in the unmistakable shape of handprints, decorated the skin of her arms. Even larger bruises of various healing stages painted her thighs and waist. Isolde gently lifted the broken body into her arms, careful to not touch her back that had been split open.

A small cry of pain whimpered from her cracked, pale lips.

"Shh," Isolde said, her voice barely a whisper. "I'm getting you and your family out of here. What is your name?"

"Martha," she said, her eyes opening slightly. Stunned relief flooded her gaze when she saw whose arms she was in. "I was praying you would find us."

"I'm sorry I didn't come sooner." Yet another guilt Isolde knew would haunt her.

"My son," she asked, her eyes darting around. "Where is my son, Cadoc? My mother?"

"They are with us. We are getting you somewhere safe, somewhere no one will ever hurt you again."

Tears sprang from Martha's eyes as she rested her head on Isolde's shoulder. Isolde hurried back up the stairs, Blyana keeping close behind with the two others in tow.

"I was just doing what he asked," Martha said, her voice cracking. "He ordered me to clean his figurines. The beautiful glass ones in his bedroom. I did the best I could," she cried, "I can't hold them properly like I used to."

Isolde nearly missed a step as she gazed down at the mutilated hands curled against her chest. Bits of her fingers were missing, and others were permanently bent in abnormal angles.

"Did he do that as well?" Isolde asked, a familiar cold fire stirring in her chest.

"He forced himself on me," she said, fresh tears bleeding into Isolde's black coat. "And said he would hurt Cadoc if I did not do as I was told. I cried...and that made him angry. So he took my hands."

The creature prowled once again in her mind, angry and hungry. "It's over now," Isolde said, coming up onto the landing. "That will never happen again."

The grounds were quiet; not a single guard prowled the yard. Even the rain had stopped, stealing the cover they needed. Keeping to the shadows, they made it through one of the side doors of the south wall. Isolde's heart hammered against her ribcage. The smell of Martha's blood soaking into her jacket made it impossible to sniff out any possible intruders.

She glanced back at Blyana who nodded, urging her to move. Cadoc and the old woman kept pace with her, their eyes wide with fear.

At last, they reached a small door next to the large, grated gate. It groaned as Isolde carefully eased it open. She looked around quickly, her hearing pushing into the night for any sign of disturbance. When nothing stirred, she hurried the others through. Making their way underneath the drawbridge, they moved south where two boats waited.

Two figures emerged from the bushes, their eyes glowing. A faint growl filled the night air. Bodies lined the riverbank-some human, some beast.

"Put up a fight, did they?" Isolde asked, stepping over the carcass of a massive coyote. Blood coated the fur at its neck; a wide, gaping wound from an axe disturbed the flow of warm amber hair.

"Somewhat," Malaki murmured, his eyes roving Martha. "You can tell they haven't trained in a while. Lost control within the first few seconds of transforming."

Isolde gently set Martha down on one of the cots in the first boat. Her leather coat stuck to her wounds.

Cillian stepped forward, his jaw tensing. A harsh curse pierced the night as his eyes found Blyana, who was helping Cadoc onboard. Isolde forced him from her mind, knowing all too well what memories were playing out in his head.

Malaki's hands rested on his hips as he looked downriver. "We will keep to the smaller streams until we reach the next stop. I don't want any chance of them getting their hands on her or them again."

Isolde nodded. "Her back is destroyed. See what you can do about healing her. And…whatever other injuries she has."

A pair of arms no larger than twigs wrapped around Isolde's middle. She fought the urge to sling them off. "Thank you," Cadoc said.

Isolde forced herself to relax, to allow her hand to fall on his head. "It was my pleasure, Master Cadoc."

He looked up at her, his gaze searching. "You aren't like the other one."

Isolde shot a look to Malaki, who returned her stare.

"Your eyes," he continued. "They're different."

"Is that so?" Isolde squatted, her eyes level with his. "And whose eyes do mine put to shame?"

"The other hooded man."

"There's two of me?" The tight band around her torso meant to flatten her breasts seemed to grow tighter. It had been Malaki's idea to hide the fact that she was a woman. The band and mask that distorted her voice had done their job well. They were another layer of overly cautious security he had insisted on.

Dimples formed in Cadoc's cheeks as he smiled. She couldn't help but think how adorable he was. "No, he was different. His eyes were black as coal. He was hooded, but the others with him were not. And he wasn't nearly as kind."

"Where did you see these men?" Malaki asked so gently it drew Isolde's attention.

Cadoc looked timidly at the towering figure beside him. "On the road to Foxclove. We were taken from our homes and thrown into Lord Dagan's service when Papa couldn't pay the taxes." He turned back to Isolde. "The other man though, he and his group rescued some of the others bound for here...but not us."

Isolde rubbed her gloved hands together. "Well, I'm glad to have succeeded where he failed. What did these men look like? The ones without masks."

"Dark hair, dark eyes, skin golden...like a warm sunset."

Isolde looked to Malaki again. He dropped his chin in understanding and placed a comforting hand on the boy's shoulders. "Thank you for the information Cadoc," she said. "I hope our paths cross again someday."

He smiled once more before allowing Malaki to steer him towards the cot where his mother slept.

Isolde slowly rose, her knees aching. *Another sighting.* It wasn't the first time this other masked criminal had turned up. Something told her it wouldn't be the last.

"That's interesting," Malaki said, stepping up beside her. His arms were crossed over his chest in a tight knot. "We'll need to tell the others."

"We will." Her voice was low, her mind far away from the shore of the Lenda River.

Malaki nodded with grim understanding, his fingers twitching on the handle of his axe. "Come with us," he said, his voice pleading.

"And where would the fun be in that?"

The moment she saw what state the humans were in, there was nothing in all of Arnoria that would get Isolde to leave. Punishment would be dealt out tonight. Brutal, unyielding punishment. She could see Malaki shudder. The fear and sorrow rolled off him in palpable waves.

She could feel his eyes on her as she counted the arrows in the quiver hanging from her back. Her fingers worked at the straps of her daggers, ensuring their security. Death would be her only companion tonight, and she knew Malaki loathed it.

"Are you really going back in?" he asked.

"You know I am, Malaki."

He opened his mouth, but quickly shut it, having thought better of the words dangling on the tip of his tongue. He nodded reluctantly, swallowing the words he wanted to say in one prideful gulp. "Need someone to stay and help?"

She looked at him sideways, eyes narrowed in a challenge. A small growl echoed through the night.

"Fine," he said, his jaw twitching. "The Hood hunts alone."

Born from the mouths of those she first freed and those who feared her, the name had stuck. In no time at all, she had become public enemy number one to the king of Arnoria, the most sought-after traitor of the kingdom. In the eyes of the sovereign, she was a human sympathizer, someone bent on undermining his rule.

"I won't be far behind you," Isolde assured him.

"If you don't show up by the time we reach the Split," Malaki said, jumping onboard, "I'm coming back for you."

"I don't doubt it."

"Be safe." His words were hushed, a plea to not be reckless, to not get herself killed. "Please."

She nodded, her gaze softening. "Always."

Malaki and two other humans pushed off the muddy bank, their oars working with the current. A tiny shadow hovered downriver. Cillian and Blyana were waiting for the others at the bend in the river.

Isolde turned back to the towering wall. Now freed of the burden of getting them out safely, a familiar feeling emerged. Breathing deeply, she let the cool, wet night air fill her lungs. The cold fire crept forward, blackening her heart. The side of the Hood many feared was falling into place once more. Her power stirred, claws racking against her control, demanding blood...demanding death.

The answer to her question presented itself.

Do I let the bastard live?

It was etched in the rivets on Cadoc's back. The mutilated bones of Martha's hands. The pieces of her soul Dagan stole. The despair of those onboard the boats heading for freedom. And those lost souls cast into the river.

It burned in Isolde's mind as the flames licked at her resolve, stoking her fury. Yes, she had an answer.

She smiled and the monster within...smiled back.

CHAPTER 4

Two men sauntered into the downpour, heavy blades swinging at their hips. Isolde's stomach rolled at the smell of liquor and body odor.

"Lord Dagan really did a number on her tonight," the taller one said, his boots sloshing. "It'll be a miracle if she's able to stand straight again after he opened up her back like that." Isolde held her ground. They were talking about Martha.

"Maybe the bitch will learn to not break things when cleaning them next time," the smaller one sneered, his beady eyes probing the grounds. "Especially if they're some of the Lord's favorites. Stupid humans are completely worthless."

"Well, not completely worthless, Barrow," the other jeered, a sickly tone in his voice that made Isolde's blood freeze.

"That's true," Barrow said, a wicked grin forming over his pock-ridden face. "There's still use for some of those whores. I might find use for one or two of them tonight now that you mention it."

Isolde's fingers ran down the feathered tails of the bloodstained arrows nestled in her quiver. The animal deep within her prowled along her mind...her bones...her blood...begging to let the arrow find its mark deep between his legs.

Not yet. She slowly released the tension in her shoulder, letting the arrows drop. No, she wanted Dagan punished first. *But soon.*

Isolde wasn't surprised to find Dagan's chambers just as easy to sneak into as the dungeon. Not a single guard stood at post outside their master's door. His arrogance and false sense of security had only grown since the passing of his father. She pushed inside and secured the lock quietly behind her.

His scent, overly sweet cherries and rot, filled the room. Dagan's chest rose and fell in peaceful slumber beneath the four-poster canopy bed. The fine silk sheets were crumpled up around his puny form.

Isolde's lip rose over her teeth. Her hands already ached for the blades at her sides. The dark, open wounds on Cadoc's shoulders branded her mind. Martha's blood still soaked her leathers.

Not yet, she told herself, forcing her body to take a seat across the room, next to the slowly dying fire. All the while doing her best to ignore the crackling flames.

Crossing one leg over the other, she hummed softly, her eyes roving the room. Satchels overflowing with gold coins and jewels littered the messy desk to her left. Various paperwork was scattered throughout, numbers and details scrawled across their surfaces.

A small, gilded mirror balanced on the table's edge. Light from the fire winked as Isolde turned it to face her. Glowing emerald eyes stared back. A ring of rich silver encased her pupils and stretched out, shining in a bed of green. They were eyes from the past, eyes of another long since turned to ash.

Gritting her teeth, Isolde secured the mask farther up and pulled the hood down into place. Not that it mattered if the lord saw who she was. He wouldn't have time to tell a soul. Gingerly, not wanting to wake him, Isolde discarded the mirror and pulled a dagger from the pile.

What a fine specimen. She took in the large emerald encased in silver on the pommel. Tilting the blade slightly, a faint sheen whispered from the rivets of metal in the light of the fire. "Elithrium," she said quietly. "That is a surprise."

Only those deemed worthy by the crown possessed such a prize. "What did you do to deserve this?" she mused, her voice audible only to her. It made acquiring the coveted element that much more difficult for her cadre to steal.

Her patience and the sleeping Dagan's time had expired. Looking around once more, she found little interest in what she saw.

"Time to wake up," Isolde said, hammering the edge of the desk with the blade, sending a few rogue gold coins spilling onto the floor. Their metallic music echoed off the stone walls.

Lord Dagan shot up, his eyes heavy with sleep.

"Oh, I'm sorry, did I wake you?"

Exhaustion instantly evaporated from Dagan's eyes and was replaced with what Isolde thought was an amusing attempt at bravery. Jumping from beneath the sheets, he lunged for the sword at the bedside. She laughed at his attempt to free it from the scabbard. It looked ridiculous in his weak, untrained hands.

"You dare break into my manor!" he roared, his voice raspy. He pointed the sword's iridescent tip at her heart.

She smiled beneath the hood, her legs still crossed before her in complete relaxation. "Come now, it's not like I haven't before! You remember." A casual hand brushed her face.

Dagan's palm instinctively flew to his pale cheek, covering the long scar that blazed a trail from his temple down to his less than impressive jawline. A scar on the other cheek matched perfectly. He snarled in response, the sword's tip dropping to the floor, its weight too much for a single hand to bear.

"Do be careful not to cut yourself on Daddy's sword now, little lord. Wouldn't want to get blood on his nice things." She remembered that sword well.

Estetul. *Peace Bringer.*

Even dull from improper care, it would still hold a threat if wielded by someone of consequence. The same fine sheen of elithrium glowed beneath the years of tarnish.

"Shut up," Dagan growled, daring to take a step closer, raising the blade once more. "I am Lord of Foxclove now. Not that weak old man."

"That weak old man was a far better leader than you will ever be."

"Is that so?" Dagan sneered, his malicious eyes cutting. "And where is he now? Oh, that's right, he's rotting away in some field among the bodies of those worthless humans he cared so much for."

Isolde's head tilted to the side. "You didn't even have the decency to bury him in the family crypt?"

"And have him soil our family name?"

"Seems like you're doing that just fine by yourself. Murdering your own blood and all."

His eyes narrowed, lip curling with disgust. "Those mutts were an abomination. The worthless whores knew to take the tonic. Every slave of mine does. If they had just taken it, those children would have never been born. Their deaths are on their filthy hands."

"Whores," Isolde mused, her fingers pressing together. "Worthless…Clearly you didn't feel that way when you found yourself dick-deep in them on a regular basis. If that's your true opinion of them, Dagan, it sounds like you're the one who's desperate."

He hissed but did not dare come closer.

"What's the matter, little lord? Can't get a woman of higher standing in your bed or at least one you don't have to force?"

The sword shook in his hands. *At least he has the mind to be somewhat fearful of me.* Few failed to see how serious she was even after issuing her messy, bloody warning.

He was so pale and fragile in the light of the moon. A sad comparison to what his father used to be. "I must say, I don't see much of him in you. More so your mother, the viperous bitch she was. What a shame," she said.

"You are nothing," he sneered, the copper mustache twitching. "A common street rat who likes to play hero."

"How observant of you. And I'm sure you are well aware of why I am here." Her gaze dropped to the dagger, as if to inspect its blade. The point rested on the tip of her finger.

"Because you're a bleeding heart for useless human trash hiding behind a mask." Beads of sweat rolled down his milky white skin, as he looked longingly to the door. "My father would have loved you."

"Oh, I have no doubt," she said. If only he knew that she had met Theort as the Hood once. That he shook her hand and offered sanctuary if she or the others should ever need it. "Far more than the pathetic excuse for a man before me. A man who took what his father built—a thriving territory of peace and prosperity—shit all over it because you couldn't stand the idea of living side by side with others who were different than yourself. What weakness."

"Bastard!"

"My, my, what manners," Isolde said, her eyes finding his once more. "I see most of your father's men left you. Only the trash stayed behind. Like does call to like, after all."

A small hiss slithered between his bared teeth as a set of fangs descended. "Those who are loyal to the true heir of this place stayed. The others met the same fate as that old man."

"I doubt that very much," Isolde pressed, a grin pulling at the edge of her lips. "Your men wouldn't have stood a chance against Lord Theort's."

Dagan's eyes slowly morphed into slits, and scales began forming above his eyebrows, down to his cheekbones.

"Oh, yes," Isolde mused, her lips turning in disgust, "you most certainly take after your mother."

"You have no idea who you are meddling with. The friends, the power that I now wield."

"Oh, I'm shaking." Isolde's tone was bored, hollow as she leaned back farther into the chair.

"The king has plans for you," Dagan said, licking his thin pale lips. "Plans he has worked tirelessly to perfect. It's going to be so much fun to see your cluelessness righted."

"Oh, no," Isolde said leaning forward to brace her elbows on her knees. "I believe you are the clueless one here. I'm sure you've heard stories, tales of what happens to those who don't do as they're told."

Fear shined in his viper eyes, but she didn't give him time to ponder.

"I gave you ample opportunity to change, Dagan. To be what your father was. Every time you looked in the mirror, in fact, was a reminder. Or did you not understand my instructions? You seemed to that night, when you were begging for your life with piss rolling down your legs."

Dagan struck, his fangs fully extended as he plunged the tip of the sword forward, his voice roaring in anger. Slipping to the right, she dodged the tip with ease as it embedded in the velvet chair. With her fist still locked around the hilt of the dagger, Isolde slammed it into his jaw. The crunch of bone beneath her hand was pure pleasure, drawing out a smile.

He yanked the sword free and charged once again.

The dagger held up against the sword's pathetic blows. She doubted it would have against his father, a bear of a man whose power was one and the same. Venom dripped from Dagan's fangs as he lunged and struck, fighting to get close enough to land a fatal bite.

A great commotion erupted outside the hallway as guards attempted to bust through the massive oak door. *Now they arrive?* A spring of annoyance pricked her mind.

"What a shame. I had intended for us to have more time together," Isolde mused, the blade twitching in her hand, as if it too wanted to bathe in blood.

"I warned you, Dagan," she said, her voice muffled by the mask. He brought the sword down on top of her. As the sword and her dagger collide mid-air, the vibrations ripped through her arm. The glowing, sharp edge of Estetul was only a foot from her face. "Remember that."

A flash of silver whipped through the air and imbedded itself beneath Dagan's exposed ribs. He gasped in pain, the massive sword fell to the floor as he clutched at the hilt of her blade. One of the twins she always carried as the Hood slipped in his grip. Blood pooled around his wet, fumbling hands.

Fear now shined in his eyes as they looked into the Hood's. Hers only stared back in indignation. There was always some form of guilt, a whisper of shame at each death.

But not this one. No, this was an exception.

"I know what you did to Martha," Isolde whispered, leaning forward, her gaze penetrating his. "I know what you have done to all of them." The blade twisted in her grip, drawing out a whimper of agony from his blood-slicked lips. Her power stirred in delight, purring in approval. "Be grateful we didn't have more time."

She shoved him away, yanking the blade free. Blood gushed from between Dagan fingers, spilling out onto his torso. He fell to the floor and did not stir. A stream of blood trickled from the corner of his mouth to join the pool forming around his body.

Isolde wiped the blade on the satin bedsheets and paused at the ornate desk.

"We wouldn't want this to go to waste, now would we?" she said, plucking as many bags of gold as she could carry. She shoved them into one of the leather bags hanging from the wall. As she perched on the lip of the slick windowsill, the door exploded, sending bits of a wood and iron raining down on the lord's chambers. A guard, whose head was rounded with curved massive horns looked around, his ram eyes widening at the sight of his dead master.

Before plunging to the balcony below, Isolde nodded, her hand waving before her in a sarcastic bow, "The Hood thanks you for this fine bounty, gentlemen."

Isolde was out the window and running before any of them moved towards her. Adjusting to the extra weight from the gold, she sped through the bedroom attached to the balcony and turned a corner. She was met with a group of stunned guards. For a moment, everyone froze. Streams of firelight from the windows lining the hall danced off the armor decorating their chests and shoulders.

"One, two, three," Isolde said, her bloody finger pointing at each one in turn. "Unfortunately, there's nine of you and only eight arrows, so looks like some of you are going to have to share."

Then chaos erupted.

Arrow after arrow sung from her bow. The elithrium arrows split the air, finding their marks as guard after guard began to morph. Coyotes the size of small ponies surrounded Isolde.

Her arrows did not falter. She would hold off on transforming as long as possible to save her energy...and sanity. Eight of the nine fell with arrows protruding from their eye sockets. Blood filled the rivets that ran along the stone floor.

A cruel grin hidden by the mask formed as the Hood pointed the final arrow at the remaining guard. "Look at that; I did have enough after all." A dark chuckle leaked through as she made to fire but paused as the beast tucked tail and ran, a small whimper escaping him. She laughed to herself and yanked the arrows free from the carcasses.

Isolde walked under and through the fortress gates. The bags of gold coins were jingling as she came to an abrupt halt. The whipping post stood before her. It was the same one they had spotted earlier, only now she saw the backside of it.

Another beam was nailed between the two back poles on either corner. From it hung nooses far too small and close to the ground to hold anything but a child. Cadoc's face flashed in her mind. As did the woman who inspired her to come. Isolde still felt the burn of the woman's tears as she wept and begged her to help the rest that remained. Had her child died this way? Was their blood painted here too?

Without a second thought, Isolde deposited the gold off to the side behind a discarded crate and ran back into the manor.

An hour had passed before she was nearly done. Dagan's lifeless body hung from the noose at the top. His eyes were open and staring from a scarred, pale white face. Each pole held two fallen soldiers. Their hands were bound and fashioned over their heads.

Large slits decorated their cheeks, blood flowing down their faces as if they were weeping blood. The Hood's calling card.

Satisfied with her work, Isolde placed a hand and foot on the side of the platform preparing to jump down.

"Hold it right there, you bastard!"

Isolde froze, irritated by the delay. Her back was aching from the weight of carrying the bodies. And she was starving. Not to mention Malaki, who was undoubtedly growing anxious and impatient at her absence. Climbing back down, she faced the new comers approaching her from the gate.

She recognized one as the guard from earlier who had emerged from the dungeons. His small form and beady eyes glistened in the fire from the surviving torches. The other was the one she spared, the one with sorrow on his face, the same sorrow that still lingered.

"Is that any way to talk to a guest?" she asked, her head cocking to one side, a hand resting on her hip. She didn't recognize the scent, but she assumed they were some sort of predator. "At least not until you introduce yourself."

"Barrow. Not that it matters much to you. Just wait until the king gets a hold of you," he said, his teeth bared. "You killed a lord."

"Oh, I'm sure His Majesty will find someone else to take his place. Perhaps someone far worthier of the position, but I have my doubts."

"We have ways of dealing with the likes of you in the capitol," he jeered taking a step closer. "Which is where you are going after we have our fun with you. Isn't that right, Victor?"

The other man remained silent, his eyes wide with fear. The grip he had on the sword was bone white.

"Sounds exciting," Isolde bit back, placing a hand once again on the wall. "But I really must be off."

"You're not getting past me, Hood." Small teeth had begun to poke through Barrow's gums, and thick black fur spread over his arms and neck.

"How do you know there is only one Hood?" she asked over her shoulder. Confusion halted his transformation.

Allowing the power to come forth, flowing as easily as water covered a rock, she focused in on what she wanted. A plume of air passed over her skin like silk and grew. She forced the gust out, knocking the two guards off their feet. They landed with a crack against the wall and slumped forward.

Exhaustion forced her to lean against Dagan's dangling body for support. Much like her ability to transform, using her power to manipulate the wind took its toll on her as well. When at last she caught her breath, Isolde leapt from the platform and strolled to the two guards. Her black cape billowed behind her.

Barrow stared forward; the back of his head was crushed. The other, to Isolde's immense surprise, was still breathing. Looking back at the platform, she noticed room for two more spots.

Victor struggled against his bonds, his eyes darting between Isolde and the bodies that surrounded him. "Please, please don't kill me."

"Why not?" she asked, her fingers tightening around the slick, frayed rope. "You make a rather nice edition beside your fearless leader. The one you chose to follow."

His body swayed in the dying rain. Drifts soft mist floated between the barracks.

"Please," he begged, his finger pulling uselessly at the elithrium filled rope digging into his skin.

"Is that what she said?" Isolde asked, dragging Barrow into position. It didn't take long. The dead didn't fight as much as the living. Still, he could have done her the courtesy of not being so heavy. He hung to Dagan's left. "You should have thought about that before you decided to assault an unarmed woman."

"I-I didn't," Victor stammered, snot dripping from his nose, spittle slipping between his lips. "I couldn't do it."

"Even if you didn't, you were still there. And did nothing to stop it." It was purely an accusation. One Isolde knew was correct.

The man closed his eyes and wept. And with that, she kicked the chair from beneath his feet. His body fell through the trap door, the skin of his neck tugging.

The rope frayed then finally snapped at the slit she had created, causing him to fall face first into the mud. A hacking cough exploded from his lips as air found its way once again into his chest.

Before he had a chance to recover, Isolde shoved him against one of his fallen comrades already cooling. "You will not touch these bodies, or any others you may find."

He whimpered slightly, piss soaking his pant leg.

"You will tell whoever arrives that the Hood was here. That he took the justice His Majesty was too cowardly, too lazy, to extract himself. That this is a warning to all of Arnoria. Stop the abuse of humans and half-bloods or suffer the consequences. Have I made myself clear?"

The man nodded again, this time tears streaming from his face.

"You're lucky," Isolde said, pulling the noose away.

"Why?" he asked, his lips trembling.

"If you were guilty of what these bastards did," she said, her chin jutting to his dead comrades, "well, let's just say your balls wouldn't be found in your pants anymore. But a man who would do that to someone doesn't take the time to stop in the pouring rain and look back with remorse."

"I'll do whatever you ask, Hood," he said. "I am in your debt."

The tears continued to flow as she lightly patted his dirty, unshaven face. "Good boy. Don't forget now."

A force struck her left shoulder, causing her to fall back off the platform. Twisting her neck away, Isolde landed on the injured shoulder. A cry of pain exploded through her mask as the bone dislodged from its socket.

"I got him!" a guard yelled from a top the wall. "I got the—"

His words shifted into a fit of screams as Fane cut through the night sky. His merciless talons tore at the guard's eyes as his beak tore flesh from bone. A screech of fury ripped through his beak as a blade embedded itself in the man's throat. Fane hovered for a moment before taking off into the trees. His beautiful, white feathers now covered in blood. To Isolde's dismay, the guard fell back over the wrong side of the wall, taking her knife with him

"Damn it," Isolde growled. Commotion erupted along the wall as more guards emerged. Without waiting, she gripped the shaft of the arrow protruding from her back and yanked. Fire raced through her arm and back. But her lips stayed sealed. Weakness was never shown by the Hood. Or by Isolde for that matter. She looked to Victor, waiting for him to attack in her vulnerable state. But he merely shook his head and whispered, "Run."

Pain ripped through Isolde's arm as she bolted. Blood, warm and thick, slid down her back, soaking her shirt and pants. Veering to the left, she retrieved the bags of gold she had stashed away and broke for the edge of Blackford Forest.

A volley of arrows chased at her heels as shouts from the remaining guards echoed through the trees. The forest floor was a blur beneath her feet. Isolde's shoulder hung at her side, useless and throbbing. The trees seemed to part, allowing her escape from the wave of death she had just unleashed on her neighboring territory.

CHAPTER 5

"She should be here by now." Malaki's gaze cut across the bank and into the trees of Blackford Forest. Not a sound echoed past the veiled darkness.

"She'll be here," Blyana said, her voice low. "You saw her face. I'm sure Dagan is taking longer than she thought."

"That's part of my concern." He knew the need for revenge that plagued Isolde, that had festered in her for so many years. It engulfed his senses as well, but not beyond reason.

Blyana continued to row, her grip on the oar sure and steady. "Isolde is fifty-five years old. You worry too much. She can take care of herself."

"I wish you and Cill would stop saying that!" he snapped. "I worry just enough to keep her alive. You weren't there. Neither of you were." His hands flexed on the handle of his axe, his eyes flickering to Cillian in the other boat. "When we nearly lost her, when I nearly lost who she really is…I can't let her get to that point again, Bly. None of you get a say in how much I should or should not worry about her."

Blyana's fell silent. She was family—Malaki had said as much. But it still didn't change the fact that she had not been there at the beginning. An outsider. Malaki ignored her, seeing her eyes fall before she continued to row. He refused to acknowledge the sting of regret he felt for his words.

A few minutes passed, and he sighed in frustration. "I'm going ashore."

Without waiting, he threw the axe over his shoulder and plunged into the chilly river. His skin sung with relief as the water bled through the layers of blood-soaked leather. He crept just inside the tree line, keeping up with the boats and their refugees as they passed in the night. Solitude had always been his place of refuge and torment. As the silence wore on, doubt inevitably founds it way into his mind.

Was I being too hard on her? He thought back over the years, retracing her footsteps along the way. When Isolde first mentioned this crazy idea of becoming the Hood, it had almost come to blows. He nearly left, refusing to watch as she tore herself apart with grief and bloodlust.

But the night he had decided to leave, needing to see her one final time, he found her in the library. Fast asleep, she had nestled a pair of boots to her chest. His boots. It was an old joke, one that brought a smile to his face. As a child, when it was time for him to go, she would steal his boots, claiming he couldn't leave with bare feet.

She was still that same girl. That same child he made a vow to decades ago. A vow he could never bring himself to break.

A sound off in the distance brought him up short. It was faint but distinct…footsteps. Ripping off his hood, Malaki allowed his power to stir, allowed the animal to come forth on a short, thin leash.

As the sound grew closer, his anger rose, muddling his thoughts into one thing only: kill. A fierce growl ripped through his elongated teeth as the footsteps halted behind a thick brush upstream. Fur splintered through his skin, bones began to bend, and tiny fractures erupted through his frame.

"Is that anyway to welcome me back?" He knew that voice; it was what drew him back into himself. What anchored him to his humanity. The growl morphed into a rumbling chuckle, and relief flooded him.

His magic reached out to her, forcing limbs and weeds to part as she strode forward.

"Trouble?" she asked. "You don't normally ditch your hood so soon."

"I do when I think I might have to transform," he retorted, walking forward, his words laced with annoyance. "When I know I might have to save you from your stupid ideas."

A growl of her own ripped through Isolde's teeth, the lights of her eyes igniting. "You love my stupid ideas."

"Only when they don't get you killed." His hands worked to remove the satchels but stopped at her hiss of pain. "Or hurt." His mind raced with thoughts of anger and concern.

Readjusting the straps on her shoulder Isolde let out a frustrated sigh, ignoring the pain. "It's nothing."

"It's never nothing with you," he muttered. "Let me see."

"It's fine!"

"Isolde, let me see." Sternness coated his words, but bits of worry resided there as well. It wasn't the first time he had seen her hurt, nor would it be the last. Still, each time was like a fresh wound to his heart, a beat of failure hammering into his mind. Even one drop of her blood spilled was too much.

Rolling her eyes, Isolde turned around and pointed to the gaping hole of her cloak. His gentle fingers probed her shoulder that hung at an odd angle. His touch was light, thoughtful.

"Are you tired? From helping the others?" she asked.

As if being summoned, exhaustion raked his nerves, coating his very skin with tiredness. Still he didn't acknowledge it, his mind fully focused on her. "As you are so fond of saying…I'm fine."

He worked his fingers around the edges of the tear and pulled. The fabric tore away like paper, revealing the nasty wound. A small sigh echoed through his lips, the tips his of fingers pushing the edges together. *So close.* Far too close to a point he would not have been able to fix.

"Two more inches and you would have been beyond even my skill to heal, Isolde."

"Good thing Foxclove doesn't train their archers well. Really, Malaki it's fine. I'd rather you help someone else. I'll heal."

"No, you won't," he bit. "A wound from an elithrium weapon leaves your wound to heal like a human's. It would be days before you would fully heal from this."

"You can tell it's elithrium just by looking at it?"

"There's a faint sheen in your blood. Iridescent." He continued to poke and prod. "But thankfully, there wasn't much in the arrow itself. Otherwise, I would have needed the remedy to extract the elithrium first."

He knew she could hear his stress, his concern. There was only so much his power could fix. He was powerful, one of the most powerful earth wielders in Arnoria, but even he had his limits. By helping another, payment was demanded, whether it was from the earth or from his own body. *It's a small price to pay.* He continued sending his strength into her, the tiny fibrous muscles slowly knitted together beneath his touch.

"I'm sorry but it will scar," he said, his hand coming to cover the wound. Hints of elithrium still remained, small hints of the poison he couldn't fully extract. He didn't miss Isolde's hands balling into fists to keep from raking her nails down her back.

"What's one more scar?" she rasped, her voice dark and sarcastic.

One more scar. She had so many. Far, far too many. Malaki continued to work, his breathes growing quick with exhustion. His hands dropped to his side, arms heavy with exhaustion. "Done."

"Thanks," she said with a sigh. "Good as new."

"Not quite," he said, forcing a hand to the crook of her elbow, and the other resting on her shoulder. "You can't walk around with a dislocated shoulder."

"I won't," she said, pushing out of his grasp. Before he could protest, Isolde headed for the nearest tree and slammed her shoulder into the side, shoving the bone back into place. A grunt of pain escaped her clenched teeth.

"Completely unnecessary Isolde," Malaki ground out, pushing a heavy, tired sigh through his lips and placing his hands on his hips.

"Yes, well," she said, with a half-hearted shrug. "Just like I can't walk around with a dislocated shoulder, I can't have you drained of all your strength. We still have to get them to the checkpoint." She slid the hood back into place.

Malaki bit his tongue, watching her struggle to pull the blood-and-sweat soaked leather back into place. *Stubborn woman.* He kept pace as they followed the riverbank. He knew she didn't want him to expend any more of his energy, but this was insanity.

They worked in silence, their steps dancing across the smooth stones of the riverbank. Not a soul made their presence known as the hours ticked by. The bow rested casually in Isolde's fingers, an arrow notched into place, ready to fire at a moment's notice. The familiar, worn handle of Malaki's axe rested snugly in his grip.

Before long, the landmarks grew more familiar. They turned the corner of a bend. Hidden in the shadows of early dawn slept the small outpost, Yuek.

With less than five hundred occupants, the town of Yuek would be hard-pressed to catch the attention of the kingdom. The inhabitants mostly kept to themselves, which was one of the reasons Isolde chose this location as an outpost—along with their long-standing hatred for the king.

Blyana and Cillian, with the help of the humans, guided the boats into the docks on the left. Wood scraped against the frame of the vessels, the sounds echoing across the water.

Crouching behind a plume of river grass that grew at the edges of the water, Isolde and Malaki watched the group disembark. The humans remained quiet. He could see their eyes were wide with fear.

"Any news of the other outposts?" she asked.

"You know the information goes no further than this," said Malaki. "It's safer that way for all of us. If one of us is captured, that's a liability to the whole operation. It's best to keep the next link in the chain a mystery."

Isolde sighed, knowing this to be true. Still not knowing where the now freed humans were going grated on her nerves.

"But," Malaki said, his tone softer, "if something had happened, if the operation was somehow compromised, we would have heard. The news would have reached us one way or another. There have been precautions taken to ensure a warning would be sent up and down the chain."

Within minutes, the humans were escorted off the boat and placed into another. A painting of a fish was plastered across its side. Malaki shivered with disgust, wrinkling his nose. *Well, it won't be a pleasant-smelling journey. But at least they will be safe.*

"Another success."

The happiness and contentment in Isolde's voice caused Malaki's heart to ache. "You can't keep doing this, Isolde."

"I beg to differ," she said tugging at the cuffs of her black, leather jacket. "I've been doing this for decades. I don't see any reason why I should stop now."

"Because it's going to get you killed," Malaki shot back.

"You doubt the training you've put me through over the years, Malaki?" Isolde said, her voice laced with a chuckle she knew dug into his tanned, inked skin.

"What do you want, Isolde?" Malaki asked not taking the bait. Leftover drops of rain cascaded down the brown leather hood as he shook his head. "Why do you continue to do this?"

"You know why," Isolde said, all humor leeching from her voice.

"It can't be only to help the people," he said, "This goes far beyond that." Isolde's shoulder shrugged. "Maybe I enjoy it. Everyone needs a hobby."

"Your hobbies are disturbing," Malaki said, resting an arm on his knee. "Murder...stealing...sabotage. Not very becoming of a lady."

"Good thing I'm not a lady," Isolde said. "That sounds incredibly boring."

"There has to be a time when this ends," said Malaki, with an air of irritation. "You can't keep doing this forever."

"How fortunate for us, and the people of Arnoria...today is not that day." Isolde's tone held a hint finality that could not and would not be disputed.

"When then?" Malaki demanded.

Isolde ground her teeth together. Bringing an end to the havoc they plagued upon their homeland was a conversation he had begun to drudge up more often. He had to make her see that this could not go on forever. That eventually their luck would run out. Or her heart would turn so cold there would be no fixing it.

Isolde turned to meet his blazing stare and held it. The same light of power shined in her gaze to match his own.

"When I am no longer needed."

A heavy, defeated sigh ghosted along the riverbank. "That will never happen," Malaki said, his voice losing its bite. Sorrowful disappointment thickened in his blood. A sense of failure descended on him like a wall of stone. "The people will always need you. In one way or another."

"Sounds like you just answered your own question, Malaki."

Cillian and Blyana shook hands with a man Isolde assumed was their point of contact and boarded the boats shoving off into the river.

"Come on." Malaki rose, his back bent to keep well out of view. "We'll meet them down river."

Just as the sun broke over the tops of the canopy, Blyana and Cillian ditched the boats, allowing them to float down river heading south, away from Thornwood. Martha's blood was still smeared over the boards of the one in the lead. The last thing they needed was the scent of an escaped slave making its way back to Thornwood.

The four of them ran for a solid hour before stopping at a cluster of boulders hugging the riverbank. "Let's see it," Cillian said, taking a seat next to where Blyana perched on a boulder, her blue eyes reflecting in the dying night.

"Is that all you care about?" Malaki asked, yanking the satchels from his shoulders.

"I am a thief," Cillian said, his arms wide as if in awe of himself. "Coin and jewelry intrigue me."

"That better not be all that intrigues you," Blyana smarted, her lips turning up. Before Cillian could answer, Malaki threw the bags to the ground, allowing the contents to slip out before them.

"Dagan was certainly doing well for himself," Isolde said, nesting down by the pile.

Malaki nodded in agreement as he squatted down beside her, his fingers searching. "Especially for a lord who wasn't doing much of anything besides enjoying the spoils of his father and position."

Blyana descended from her perch to claim a spot next to Isolde. Reaching out, she extracted a large ring. Its band of solid gold danced in the light of the rising sun. An impressive ruby fashioned into an octagon nestled in its center.

"Here," she said, tossing it to Isolde. "You're the one with the taste for shiny things."

Isolde chuckled and slid the gaudy monstrosity onto her ring finger. She looked at from all angles, her eyes assessing. It looked odd next to the gold band that held a diamond she always wore on the middle finger of her right hand.

"Too recognizable. What a shame," Isolde said. Still she left it in place, admiring the weight. She continued her search until she came upon a piece of parchment, a smudge of wax clinging to the top. Her blood ran cold when she recognized the seal.

The royal seal was easily seen in the shimmering black wax. A golden triangle encasing a serpent's eye stared back at her. Unfolding the paper, she scanned the elegant letters, also written in gold:

Lord Dagan,

His Majesty sends his appreciation for your cooperation and continued loyalty. Your devotion will not soon be forgotten.

Isolde read it again, suddenly wishing she hadn't rendered Dagan unable to answer questions. "It seems Dagan has made some friends in very high places." Without explaining, she passed the note to Malaki. A grim line formed on his lips, his nostrils flaring. Without waiting, Blyana snagged the note from his fingers.

"All of this is from the king then," Malaki said, sitting down. His arm rested on a knee as he rubbed a silver coin between his fingers.

"It would appear so," Cillian said, his eyes losing a hint of humor as he read. "Whatever he did for the king, he was paid handsomely for it."

Isolde reached once more into the bag. A sharp pain ripped through her hand as her fingers closed around what she believed to be stone.

"Ow!" she cried, causing them all to jump.

"What?" Malaki demanded, his eyes glowing, hand already on the handle of the battle axe on his back.

Burns covered Isolde's fingers and palm. The pain radiated up into her arm, igniting every nerve ending in a blaze. Looking down, she saw a small piece of raw elithrium glowing faintly in a bed of gold. She gripped her wrist as if to stop the pain in her hand as she stared down at it.

"Malaki," she said, not looking away.

She heard the growl rumble through the air. Blyana jumped back, her eyes blazing at the sight. "I've never seen a piece of raw elithrium."

"Neither have I," Cillian said.

"Good thing our blades can't do that" Blyana said, her fingers trailing the holsters of her daggers.

"Because it's been altered," Malaki said. "Once elithrium has been combined with another element, it loses a lot of its potency. The amount the blade contains is a factor of course. The more elithrium used, the deadlier the blade. Still, even a little can cause us serious problems."

His eyes slid to Isolde, who rolled hers in return. The freshly healed scar still ached, the elithrium arrow's annoying token of remembrance. Carefully covering the small piece of fiery stone, Malaki placed the jewels and note back into the bag.

"Why did someone like Dagan have it?" Blyana asked, doing well to keep a healthy distance between herself and the satchel.

Malaki sighed, his eyes finding Isolde's once again. "I'm not sure. It couldn't have come from anyone except the king. He runs the only supply in Arnoria. Unless another pocket has been found, but I feel we would have heard of it by now."

"Alaric will find that most interesting," Isolde said, rising. Her hand continued to ache. Malaki reached towards her, intending to take her hand in his. "No," she said, stepping back, clutching her hand to her chest. "You have done enough today."

"Isolde." He sighed, his jaw tensing with impatience.

"You are exhausted, Malaki. It's only a small burn that will heal just fine on its own. Besides, it's rare elithrium. Only the antidote or time can heal it."

He ground his teeth, but the exhaustion was all too apparent on his face. "Stubborn ass." The word rolled over his tongue like gravel. Her eyebrows arched, a small incredulous smirk spreading across her face.

"Anyone up for breakfast?" Cillian asked, effectively breaking the tension.

"I'm up for a shower," Blyana said plucking a twig from her hair.

"That too," Cillian murmured, his arm wrapping around her hip, pulling her to him.

"I have to make a delivery," Isolde said, not fighting the smirk as she pulled the bags from Malaki.

"That can wait," he said, his hand gripping the straps. "If you say I need to rest, you most certainly do."

"As you are so fond of hearing me say it, I'm fine." She pulled the bag from his grip and took a step back. "You know what I have to do. I might as well drop this off while I'm at it."

Malaki opened his mouth to argue but simply nodded, for which Isolde was grateful. Enough discord already existed between them. She knew Malaki was well aware of where she was going. That she needed the privacy…the time.

"Be safe," he said. A heaviness fell on his face, an old pain inflicted by memory darkening his eyes. "We'll see you back at the manor."

"See you there," she said before taking off into the forest without looking back.

CHAPTER 6

Light of the morning sun penetrated the tumbling waves of the waterfall, illuminating the cave's opening. Repositioning the bags along with her bow and quiver, Isolde stepped into the darkness. The path wound left, right, and up. Each step was sure and perfectly memorized.

Small beams of sunlight broke through crevasses in the rock's surfaces, dancing across the now dry walls, highlighting her way.

The Hood's lair resided deep within the Blackford Forest, nestled safely at the point where Briarhole, Foxclove, and Thornwood's boundaries met. It was a healthy distance from all three, leaving room for suspicion if it was ever discovered.

Isolde made the final left turn, the ceiling of the tunnel rising into a colossal open cave. A single hole penetrated the top allowing light to pour in and fall on the lavish furnishings within.

Massive beds rested along the far corners of the open space, each with its own armoire, overstuffed chair, and table. Malaki had insisted it was overkill, claiming it was a waste of resources. Granted, it was rare they needed to stay here overnight, but Isolde refused to allow them to sleep on anything but the finest beds and linens. In their line of work, luxury was something you took when you could. She most certainly wasn't going to sleep on the ground if she could help it.

Isolde's footsteps echoed off the walls, coins danced in their satchels. Reaching the large bookcase carved into the side of the cave next to her bed, as far from the roaring fire as possible, Isolde slid down to the floor. A rise of familiar panic slammed into her, but she was too tired to acknowledge it. Exhausted, she ignored the flames and pulled the hood free from her face.

"So," a voice said, its melody bouncing off the walls in piercing bells. Isolde's fingers flew to her bow and quiver, an arrow fitting in place as the tip moved towards the sound.

Galaena lounged in one of the lush chairs just on the other side of the fireplace. A cushioned stool nestled beneath her feet as her hands gingerly held a book before her. Taking a deep breath, Isolde lowered the bow, her gaze heavy with a relieved annoyance.

"You really shouldn't do that to me, Gal," Isolde said, setting the bow and arrow down. She rested against the wall, willing her heart to stop racing.

"You really should learn to look at your surrounding before slipping that thing off," her aunt said, her eyes not leaving the page. "How was last night?"

"You tell me."

Isolde tossed the cargo of gold before the fire, and flames danced across their shimmering surface. "Should be able to keep the people fed for at least a month or two."

Galaena's fierce gray eyes softened. Whether it was at the prize before her or the exhaustion in Isolde's face, it was impossible to say. Setting the book aside, Galaena rose to slide down the wall and gently freed the braid from Isolde's soiled jacket.

"Are you alright?" Galaena asked, fingers working to loosen the strip of leather from its knot at the end of Isolde's braid.

Isolde nodded but looked down at her burned hand. She did not wish to talk of Dagan right now or repercussions that would undoubtedly follow.

"And the humans?"

"We got most of them out," Isolde said. She felt Galaena's sigh of relief, a wave of anxiety dissolving in the air. "There is something else."

Gently lifting the bag, careful to only touch the fabric, Isolde dumped the rest of the contents on the floor. The elithrium rolled to the edge of the fire's light. It glowed more brightly, its greenish hue playing against the black leather and splotches of dried blood on her pant legs.

Galaena's hands froze, her body going noticeably rigid. "Where did you get that?"

"It was in His Lordship's bag," said Isolde, her fingers gently grazing her palm. "Along with this." She handed over the note from the king and waited while Galaena read. A thin line formed on her lips as a heavy sigh pushed from her chest.

After a moment, her aunt simply nodded and folded the note. "Alaric will come remove that," she said, her gaze darting to the offensive mineral. Galaena had come into contact with it before and she had no desire to ever do so again. A wide, linear scar across her throat laid truth to that fact.

"For now, you need to get ready," Galaena said, her eyes hovering on the blood and gore. "Any of that yours?"

A grim smile formed on the corner of Isolde's full, expressive lips. "Maybe just a tad."

Galaena rolled her eyes. "Come on, let's get back before the others wake up." Leaving the hoard of treasure to rest by the fire, they walked through the tunnel and out into the awakened forest.

"I'll be right there," Isolde said, her feet leading her to the right. She did not wait for a response. Her aunt knew where she was heading. A small path wound around the large boulders that served as an entrance to their hideout.

It moved through the forest for a short distance, then widened into a small clearing. On the far end stood a large andacovie tree. She had picked it out specifically, even snuck into Arnoria's capital, Elenarta, to steal one from their nursery. They were sacred to the virya, reserved only for those the crown deemed worthy to have mark their final resting place. Not even the test of time could touch its bark.

It was out of place, not fully belonging to Blackford Forest. Mindful of her steps, Isolde brushed aside the swaying limbs. Beams of sunlight softly caressed the petals of the roses that grew around the back side of the trunk.

The scent hung heavily in the morning air-sweet and full of memory. A lump formed in her throat, as it always did when she visited. It was a sadness that could not be explained, a wound that would never heal. Dropping to her knees, Isolde's fingers lightly grazed the smooth bark.

Swallowing hard, she whispered, "We got them out. Most of them." Tears flooded her cheeks, their trails burning her skin as they fell. "I killed him…a lot of them." She tried not to think of it, the sadness that would paint his perfect, handsome face. The face she had not seen in almost forty years…a face she would never see again.

"I miss you," Isolde said, her voice breaking as the familiar, unforgiving pain pierced her heart. A crack so vast and deep cleaved its way through her chest. There were some wounds that time could not mend, no matter how much she wanted it to. Kissing her fingertips, she lightly grazed them over the lush grass that grew at the base of the trunk.

"I do not bow to fear," Isolde whispered. "It bows to me."

A soft breeze blew through the limbs, its gentle touch kissing the trail of tears on her cheeks. She sighed heavily, her eyes squeezing shut as she forced herself to stand. Touching the bark, she took a deep breath, and buried the pain once more as she turned and left.

Each layer was put back into place, every ounce of pain buried beneath a bedrock of anger. She whipped her face clean of tears, not wanting her aunt to see her this way. She followed the path back around to where the Lady of Thornwood waited patiently.

Isolde ignored her worried gaze as they walked on. It was her burden to bear, no one else's. A hundred yards into the forest stood a massive oak, its trunk impossibly large.

"I still can't believe Malaki was able to do this," Isolde said, her fingers lingering over the various knots on the bark. There was one just at her eye level that would open up a doorway.

"You should have seen him in his prime, before…" Galaena stopped, her lips tightening. "Before Aurora died."

Isolde's finger found the knot and hovered over it. "I wish I could remember her. She must have been quite amazing."

Galaena smiled, the light warming her gray eyes into living metal. Nodding, she said, "She was. Being a human was never a burden to her, only a gift. Malaki thought the same."

Aurora had been Galaena's lady-in-waiting, a ward that had turned into a trusted companion as time moved on. Galaena had taught her how to fight, how to wield a sword. It was how she snagged Malaki's heart.

"It didn't matter that she was human," Isolde said, her finger pressing into the knot. It gave way without resistance. Malaki had instilled the bark with their cadre's scent, allowing only them to use this passage.

Galaena shook her head. The dawning sun's light danced across the waves of her hair that fell down the length of her back in honey colored waves. "Not for a single moment."

"If only everyone else thought that way."

Spiral steps made from the tree itself led down to the tunnel which ran beneath the forest and ended at Thornwood. She remembered the months it took Malaki to form it with the intent of it serving as an escape route if the need ever arose. She highly doubted he would have complied with her plan of turning it into the Hood's escape route.

Striking a piece of flint, Galaena lit one of the many torches resting at the bottom of the steps next to a bucket of water. Isolde's arms automatically flinched at the flame, forcing her to step back.

"Sorry," Galaena murmured, turning towards the tunnel's opening, her eyes lowered. Isolde forced away the familiar fear and followed. Damp air accompanied them as they worked their way home, the darkness bending to the light.

"He was mentioned again." Isolde's voice echoed off the circular walls.

Galaena's silence stretched out before them, thick and full of palpable worry. "His reputation is spreading."

"This is more than reputation," Isolde said, her teeth grating. "A human boy saw him."

Galaena stopped short, her eyes humming with power. "He saw him?"

"It would appear so," Isolde sighed, leaning against the wall. Her arms knotted over her chest as exhaustion seeped further into her bones. "Apparently, my eyes are more appealing than his. Which is no surprise. I mean, they are quite remarkable. Extraordinary really."

A signal brow rose on her aunt's slightly wrinkled forehead, her gaze narrowing with annoyance.

Isolde rolled hers in response as the tip of her boot tapped the packed dirt. "He described them as dark. Like the night, black and shining." Her tone was slightly annoyed.

"Nothing else?"

Isolde shook her head, loosening a few blood-cracked strands. "He did have others with him. Unmasked."

"And?"

"He was just a child, but the way he described them made me think of those who dwell in Endurmure."

Galaena's brow furrowed in thought. Without answering she began to walk, taking the light with her. Sighing heavily, Isolde shoved off the wall and followed.

"You think he is from the Forgotten Lands?" Isolde asked. She knew very little about the region that inhabited the western coast of Anroria or its people. They were said to be nomads. Virya, humans, and half-bloods who wondered the great sand dunes of the Anar Desert and haunted valleys nestled inside the Vailoron Mountains.

"It's possible," Galaena said, her eyes forward and mouth set. "I'll speak with your uncle about this but for now you must be careful Isolde. The last thing we need are competing masked crusaders tearing apart Arnoria."

"As if it would be a competition." Isolde scoffed, picking flakes of dirt and blood from her hood.

"Let's not test that theory, shall we?" Galaena picked up her pace, her footsteps nearly silent beneath the sway of the gray silk dress that hung from her slender, athletic form. It was easy to still see the fierce warrior beneath the Lady of Thornwood exterior. Trained from birth, Galaena had been raised to defend Arnoria. To sacrifice anything and anyone for its survival.

She swept her eyes over Isolde's form, landing on the gaping hole stripped across her back. The fresh red scar burned in the light of the fire.

"Besides," she said in a patronizing tone that grated Isolde's nerves, "it looks like you could use some more time with Malaki in the Pit if a lone archer from Foxclove of all places can land a blow."

"Afraid I'll lose?"

"Not at all," her aunt said, the ghost of a smile playing on her lips, "I just don't want to risk my niece or the future heir of Thornwood."

Isolde's teeth ground together, the sound bouncing off the smooth, beautiful walls.

"You are set to leave for Briarhole tomorrow morning," Galaena said, her eyes sliding to Isolde. "It will be your first attendance at Lestahere as heir to Thornwood."

Lestahere: an annual three-day meeting for the lords and ladies of Arnoria to discuss trade deals, land disputes, and slave labor. Three days of having to wear a mask, pretending to be one of them.

Isolde fought the growl growing in her chest. "Is that truly necessary?"

"You know it is. Alaric wants you to learn the political side of things. He knows you can more than handle yourself with or without a weapon. He wants you prepared mentally for the job. We both do."

"I wouldn't have to if you would change your minds," Isolde said, not even attempting to hide the contempt in her voice.

"It has been years since either of us has morphed, Isolde. Can you imagine how painful it would be now? Especially with his leg?"

No. She flinched at the thought of morphing even at that moment. Memories of bones shattering and skin tearing ghosted through her mind. Her uncle had been injured, punished for his stance in the war against the current king. His left leg had been permanently maimed, leaving him with a limp and a cane as his forever companions. It made the task of transforming far more excruciating.

"Two hundred and sixty-three years is plenty. We have lived a good life and it doesn't appear that things will get any better. So why not live these last twenty to thirty years of relative peace as our last?"

Isolde shook her head, not at Galaena and Alaric's decision, but at the reality of it. "In order to die, you must forfeit your power. I suppose there is irony in that."

"Perhaps some," she said. "As long as we do not transform, we will continue to age. Its far easier for a virya who only has the power to manipulate the elements to control their power. But for those who can transform…That is an entirely different monster to control. It goes against our very nature."

It had been hard on them. To deny something so natural…It was a part of their very being. There had been a time Isolde had decided to forsake her immortality too. But fate had other plans. Isolde was just a child then, with no knowledge of what went into the decision, only the decision itself. Still, it was their choice, not hers, to make. "And if you do?"

"Then we revert back to the time we stopped aging. For most virya, our maturation was reached in our late twenties. Our minds and powers continued to develop but our bodies remained frozen."

Isolde had begun to notice the minor changes in Galaena's face. Even now, in the torch's unforgiving light, small wrinkles shadowed the corners of her eyes and forehead. Tiny strands of gray shined through her golden hair.

"How many years does it take to start showing signs?"

Galaena shrugged. "It's different for everyone. The more powerful a virya, the longer they can go. For us it has been nearly thirty years, and we are just now starting to see the changes…to feel them."

An anger filled Isolde's heart. An anger she knew was covering up what she really felt, which was fear. Fear of losing the two people who had raised her, taken her in, and made her their own. "It's not fair."

"It is how the gods made it."

"The gods are bastards."

"Enough, Isolde!" Galaena barked, her glowing eyes cutting. "Do not speak ill of the gods. It is the way things are." Galaena had never held any love for the gods. Just healthy respect that reprimanded Isolde's blatant insolence. Immortality gave one the illusion of infinity, never having to face the loss of a loved one. She swallowed the lump in her throat. *It was cruel.* Their immortality was a curse disguised as a gift.

A small light appeared up above, a tiny beacon welcoming them home. "Leave the suit, and I will see what I can do about repairing it."

"Don't waste your time," Isolde said, her voice suddenly hollow. "I'm wearing more blood than leathers at this point. It's not worth saving."

"We'll, see."

Isolde could still feel her eyes searching. Galaena had always been like a mother...Perhaps mending her clothes no matter how blood-soaked they were, was a way to hold on to that.

At the end of the tunnel lay another set of stairs. Intricate slabs of dirty marble led up to a small latch in the ceiling. While Galaena doused the torch in the full bucket, Isolde shoved against the door. Her shoulder ached in pain, despite having used her good one. It gave way without issue, flipping open with a bang.

The massive cellar nestled at the base of Thornwood was deserted, save for the various fruits, vegetables, and dried meats that hung from the ceiling. Off to the right rested barrels of some of the finest wine in all of Arnoria. Isolde and Cillian kept close tabs on their stores.

"I assume Nan is finishing up with the cookies for the children," Galaena said as she followed Isolde up the stairs and replaced the trap door. "She will be up shortly to see you."

"Fine," Isolde said, desperate to get out of the suit. "Are the children there already?"

"Most arrived before sunup. Their parents were more than eager to drop them off just to get a reprieve from being asked to come to story hour."

Isolde could not fight her smile. Every week she hosted a story hour for the children of her area in the Thornwood library. Much to the dismay of those in prominent roles in the community, all were welcome to participate. Even humans and half-blood virya.

"Why do you think the king made reading illegal for them, Gal?" Isolde asked. She had her own theories, but none that spanned beyond pure bigotry and cruelty.

"I don't know." Galaena sighed heavily, her hands moving over the ears of corn nestled in one of the baskets. "Hatred has a way of tricking people into doing unspeakable, unexplainable things."

"As does bravery," said Isolde, her eyes suddenly guarded. "It's no wonder Malaki is on the verge of having a stroke at every mission."

"It's because you put him in those positions, smart ass," Galaena said. Her eyes narrowed, the warm gray turning into solid stone. "Let that soak in the tube when you're done." Her hand waved at the suit. "Even if it is soaked in blood, there might be enough left to make a new hood or two."

"Why do you think I picked black?" Isolde asked over her shoulder. "It wasn't to match my beautiful soul."

Isolde chuckled as a laugh pushed through the thick, earthy air. She took the steps two at a time, fighting to ignore the annoying itch in her shoulder. Breaching the cellar door, Isolde crept through the vast kitchen, ducking beneath the counter to avoid the cook's gaze. As they stooped to place a tray of cookies into the oven, Isolde pushed through the double doors and out into the hallway.

Keeping out of sight was slightly harder than normal for today. Children ran through the halls, their peals of laughter both alarming and joyous came from all directions. Still, it would not do for one of them to see the Hood lurking about Thornwood unchecked. With minds set on story hour, she was able to sneak past without issue.

Facing the east, Isolde was met with the full brunt of the sun's light as she walked through her bedroom door. Alaric had assigned her the room for this very reason, making it impossible for her sleep in.

She stowed the full quiver and bow into one of the many hidden compartments placed around her room before heading to the bathroom. She looked longingly at the silky blue covers, wanting nothing more than to dive in and sleep the day away.

Isolde turned the knobs of the deep, copper tub, allowing the scalding water to flow as she peeled away layer after layer and tossed them aside for Galaena and Nan's later inspection. Small bits of dried blood snowed on the white marble floor in flakes. The full-length mirror showed an image of death itself.

Isolde wasn't sure how the blood had seeped through so many layers. Dark streaks ran down her sides and across her stomach. A smear raced from her defined shoulder up to her neck and jaw. Turning around, she assessed the wound on her back. It was red and sore, but at least it was nearly closed. A frozen waterfall of red fell down her back and onto the back of her thighs.

"Damn Dagan for giving his soldiers elithrium arrows," Isolde said to herself, the tips of her fingers pushing at the forming scar. If it had been potent, a nasty hole would still be smiling at her, with the promise of an uglier scar to follow. New skin would cover this one by tomorrow, with only a small hint of what had happened that night remaining. Malaki was right, just a few more inches to the right and…Doubt leaked into her mind, the power within growling in response.

Isolde's eyes quickly fell from her skin, avoiding the rest of her back, and followed the trail of blood to the front. The large, angry gash on her thigh still throbbed as if the spear of Odesious, Lord of Marsh Hall, was still there. Not a curve was spared a nick or slice except for her face, neck, arms and chest. Those had somehow miraculously remained untouched, unblemished.

Before diving in, she added few drops of rose oil into the steaming water. The sweet aroma filled the room and instantly relaxed her muscles. Gingerly, she slipped beneath the surface of the near scolding water with a sigh.

Resting her hands on her chest, Isolde nestled against the hot, copper tub. A few bubbles from her lips scrambled to the surface. She closed her eyes and the faces of the dead met her in the darkness. Their eyes were cold and lightless.

It was inevitable. They each left their mark on her in some way. A scar forever blemishing her soul. It had been years since she had taken the life of a lord. There would be repercussions, severe ones. Yet when she thought of Martha and Cadoc, there was only peace with her actions.

Her thoughts of the night were interrupted by a small knock at the door. She smiled, knowing that knock from anywhere. Breaking the surface, her now clean hands rubbed the water from her eyes. "Come in."

A pint-size vessel of fury and wisdom, beamed at her. "How are you, my rose?" An oversized towel was held in her arms. Streams of light danced on her graying black hair that was arranged in intricate braids around her head.

"I suppose I could be worse, Nan," Isolde said leaning back, wanting to hide the wound. Worrying Nan was something she avoided at all costs.

The old woman crept to the stool Isolde kept purposefully beside the tub. A small ache thumbed through her heart at the sight of her slowly, almost painfully lowering herself down to the seat.

"Thirty years at this, and you still can't keep from hurting yourself," Nan said, her eyes finding the burn on Isolde's palm. *You have no idea, Nan.*

"Thirty years, and I still haven't found a suitable chair for you to sit in."

"This chair is just fine," Nan said, taking Isolde's hand, her brow furrowing in unnecessary concern. "It's my hips that are the problem."

For as long as Isolde could remember, Nana Bara had always been there. She was a human who posed as a slave for appearance's sake only. It was dangerous for her…for all of them for Nan to pose as anything else. Being accused as a human sympathizer was nothing short of treasonous.

They were quiet for a moment, then Nan spoke. Her voice was soft and cautious. "Did you get them out, my rose?"

Isolde nodded, her thoughts reverberating back to the night before. "Most of them. But I was too late for one. I don't know if she will survive. Even if she does, she will be crippled."

Nan was quiet as she moved behind the tub. Her warm, sure fingers picked up where Galaena's had left off, undoing the mess the braid had left. "You got them out. That is what matters."

Isolde bit the inside of her cheek, her eyes fighting against the tears threatening to spill over. "He would have been ashamed of me, Nan."

Isolde felt Nan's hands still. She knew to whom she was referring. In the mirror, Isolde watched as Nan's eyes turned to the window. Their hazy blue gaze looked past the trees that lined Thornwood manor's well-manicured lawn. To the andacovie tree…to the grave that sat just outside their hideout. Her son's grave. "No, my rose."

"He would have. Not for the act of it, but for how I feel about it. I killed them," Isolde said, her voice hardly a whisper, "and I don't feel an ounce of regret about it."

Nan dipped her fingers in the water, her skin stained red. "The life you have chosen, Isolde, is not one of ease. Hard decisions must be made and you are willing to make them, no matter the cost to you. I would say the path you turned from would have been just as difficult. He would never be ashamed of you."

Nan's blood-stained fingers combed through her hair. Isolde closed her eyes, regretting bringing him up in the first place. The familiar cold fire stirred within her chest. Its merciless flames licked at her self-directed pity, stirring her hatred.

"I should have cleaned out Foxclove," Isolde said. "Should have purged that place of such evil."

"Do not regret allowing someone to live, Isolde," Nan said, working into her scalp down to the tips of her dark brown hair that held a hint of rich, ruby red. "There is no hope for the dead, only for the living. You have so much life left to live, an infinite amount. Do not waste it on hate and regret." With a silent command, Nan pushed Isolde beneath the water.

They remained silent as Nan gently washed away the blood and grime. She would miss moments like this. Nan's mention of infinite time was like a blow. It had not escaped Isolde's notice that Nan was getting older. The evidence was so apparent. She wondered how many more days like this they had left.

Time played cruelly with humans, but it had been gracious to Nan. At nearly eighty years, she was still as strong as ever. She had been Isolde's nurse when she was born nearly fifty-five years ago. Ever since, Nan had been her confidant in every way.

She looked ahead at her reflection. Eyes of brilliant emerald ringed in the purest silver looked back. She was strikingly beautiful, that much was true. Still, it was a mask. A disguise for the monster that lived within...who she truly was.

Peals of laughter erupted from somewhere downstairs, pulling Isolde from her thoughts.

"Those children are going to riot if you don't get down there soon." Nan touched her cheeks then handed her the luscious towel. "Tanor is there as well, waiting for his lessons."

Isolde nodded and toweled off quickly, being sure to keep her back out of Nan's line of sight. Pulling a gust of wind through her fingers, she dried her hair, sending heavy waves of dark brown flowing around her shoulders. The ring on her middle finger snagged at the strands. A pair of golden wings served as the band that held a single diamond in place. Its flawless core echoed a hint of blue and silver, as if the wind itself lived within.

"A few new children arrived today," Nan said walking to the door. "Do try to not scare them."

Isolde chuckled. "Fear is what I do best, Nan."

CHAPTER 7

"Lady Isolde?"

"Tanor, how many times have I asked you to just call me, Isolde?" Her eyes never left the page. She and Malaki had stowed away for a few moments of peace. To allow the children to calm down and take their seats in the library.

"Forgive me, as always," the boy said with a nervous chuckle. "There is a...favor, I must ask of you."

"A favor? And what is the nature of said favor?"

"Well, it involves a...um..." His voice shook, a small nervous laugh dancing across his words.

Isolde recognized that tone. That nervous excitement. "A girl?"

He nodded, a pink blush blossomed across his freckled cheeks.

"Do tell," she said, snapping the book closed.

Blond curls fell into his eyes as he stepped forward, his hands wringing together before him. "Well, it's quite a large favor."

The ghost of a chuckle breezed past her lips. One similar echoed from Malaki who lounged off to the side. "Let me be the judge of that," she said.

"Could she...could—"

"Spit it out, Tanor," Malaki grumbled, not looking up as he turned a page in the book nestled in his hands.

"Could she join us?"

Isolde went still, her mind racing with possibilities. Impossibly dangerous possibilities. "Do you mean at story hour?"

Malaki peered over his own book, and his eyes, once alight with amusement, darkened. Tanor looked nervously between them. *He has every right to be terrified.*

"Please tell me you mean story hour, Tanor. Please tell me you did not tell this girl that you know how to read." Isolde was on her feet now, hands balling into fists at her side. He cowered into the back of the room; his eyes locked on hers that were now ignited with power. A hint of what lay beneath the surface.

"Does she know you can read?" Malaki asked, his voice deathly calm, the only hint Isolde needed to know just how angry he was.

Tanor dropped his gaze, a line of silver forming at the crease of his eyes. He didn't have to say it.

Isolde swore. Her fingers locking around the back of her neck as she paced.

"How could you be so stupid, Tanor?" Malaki asked.

"I don't know, I was just—"

"Just trying to impress a girl," Malaki said, rising. "Was it worth it, betraying Lady Isolde?"

She hated the sound of her formal title rolling off Malaki's tongue. But it had the desired effect. Tears now streamed down Tanor's face as a look of shame blazing from his eyes. "I'm so sorry Lady Isolde, but I…I love her."

"Love," Isolde said, scoffing. "You don't know what that is."

"I do," he said boldly, jaw locking. "I love her more than I have loved anything else in this world. Haven't you ever loved someone?"

A chill filtered through the room as Malaki slowly rose, the chair creaking almost painfully. Isolde shoved away the memories, the unbearable pain fighting to break free and tear this child apart. He must have seen something in her face, for he took a step back. A look of fear and of utter shame grew on his face. The mask she worked so hard to keep in place had slipped, revealing the despair beneath.

"If that were true," Isolde said, stepping toward him, like a predator stalking its prey. Her voice low and even. "You never would have told her. Because now, if the truth comes out, you have doomed her too."

Terror chilled his gaze, a slight tremor playing into his bottom lip as he spoke. "She would never."

"You don't know that, Tanor," Malaki said. "Not only have you put yourself and this girl in danger, but your father, Lady Isolde, and all of Thornwood as well. It is well known that she reads to the children. It won't be hard to guess who has been teaching them to read as well."

Paleness swept away the blush in Tanor's cheeks. He swallowed thickly as the realization set in. "What do I do?"

Isolde sighed, her eyes slipping to Malaki, who met her gaze. Long had they been able to communicate this way. It was a secret language they had created, one that started out as enjoyment but had morphed into one of survival. She knew the look in his eyes, the one that said there was no easy choice.

"I don't believe you would think well of me if I killed her," Isolde said, turning back to the boy. A bolt of fear and a hint of anger flashed in his eyes. Isolde hid a smile; perhaps he did love her. "So, the only option is to have her brought here so she can learn too."

The excitement blossoming on Tanor's face was short-lived. Malaki moved, his form a blur in the dim light of the secret library. He stood a good two feet taller than Tanor, dwarfing him in the wake of his shadow. "Do not smile at this, Tanor," he said, his words grating around his bared teeth. "You have put us all in danger. If she tells anyone about this, she will be the first to meet the blade."

Tanor's eyes moved immediately to Malaki's side, to the sheath that housed Secrettaker. A famous blade in its own right; one no one wanted to face. He swallowed again, his resolve returning. "She won't say anything Master Malaki. She won't. If she does betray us," he said, his eyes moving to where Isolde stood by the lifeless fireplace, "if she betrays you, my lady, I will kill her myself."

Sadness crept into Isolde's heart, but she stomped it down. Her face remained impassive as if his words were just that: words. "Let us hope it does not come to that, Tanor. You have already broken one promise to me. Do not break it a second time."

Despair once again found its way to the boy's now reddened face. "Forgive me, Lady Isolde. She's here today for story hour if you wish to meet her."

"Very well. I'll see you in the library."

He nodded once more with the same stiff, awkward bow Isolde once found so endearing and ran up the steps, having to side step Malaki's piercing, unforgiving gaze as he went. The door above clicked closed, and Isolde fell into the arm chair. Running a hand over her face, she sighed. "This complicates things a bit."

"A bit?" Malaki said, his words laced with mocking amusement. "I would say this puts us in a very difficult position." Snagging two glasses he poured them each a glass of whiskey.

"Still the heavy pourer, I see," Isolde said, her fingers encasing her half-filled glass.

"You've never complained about it before."

"I never will," she murmured as the warm liquid bit her tongue. The burn was a welcomed torture. A familiar, cozy pain that cascaded down her throat and into her chest.

"What are we going to do?" he asked, draining his glass in one gulp.

The cuff of his fresh, clean tunic pulled away from his wrists, hinting at the swirling thorn-covered vines that wrapped up Malaki's forearms, shoulders, and down his back. Each branch held a name in an old language, one that existed long before the virya came into existence. Each name etched into his skin, was a reminder. A haunting remembrance of someone he had failed to save.

Isolde balanced the glass on the edge of the cushioned arm of her chair. "I know one thing we aren't going to do," she said. "If this girl talks, we can't let him kill her."

Malaki stared into the glass. "No, we cannot."

That only left one option, one choice to be made. Who would be the one to end the girl's life? "It might not come to that," she said, not at all convincingly.

"We've never done well in the hope of a might, Isolde."

"We've gotten by well enough so far."

"So far." He shook his head before pouring himself another. "It was bound to get out eventually."

"It was a risk I was willing to take." And it was. Any chance of freedom was worth the risk.

"And what will it cost you?"

"Freedom is never free, Malaki. We of all people know that better than most."

"Indeed, we do." Easy smiles formed on their lips. Setting her glass down, Isolde rose to sit at Malaki's right side and wrapped her arms around his neck.

Memories of her as a child flooded her mind as his strong, safe arms wrapped around her shoulders. The same arms that had guarded her for fifty-five years, the same arms that would not stop protecting her until he drew his last breath.

"I'll do it," she whispered, her arms tightening. "I'll be the one, or rather the Hood will be."

Malaki kept silent and only held her tighter. There was no doubt she would; it was a fact not a possibility. She felt his shoulders move. His voice was a whisper, a promise at her ear. "I'll be there with you."

Seated in her usual wingback chair next to the cold, lifeless fireplace, Isolde closed the book and scanned the library. There were even more children here this week, four more to be precise. They sat with legs crossed and eyes wide, staring up at her. That was the mask she wore today: Lady Isolde Cotheran.

Isolde knew she had to exercise caution, a great deal of it in fact. Eyes of the king were ever watchful, itching for the opportunity to report a human sympathizer in order to gain his favor.

"Just don't read anything out loud that encourages rebellion," Alaric had warned. "You never know when someone will find offense and report it to the king."

She had agreed, not wanting to put her feelings about that bastard onto children. They would form their own opinions soon enough if they hadn't already. More so, she wanted to give them an escape from the life the gods had condemned them to.

They looked to her now, their eyes shining with wonder. A few gazed out the window. Isolde could practically see their imaginations at work, turning the story over in their minds. A boy in the back chewed on his thumbnail.

"Alright, everyone," Isolde said, setting the book down on the already crowded table. "Nan has a treat for you all waiting in the kitchen. Will and Silva, would you show our new friends the way, please? I'll see you all next week."

Needing no further instructions, the horde of children stampeded down the hall. Will and Silva led the four new comers, whose eyes were still wide with excitement. Two remained seated, their eyes glued to her.

"Tanor," Isolde said, "I believe introductions are in order."

Tanor nodded, his eyes shining. A grin formed on his expressive mouth. "Lady Isolde, I would like you to meet, Mary." A soft tone caressed her name as it left his lips. A faint blush blossomed over her pale, freckled cheeks. Tanor had talked about her frequently. She was the eldest of five siblings with a mother who did what she could to provide for them. Leaving Mary, a child herself at thirteen, to raise the others on her own. Isolde hid her knowing smile and walked forward, her hands clasped in front of her. Ringlets of red fell about Mary's shoulders, framing her freckled, pale face in a storm of wild fire.

"Very nice to meet you, Mary," Isolde said. "Now, if you will follow me." Isolde strolled to the fireplace, her hand resting on one of the small decorative stones.

Mary looked to Tanor for instruction, her eyes filled with uncertainty and apprehension. He nodded earnestly and followed. Isolde pushed gently, allowing the trap door to swing inward. Without looking back, she descended a dark, spiral staircase.

"Do mind your step," she said over her shoulder, the hem of her lavender dress brushing the worn floorboards.

The stairs gave way to a wide room below. A large mahogany table resided in the center. The surface danced with the light of a humble fire. Books and parchment decorated the top. Four chairs lined the table, and a fifth sat in the head.

"Malaki," Isolde greeted. The students filed in, the girl stiff and wide-eyed.

"Lady Isolde," Malaki said, rising. Mary's eyes widened further as she took in Malaki's intimidating form.

"Please take a seat," Isolde said, waving a hand to the empty chairs lining the table. She caught a glimpse of Tanor who took the seat on her right. He was fighting to hide the grin on his face. Careful of the force, Isolde kicked him beneath the table, and the smile disappeared instantly. It had not been that long ago the same fear showed in his eyes at his first lesson.

"It is my understanding," she said, her attention turning to Mary, "that you wish to learn to read."

After a moment, Mary nodded, her eyes diving to the table. "Yes, my Lady," she said.

"Why?" Isolde demanded, a hardness creeping into her words.

Tanor's eyes moved between Isolde and the new comers, a firm line forming on his lips. At last Mary said, "Because I want to."

"Not good enough," Malaki bit, his voice booming in the confined space, making the children jump.

"You do understand the seriousness of the situation?" Isolde asked. Her eyes, blue with a hint of gray, dropped to the table. "Look at me!"

She could feel her power stir, the light in her eyes shining in their own. Isolde needed Mary to understand just how serious this was.

"This is not a game. It is a matter of life and death. You will not be able to use this gift openly; no one outside this room can know."

Isolde let her words settle for a moment, her gaze flickering to Tanor who sat up straight, his gaze hard. He knew the severity of the situation, the importance of silence on her part.

"Now, I'll ask you again, why do you want to learn how to read?"

"It's a way to stand up to the king," Mary said, holding Isolde's piercing stare. Her chin rose ever so slightly. "A way for us to fight back."

"What if you are accused?" Malaki demanded, his hands resting on the backs of their chairs. "What do you do if a soldier shows up at your doorstep...and accuses you of this?" Mary looked to Tanor, then to Isolde, then back again, unsure of what to say.

"You keep quiet," Tanor said. "You do not mention Lady Isolde or Thornwood." Mary licked her lips, her cheeks blazing.

"If you do not expose yourselves, this shouldn't be a problem," Isolde said. "Which isn't going to happen correct?"

"Correct?" Malaki growled, the wood groaning beneath his hands.

"Yes, my lady," she whispered.

"Good," Isolde said. "Now that that is cleared up, let's begin." She passed Mary a palette and a single piece of chalk. "We are starting with the basics. Each word is made up of a combination of letters. Today, you will begin to learn those letters. Their shape, order, and sounds."

She pushed a stack of papers between them, the letter A sprawled across its surface in bold, elegant writing. "Let's start from the beginning."

"Never gets old, does it?" Malaki asked, pushing away from a bookcase resting in the back of the hidden classroom. Tanor had offered to show Mary to the door by way of the kitchen. A book was tucked into the lining of his pants. A loan for having taken up his reading time for the day.

Isolde smiled, pushing up from the chair. "Not even a little bit." She collected the letters of alphabet and placed in them onto one of the bookshelves and began dusting away the chalky remnants of the children's work on the palettes. "I take it everything went well?"

"It went fine. Our connections in Yvek have received word they are only four days from their final destination by now. Wherever that is. The current must strong if they are that far along."

"How is Martha?" Isolde asked, her voice low.

Malaki's face fell, his eyes hardening. "She'll live," he said, "but only just."

She nodded, any regret for having killed Dagan evaporating instantly. "She's alive Malaki; that's what matters."

"What matters," he said bitterly. "What kind of life will she have? Crippled, unable to stand properly, unable to use her hands...What kind of curse have we put on her?"

Isolde licked her lips, not really sure how to respond. "You gave that boy his mother back. She can be there for him, watch him grow. That's a gift...not a curse."

He looked at her, his eyes softening. It was easy to forget how old he was. Impossibly handsome and chiseled from stone itself, he had served as the previous king's Right Hand.

His second in command. Entrusted with the task of leading the king's armed forces, Malaki had also been in charge of ensuring the safety of the royal family. Isolde knew this particular failure haunted him, nearly as much as not reaching Aurora in time. Their names decorated his skin, hidden amongst the thorns and branches.

"Where are Bly and Cill?" Isolde asked, desperate to steer his thoughts away from the torture he endured within himself.

"At the Pit," he said nodding to the north. "Awaiting our arrival."

"Seriously?" She rolled her eyes, the weight of the night pressing down on her even more.

"Call it nervous energy. The adrenaline hasn't quite left them yet. I'm sure you know the feeling."

"All too well."

"Care for a few rounds?" he asked, a devilish grin playing across his face.

She absently rotated her shoulder. The wound sang with a ghost of pain. Declining would spark suspicion and she was not in the mood to deal with his interrogation.

This is going to hurt. "If your old hands can keep up."

He growled with anticipation stepping aside to pull the door open for her. Children's laughter echoed down the hall to the kitchens. "So, a new one," he said. She rolled her shoulder once more and walked to the door. He trailed behind her. "I'm still not sure about this."

"We couldn't turn her away, Malaki," she said.

"Can we trust her?"

"I don't know yet." She prayed to the gods she hated that they could. Otherwise…She refused to let the thought go on. "Tanor has vouched for her silence. We will have to trust that…for now."

Tanor had been her first student, a favorite from their first lesson. He resided with his father, Tarvo, at Thornwood. Tarvo had joined them from Whisper, one of the central hubs of trade for Arnoria. Tanor's father had served as one of the most talented blacksmiths in the area.

However, being human left him and Tanor subject to much abuse. Patrons would place orders, then refuse to pay the agreed upon price at their completion. The law was never on his side; it was designed against him. Often times, Tarvo was left empty handed and bleeding on his shop floor.

Isolde had laid witness to such an event. She offered him a contract at Thornwood, and he served as their lead smithy. As time progressed, Tarvo became more comfortable, even offering up his opinion on the king. Isolde grew to trust him as well, even approaching him about working with elithrium.

Tarvo confessed he was experienced in the art of handling the deadly material but that he would need something in return. "Teach my son to read."

It had taken Isolde by surprise. "Why?" she had asked. "If he is caught reading, or if anyone finds out…. he will be put to death."

Tarvo nodded, his hands rubbing together. "My wife had begun teaching him when sickness took her. It was her dream that he learn. He knows the law, Lady Isolde. He understands what it would mean for us and for your house if he were ever caught."

She had always been fond of Tanor. His curious nature was a breath of fresh air at Thornwood. Nodding, she extended her hand to him, "You have a deal."

Isolde smiled at the memory. He had come a long way in the past ten years and his appetite for knowledge had only grown. Alaric had taken a liking to the young man, even going so far as to search out new books not only for Isolde, but Tanor as well.

Malaki stopped at the table at the front of the library. His eyes still troubled. A grin tugged at the edge of Isolde's lips. "You keep scowling like that and no amount of virya power will save you from wrinkles."

His upper lips raised to expose a row of teeth, set. "You are far too reckless."

Isolde bit the inside of her cheek, her annoyance rising. "And you are a pain in my ass."

A faint growl filtered through the library. They both knew the conversation about changing the plan was coming but it would have to wait until their dangerous energy was spent.

A plate of raspberry jam sugar cookies rested on the table between them. Warm jam trickled down the white powdered sugar, creating warm pink pillows of icing. Isolde stuffed one into her mouth, the sugar melting on her tongue. She closed her eyes as a moan of pure pleasure erupted from her throat.

Malaki reached over, his fingers closing in on one. Striking with the quickness of a serpent, Isolde smacked his hand away, and pulled the plate to her. "These are mine," she said, stuffing another into her mouth. "Get your own."

Malaki seethed. "Don't make me take it." She stuck her tongue out at him, bits of cookie and jam falling to the table. "You're such a child," he said. "I only want one."

"Nan made them for me."

"And you can't spare one cookie?" he demanded.

"Nope," Isolde said, tossing another into her already stuffed mouth.

"Give...me...a...cookie!" Malaki's voice rumbled through the library. Looking him dead in the eye, Isolde lifted a cookie, inspected its star-shaped surface...and licked the jam. She repeated this until the jam was licked free from each one. Malaki watched, his jaw feathering in fury as she carefully placed each cookie back onto the plate and pushed it towards him.

"There you go," she said, grinning. "The rest are yours."

A smirk played out on Malaki's lips as he fisted the now jamless cookies and crammed them all into his mouth. Crumbs littered the table and dusted the stone floor.

"Five minutes," he said, turning on his heel heading out the door to wait. She bit back a laugh, knowing good and well he could still hear her. Pulling herself away from the table, she hurried up to her room to change.

Her training leathers fit perfectly to every curve of her hips, thighs, and chest. They had been specially tailored by Nan and Galaena. Turning to leave, Isolde caught herself in the mirror and a smirk formed on her lips at the sight of her backside in leather. She was by no means small. No, she had never been accused of that. Instead, beautiful curves decorated her body and she relished in it.

Malaki was leaning against one of the pillars in the foyer. Two long swords, one in each hand, glistened in the light of the early afternoon sun. Exhaustion rattled her bones, draining every ounce of energy from her muscles. Without a word, he tossed the smaller of the two through the air. She caught it with ease, ignoring the barking pain in her shoulder.

"Long swords?" she grumbled, her lip turning up at the plaything in her hand. "I hate these things. Why do you get the bigger one?"

"Because I'm the oldest," he said, with a triumphant grin, swinging the blade over his shoulder. "And you need to practice. Try and keep up." He said with a grin as he took off in a sprint, creating a blur over the back of the well-manicured lawn and into the woods.

Fire ignited in her blood. It was a challenge to her power. No matter how tired she was, it was a challenge Isolde would never ignore. She followed, her legs pushing and her arms pumping. A few seconds in, she heard his steps less than one hundred yards away, veering left.

A snarl ripped through her teeth, her competitive side erupting. The sword might as well have not been there. She felt nothing. Nothing at all except the need to catch him. Her power surged, forcing her to move faster. It bubbled to the surface, fragments breaking through the tight hold she constantly kept in check.

She spotted the Pit up ahead. The large field Malaki had cleared years ago for them to train in was littered with sporadic mounds of earth and gaping holes. It was not proper for a lady to be trained in the art of combat. Making the Pit's proximity to Thornwood not ideal. However, it would not do for her to transform into a savage beast and kill everyone in sight if she lost control.

They had little choice in the matter with Thornwood being the smallest territory. Space was a commodity they were not afforded.

Isolde broke the tree line and spotted Malaki on the edge of the forest, his ebony hair windswept. He was watching Cillian and Blyana exchange blows with a look for scrutiny. Their eyes were ignited, glowing with their own power. Blyana dodged a well-placed strike, her side becoming too exposed.

"Watch your right!" Malaki barked. But it was too late.

Cillian shot forward. His sword, while harmless, landed a painful blow to her exposed ribs. She hissed and whirled around, her arm swinging wide. The blade passed just inches from his grinning face.

"Come on, love," Cillian chided. "You can do better than that."

Blyana bared her elongated teeth and launched at him, the tip of her sword aiming for his heart. He blocked it with ease, his feet shifting to match hers as they moved around the clearing. Their steps were mindful of the holes and rocks scattered about.

They were wielding long swords as well. A weapon neither Isolde or Blyana cared for. However, Cillian was an expert in anything that had a blade. It sung in his hands, creating a lovely melody of steel and wind. They continued on until Isolde could see Blyana's control beginning to wane.

Swinging wide, Cillian blocked her strike and grinned in her face. A shriek of fury pierced the air as she launched into another attack.

"Enough," Malaki ordered, his hands sweeping over the clearing. The earth reacted as he commanded, creating a fissure in the ground. They stood on opposite sides of the newly formed crevice. Their chests rose and fell, exhaustion pouring from their shaking shoulders.

"I almost had him, Malaki!" Blyana panted, her eyes narrowing at Cillian who smiled back.

"I adore your imagination, love" Cillian said with a wink. She hissed in response but sheathed the battered blade.

With his sword already unsheathed, Malaki strolled to the center of the field and turned back to Isolde. His eyes were guarded, power igniting in his gaze as he sealed the earth once more.

"See if you can at least land a blow this time," he barked pointing the blade at her chest.

Isolde's eyes narrowed as she ripped the blade from its sheath. Exhausted control blanketed what felt like an endless well of power. Its surface churning and pushing against the carefully placed restraints in her mind. Isolde felt the feathers beneath her skin. The sharp keen eyes hone in on her opponent as Malaki brought the massive iron sword down.

The pain in her shoulder did not register as vibrations cascaded down her body. She shoved against him, their swords separating only for a moment before colliding once again.

"Don't let it control you," Malaki said through gritted teeth. She growled and shoved against him again. They danced around each other, moving too fast for a human or even some half-bloods to truly follow. "Force it down!"

This was Malaki's favorite time to train her. When she was sleep deprived and at the brink of losing control. They continued this way for a while, each matching the other blow for blow. When she struck, he would block. His sword was met with hers at each turn. Eventually, their swords became chipped and warped.

They continued on until Isolde's foot took a wrong step. Malaki launched forward, knocking the blade from her grasp and driving her into the dirt. She snarled up at him as he pressed the armless, dull blade against her throat.

"Dead." His voice lifeless, serious as if it had been a real battle.

"I beg to differ." She thought about driving her foot into his crotch, just to prove her point but she saw the warm, hazel eyes once more. He had reined it in.

"Time for a break," he said, his teeth still clinched, holding the blade against her throat.

"So soon?" she said, her arms shaking with exhaustion. The power held strong, her controlled grip on the beast grew weaker and weaker.

"If we don't stop soon, we'll be coming to blows with claws and talons. Take a breath."

She did, in through her nose and out through her mouth. With each exhale, she tried to imagine her aggression going with it. Malaki still held his sword tightly, its edge not allowing her any room to move. He knew better than to let his guard down around her when she was trying to bring herself down.

Each breath placed a bar in front of the beast in her mind. The hideous creature growled at the restraint, its need to be set free clawing at her will. A slight wind brushed her cheek and she sighed. At last, the final bar was placed, securing the creature within. Flexing her fingers, she withdrew her battered sword and took a step back.

"Are you alright?" Malaki asked the grip on his sword still tight. Isolde did not take offense. She knew she was dangerous.

"It's getting there," Isolde nodded and pushed the ruined hunk of metal aside for good measure.

"I'll say," Cillian said, "I'm a little disappointed. Would have been nice to see the old man put on his ass again."

Malaki narrowed his eyes at him. "Would you care for a turn?"

Cillian merely grinned, his fingers playing with the loose strand of Blyana's hair. "I would hate to deprive Isolde of having the pleasure."

Blyana chuckled, her shoulder bumping into his chest. "Oh please, you know you're scared of Malaki. You would be a fool if you weren't."

"Anyone would be," Isolde said, her power pushing against its bars in response. "Let's get a drink." A small brook snaked through the forest just a few yards beyond the tree line. Isolde welcomed the sound, blocking out the snarling ripping through her skull. Perching on a boulder, she splashed the cool water onto her face. Ribbons of ice slithered down her neck and chest. She sighed in relief.

"An interesting report came through the grapevine," Cillian said, dumping a handful of water down his back. "There have been more rumors of a masked vigilante sneaking around Arnoria."

"Is that so?" Isolde said, plopping down. Tearing her boots off, she sunk her feet into the cool, rippling water and sighed once again. "A child from Foxclove mentioned another masked crusader. Do we have a name? It better not be the Hood. This imposter has capitalized off me enough."

"From what I understand, they call themselves Helurtu."

"I've heard the name," Blyana said, her lips parting. "It was commonly heard at Madame Vara's in Whisper."

Malaki's eyes darkened, a low growl echoing through his chest. "That doesn't put them in a good light if their name is common in that particular establishment."

"No, it doesn't," Cillian spat.

"I don't recall them being a regular," Blyana said, her eyes dropping to the small, viper tattoo on her thumb. A constant reminder of the past. "Just whispers…rumors."

"Still," Isolde said, trying to draw Blyana from the past. "This Helurtu sounds like another friend for the Hood to meet."

"You just killed a high lord, Isolde" Malaki sighed. "Can hunting down a possibly phantom slave trader wait a day or two?"

Her eyes narrowed, a retort dangling on the edge of her tongue. But the pain in her back had returned along with new pains elsewhere. "One day," she said. Her fingers broke the water again. This time a soft, almost caressing hand responded, like the touch of a lover. Tiny streams of water, no bigger than a piece of thread, began flowing up her hand and around her wrist. She jerked her hand back, shaking the invasive droplets free.

"What is it?" Malaki demanded, his eyes lighting instantly.

She shook her head, drying her hand on her pant leg. "Nothing," she said, forcing a smile. The touch echoed on her skin. A part of her longed for the water once more. As if a piece of her soul was pulling, tugging her back into its embrace. It wasn't the first time. Flashes of the past rushed forward.

Columns of water danced around her, forming into whatever shape she wished. Eyes of those she loved most looked down at her in both fascination…and fear. Pain ripped through her like blade at the memory. Isolde shoved it away, burying it into a part of herself she rarely allowed herself to think of.

Malaki rolled his eyes and sighed heavily. "We need to get back. Alaric and Gal will be needing help with the packing. Tomorrow we leave for Briarhole."

Isolde groaned and fell onto her back. An arm covered her eyes to block a beam of light penetrating the canopy of leaves. "Can't you make them see reason, Malaki? I don't want to be Lady of Thornwood!" She hated how whiny she sounded but despised her new role even more.

"Quit complaining," he said, poking her in the ribs. She swatted at his boot. "This is their choice. Be the grown-up I know is in there."

She stuck her tongue out at him and pushed off the ground.

"Did you forget my threat?" Malaki asked, coming to his full height, hands resting on his hips. A hint of humor danced across his face.

Isolde rolled her eyes and crossed her arms tightly. "You must be eager to lose your tongue by sticking it out where I can chop it off," she said, her voice like a petulant child, mocking his deep, husky tone.

"It still stands," Malaki said, already walking back to through the clearing to fetch the ruined swords. She stuck her tongue out at him again, adding a hand gesture for good measure.

"I saw that," he called.

Isolde shook her head and followed after him. Cillian and Blyana were not far behind. A sense of dread had slowly begun snaking its way into Isolde's gut. It was the realization that a new life was about to be thrust upon her and tomorrow was the first push. Tomorrow, she would put on another mask. One that was more foreign than the Hood.

The mask of someone who willingly danced with devils. The mask of Lady Isolde Cotheran, heir to Thornwood.

CHAPTER 8

erritory after territory passed beneath the company of Thornwood. Wagon after wagon followed, each one containing an infinite amount of supplies.

"How much longer?" Isolde whined, arching her back.

"We probably would have already arrived," said Malaki. "If we weren't lugging enough dresses to outfit an entire army behind us."

"I need options." Isolde ground her teeth in annoyance. "How am I supposed to know what I want to wear a few nights from now?"

"We are there for three nights, Isolde," he said. "You pick three dresses, pack them, then wear them. In whatever order you desire."

"Your sense of fashion is as frightening as your lack of skill with a bow."

"As is your temper," he retorted, a hint of a growl lacing through each word.

"It's no use," Blyana said, leaning over Isolde's saddle, her eyes humorously appraising Malaki. "He's too far set in his ways of life as a soldier."

Isolde had tried countless times to get Malaki to try something other than his britches and worn white tunics. Yet the more she looked, the more she couldn't imagine him in anything else. The white fabric of his tunic stood in stark contrast with his deep, russet skin. Vines and names of the dead ran along the chiseled lines of his muscles in deep, black remembrance. He was the very picture of comfort, of familiarity.

He was home.

"Is all of this necessary?" Isolde scanned a wagon filled with luscious, expensive wine. Each bottle was capable of feeding a family for at least a few days. Or at least allowing her to slip into oblivion for a while.

"I don't like it any more than you," said her uncle, Alaric, from where he rode up ahead. The high, afternoon sun shined in his golden hair. "But it is expected. This particular gathering is a power play, a display of wealth."

"I wasn't aware we were dick measuring—"

"Isolde!" Alaric's gray eyes flashed. "You will watch your tongue. This is not the proper behavior for the future heir of Thornwood."

"Oh? But emptying our coffers and showing off to nobility is?"

"It's not about emptying the coffers," said Cillian. "It's about the image, the illusion of power that possession seems to display." A hint of distaste peppered his words. Turning around, Isolde caught the faintest of scowls set in the corner of his mouth.

"He's right," Alaric said, turning back around. "This is merely a formality and we need to make an impression. This is your first time before the council. I want you to learn the room and be watchful of who speaks, their body language towards one another."

"So, you want me to learn to be like one of them?" Isolde asked, her voice cutting with annoyance.

"You know that's not true," Alaric said, his tone reproachful. "But you need to learn what kind of people you will be dealing with."

"I wouldn't have to if you would just use your power," she grumbled. The old anger and heartbreak were made new. "If you don't, you will die, Alaric."

He was quiet for a moment, his head dropping slightly. After a moment, his voice drifted back to her. His words cushioned with patience. "Your aunt and I have lived long enough. It is time."

"It's time," she chided, her grip on the reins tightening. "There are plenty of others who have lived far longer than you two."

"That is not what we want."

Isolde sighed sharply, hoping to dispel some of her frustration.

"It is not your choice, Isolde," Alaric continued. "Yes, Gal and I are giving up our immortality to enjoy the years we have remaining in peace. I want to make sure Thornwood is left in the best hands possible," he said, his tone much lighter, much like the Alaric she remembered from childhood. "You are the only one I would trust with our people."

Isolde shook her head. "Not once have you asked what I want Alaric, I don't want anything to do with it!"

"And you think I did?" he demanded. "I never wanted to rule Thornwood either. It wasn't a choice. But I dealt with it because that's what needed to happen!" He sighed again before straightening up in the saddle, his eyes forward. "Sometimes…We don't have a choice in the glory that is thrust upon us, Isolde. Sometimes our lives are not our own."

Isolde ground her teeth, forcing down the lump in her throat. She refused to speak, refused to acknowledge him as they rode on. She wished she could talk with Nan, needing her infinite wisdom on the subject once more. But Isolde knew what her words would be, what they had been before.

"It is their choice, my rose," Nan had said the night they had delivered the news. "You will have to make such a choice as well one day. Just pray that you have the opportunity that they do, to leave this world on your own terms and no one else's."

She shook her head, clearing her mind of Nan's voice. Nudging Versa forward, she pushed past the guard and led the way of the caravan. She needed time to think, to rein in her anger.

After a while, hooves sped to her. Isolde knew who it was without even having to look up.

"I don't want a lecture," she said through her teeth.

"I'm not giving you one," Malaki said, bringing the gentle gilding next to her. It sniffed at Versa who snipped back.

"Nor do I want to hear that it is their choice. I understand that, but it doesn't mean I have to be happy about it."

His jaw feathered. "You're being selfish."

"Excuse me?"

"You heard me," Malaki said, his eyes cutting. "I've known you your whole life. You are so much more than this. And you are wasting what you could be...what you were born to be—"

"Enough," Isolde growled, causing Versa and Malaki's horse to startle. "I was born to be exactly who I am, Malaki," she said, her power flowing, heating her blood. "And nothing will change that." Driving her heels into Versa's sides, she shot forward without a care if she was followed or not.

Miles passed beneath their feet. Endless miles filled with nonstop instruction from Alaric.

"You mustn't speak unless directly addressed," he said, knowing full well she would.

"Yes, the females are to remain silent like the good little decorations we are," Isolde said with the roll of her eyes.

"None of the heirs have an allowance to speak unless invited to." His eyes narrowing. "Not even the males."

"How very equally opportunistic of you all."

"Take it as a challenge," Malaki said, the hint of a smile playing at his lips. "Try to remain quiet as long as possible. I know it's difficult for you."

"I find it hard to remain quiet in the face of stupidity," said Isolde, her fingers gripping the reins.

Malaki's brow rose. "My case in point."

Emerging from the tree line, leaving Blackford Forest behind, they halted. Strange sounds echoed across the rolling hills of the northernmost territory. Unease settled into Isolde's bones.

"What is that?" Cillian asked, his eyes hard on the road ahead. It veered down and to the left, disappearing into the rising sun.

"I'm not sure," said Alaric. His tone was hollow, and it filled Isolde with dread. Driving his heels in the flank of his chestnut stallion, Alaric rode forward with three guards at his back.

He's lying...he knows. Her hands gripped the reins. Malaki shifted closer to her, his horse bumping Versa. She whined and snipped in frustration to which the gelding ignored, his mind eased by Malaki's power.

Cillian and Blyana slid closer as well. Their eyes scanned the horizon.

Upon reaching the top, Alaric froze in the saddle. He was so still, so focused on what lay beyond. The guards looked at each other, their eyes wide with disbelief-and horror. Just when Isolde couldn't stand it anymore, Alaric turned. His eyes, so full of fury and sorrow, slid from Isolde to Malaki. Without waiting, her second-in-command reached over and gently placed her hands on the bridged horn of her saddle.

"Mal—"

"Whatever you do," he said, wrapping the reins between her fingers such a way that they would not fall from her grasp. "Do not let go." The sounds grew louder...familiar...agonizingly recognizable.

"Malaki," Isolde said as the sound repeated over...and over...and over again. The crack of whips...wailing...crack...wailing...crack...wailing.

She turned her face to Alaric. He was still looking at her, a faint line of silver shining from his eyes. It glistened off the light growing in the depths of his haunted gaze.

"Look at me, Isolde," Malaki said, his fingers gentle but firm as they pulled her face back to his. "Only at me."

"I know that sound," Blyana said, her eyes wide and glowing.

"Bly," Malaki rasped, his eyes piercing into Isolde's, which were now wide. Cillian remained silent, his jaw set and coal colored eyes hard as obsidian stone.

Screams carried over the gusts of wind, bellows of agony that sent tears falling down Isolde's cheeks as she tried but failed to look.

"Malaki," she said again, her voice a grated, hollow rasp.

"I know," he said, cradling her face in his hands. She felt his warmth, his peace spread through her muscles, loosening the tension. "I do not bow to fear," he whispered, his forehead resting on hers.

Agony swept through her heart like a winter's punishing chill. *My heart is bleeding, surely.* Her fingers gripped the horn, the wood splintering...the leather stretching.

After a moment, Isolde paused to shove the memories of her childhood at Briarhole, along with the ones from before, back into the pieces of her soul that belonged to only one. To the person buried back in Blackford Forest, beneath the tree that did not belong. She allowed that sorrow to turn. The winter's biting cold melted and turned into a scorching heat of hatred. A fire that threatened to consume her body and soul.

A shaky sigh ghosted through her clenched teeth, her eyes squeezing shut as she whispered back, "It bows to me." She looked once more into Malaki's eyes. He must have seen the fire, the flow of furious resolve that burned deep within. After a moment, he planted a kiss on her forehead and leaned away.

Blyana moved to cover Isolde's left as Cillian pulled to cover her back. They too were looking forward, the same hatred igniting in their eyes.

Breaching the top of the hill, Isolde couldn't hold back the shuddering cry of sorrow that erupted from her throat. Bodies...There were so many broken bodies. They seemed to stretch onward, a never-ending wave of suffering.

Backs bent as they picked and harvested the fields of Briarhole. Backs shimmered with fresh blood running from new rivets in their flesh. The once beautiful territory known as Arnoria's stronghold, was nothing more than a slave encampment. A death camp.

At various points along the rows of labor rode a virya. Each was armed with two whips, one for each hand. Their tips were stained black and red.

"Move it!" One shouted from the right, causing Isolde to jump. The whip rose and fell over the back of an old man, his back jerking from the blow. He landed on his hands and knees, his scarred flesh torn a new.

"On your feet, old man!" the guard roared, his hand raising once again.

Malaki moved before she could. His hand gripped hers as it reached for the blade at her side, constricting it around the horn. She bared her teeth at him, her anger now aimed solely at him. But the look on his face stayed her fury. It was the look that told her he knew, that he understood...that he felt the same.

Grinding her teeth until she thought they'd shatter, she pushed Versa forward leaving the sound of pleas for mercy and cries of agony behind her.

It took another hour to reach the stronghold. An hour of cries and pleas to berate and torture her. Eyes...so many eyes stared as they passed. Eyes so hollow Isolde wondered if a soul remained behind them. The scars and wounds on their bodies could not compare to the horror inside.

Every face said the same thing to her. Each one was crying and seemed to say, "You have failed me...you have failed me...why have you failed me?" Plan after plan formed in Isolde's mind. Ways to save them from this nightmare. And plan after plan crumbled into ash. It was impossible. There were just too many.

She swept a glance back at Cillian. His dark eyes filled with worry were fixed on Blyana who stared straight ahead. The thin line of her lips did not waver, did not move even as a woman fell at her horse's feet.

"Stupid whore!" a virya roared, his large boots stomping through the mud. He fisted a handful of her strawberry blonde hair and yanked her up to her feet, wringing a straggled cry from her parched, cracked lips. "I'll make sure to pay you a visit later tonight."

A growl rumbled through Isolde's teeth as the virya's eyes rose to meet Blyana's. He blew her a kiss and pulled the woman back to him roughly. "Like what you see?" he asked, his eyes roving over Blyana. "Don't worry, you'll get a taste. After I'm done with her."

Isolde's vision turned crimson as her anger exploded. Ripping away from Malaki's grasp, she spurred Versa forward, forcing Blyana behind her. The guard shoved the woman to the ground but wasn't quick enough to escape Isolde's reins. They constricted around his neck and squeezed. She pushed Versa forward, throwing the man off balance to dangle in the strips of leather.

"Isolde!" Alaric rode forward, his stead nearly colliding with Versa's flank. "Release him. Now."

"He threatened Blyana," Isolde rasped, every word laced with vengeful malice. Her eyes turned back to the man struggling. His face was turning a shade of purple that made Isolde smile. Her power stirred, feeding off her anger. The light in his eyes began to fade, his fingers fumbling against the reins.

"And I'm sure he regrets that now," Alaric said carefully. "But killing him will only cause problems. Is he worth that trouble?"

She wanted to say yes, that his death was worth whatever issues would come. But reason slowly worked its way back to her. Isolde let the man struggle for only a moment longer before reluctantly jerking the reins free. He fell to the ground in a heap. His meaty hands cradled his throat as dry, rattled coughs fought their way out of his chest.

"Come," Alaric said, his tone thick with the weight of Thornwood's lord.

Isolde stole one last look at the man still kneeling in the mud. He looked up at her, his eyes blood shot and furious. Clicking her tongue, she urged Versa forward. A small, cruel smile spread across her lips as she looked back and said, "We'll see each other again."

She turned away just as Cillian rammed his horse into the guard, sending him flying face first into the mud, manure, and piss. Up the path, Blyana murmured, "You shouldn't have done that, Isolde."

"There are a lot of things I shouldn't do," Isolde said, pointedly ignoring Malaki's gaze. "Has that ever stopped me before?"

"They were only words," Blyana said, her eyes falling to her hands. The knuckles were bone white as she gripped the reins. The pad of her finger began to rub against her left knuckle.

"Words that he won't say again."

"Don't even think about it." Each word rumbled through Malaki's chest. His eyes held a slight glow.

"Too late," said Isolde with a shrug and a smile that promised violence.

"I mean it, Isolde!" Malaki said, his hands clenching around the reins. "This isn't Foxclove."

"I'm well aware of that, Malaki," Isolde said. "I grew up here, if you'll recall."

"Yes, you did. Forty years ago. There's no telling what changes Volkran has made."

She ignored Alaric's backward glance. He knew what she was thinking, what her power now demanded. A slight shake of his head told her enough.

"Looks like I'll be breaking the rules again."

"Not just you," Cillian said. His eyes, usually so bright with laughter, were now flat with quiet fury. A fury that only rose for one person. Blyana's gaze drifted back to him. It was a look she only shared with him, one of understanding, of safe assurance.

"Of course, not without you, love," he said with a flicker of amusement breaking on the edge of his lips.

"That's what I thought," Blyana said, turning back around.

Isolde grinned at Malaki's heavy sigh. His fingers pinching the bridge of his nose.

"Are you going to worry the whole time?" she asked.

"With you plotting and scheming in the lion's den?" he said, his eyes tired. "Worrying won't cover it."

"You expect me to let this go?"

"I expect you to learn which battles are worth the sacrifice...and which ones are not."

"Tell me," said Isolde. "Would you have let it slide if his words were aimed at me?"

Malaki fell silent, eyes flashing with a spark of anger. His lips pressed firmly together, refusing to say the words. Isolde snuck a glance at Blyana, who immediately dropped her gaze from Malaki. But she saw the look of hurt etched in her friend's face.

Isolde knew good and well what Malaki would have done if the man had said that to her. His wrath would have been unleashed in a wave not even Alaric could have stopped. But for Blyana...Isolde saw the look of shame on Malaki's face and she shook her head at him. Blyana wanted Malaki's approval, was desperate for it. For him to see her as one of their own and not an outsider.

The rest of the journey passed in strained silence. Isolde focused on keeping her eyes forward and hands firmly knitted around the reins.

"Welcome House Cotheran of Thornwood," a man greeted as they rode under and through one of the massive elithrium iron gates of Briarhole. Forty-foot walls spanned the fortress in each direction.

"Thank you," Alaric said sliding down. His teeth clenched when he touched the ground, his mangled left leg folding beneath him. The firm grip on the reins was the only thing keeping from landing flat on his backside.

"Let me help you—"

"Leave me," said Alaric, smacking the man's hand away. A yelp of pain echoed through the courtyard as the man scurried back, hiding his hand behind him.

Alaric gazed around and met Isolde's hard stare. Looking away quickly, he turned to the trembling man as he yanked his cane free of the saddle and hobbled by. "See to the horses, men, and luggage, please."

"Y-yes s-sir," the man stammered his eyes downcast.

Descending Versa, Isolde walked over to him and pushed a bag of coins into his uninjured palm. "Forgive him," she said gently, the corner of her lips tilting. "He's a grumpy old ass."

Fear shined from his eyes but quickly faded to humbled understanding. "My lady," he said with a deep bow. "If I returned to see my home like this," he said, his eyes sweeping over the keep, "I can't say I would not do the same."

She felt Malaki's warmth brush her arm. "May I?" he asked the old man, holding his hand out to him. He looked at Malaki with fear and distrust but quickly relented. Isolde wasn't quite sure if it was out of fear of disobeying him…or if he saw something in Malaki that put his mind to rest.

His hand looked so small, so fragile in Malaki's grip. But a look of ease soon loosened the tension in the old man's face as Malaki's magic slowly, tenderly reformed the bones. After a few more moments passed, Malaki relinquished his grip and took a step back.

"Thank you, sir," the old man said, flexing his now newly healed hand before his eyes. "You truly are a blessing from the gods, my Lord Malaki."

"I am no lord," said Malaki, the words rushing from his mouth in panic as he looked around the courtyard. "Not anymore."

The old man stared at Malaki. His hazy eyes crinkled at the edges as he bowed to him. "As you say, sir." He bowed once more to Isolde as a warm, grateful smile broke across his face. "My Lady Isolde." A blanket of sadness covered her heart as the man left to carry out Alaric's orders.

CHAPTER 9

Alaric stood at the bottom of the large staircase, just outside the entrance to the ballroom. His dark golden hair, laced with fine lines of gray was swept back in waves that nearly touched his shoulders. He wore the colors of House Cotheran with absolute perfection.

A maroon-colored jacket set with golden embroidery displayed the hard physique one only earned over a lifetime of ruthless training. Cream colored britches were neatly tucked into his perfectly polished brown, leather boots. Gold shined from the buckles at his chest, waist, and ankles. Isolde paused at the top of the stairs. *What a warrior he must have been.*

His eyes turned from happy to disapproving as she descended. A knowing smile blossomed on her freshly painted lips. She knew she had chosen the right dress.

Deep crimson silk clung to her form. It left little to the imagination and plenty for the eye to absorb. Flowing over her hips, the delicate fabric hugged every curve. It traveled from her thighs, continuing up her waist to her breasts that were surrounded by a stream of intricate embroidery.

Sweeping across the low neckline, golden roses surrounded by thorny veins wound up her left shoulder and down the length of her back to brush across her right hip. They ended at the hem that trailed behind her. The neckline kissed the top of her shoulders, ensuring her back was covered, as it always was.

Alaric's lips hardly moved as he offered her his arm. "You are here to learn how to run a territory, not give them something to look at."

Isolde gripped the sleeve of his jacket and smiled innocently. "I'm not here just as a distraction?" she asked, her eyes wide with exaggerated confusion.

He growled lowly, his grip tightening. "You know that's not it at all, Isolde."

"I want to know what kind of men I'm dealing with, Alaric. This is one way to find out." She brushed a wave of her dark brown hair over her shoulder. Two golden hair pins set with tiny rubies kept the sides swept back from her face.

"Dagan's ruby ring would have matched this perfectly." Blyana had said while getting ready. "What a shame."

"There won't be much talk with you dressed like that," Alaric said.

"Good." She smiled. "Then this will be quick."

"From Thornwood," the servant at the entrance to the ballroom announced, his eyes forward and his attire impeccable, almost painstakingly so. As if his life depended on it. Perhaps it did. "Lord Alaric Cotheran and his niece and heir, Lady Isolde Cotheran."

Gripping Alaric's arm, Isolde stepped into the den of vipers. Her dress stood out against the dark, ebony wood. A drop of fresh blood against a wall of night. Isolde noticed Alaric's eyes wandering over the vast changes that had been done to his home.

The walls were now black and set with gold trimmings. Silk-covered furniture was stationed around the room. No expense was spared, something Isolde knew, Alaric detested. Eyes watched their arrival, most she recognized. Lord Milt of Harrow Hall, a friend and ally of Thornwood, lingered by the finger foods. Isolde smiled at seeing his jesting gaze.

"Alaric," Lord Milt said, beaming. He extended his hand and Alaric shook it warmly. "Always a pleasure to see you." A giant of a man, Filippus Milt stood well over six and a half feet tall. Yet every muscular inch of him exuded nothing but gentle warmth.

"As it is for me, my friend," said Alaric, returning the smile.

"And of course, we mustn't forget the jewel of the night," Milt said, turning to Isolde. His eyes ran the length of the dress but held no look of lust in his gaze. "And in that dress, I have no doubt you will be."

"I can only look to you for guidance in that department," said Isolde, waving a causal hand at Milt's incomparable style. He stood a foot taller than Isolde, and every inch was perfectly arranged, not a hair out of place nor a wrinkle present in his attire. A thick, brown beard, perfectly trimmed spread over his square, strong jaw line.

"Cotheran!" boomed a voice from across the, crowded room. Everyone turned to the sound, to the dais where Lord Volkran of Briarhole lounged. He pointed a finger before him, beckoning them with no more respect than one would a dog.

"Excuse us," Alaric said, pulling Isolde away. She shot a wink at Milt who returned the gesture.

Dressed in various shades of black velvet and leather, the Lord of Briarhole gazed at Alaric in obvious disdain. His lip curled at the click of Alaric's cane against his precious marble floors. "When you are a guest in *my* house," Volkran sneered as they stopped before him, "you will greet me first. Or have you forgotten decorum since leaving here?"

A muscle in Alaric's jaw twitched. "Certainly not, Lord Volkran. I do apologize."

Volkran grunted, his gaze turning to Isolde. "And who is this?" he demanded, his eyes lingering on her breasts. "Your new whore?"

Isolde felt someone slide beside her-a presence and an anger, she would know anywhere. A low rumble shook Malaki's chest. Volkran slid his eyes to Malaki. A look of pure hatred darkened in his gaze as his meaty hand ran over the pommel of the sword resting at his side.

"No, my lord," Alaric said, attempting to draw his attention from Malaki. "This is my niece and heir, Isolde Cotheran, as the page just announced."

Isolde's face radiated a sarcastic grin as she slid into a curtsey. "And even if I was a whore," she said sweetly, "I doubt anyone in this room would be able to afford me. Including you, Lord Volkran."

Volkran balked in shock, his eyes glowing with fury at such disrespect. Her smile only grew. Before the furious man could say anything else, Alaric swept her away to one of the vacant tables at the far end of the room. "You can't say things like that, Isolde," Alaric rasped.

"And why not?" she demanded, "Am I supposed to stand there and take it? That might be your method, Alaric, but it certainly isn't mine. Nor will it be when I rule Thornwood."

His teeth ground together in frustration. He looked to Malaki for help who merely crossed his arms and shook his head. "You too?"

"Just be thankful she didn't kill him, Alaric," he murmured with the shrug of his shoulder.

"The night is still young," said Isolde, taking a glass of wine from one of the servants as they passed. "I'm not making any promises."

The evening continued with introductions and revelry. Music filled the great hall. Isolde always thought Briarhole was perfect for hosting such grand events. Blyana and Cillian danced the night away, their eyes rarely leaving each other.

Malaki lingered near where Isolde danced with partner after partner. She smiled at the new tunic and pants she had convinced him to wear. A fine, dark green jacket, fitted with hidden pockets that held blades, covered his broad shoulders. Occasionally, she would see him flex his arms or tug at the collar of his shirt. Discomfort radiated from his every movement. A light laugh danced from her lips at the sight.

As the music faded, Isolde bowed to her partner, allowing him to plant a kiss on her hand before making her way over to her fidgeting second-in-command. She plucked a goblet from the table and lifted it to her lips, drinking down the rich, foreign nectar. It warmed her blood and numbed her anxious energy.

"Go easy on that," Malaki said.

"Mind your own business," she said, dragging the back of her hand across her mouth.

"You are my business," he said. "And it's not in your best interest to be drunk the first night. Let alone with people who are enemies in more ways than one."

"Come now," she said, chuckling, "they aren't *all* enemies."

"They are, whether that is towards you or your…other form."

Isolde shrugged, looking around again until she spotted the one person she had been most anxious to see. Poised behind her husband on the ridiculous dais, her arm draped casually over the back of his throne, stood Zibiah.

The gold of her gown made her the brightest star in the room. It fell in tiny chains that gathered at her breasts and hips, providing at least a hint of modesty. The sword Isolde had seen her wield with terrifying talent rested at her side. She was a wife second and personal guard to her husband first.

Their eyes locked from across the room. The hint of a smile formed on Zibiah's otherwise neutral expression. She leaned over Volkran's shoulder and whispered into his ear, interrupting a conversation with one of the other lords. He dismissed her with a scowl of annoyance.

"I'm going to mingle," Isolde said, setting her glass down. "Continue to stand there and brood if you must." She left Malaki's side before a word of retort left his tongue and worked her way through the throng of onlookers to the door Zibiah had disappeared behind.

Stepping through the doorway, Isolde looked back and forth down the deserted hallway. A small crease formed on her brow as the unmistakable touch of a blade ghosted across her throat in a cool, sharp kiss. "So unlike you, Lady Isolde," the voice purred. "Usually, you're always on your guard."

"And do I need to be on guard around my friends?" she asked.

"Especially around your friends." After a beat of silence, the blade lifted and quiet laughter broke through their lips. "It's so good to see you." Zibiah folded Isolde into her strong grasp, hugging her close.

"You as well," Isolde said, hugging her just as tight. "Even if you look like you're wearing the wealth of Briarhole."

Zibiah sighed. The golden ring on the left side of her nose shimmered as her full lips curled in disgust. "You know it wasn't of my own choosing. Volkran loves to show off."

"Indeed, he does. You might stand a chance against me in that, Zib."

Challenge shined in Zibiah's golden eyes as her accent thickened on the words. The o's stretching as she spoke. "Would you like to find out?"

"What do we have here?" a voice called from the darkened hallways. A figure emerged, one Isolde had never seen before. While he was tall and handsome, there was something Isolde did not like.

"Don't be rude, Zibiah," the man slurred leaning against one of the pillars framing the entrance to the ballroom. "As hostess, it is important for you to introduce me to the ladies of other territories."

Zibiah's eyes hardened, her jaw working.

"Very well Lauram, this is Lady Isolde of Thornwood, Lord Cotheran's niece and heir. Isolde, this is Lauram, Lord Volkran's heir."

Lauram's blood shot eyes ran the length of Isolde's dress, his top teeth scrapping over his bottom lip as he smiled. "Very nice to make your acquaintance, Lady Isolde. I did not know the shit territory of

Thornwood held such a beauty in their midst. Otherwise, I would have visited a lot sooner."

Isolde smiled coldly. "I can't say you would have done well there, Lauram. Women and men of Thornwood don't take kindly to being ogled by someone who can barely stand on his own two feet."

"You're a sassy bitch, my lady," Lauram said, shoving away from the wall. He teetered but kept himself upright as he stalked forward. "That mouth of yours needs to learn some manners. I have a tool just for the job."

"Oh, I doubt it's sufficient for that, or any job for that matter."

Lauram took another step toward her, his eyes burning in fury. "How dare you…in my own house!" At that time, the music switched over to something far more intimate. The long, drawn-out notes filtered through the door as partners began to move slowly…closely around the dance floor.

Mischievous malice danced across Lauram's face. "Dance with me, Lady Isolde," he said, extending his hand. "Dance, and I will forget this insult on Briarhole."

"I don't dance with impotent, little men," Isolde said, her lip curling in disgust.

"Little bitch," he spat reaching for her. "You will dance if I deem it so!" He was far quicker than Isolde had anticipated. His fingers hooked around the edges of her dress, intent to pull her towards him. The fine silk fabric gave way, ripping part of the front of her dress and down the sleeve.

Fire ignited in Isolde's eyes that stilled Lauram's hand but only for a moment. Zibiah stepped in as Lauram reached for Isolde yet again. Her hand was placed on the hilt of her sword in warning.

"I'm sure Volkran wouldn't be pleased to hear of you assaulting another heir, Lauram." Her voice was thick and cold as steel. A look of pure hatred broke through Lauram's drunken haze as he took in

Zibiah. His gaze fell to the sword at her side. To the sword, Isolde had no doubt he had witnessed being used before.

With a sigh of frustration, Lauram's hand dropped back to his side. Casting one last look at Isolde, the drunken heir of Briarhole stumbled forward into the ballroom as he pushed back mutinous strands of bright, auburn hair.

Isolde held her dress up, covering her chest as much as possible. Anger seeped through the cracks of her control, her teeth clenching. "I need some air." Taking deep breaths, she turned to one of the side doors.

"Isolde," Zibiah called, her eyes bright with worry.

"I'm fine," Isolde said before disappearing into the night. Her fingers laced around the fringes of her dress, clutching them to her.

She fled, something she had only done once before. In another world, in another life she would rather forget. It wasn't a choice. Either she leave and collect herself, or slaughter the heir to Briarhole. Which would put Zibiah in the awkward position of having to execute her.

Crossing the courtyard, she noticed a strip of light stretching across the cobblestone path like a beacon in the night. The doors to the stables were slightly ajar.

The air was filled with the faint sound of music. Not just any music. Isolde's cautious steps moved silently toward the sound, her heart racing. She knew that song, knew those words from a world that had long since turned to frozen darkness. Pushing the door open just enough to slip through, she spotted its source.

A girl, no older than six, sat beside one of the stalls. Her back was to the door, her hand reaching up to pet the snout of the steed who stretched toward her. Not just any horse, her horse. Versa's mane fell over her face like a wave of midnight. Her grey coat shined in the light of the lantern like a storm out at sea.

Isolde leaned back, her head resting against the warm, polished wood. *How did she know that song?* Isolde's nails dug into the flesh of her chest. It was a song that would end this girl's life if heard by the wrong ears. It held the story of the past, one the king had deemed treasonous to repeat. The words flowed over the girl's tongue like sweet torture. Memories and ghosts filled Isolde's mind. Each note brought her to the point of breaking…of remembering.

Unable to stand it any longer, Isolde's patience broke. "Enough!"

The girl jumped so violently she overturned the bucket, causing Versa to whine and throw her head in anger. The sleeve of the girl's worn, filthy dress fell down as she stared at the floor. It seemed to swallow her whole.

A small tremble racked through her emaciated body as she said, "Please forgive me, my lady."

Isolde walked forward. Her footsteps must have sounded like the pounding of drums to the small creature, for she shook all the more upon her approach. A small cry slipped through her lips as a tear fell to the straw-covered floor. Isolde extended her hand, intent on fixing the girl's dress but froze.

Scars, both new and old, decorated her skin.

"Did they do this to you?"

"It was deserved, my lady," said the girl in a rush.

"None of this is deserved." Isolde slowly, carefully replaced the girl's dirty sleeve, mindful of any new wounds that might be hidden underneath.

"What is your name?"

"Nyla, my lady," she said, her bare feet shifting nervously beneath her.

"That is a dangerous song to sing, Nyla," said Isolde. "Especially in Briarhole."

The girl sniffed, her head falling impossibly lower. "It is the song my father used to sing to me. His grandfather sang it to him when he was a boy."

"Who was your grandfather?"

"Fintan...Fintan Abbott." Isolde went still. Her eyes were wide and her teeth set. "He used to work in Briarhole. In these very stables," Nyla continued.

The flash of a face sparked in her mind. The kind, old man who held her up to feed the horses at the fence line. Who taught her how to put on a saddle...how to ride.

"I remember him," said Isolde, the words lodged in her throat. "He was a great man." The words came out choked, refusing to move past the lump in Isolde's throat.

"My father said as such." The hint of a smile played along her words. Nyla glanced up, her eyes wide but cautious. They looked far too big for her small face.

"Your father should have taught you that particular song isn't one to be sung in the open." Isolde sat down on the bucket and leaned against Versa's door. "No matter how beautiful your voice is."

Nyla nodded, her small hands folding behind her back as she rocked back and forth on her heels. "Do you sing, my lady?"

Isolde smiled to herself as Versa nuzzled her shoulder. Her hot breath kissed the skin exposed by the tear in her dress. "I did...once upon a time."

Nyla bit her lip. "Will you sing something now?"

Isolde chuckled at the boldness of the little girl. "I'm afraid I'm out of practice."

"Please?"

Isolde sighed, her fingers grazing over Versa's velvet, gray chin. A snicker trickled from her snout. "Another time." It had been years since she sang. The last time had been at a grave. Notes played in her mind, as words danced across her tongue, itching to be set free. But she couldn't bring herself to. Even when Nan and Galaena begged her...she could not.

A bell struck off in the distance causing the girl to jump.

"I must go," Nyla said. "I can't be caught outside after the tenth chime." Fear etched into Nyla's body as she bowed to Isolde.

"Take this." Isolde plucked a jewel from her hand and held it out.

"I cannot," said Nyla, taking a step back as if the jewel would strike. "That is far too pretty for the likes of me."

"It is not good enough for you, Nyla," said Isolde, the ring still aloft. "Please. I want you to have this and remember that you do have friends in this world."

Cautiously, she reached forward and gently pulled the ring away. She held it before her eyes. "It's the most beautiful thing I have ever seen. It looks just like the one Lady Volkran has."

"This is its twin," said Isolde. "You can trust her as well."

Nyla smiled. "I like her. She's nice to us."

"She is indeed," said Isolde, suddenly nervous for girl. "Now, run along. I don't want to be the reason you're late."

Nyla bowed once again, her eyes widening. "Thank you, my lady." Without waiting another moment, the brave little girl slipped through the back door of the stables and disappeared into the shadows.

Leaning back once more, Isolde rested against Versa's door. She toyed with the remaining ring on her right hand. A pair of golden wings forming the band held a diamond aloft. It had been a comfort for her for many years. Since Galaena had given it to her on her twenty-fifth birthday. "It was your mother's," she had said. Isolde had not asked questions. The ring fit perfectly on the middle finger of her right hand and had been there ever since.

"Well," said a familiar voice, pulling her from the past. "That was most unexpected." Versa stomped at the sound of her former owner's voice. She tossed her head in his direction.

Lord Milt sauntered forward, his thumbs resting easily in the loops of his belt. Everything about him was at ease, even the kind smile he wore on his handsome, bearded face. But his steps fell short when his eyes pulled to the rip in her dress. Their gaze grew hard and glowed with fury.

"Don't tell Alaric or Malaki," Isolde quickly said. "It's taken care of."

Milt looked her up and down once more, drawing a sarcastic smile from her face. Sighing heavily, he shrugged out of his jacket and draped it over her shoulders. "I suppose that's wise. Malaki wouldn't take well to being arrested for killing one of Volkran's men. Neither would Alaric."

"You're probably right. Which part did you find unexpected?" Isolde asked, smiling up at him in thanks, keeping her hands secure over the fabric. It smelled of freshly cut grass and sunlight.

"You giving up a piece of jewelry." He turned to Versa, who pushed against his chest.

"I have been known to be generous," she countered, her finger feeling light with the lack of expensive weight.

He chuckled. "Not with your jewelry you're not."

Isolde shrugged. "It looked better on her."

"That's a good enough reason, I suppose," he said with a knowing smile. He ran the palm of his hand down Versa's face. His power moved through his skin and into hers, calming…reassuring. Where Malaki's power pulled from the earth, Milt's was geared towards animals. His very presence was a balm, a place of refuge for them. While they were both earth wielders, Milt and Malaki's powers were two different facets to the same gem of power.

"How does she fare?" he asked.

"Quite well. Very spirited."

Milt nodded, a grin playing at the edges of his mouth. "Then she suits you perfectly."

Taking a seat beside her, he rested his forearms on his knees. "I am told that you are to be heir of Thornwood."

Isolde scowled. "Unfortunately."

"You aren't happy? Surely you of all people are up to the challenge."

"That's not what I want for myself."

"Is being Lady of Thornwood so bad? Think of all you could do for the people of Thornwood. They adore you."

It felt so undeserved. She had heard it so many times yet she never truly believed it. "Like what?"

"Well," he said, shrugging. "One way is finding a solution for our Hood problem."

Isolde kept her face neutral, but her heart galloped. "How do you propose I do that?"

"By any means necessary." A silence fell between them, leaving only the sound of horses to fill the space.

"Why do you hate the Hood?" She intended to sound bored, but it fell from her lips in a desperate whisper.

"He is a menace, Isolde," Milt said, his lip curling. "A menace to the realm and the people of our territories."

Isolde pulled Milt's coat tighter around her shoulders. "What has he done to harm the people?" Milt's jaw flexed, his teeth grinding. "In Thornwood, while he does take from the House of Cotheran, he gives to the people of Thornwood."

"That is not the way," he said.

"Perhaps it should be."

Milt was silent for a beat, his fingers tapping against the fine leather breeches stretched across his defined thighs. "What are you saying, Isolde?"

She knew she needed to tread lightly. Milt was a friend of Thornwood, a friend to her…but that only went to so far. Still she found herself saying, "The Hood's priorities seem to be centered around taking care of the many. Not the minor troubles of the very, very few."

He held her gaze, searching. *Could he see?* She was suddenly terrified. The blade strapped to her inner thigh was cold against her skin. They had met on more than one occasion during her visits to Harrow Hall. Her disguise did well to hide her from the world, but her eyes had always been a beacon for who she truly was.

To her relief, Milt merely sighed. His wide, impressive chest pressing forward as he looked up to Versa who tossed the perfect chocolate brown waves of his hair.

"Perhaps you're right." He gently stroked her chin. "But that doesn't excuse his actions. Nor will it save him from the hanging post if caught in my territory. You would be wise to do the same when you sit as Lady of Thornwood."

A sharp pang of sorrow scorched her heart at the thought of Lord Milt ripping the hood from her head, at the betrayal on his face and agony as he led her to her death. Malaki was right. Not only did she have enemies as of Lady of Thornwood here...but as the Hood as well.

"I'll keep that in mind," she said, a halfhearted smile stretching itself into place.

Milt braced against his knees and stood. "We should probably return," he said, wiping off his backside. "Wouldn't want any rumors started about finding us here...together...our backsides covered in hay, and you in this state of undress."

A wide smile stretched across his face, spreading to her own. She placed her hand in his and stood. "What a scandal that would be."

"Just for once," he said, leading her to the door, "I would prefer the rumors at this meeting to not all be about me."

"You don't like being the center of attention?" Isolde asked, bumping his shoulder.

"My dear Lady Isolde," Milt said with a mischievous grin. "I will gladly leave that particular torture to you."

CHAPTER 10

Alaric squeezed Isolde's hand as they entered one of the grand rooms selected for hosting the first meeting of Lestahere. Circular walls were lined with bodies, some familiar, some not. Most nodded at their entrance. A few remained standing. Their faces hard and unwelcoming.

"Lord Cotheran and Lady Isolde of Thornwood," the servant from the previous night announced.

Alaric moved them over to their designated seats in the back corner at the far end of the table, away from the large black velvet throne that resided at the head.

Milt nodded to them, his eyes glancing momentarily over Isolde. Much to her appreciation, his eyes held nothing of their conversation from last night or the state in which he had found her in. The others ignored them altogether, busy in their own conversations.

At the far wall, next to the decanter of various wines was Ferden, Lord of Dolinmere. Isolde found it impossible to draw her eyes away from him.

Molten steel shined from his eyes as he took in the room. The pale, golden mustache twitched ever so slightly as he sniffed the wine held delicately in his hand. A look of distaste maimed his otherwise handsome face. Setting the goblet down, he leaned against the wall. His long arms crossed over his chest. He was a force of quiet power, one clouded in mystery. No one knew what kind of power Ferden possessed, making him incredibly alluring…and dangerous.

A look of boredom masked his features with ease, as if this summit was beneath him, a complete waste of his time and efforts. It had been so long since their last encounter. Of course, Ferden had been completely ignorant to who she truly was. All he saw was the Hood, with arms full of his treasure. Isolde smiled inwardly.

Alaric followed her eyes, his own golden-speckled jaw feathering. "Lord Ferden," he said. Isolde nodded, a small smile creeping onto her lips.

Alaric's eyes rolled as a sigh escaped his slightly parted lips. "I take it you have met."

She shrugged. "Once upon a time, under very different circumstances."

Her uncle glowered at her, teeth grinding.

"Lord Cotheran." A woman of impeccable beauty sauntered forward, her movements fluid and well trained.

"Lady Helm," Alaric said with a bow, "a pleasure as always."

Lady Yvaine Helm of Blackwater stopped before them. The hem of her peach satin dress brushed against the marble floor. It looked off putting against the soulless black. Like a puddle of vomit. A waterfall of blonde curls embedded with strings of tiny diamonds fell over her left shoulder.

"The pleasure is all mine," she said in a small curtsy, her eyes roving over him hungrily. "I take it Lady Cotheran did not make the trip with you this time."

Alaric shifted his stance uncomfortably, his eyes darting down to Isolde momentarily. "Unfortunately no, there was much to tend to at Thornwood."

"I see," Yvaine said breathily, a predatory smile forming to show a row of perfectly white teeth. "Her loss then." Isolde bit back a growl rumbling through her chest.

"Allow me to introduce my niece, Isolde."

Hardness crept into Yvaine's dark brown eyes as they took in Isolde. They fell on Isolde's hand that was clutched in Alaric's grip. A sneer hardly detectable fell on her mouth. Isolde had chosen another silk gown. This one, a royal blue set with a river of sapphires that swept over her hips and lower back, accentuated every curve. Delicate silver lace ran along the neckline and covered her arms.

"What a pleasure to have such…young blood in our midst this year. No matter how they might dress."

"The pleasure is all mine," Isolde said, her blood-red lips turning up as her power stirred. "And what a privilege it is to meet someone such as yourself, Yvaine. I would never have known such a color had come back in style. Youth does deprive one of things that are considered outdated. How brave of you try and bring dead fashion back from the grave."

A small light flickered in the depths of Yvaine's gaze. Her hands bunched into claws. Isolde's power rushed forward, her hand clamping down on Alaric's as a growl escaped her chest. Off to the right, a small chuckle broke the tension. Ferden did little to hide the grin that broke out on his face.

"The only thing more entertaining than women's spouts on fashion are their spouts over males."

Yvaine eyes cut, her teeth bared to Ferden, who merely grinned wider. Turning her attention back to Alaric, she seethed. "You would do well to keep your niece on a leash. Before someone else does it for you."

Malaki moved forward, his face stern.

"Or is it you who holds her leash?" Yvaine's polished finger grazed down his shoulder. "The Bastard Prince...I've heard stories of you."

Her eyes raked over Malaki, the tips of her nails drifting over his chest.

"All exaggerated," he murmured, looking anywhere but at her.

"Come now." She chuckled, taking a step closer. "That can't be true. Especially not the ones that come from the bedroom."

"What a spectacle you make of yourself," Isolde spat. "And here I thought you were a woman of noble stock." Alaric's gaze slide to her, to the undertone of cold rage barely contained beneath the surface.

"Jealous, are we?" Yvaine said, her eyes cutting to Isolde. "What? Did you venture into the gutter too once? Take a tumble in the hay with the legendary warrior, and leave him wanting?" Her hand traveled lower. Malaki tried to take a step back, but she gripped his belt, holding him in place.

"I must respectfully decline, my lady," said Malaki.

"Don't be shy."

"I said," Malaki repeated, his voice gaining an edge. "I decline, my lady."

"I do like those who play hard to get."

"Take your hand off him," said Isolde, her voice lethal and cold as death itself.

Yvaine turned her gaze at Isolde, her face a mixture of shock and incredulity. Malaki tensed, his eyes shooting a warning to Isolde. "Excuse me?"

"I didn't stutter," Isolde said, taking a step closer. She dropped her arm from Alaric's grip, her face inches from Yvaine. "But I'll repeat myself, seeing as listening is a problem for you." Light flickered in Isolde's eyes, and her voice was edged in steel. "Remove...your...hand...*now*." The final word came out in a feral growl.

"And if I don't?" Yvaine cooed, cupping her hand to Malaki's crotch.

Isolde's fingers curled and bent into a claw. Strips of air found their way through the groves of her fingers, pulling the air into her grasp, the very air that once lived in Yvaine's chest. The Lady of Blackwater dropped to the floor with a gasp, her hand clawing at her throat.

"Isolde," said Malaki, reaching for her. But he was met with an invisible wall of air. A steady stream of wind pulsated around them, encasing Yvaine and Isolde together.

Isolde leaned forward, her lips pulling back over her teeth. "If you ever lay a hand on another man or woman without their explicit consent again...you will lose that hand." Yvaine's eyes burned with petrified hatred. "Is that in any way unclear?" Yvaine's fingers gripped her throat. They dug into her skin, desperate for air.

Off in the distance she heard Alaric screaming her name. "Isolde! Enough!"

"Say it," Isolde demanded, releasing just enough air to return to Yvaine's lungs. She gulped down what Isolde gave her and pressed her shaking hands into the marble floor.

"I understand," Yvaine snarled her eyes shining with the promise of vengeance.

"You can listen," she chided, releasing her power. The corners of Isolde's lips turned up into a smirk as her hands fell to her side, the air finally calming. A servant ran forward to help Lady Blackwater to her feet.

"Get your hands off me, filthy human," Yvaine said, seething, her eyes bright. "Who wants to fuck a bastard anyway." She turned to Alaric, "As I said, leash her...or someone will."

Isolde made to follow, her hands curling up once more. But before she could move, Malaki gripped her shoulder, holding her firmly in place.

With one last look of hatred, Yvaine stomped off to where Milt was discussing business with Lady Circe of Marsh Hall.

"Must you provoke them on your first appearance?" Alaric asked.

"She started it," Isolde grumbled, pushing a few stray stands of hair behind her ear. "Besides, I thought it only fair to give them a taste of what awaits them," she said, her eyes still locked on Yvaine. "She seemed quite taken with you both."

"Let's just say your uncle and I were very popular bachelors at one point in time," said Malaki, an all-too-knowing grin forming. A small smile crept into Alaric's face as well, and a light returned that she had not seen in so long.

"Yes," Ferden said, strutting forward. "You both were quite popular in Elenarta. And you see how that well that turned out. A dead royal family and a kingdom in turmoil."

Malaki snarled, barring his teeth, not even attempting to hide the aggression. Alaric's jaw tightened, his eyes glowing ever so slightly. Ferden merely grinned and said, "Careful, old friend. Would be a shame to transform now only to have to start all over again."

He gave Isolde an appraising look, the hint of an amused smile playing on his lips. "Impressive."

Before she could utter a response, he moved to take a seat at the table. His movements were graceful and feline. A sense of unease coated Isolde's senses but she couldn't put a reason to it. No lust or revile lingered in Ferden's eyes, but something else did. Something ancient lurked in his cool, penetrating stare.

"Lord Volkran and Lady Zibiah," the page announced, and a hint of fear lanced in his voice. Isolde's stomach turned in excitement and nervousness as the Warden of the North stalked forward.

His black eyes roved the crowd and narrowed on Alaric as he took his seat at the head of the table. Zibiah stood at his side. Isolde could not hide her smile.

Long trims of shimmering gold cascaded down the length of her body. A belt of solid amethyst held them together at her waist. Every inch of her ebony skin held a shimmer to it, as if covered in a light layer of powdered gold. Beautiful, long braids that started at the base of her scalp, fell over her chiseled shoulders. Small gold and silver trinkets shined from their tips like stars in a vast blanket of night.

Zibiah's warm, golden eyes smiled when they found Isolde. She would not dare wave to her friend, not here. Isolde knew this all too well and took no offense.

"Sit," Volkran ordered, his voice deep.

The mass of bodies took their seats, six around a massive oak table. The symbol of Arnoria was branded in the center. It possessed three circles; the top, holding the outline of a bird in flight, the center over lapping the circles above and below it, contained the outlined mountain peaks of the Oronilma Mountains; and the bottom housed colossal waves. Each represented the virya- those of sky, land, or sea- as a united whole.

Isolde took her place near the back of the room, just to Alaric's right. The ladies or mistresses of the lords stood as well, their backs to the wall. Circe and Yvaine had taken their husbands' places, death having hindered the men's presence.

Light flooded the space from the large chandelier that hung directly over the center of the table. There were no windows in this room, giving Isolde a rather claustrophobic sensation, like she was caged with monsters.

There was, however, one chair that remained empty.

"Cotheran!" Volkran barked, his tone biting. "Explain why this woman is here," he demanded, thrusting a gnarled, callused finger at Isolde. The creature growled in her head, her lip fighting to hide the snarl. "There are far too many in here as it is."

Malaki, who stood at Alaric's left, bared his teeth in rage, his hand squeezing the pommel of his blade. Alaric's lips drew into a tight line, his temper already pushing to its limits. Isolde merely smiled mockingly.

"Do you have a problem with women being at your table, Lord Volkran?" Lady Circe asked, her piercing eyes staring daggers into

Volkran. Isolde read the threat, the subtle implication that he did not deem females worthy of sitting with men.

A low growl crept through Volkran's teeth. "I have every right to question anyone in my house. No matter what might or might not be between their legs." His eyes cut to Alaric to see if the words had hit home. If they did, Alaric would not dare show it. In fact, he had slid on a mask of boredom, his cheek resting in his hand.

The growl was the only warning Circe granted before launching out of her chair. Zibiah, with grace so few possessed, caught Circe's blade against her own, just inches from her husband's face. Isolde had always marveled at Zibiah's abilities. Even as a water wielder, her powers translated flawlessly onto land.

"Attacking one's host is not very ladylike, Circe," Zibiah said, her voice calm. "You would think someone of your standing would know this." Her golden eyes flashed with amusement at Circe's rage. Isolde swallowed the smile dancing on the corners of her lips. It was ludicrous to think this old bird would be any match for the Lady of Briarhole.

Shoving against the elithrium sword, Circe regained her seat, her own blade sheathed. Volkran had not turned his eyes from Alaric.

"Isolde is my niece, here for the same reason I am sure Lauram is," Alaric said, his hand sweeping lazily to the large male at Volkran's back. "She is the heir to Thornwood, here to learn the ways of the council. As she will be a member in the future."

Isolde bristled slightly at the implication of being one of them. The corner of her mouth turned up as she stared at Volkran. He returned it with hatred, "She is of your house? Your blood?"

"Is Lauram of yours?" Isolde asked, her voice sarcastically questioning. It was a sore subject for him, having not been able to produce an heir of his own. A sore spot that Isolde took great pleasure in poking.

Fury raged in Volkran's eyes, but he kept his seat. "Fine, learn what you can, girl. We will see if you have what it takes to be at this table soon enough."

"How kind of you," Isolde crooned bowing her head.

A chuckle echoed from behind Volkran, to which he ignored. Lauram scratched his chin as if to hide the grin. He was staring at Isolde, his gaze curious. She shot him a bored look.

"Let's not sidestep the elephant in the room," Volkran grunted, his hands coming to rest before him. "I'm sure most of you have heard by now but for those of you who haven't, Lord Dagan of Foxclove was found dead in his home three nights ago."

A soft murmur broke out over the room. Isolde watched their eyes. None of them were looking at her. She released a silent breath of relief. Not that she was expecting them to. Still, it put her mind at ease, for the most part.

"Was it the Hood?" Yvaine asked.

"Who else?" Ferden said, his tone filled with disinterest. "He is becoming bolder as of late. All the more reason we should make finding this criminal a top priority." A few clapped their hands on the table in agreement. Alaric nodded along. He knew how this game was played.

"The king himself," Volkran bellowed, "has demanded that this matter be resolved...*swiftly*. It has not only affected our houses but now the kingdom suffers. Lady Circe, how have you fared since the Hood's involvement?"

Isolde cringed inwardly, remembering her night at Marsh Hall. The birdlike creature still looked just as ghastly as before. The scars Isolde left behind stood out so strikingly against her pale porcelain cheeks, making her look all the more gruesome. She had once been a beautiful woman, one pursued by many hopeful suitors.

Circe dropped her gaze to the table, her long, bony fingers tapping the rich, black wood. "I wouldn't mind having a few spare minutes with the Hood myself before turning what is left of him over to the king. My lumber yards have become far too overgrown and silent without the human labor."

Marsh Hall had been her first excursion as the caped crusader. Isolde scowled at the memory and her clumsiness. Still, she was relieved to hear the treatment of humans had improved since her last visit nearly twenty-five years ago.

"Lady Helm?"

Blackwater's overseer squirmed in her seat. Isolde could tell she was not used to being addressed at the council meetings, her eyes darting from one member to the next.

"Productivity has decreased," she admitted. "The Hood has given the humans a spirit to fight back. To refuse to work unless taxes are decreased. Not to mention the storms that have ravaged the coastline. We will be under the mark significantly for the king's required amount of pearls and shellfish, I'm afraid."

Volkran leaned back in his chair, his chin resting on his bare fist. Isolde's eyes were on Lauram, who seemed to take his benefactor's silence as his signal to handle the matter. "How many free humans remain in your territory?" he asked.

A small crease formed on Isolde's brow. Her eyes darted between Lauram and Volkran. But Volkran merely watched, his eyes tight. "With the new increase in human taxes, there are very few who could pay them this year. Most of the humans and half-bloods in Blackwater are slaves."

"Have you tried the whipping post, Yvaine?" Lauram asked. "I find a slave will do as they are bid if you take a little bit of flesh from their backs."

Isolde's teeth ground, her fury rising, stirring the creature in her mind. It prowled just along the edges of her control, always looking for a means of escape. Malaki shifted beside her, his only warning for her to stay calm.

Yvaine smiled wickedly. "Oh, rest assured, Lauram, they are punished swiftly for their disobedience. However, in Blackwater, we have other means of punishment." Fear crept into Isolde's muscles at the smile that slowly spread across Yvaine's face. The Hood would have to visit Blackwater, and soon.

"Lady Isolde."

Her attention was forced back into the present to find all eyes on her or on some part of her anyway. "Yes?" she asked.

Lauram pushed away from the wall to stand at his master's side, as if he belonged there. His face was so expressively unnerving, the rose-red lips stretched wide over a set of large, white teeth. "I said, what are your thoughts on the matter? The Hood is a human sympathizer after all. I thought you might have some insight given your commonality."

The jab was a hard hit. Being labeled a human sympathizer was one quick step away from being called a traitor. Zibiah cut her eyes to her husband's heir, her hand resting casually on the hilt of her sword. It was payback for the night before. For denying him what he so foolishly believed was his for the taking.

"You do flatter me, Lauram," Isolde said, coming to stand at Alaric's side matching his aggressive stance. Her hips swung purposefully, heels echoing on the marble floor. If he would use his strengths, she would most certainly use hers. "But I am not the one out freeing slaves. In fact, I believe Thornwood has done an excellent job of holding on to the same ones over the years. How many do you go through in a year, Lord Volkran? I can't imagine being so wasteful is good for business."

"The matters of Briarhole are none of your concern," he sneered, hatred lacing his words. Lauram continued to lean forward, his hands bracing against the table. He looked at her as if he wanted to play, not a look of desire...but of dominance. A look that wanted to break something-or someone.

"Perhaps not," Isolde bit back, her face neutral and composed. Alaric stirred beside her but kept quiet. "I agree the Hood should be caught. He has caused enough trouble in our territories."

She draped an arm casually over the back of Alaric's chair. A smile formed on her face as a plan began to form in her mind. What was the one thing that would bring these people together more than anything else?

Greed.

"We need something that will unite the territories...and the kingdom for that matter," Isolde said, the ring on her hand twirling in her fingers. "A bounty perhaps. He is the people's champion after all. They would need some kind of incentive to give up their savior."

The room was quiet, all eyes still on her. She swept them with her own, her composure never breaking. They landed on Zibiah, whose face was stone, but her eyes were set, questioning.

Lord Milt nodded, his fingers brushing into his beard. "Agreed," he said. "I propose five hundred gold pieces."

"Each," Circe chimed, her eyes flashing around the room. Isolde nearly gasped, her heart falling into her stomach.

"Each!" demanded Yvaine and Milt, in unison. Their eyes flashed with incredulity.

Isolde's gaze immediately dropped to Alaric, who had remained silent, his jaw set. It was impossible to tell what he was thinking behind the mask of a lord. Of course, he would be furious with her for having mentioned it. The last thing the Hood needed was more attention. Malaki shifted, his eyes piercing hers. She could already hear his reprimands.

Five hundred gold pieces each! Isolde's mind was spinning. That was more than they had stolen in the past two years combined. Now all she needed was the location.

"Silence!" Volkran said, his hand hitting the table with such force a small crack formed. The well-bred lords and ladies took their seats once more, their eyes still lit with anger. A few even glowed, highlighting the power beneath.

"Three hundred gold pieces," Milt said, his eyes burning into Circe. "Not a single coin more."

Circe sneered at him, her nose turning up.

"Three hundred each," said Ferden, his voice distant and uncaring. The whole table reluctantly nodded, a few grimacing with the thought of parting with that kind of coin.

"Very well," Isolde said. "Now there is the matter of deciding where to keep the reward until the Hood is caught."

"Location?" said Lauram. "Why not just collect the money from the houses once the Hood is caught?"

"Because smart people do not trust empty promises, Lauram," she said, her voice patronizingly sweet. "Nor do they trust empty reward boxes."

"She's right," Circe said, her eyes roaming over Isolde. "If we are to catch this thief we must show the people we are serious."

"I propose the bounty be kept at Briarhole," Volkran said, his meaty hand slapping the table once more. "It is the most guarded manor in the kingdom, apart from Elenarta. That bastard wouldn't dare try to get to it here." Isolde fought to keep her face neutral, her heart plummeting. *Anywhere but here.*

"Neutrality is key," Milt said. "Besides, you aren't the most trustworthy man in the room, Volkran."

Volkran rose from his seat, his eyes glowing and mouth opening to shout when he was cut off.

"I propose Foxclove."

Isolde's gut twisted at the sound of that voice. Memories she fought to suppress flooded back in a blinding moment of anguish. Her power surged in one mighty wave, severing what little control remained. Blood red coated her vision as she turned to the door, her mind set on one thing only.

To kill.

CHAPTER 11

G age.

The Right Hand of the King stood in the doorway, his large silhouette blocking the afternoon sun. A cocky, crooked smile was spread across his infuriatingly handsome face. *I suppose he needs to be that handsome.* Visions of his dead body filled Isolde's mind. *It has to hide all the evil inside.*

Malaki sprang forward, his hand gripping Isolde's wrist as her foot raised to take a slow, predatory step forward.

"Not here," he breathed so low she barely heard him over the roaring in her head. She turned to snarl at him, but the look on his face stilled her anger. The same hatred she felt festered deep within him too.

A growl so subtle only Alaric and Malaki heard ripped through her exposed teeth. Her uncle's hand was instantly on her other wrist, squeezing in warning. Taking a shaky breath, Isolde froze the hatred and let it turn into numbness. Her face became neutral once more.

A smirk glistened off Gage's chiseled, god-like features as he bowed, his piercing blue eyes sweeping the room. They landed on Isolde as he rose. His smile grew wider, vicious.

"Thank you for the hospitality, Lord Volkran," said Gage, making his way around the table. "And to you, Lady Isolde for such an interesting proposition." He plucked her hand from Alaric's and brought it up to brush against his cool, full lips. Malaki growled in warning, but Gage ignored him, fully aware of his invincibility.

Behind him followed another, his form even bigger than she remembered. Isolde yanked her hand from Gage's grasp as her teeth bit the inside of her cheek to keep from smiling.

"Liam," she said, her head dipping ever so slightly.

Liam came to stand behind his commander. His dark brown eyes were guarded. It was the same mask he always wore in Gage's presence. The mask of a loyal soldier, an ally of the king. But Isolde knew better. She could see the smallest of smiles break at the edges of his full, expressive mouth. Dark bruises blossomed on the otherwise flawless olive skin beneath his eyes.

Liam nodded stiffly but maintained composure. The scent of teakwood and citrus bloomed around her, easing her discomfort. "Found a new recruit did you, Gage?" Volkran said, his eyes still shining with annoyance.

"Indeed," Gage said, his head tilting to Liam. "He has shown much promise, much potential." His gaze found Isolde once again and moved up and down the length of her body. Disgust coiled in her stomach at every pass, every caress of his gaze.

"Is it your intention to look after Foxclove then?" Circe said, her fingers dancing along the stem of her wine goblet.

"It is, Lady Circe," Gage said finally tearing his stare from Isolde to take the empty seat of Foxclove positioned between Yvaine and Ferden. Liam followed, a hand resting on the pommel of his elithrium blade.

"There are still many soldiers and civilians to tend to. And while there are slaves still present, their current condition isn't up to par. So, His Majesty thought it would be best for me to lend a hand."

"Very wise," Alaric said, his voice clipped. "So Foxclove has been offered as a place to house all of the coin for the capture of the Hood.

By my calculation that should be 21,000 pieces in all. Do you have somewhere on the property you deem safe enough to keep such a sum?"

Kicking up his feet onto the table, much to Volkran's distaste, Gage smiled. His teeth white and razor sharp. "But of course. I intend to keep it in the open."

A flutter of voices erupted along the table. "Are you mad?" Milt demanded, his eyes bugling in disbelief.

"Hardly," Gage answered, his gaze turning to stone. "21,000 gold pieces is indeed a massive sum. Far too heavy for even a small army to carry out. The Hood would have to return to Foxclove on multiple occasions to even put a dent in the pile. He'll be too distracted by the ease of access and won't consider the execution. His arrogance will be his downfall."

Isolde smiled inwardly, her face showing nothing. Behind Gage, Liam watched her, his eyes piercing and just as calculating. He knew her thoughts, he could read them as if she had spoken them out loud. She caught the faintest shake of his head, a warning. She merely smirked in response.

"You appear rather confident, Gage," Volkran said, his eyes on the table. "For a man who has let this thief slip through his grasp on more than one occasion."

Gage's defined jaw was set, his eyes narrowing as he slowly lowered his feet to the floor one by one. The room drew a collective breath as a heavy silence fell on them like an uncomfortably heavy blanket. Leaning forward, Gage braced his massive forearms against the table. "Do you question my judgment, Volkran? For if you do, you question the king's."

Volkran immediately dropped his gaze, suddenly finding his wine to be rather interesting. Isolde was hardly paying attention. Her mind was already at work, memorizing the layout of Foxclove.

Where would that prick keep it?

"I believe we have spent enough time on this subject," Ferden sighed, his tone lazy and bored. "All those in favor of the reward, with the amount as previously stated of three hundred gold pieces each, to be held at Foxclove until the Hood is captured."

A moment of silence then a unanimous "aye" sounded, Isolde's voice whispering with the chorus.

"So approved," Volkran rasped, his eyes still on Gage. "Now, I believe there are other matters to attend to before we dismiss for the day. We will need to raise taxes in each of the territories if we are to fund such an endeavor."

"Indeed," Yvaine said, her eyes raking over Gage with obvious interest. "Sir Gage, what do you propose?"

"Oh, I'm sure Lady Isolde has far better insight than I do," Gage said, his hand gesturing to her. "It is her plan after all." Yvaine rested back in her chair. Her eyes narrowed on Isolde in fury for having failed to steal Gage's unwanted attention from her.

Heat flooded Isolde's cheeks as the anger converged once again. Had she unknowingly placed those she wanted to protect in even more danger?

She plastered on a grin that felt more like a grimace and said, "A tax increase is an option. However, overtaxing the people will be counterproductive. Turning the humans and half-bloods into slaves is not going to drive them to want to help us, but to help the Hood instead. This is going to call for us to dig into our own pockets."

"Our own pockets?" Yvaine chided, her voice mocking Isolde's. "Foolish bitch."

"Watch yourself, Yvaine." Alaric said, his tone deathly low.

"She's right," Ferden snapped. "Offering a reward that is only made possible through punishing those who would receive it doesn't seem entirely logical."

Milt nodded, his hands wringing together. "I agree."

"As do I," Circe said. "It will be worth it to rid us of this pest once and for all."

A growl erupted from the end of the table, Volkran's hands slamming into the wood. "Fine!" he roared, the deep regret of loss reddening his face. "Taxes shall remain untouched...for now."

Yvaine remained silent. Her slender arms crossed over her chest like those of a spoiled child who was told no.

"Very well," Gage said, with a wide satisfied smile that turned Isolde's stomach.

The rest of the meeting went by in a blur. Isolde attempted to pay attention, but her mind was deep within the confines of Foxclove. Already she was formulating a plan. Luckily, no one called upon her again.

They all ignored her with two exceptions. Gage's annoying lustful stare was enough to drive Isolde mad. Malaki did his best to block her from his line of sight. But Liam kept his eyes on her as well. His presence was a soothing balm against Gage's scorching gaze.

A chorus of chairs scooting rattled through the room interrupting her plotting as the lords and ladies made their escape. Gage remained seated, his eyes roving the room, feeling out his new position. Liam remained as well, back straight and chin high.

Volkran stalked from the room, moving roughly past Zibiah and out into the afternoon sun. Lauram lingered as well, his figure towering, a black-and-purple cape billowing around his shoulders.

"Very impressive, Lady Isolde," he said, with a slight bow. "I look forward to seeing you at future meetings and at the Tournament of the Guard." A cocky smile played at the corner of his lips as he stared at her dress. A wicked glint shined in his eyes.

"I never attend those things," Isolde said with a dismissive wave of her hand. "I find them far too dull. But yes, hopefully we can work together in the future for the benefit of all."

Lauram grinned, his light brown eyes were cold and unfriendly. "Better for those who matter anyway."

Before she could respond, he was out the door, tailing his master. Quiet as the night, Zibiah slid to her side and sighed. "Charming, isn't he?"

Isolde shook her head. "Gushing with it. How do you stand living with both of them?"

Zibiah shrugged, her face soft and accepting. "He is my punishment. My sentence for not giving Volkran a son." She shook her head, the golden cuffs decorating to the braids clinked together. "I suppose it is better to not have to share something like that with him. Watching him corrupt his or her heart and not being able to stop it."

"I suppose," Isolde said, her eyes boring into Lauram's back, wishing for her bow. "You know there is always room at Thornwood."

"I would come if it were possible, my friend," she said, smiling, "but I would not start a war between Briarhole and Thornwood. And the humans here have no ally except me. I could not abandon them, any more than you could your own."

Isolde nodded. She knew Zibiah was right. It would be all out war. And Thornwood would burn.

Gage sauntered over, his hand resting on the pommel of his sword. "My, my Lady Zibiah. Still as beautiful as the last time I saw you. Perhaps, even more so." His piercing eyes roved Zibiah, his gaze missing nothing.

"Sir Gage," Zibiah said. "Congratulations on your new position."

"Thank you, Lady Volkran." Gage bowed, his smile widening. "I do hope we will see more of each other now that we are neighbors."

Zibiah's lips worked to form a smile that would pass as civil but fell short. "If you will excuse us," Zibiah said looping her arm through Isolde's, pulling her down the hall to the front door. "We have a dinner party to prepare for." They left Gage and Liam where they stood. Isolde sent a small smile to Liam whose only response was a slight curve of his mouth.

"I'll see you soon, Lady Isolde," Gage called, his voice heavy with promise. She chose to ignore him, unsure of what would escape her lips if she spoke.

"I take it Foxclove was a success?" Zibiah asked, leaning in, her voice hardly a whisper.

"For the most part." Isolde's eyes dropped to the ground. "We were too late to help some of them."

"I hope you ensured Dagan paid for it." Zibiah's arm gripped tighter, the only form of comfort she could extend.

"Yes, he did." Isolde sighed. "Now the full weight of the king will be upon us. Should make things interesting."

"Am I safe to assume we will be meeting in Blackford in the near future?"

"As soon as possible." Their footsteps echoed across the marble floor that was kept so painstakingly polished. Isolde pitied the poor souls in charge of such a task.

"I saw what has become of Briarhole." Isolde's toyed with the ring on her finger once more. "What they are doing to the humans and half-bloods."

Zibiah's face hardened, her jaw feathering. "Nothing has changed. With Lauram here, things have only escalated. Whippings are a daily occurrence now."

"It sounds like the Hood needs to pay a visit." Isolde smiled inwardly at the thought. She could already feel the lust for the blood returning.

"No, not yet," Zibiah said, her lips hardly moving. "I can handle them for now. The Hood has enough trouble coming her way."

"Can't argue with that," Isolde said, stopping at the bottom of the grand staircase leading to the guest rooms. "Can you get away soon?"

"I should be able to. If not I will send word." She smiled, her obsidian skin glistening in the sunlight streaming through one of the floor-to-ceiling windows. She swept Isolde up into a bone crushing hug, "All or nothing."

"All or nothing" Isolde whispered back, her arms tightening, refusing to let go.

"Zibiah!" Volkran roared from one of the rooms down the hallway.

A growl ripped through Isolde's teeth. "Go, before I add another lord to my kill count."

Gripping Isolde's hand once more, she smiled, "I'll see you at dinner."

Isolde watched her friend's retreating figure. A hollow sadness swept through her chest. Sadness for a friend that lived a life she could not begin to fathom and one she hoped to never experience herself.

Dinner moved by in a blur.

Plates replaced plates and the food continued to pour through the kitchens in an endless stream of extravagancy. Delicacies Isolde had never seen before passed beneath her nose. Each bite was a delicious, guilt-ridden pleasure.

After the last dish had been removed, Volkran, drunk and belligerent, ordered everyone to the grand ballroom. Isolde strolled behind Malaki and Alaric, their attention lost in conversation. She felt a brush of a hand at her elbow, her muscles tensing.

"Just me," Zibiah whispered, a smile plastered on her face to hide the movement of her lips. She was dressed in a dark purple gown, its layers far more revealing than Isolde knew Zibiah cared for. "There is someone who wishes to see you, in the library."

"Is there now?" Isolde said, her teeth biting her lower lip. "I wonder who it could be."

"I wouldn't keep them waiting," she said. "They are very impatient to see you."

"Wouldn't want that now, would we?" Giving her friend's hand an appreciative squeeze, Isolde sidestepped Alaric, and headed to the stairs.

"Where are you going?" her uncle demanded, his eyes narrowing.

"Such distrust, Alaric," Isolde chided continuing up the stairs. "I need my shawl if you must know. I'll be back in a moment."

"I'll come with you," Malaki offered, his foot already landing on the first step.

"It's fine, Malaki," she insisted. "I can find my way back without trouble."

"That's not the trouble I'm worried about," she heard him mumble as she turned the corner.

Once out of sight, she took off into a sprint towards her favorite place in Briarhole. The library resided in the tallest tower of the hold. Massive, thick double doors, fit with stained blood-red windows, swung open at her touch. Fire danced in the belly of the large fireplace at the end of the long hallway. On either side, rows upon rows of bookcases ran down the length of the room, encasing the walls.

The scent of thousands of books wafted through the air, making her heart flutter happily. This had been her solace, her place of peace when Alaric and Galaena took her in. It was her rescue...her sanctuary.

The hint of the fire along with teakwood and midnight orchids lingered in the night breeze ghosting in from the open windows to the left. The air changed. His very presence pushed against her instincts...her skin.

"You've grown," Isolde said into the dark, her words echoing. A faint pulse pushed out from her skin, and her scent coated his.

"I've done far more than grow, Lady Isolde." Liam's strong hands gripped her hips before his arms slowly encased her from behind, pulling her into him. The warmth of his breath spread over her cheek, his nose burying in her hair. "I've missed you."

Her arms worked around his, pulling herself further into him. She needed to feel him, touch him. "I've missed you," she said breathily, her words nearly lost in the lump in her throat. "It's been too long."

"Yes, it has." His lips moved down her cheek, over her jaw, and into the hollow below her ear. "Far, far too long."

Heat coursed through her. A furious need she had denied in his absence burned her from the inside out. "I've had a lot of time to think about you, Isolde," Liam whispered, his lips moving to her neck. "A lot of time to think about what to do with you."

"What did you come up with?" she asked, her fingers tangling in the curls of his ebony hair, forcing him closer. The other moved his hand from her waist, along her stomach, up her torso to her breast.

His fingers began to knead greedily, hungrily. Her head fell back against his shoulder as she lost herself in him.

"So impatient." He chuckled.

"You know it's not one of my virtues."

She could feel him pressing against her backside. His body clearly displayed the same thoughts racing through her own filthy, unfiltered mind.

"I'm far better at showing than telling," he purred. He pulled them deeper into a row of bookshelves tucked away in the farthest corner of the library, encasing them in the shadows of stone, wood, leather, and paper.

Every touch was long overdue. Every kiss made up for those missed, and every contact of flesh burned away the months of loneliness they both had endured. Yet, it wasn't nearly enough to make up for the time they had lost.

"Again, I ask," Isolde said, her voice laced with impatience. "And what have you come up with?"

Without another word, he twisted toward one of the bookshelves, dragging Isolde along with him. Her back hit the shelf's edge, sending volumes scattering to the floor.

"I do believe stealth is supposed to be our game, Liam," said Isolde.

"Stealth has never been our game, Isolde," he said, pressing her back. "Or have you changed the rules?"

"Rules are meant to be broken." She grinned, her fingers latching into the mess of dark curls at the base of his neck.

How beautiful he looked in this light. Olive skin, kissed by the sun itself glowed in the light of the fire. His dark, brown eyes were piercing and ignited.

"Take off your dress," he rasped, his fingertips grazing across her breast, and tugged at the ribbons that held the expensive garment in place.

"Not that rule," she said into his ear. Her fingers moved along the lining beneath his belt. Every inch of him was solid rock, carved by training, and dedication. The narrowness of his hips pressed against her palms as he stepped closer. His body shivered at her touch.

"You are going to be difficult," he said, teeth grazing her skin as his hands drew up the ends of her dress.

"Have you known me to be any other way?"

Liam chuckled, his hands wrapping around behind her knees and tugging forward. Her hand flew to the shelf above her head to keep steady, her legs wrapping around his middle.

"Months and months apart," Liam said, a finger sliding under the edge of her undergarments pulling them loose. "And I still can't see that immaculate body of yours."

"So nosy." She grinned pushing up on his shoulders to raise her backside. He pulled the troublesome garments free, letting them slide to one side.

His lips brushed her chest, sending a wave of heat through her every nerve. "Not the word I would use." Her nails dug into his back, forcing him even closer.

The minutes slipped away as they lost themselves in each other's embrace. Isolde clung to him. Her body was shaking, desperate for every inch of him. As they moved, she felt his perfection, an undeniable beauty a god would kill for. All the while his own hands held her close, as if trying to feel her form through the layers of silk and lace.

"Liam!" His name tore from her lips. Her head was thrown back against a row of leather bound spines. Her nails dug into his shoulders that quaked beneath her touch, leaving behind tiny crescent shaped marks in his tunic and skin.

A growl, low and fierce shot through the room as he thrust once more, his brow pressed into her shoulder. His body quivered against her, waves of pleasure moving between them.

At last, he breathed. His lips grazing over the spots his fingers left behind on her skin. "Isolde." It was times like this she longed for the mating bond to fall into place. For that final piece of their relationship to be made whole. But even after years and countless nights just like this one…that part of her heart, her soul, remained quiet and vacant.

According to Galaena, "The mating bond was created by the gods as a way of keeping the gifts they bestowed upon Arnoria at their purest and most powerful. A mating bond cannot form between a human and a virya," she had explained. "A half-blood can form one with a virya if their power is strong enough. It can happen; however, the chances are slim. But never a human. Their magic, in a way, has a life of its own. It searches for mates that will produce the strongest offspring, allowing their powers to grow even more."

Damn the gods, Isolde had thought.

She had asked Blyana once about her bond with Cillian. Maybe she had bonded with Liam and had not realized it. A shy, knowing smile had bloomed onto Blyana's face. Her pale cheeks reddened. All she said was, "You won't mistake it when it happens, Isolde. There is nothing you can do but fall…with only the line that ties you to him to catch you."

Her fingers caressed his face, moving strands of curls from his eyes. A faint light burned in their depths, like a single star in a well of night. She knew a similar one shined from her own. Leaning forward, she met his lips, not rushed but slow and meaningful.

Withdrawing himself, Liam set her down gently. Feeling weak and satisfied, she leaned against the shelves. "You have had time to ponder," Isolde said, gazing apologetically at the books about her. Their leather covers glistened with sweat, and she prayed no permanent damage had been done.

Liam chuckled, his lips brushing her shoulder, before he delicately pulled the silk sleeve back into place. "Too much time."

Her fingers absently stroked his arm, still amazed at the cords of muscle that ran beneath his skin. "I thought your service was over. That you would be coming back to Thornwood soon."

"I thought so too," Liam said, his hands busy with the buckles of belt. "But it appears I have caught Gage's eye. I have been promoted to his second-in-command."

"That's impressive," Isolde said, her voice hollow, small.

"Impressive but problematic. The longer I'm under his thumb, the longer he will keep me in Elenarta. It will be a while before I am given leave to live where I wish." His fingers stroked her hair, the silky ribbons flowing over his callused skin. "Which gives me the chance to have a foothold in the kingdom. A starter for us."

Isolde's fingers froze. "We have a starter, Liam. I am the heir of Thornwood. That's all the starter we need."

"You think Alaric will be content with me living there?" Liam asked, his tone dipping.

"It won't matter what Alaric thinks," said Isolde, her fingers working again. "If he is pushing the responsibility on me to run Thornwood, he has no say in who warms my bed. So, his opinion does not matter."

"It matters to me."

The pain in his words tore at her. They forced her to look up into his hardened, pained gaze. "Liam," she said, her hand cupping his cheek. He closed his eyes his tightly, leaning into her touch, and kissed her palm.

"I only entered that damn tournament so he wouldn't have to choose who to send." The words fell in a wave of bitter regret. "So, I could spare the man I deemed a father the pain of sending another innocent person into the jaws of Elenarta. And what do I receive in return?" Liam shook his head, his mouth twisting into a sarcastic smile. "The hatred of a man I loved like a father."

"He still loves you, Liam," Isolde said sitting up to wrap her arms around his shoulders. He shook beneath her. Every muscle was tight as a bow string as he wrapped his arm around her waist, molding her body to him. "He might not see it, but he does." She could feel the subtle shake of his head, the slightest dip of his shoulders.

"And if not," she said pushing back to look into his eyes, "we'll make him see it." The finality of her tone pulled at the corners of his lips. The hope that shined in her eyes was enough to ignite his own, if only for her benefit.

"Pushy as always," he said, grinning. Carefully, as if holding a flower, he gripped her chin, pulling her to him once again.

Isolde wished they could stay like this, hidden in the protective cover of darkness and books. But she knew her absence would be noticed sooner rather than later. Deepening the kiss, she stroked his cheek needing to feel him once more before pulling away.

"We need to get back," she said.

"Yes," he said, sadly, his hands trailing her once more, as if he too had not had enough. "Malaki will be wondering what took you so long to get a simple shawl."

"I'm very picky about my wardrobe." Isolde smirked.

"That's an understatement."

Their hands entwined as they walked the long length of the bookcases.

"Isolde."

She stopped at his tone. It was one she recognized and hoped she would not hear tonight. Reluctantly, she looked at him, at the lovely darkened olive skin stretched over his face. His jaw feathered for just a moment. Patches of dark stubble decorated his strong, proud chin.

"I know about Foxclove," Liam said, eyes holding to their unsatisfied hands that wove and unwove themselves.

"And?"

His eyes shot to hers and held there. He undoubtedly saw the light slightly burning in her eyes, the determination she knew he loved and loathed at the same time. "You need to stop."

"You know I can't do that, Liam," she said, keeping her temper in check. *Why did he have to bring this up now? Why ruin what we just shared?*

"There are too many eyes on the Hood," Liam pressed, taking a step closer willing her to see reason. "And now you have earned Gage's attention. Something I have been working hard to avoid."

"It was bound to happen."

"Not like this," Liam said, his grip on her arms tightening. "He is ruthless, Isolde."

A humorless laugh burst from her lips, "You think I don't already know that? I know exactly who he is and what he is capable of."

"So why invite this?" His own anger spiked. There was a slight glow in his eyes that hid the power lurking beneath.

"Because the humans and half-bloods have no one to fight for them, Liam."

He sighed sharply, knowing there was no changing her mind. He pressed his lips to her hands, his warm breath cascading over her skin. "Then promise me something."

"Depends on the promise," she retorted, her eyes narrowing.

"Spare who you can," he said, his forehead resting on hers. "The less blood on your hands...the better."

Isolde straightened, pulling free from his grip. "I kill who I have to, Liam. Sometimes I don't have a choice." It was true, she told herself. There were very few who she went out of her way to end, few who did not haunt her dreams for ending their lives.

"Please don't bring any more attention to yourself or the Hood."

Isolde stared at him, but the familiar cold fire worked its way into her veins as Martha and Cadoc's punishments leaked into her mind. Her teeth ground as her power woke and prowled along her control anxious to be set free.

"No promises," Isolde said against his lips before dashing out the door.

CHAPTER 12

Liam's touch still burned against Isolde's skin. Every caress echoed in her bones. The very thought warmed her to the core as she walked from her room with a shawl in tow.

Sounds of revelry filtered through the abandoned corridors, music and laughter bouncing off the marble walls. Turning left towards the general direction of the ballroom, Isolde stopped midstride. Her eyes fell upon a tapestry she did not recognize.

Light from the torches lining the hallway danced over a map of Arnoria that had been split in two. Humans clashed, swords drawn, and blood spilled over the canvas. As she walked, she saw the story unfold. The gods—Nar, Kian, Ceto, and Vae-all looked down up on the land torn asunder. Nar was ignited in bright flame, his eyes blazing in malice.

Ceto was surrounded by colossal columns of water bending to her will, her long dark hair floating about in waves of chaos. Kian was covered in leaves and vines, his bright golden eyes glowing as he took in the scene below.

And Vae stared down at the world laid before her feet. Her fierce, silver eyes held a hint of serenity as her hair was tossed in a fit of wind she could command without fail.

Isolde moved farther down, her eyes fixed up on the story before her. It shifted, creating a new version of Arnoria, one inhabited by the virya. Each god stretched out a hand before them, their own power glowing as it shot to the land below, all except for Nar. His arms were knotted over his chest, his eyes burning.

Isolde tilted her head sideways in wonder as she took in the god of fire. There was something about him. Something that had her teetering on the edge of wonder…and terror.

"Find anything interesting?"

Isolde jumped at the voice. The sudden fright caused her power to ignite and the light in her eyes to shine in warning.

Ferden raised in his hands in amused surrender. A smile crept onto his face, the gilded mustache tilting to the side. "I do apologize for frightening you, Lady Isolde. It was not my intention."

"Well." Isolde sighed, annoyance leaking into her words. "Intention or not you succeeded, Lord Ferden." She forced the bars of her control down around the monster, hoping it would go back to sleep.

He chuckled again, his full lips forming into a smile. "Allow me to make   it   up   to   you."
"If you feel so inclined," Isolde said.

"Do you know the story?" he asked, nodding to the tapestry.

She shook her head and drew the shawl tighter around her shoulders.

"Very well." He smiled, placing his hands behind his back as he stared up at the tapestry. "Long ago, further back than most can remember, Arnoria existed as two rivaling kingdoms. Blood was shed for years; the very land seemed to boil in it. Eventually, the gods heard the cry of a single human." His lip turned up as if remembering an inside joke. "Listening to humans was not something they did routinely. In fact, they avoided it all together if possible. But this particular one caught their interest."

"How so?"

"Because they didn't ask for themselves but for their people." Ferden's eyes glazed over, his mouth turning slightly downward as he spoke. "He asked them for power, a power to overthrow those that all but destroyed the land and people he cared so, so deeply for. He was a young prince who loved his people very, very much. So much that he was willing to make a bargain with the gods. A bargain that would in the end…cost him everything he loved."

"He must have been truly desperate to make a pact with them," Isolde said, her own hatred for the gods breaking through.

"Indeed," Ferden said, a smile not at all pleasant forming on his flawless face. "They agreed to help him but at a price. He was very young and full of hatred for those who had killed his people…his family. So, he agreed immediately, without thinking through the ramifications of that decision. When the bargain was struck, the gods unleashed their power on the prince's people, creating our kind."

"Eventually, he won the war. In his foolish youth and need for retribution, the prince executed the rival king and his family. Or most of them anyway. In the years to come, he created what we now know as Arnoria, a united land. And through time and breeding, those gifts the gods had bestowed upon him and his people, have morphed and combined with the ability to transform and manipulate the elements."

"But we aren't really reunited, are we?" Isolde asked, her eyes transfixed on the humans that resided at the bottom of the tapestry in what the artist had deemed their rightful place. Hatred rolled her stomach at the sight.

"No, Lady Isolde," Ferden said, turning his piercing, stormy gray gaze to her. "We are not."

They stood in silence for a while, their eyes taking in the artwork. Isolde noticed the strange designs that bordered the piece. Beautiful, dark swirls ran along the top of the scene and down its sides. Tendrils of dark shadow, like wisps of smoke caressed the shoulders of the gods.

Ferden's gaze slid to her, a small crease formed between his brows. "What has captured your attention, my lady?"

She raised a finger to trail along one of the shadows that snaked across canvas. "This...I can't tell if it's a part of the design or something else."

Ferden's eyes followed to where she pointed and darkened. His jaw flexed as a sigh pushed between his teeth. "It's not merely a design," he said. She looked at him expectantly, a single brow raised as she waited for him to explain.

"When the young prince made the pact, the gods had only intended to barter their power...and their power alone. But, despite the gods' infinite and unquestionable *wisdom*—" His voice was thick with disdain and his lip curled up into a sneer of disgust. "They accidently brought magic from other realms here. Magic that was meant for only them."

Isolde turned back to the tapestry. Her eyes roved the gods and the ribbons of darkness that fell over the land. "What kind of magic?" she asked.

"The kind that no one has the right possess," Ferden said, his voice was a whisper of malice. "The ability to manipulate darkness, read minds, even implant thoughts...memories into others heads. But no such power has been seen for a long time."

"Why is that?"

Ferden's gaze softened and his mouth turned down into a sad smile. "Because a Viributhian no longer sits on the throne."

Isolde's back instantly straightened. Her eyes refusing to meet his as she asked, "What does a Viributhian sitting on the throne have to do with it?" The name all but choked her as it left her lips.

"One of the conditions of the pact," Ferden said with a shrug, "was that in order for peace to remain in Arnoria, a Viributhian must sit on the throne, or lay claim to it. The foolish prince in question, was a Viributhian. The only one in existence at the time. When the late King

Viributhian was murdered, along with his family, and Tenebraith took the throne, a fracture was created. A break in the treaty. Part of the magic...was lost. Or at least made dormant."

Isolde felt as if every frantic beat of her heart echoed down the hallway. She had not heard the name Viributhian spoken out loud in decades. The very mention of it set her teeth on edge. Ferden seemed to not notice as he continued. "The late king had such power, or at least a hint of it anyway."

"That's a lie," said Isolde. The words left her mouth before she could stop them.

The lord turned to Isolde, his eyebrow cocked at her harsh, unlady-like tone. She refused to look at him, refused to raise her eyes to meet his patient, questioning gaze. "Forgive me, my lord," she said, forcing a laugh through her teeth. "I only meant that I have never heard of the late king having possessed such power before."

After a moment, Ferden's face smoothed into one of understanding as he nodded. "That doesn't surprise me." He turned his attention back to the tapestry. "Perhaps the king did not wish for it to be public knowledge. Not many had this power and those who did were greatly feared. Either way, it matters little now. A Viributhian must sit on the throne in order for that power to be unleashed again."

"I don't see that happening," Isolde said, her voice caring a tone of indifference.

Ferden shrugged, a knowing smile tugging at the corners of his lips. "You never know. The Viributhians—"

"Are dead." She didn't hide the contempt her voice. "Perhaps it is better that such a power remains lost forever. The Viributhians are dead...they aren't coming back." Isolde remembered a time before Tenebraith, before the fall. The last time, she was truly happy. Faces flooded her mind, faces of those whose ashes now dusted the ground.

Ferden said nothing. His hands remained loosely clamped behind his back. Isolde saw the smallest nod of his head as he slowly turned back to the tapestry.

"What of Nar?" Isolde asked, desperate to change the subject.

"What of him?"

"I've never heard of a virya with the ability to manipulate fire. And in the tapestry," she said, her finger pointing to the god, "would suggest he did not pass on his gift."

Ferden's eyes hardened, his jaw clenching momentarily as if in a nervous tick. "I'm not sure," he said at last. "None of the old legends mentioned it, but we know that he had some part in it."

"How so?"

"Because in order to make such a bargain," he explained, "the gods would have all had to contribute in some way. They are powerful but not infinite."

"Then where are the fire wielders?" Isolde asked.

"I don't know. Perhaps they too are lying dormant as well. Waiting to be brought forth."

Isolde looked back to the tapestry, her eyes falling on Nar once again. His eyes were blazing into hers with such intensity she thought it was the god himself looking back. She moved onto the others, who gazed down at the world below.

Their hands were stretched out, and a single ring rested on their fingers. Each held a different stone that seemed to glow. Even Nar had one, a dark ruby set in a strange black metal that held a faint sheen.

"What was the price?" Isolde asked.

"Beg pardon?"

"The price," she said. "The one the prince had to pay. What was it?"

"Well—"

"Isolde!"

Alaric stormed towards her, his cane clicking against the glistening marble floor. His frustrated gaze turned into one of suspicion as he took in Ferden, who leaned casually back into the wall, his arms crossing over his chest.

"Good evening, Lord Cotheran," he greeted with a slight bow of his head. "Enjoying the festivities?"

"Immensely," Alaric bit, his eyes turning to Isolde. "What are you doing out here? I thought you were getting a shawl."

"I was," Isolde said, waving it sarcastically in front of his nose. "Then I ran into Lord Ferden, and he was kind enough to give me a history lesson on Arnoria and the virya."

Alaric cut his eyes to Ferden, whose posture was the very definition of relaxed indifference. "Thank you for taking the time to educate my niece, Lord Ferden."

"It was a pleasure getting to know the future heir of Thornwood. I look forward to working together soon, Lady Isolde." Pushing away from the wall, he offered a shallow bow and walked down the deserted corridor leading to the private chambers.

"Come," Alaric said, holding out his arm to her. "Care to spare a few minutes to dance with your uncle?"

"Only if you let me lead," Isolde said taking his arm. She looked at the tapestry once more, her question hanging unanswered as she followed him into the ballroom.

"Not a chance," he said.

As Alaric led her around the dance floor. They moved as easily as anyone else. With his hand firmly planted in hers, Alaric had no need for his cane. She was his support, just as he had always been hers. More than once, she caught his eyes roving the ballroom. A touch of sadness and regret darkened his face. Isolde knew why. His home had been destroyed, turned into a nightmare he had fought and bled to keep from becoming a reality. And now…it was here, a reality that was very much alive.

Giving his hand a light squeeze, Isolde said, "For what it's worth, I think you and Gal make far better decorators."

Sadness melted away from Alaric as a laugh rumbled through his chest. Light returned to his eyes as he pulled her close and just held on. "Thank you."

As the final notes of the piece died away, Isolde noticed a few people missing in the audience. Gage, Lauram, and Volkran were nowhere to be seen. She knew that meant only one thing. Somewhere, a meeting was taking place she had no intention of missing out on. Pressing a hand to her forehead, Isolde forced a yawn from her throat. "I think I'm going to retire. Too much wine."

"Tired...you?" Alaric's eyes narrowed in obvious suspicion. "Off of wine?"

"Exhausted." Isolde grinned. "Bly and I are turning in."

"Take Cillian with you." Alaric nodded to the corner where they lounged by one of the fireplaces. "To your room," Alaric said, his finger pointing. "No detours, shortcuts, or side passages. Straight there."

"Of course, Uncle," she said reaching up to plant a kiss on his cheek. "I wouldn't dream of going anywhere else. Catch up with Milt. He's the least venomous viper in this den."

Without waiting, Isolde stole across the now deserted floor to where Blyana and Cillian sat in a silken chaise. "Care to escort me to my room?" Isolde asked. Her lips perked into a grin they had seen many times before.

"I very well can't let my lady walk about this fortress at night on her own," Blyana said, matching Isolde's smile as she looped an arm through hers.

Cillian rose to his feet with the grace of dancer. His sharp, dark eyes glistened with wine and mischief. "And what kind of gentleman would I be to let two beauties such as yourselves sneak around without a male escort?" He worked his way between them, securing them in his arms. "Of course, the most beautiful must take the center spot."

Isolde rolled her eyes and rushed them to the door.

Once out of sight, they sprinted up the stairs, and threw open the door to Isolde's chambers. Without waiting, Isolde rummaged through her trunk at the foot of her bed and pulled on the secret compartment that held her hood.

"I was joking about the mischief part but it seems you are taking it literally," Cillian said, folding his arms. "Quite literally in fact."

Isolde ignored him, already working on the ribbons of her dress.

"And where do you think you're going?" They spun around, hands going for the daggers on their hips and thighs. Malaki leaned against the bathroom door, his arms crossed.

Blyana shoved the handle firmly in place, her eyes seething. "Do not do that, Malaki!"

"I thought she," Malaki said, his gaze shooting to Isolde, "might try something idiotic tonight...but not you two."

"There is a meeting going on right now that I don't intend on missing," Isolde said. She continued undoing the ties of her dress. She looked over her shoulder and said, "I know it wouldn't be the first time you've all seen me naked, but do you mind?" She twirled her finger in the air.

Cillian rolled his eyes as he swiveled around. Blyana moved behind her and took over unfastening the straps. Black lace fell about the floor, a pool of death at her feet.

"I'm going with you," said Malaki. He stayed facing forward but averted his gaze.

She laughed, pulling the corset over her head. "One is far easier to sneak around."

"Not when it comes to you."

"I'm going alone, Malaki." Once her black britches and tunic were in place, she slid the leather jacket and cloak over her shoulders, and fastened the blades in place at her waist.

Isolde turned and noticed he was already dressed in his own cloak and hood. A set of elithrium daggers hung at his side, along with the mask meant to cover his face and Secrettaker.

Blyana had moved to the door and turned the lock. "I'll try not to be insulted you were planning on leaving me out of this. Oh look," she said, "I failed."

"You aren't going," Isolde repeated, pulling the mask and hood into place. Malaki and Cillian stood shoulder to shoulder, both of their arms crossing in unison.

Isolde sighed, her fingers pinching the bridge of her nose. "This won't take long," she said. "This is purely to gain information."

"We've heard that before." Cillian nudged Malaki with his elbow. "When was it...oh that's right...when you scarred Lady Circe. That was purely for information gathering."

Malaki grunted in agreement, causing Isolde to grind her teeth. Not wanting to waste any more time, she sighed in resignation. "Fine!"

With a look of smug satisfaction, Blyana and Cillian slunk to the other room to change. Malaki continued to stare, and the vines decorating his hands peeked out from beneath the cuffs of his jacket as his arms knotted over his chest. "Don't give me that look," Isolde rasped, her fingers dancing across the handle of her daggers.

"What look might that be? I have many."

"The look of smug victory," she said. "Does it make you happy to always undermine me?"

"I never intended to undermine Isolde." His voice was far too soft, far too quiet for her liking. Turning to face him, Isolde saw a shadow fall on his face.

"I don't want to put you or Bly or Cill in any more danger than I already have."

He nodded, his chest rising and falling with a sigh. "It's not up to you."

"It is! I am the one calling the shots. I am the one who should take the risks. I can't lose any of you!"

"And what if we can't lose you?" His voice rang through the room, ricocheting across every polished surface. She simply stared at him, at the furious sorrow in his face.

He ran a hand over his mouth and sighed. "You are far more than our leader, Isolde." He took a step toward her, gaining his full height. "Far more than simply Lady of Thornwood. To us..." He shook his head, causing strands of ebony hair to fall into his eyes. "You are far, far more."

She swallowed against the lump in her throat. Refusing to meet his eyes, she managed a small nod. Words refused to move over her tongue. The unworthiness of what he was saying was too much for her to bear. She didn't deserve them.

"I will follow you," Malaki said, stopping before her. He rested his forehead against hers. It was a familiar gesture, one that said, he was there—that he saw her. "I will always, always...follow you. No matter what dangers you face, you will not face them alone."

A shiver ran through her, making the lump grow even more. "And I you." She smiled against the mask, her hand resting on his shoulder. "Does that mean you will listen to me from now on and stop second-guessing me?"

"I will never stop trying to save you from your own stupidity, Isolde. But I will listen."

A small chuckle broke from her throat. "I suppose that will have to do." Isolde pushed away from him and headed to the door. "For now."

Once Cillian and Blyana emerged from their rooms, clad in leather and steel, they crept from the chambers. Thanks to the distractions downstairs, the hallways were mostly clear, allowing them to move freely through the shadows.

"How do you know it's taking place in the library?" Cillian asked, his finger grazing the handle of his throwing knife.

"Zibiah," Isolde said, looking around the corner. An empty hallway stood before her. Flickers of candle light danced across the black marble floor. "She said Volkran always takes his meetings in the library. No secret passageways for unwelcomed guests to listen in on private conversations. At least...not ones that he knows of."

She remembered the path to the hidden room off to the side of the library. A small closet, stuffed with brooms and mops lay three doors from the library. Easing the worn door open, Isolde motioned for them to follow. Once they were all crammed inside, dodging broom handles and buckets, Isolde pushed a stone into the wall. It gave way, releasing a small hatch to reveal a single window. Moon light flooded the crowded space, the rays dancing across the blades at their waists.

"Don't look down," Isolde said, swinging the window open and climbing through.

"You've got to be kidding me," Cillian said, his eyes growing wide.

"You can do this," Blyana said, her hand grazing his shoulder.

Cillian swallowed, his throat bobbing as a faint sheen of sweat glistened on his forehead. "I can't. There has to be another way in."

"There isn't," Isolde said swinging a leg out over the window seal causing Cillian to suck in a breath. "Just follow Bly. You'll be fine."

"Isolde," Cillian said, his voice strained as he looked at her leg draped over the side, his chest rising. Panic shined in his eyes. "Isolde...I can't."

Malaki's firm hand landed on Cillian's shoulder, his fingers pressing into the leather. "Are you really going to let an old man show you up in front of the woman you love?"

Cillian's chest stilled and his hands relaxed at his sides. Isolde could feel Malaki's magic in the air. His calming presence eased into Cillian's muscles, drawing out a look of resolve from his eyes. A hint of unease still lingered in his gaze but he gave Isolde a stiff nod as his plucked the climbing daggers from his belt.

"You'll be fine," Blyana said, the corners of her eyes crinkling as she smiled. "I'll be right there the whole time."

Cillian swallowed once more but nodded. "Okay, love."

One by one they followed Isolde out the window, driving their knives into the perfect stone wall. A hundred feet of air was all that stood between them and the unforgiving ground below. Isolde looked back every few seconds to check on the others.

Blyana and Malaki kept Cillian between them, no more than an arm's length away. His hands shook as he pulled the dagger from the stonewall and slammed it down once more. His eyes were glued to the spot directly in front of him. Every muscle was locked between each stab of his blade. Isolde could hear words of encouragement from both Blyana and Malaki riding the night wind.

They scaled the side of the fortress and slid over the edge of the wide, ornate balcony leading to the library. Cillian planted his hands on the balcony floor and took a deep, silent breath. Malaki rested his hand on Cillian's back. "Well done," he whispered directly into Cillian's ear.

Whispers of conversation ghosted into the night air, drawing their attention inside. Keeping as silent as possible, they crouched just outside the double doors that stood open.

Gage's voice carried through the doorway. "The king has many plans," he said, his tone biting.

"What sort of plans?" Lauram demanded.

Peeking through a slit in the curtain, Isolde scanned the room. Gage, Lauram, and Volkran sat around one of the large tables next to the fireplace. Golden goblets and precious jeweled pitchers of wine decorated the surface. Her breath caught in her throat as she found Liam.

He stood behind Gage, his hand firmly grasping the sword at his side. She couldn't help but gaze just to his right at the shelves...floor...and books they had just desecrated not an hour before.

"Ones that do not concern you." Liam's tone startled her out of her fantastic, inappropriate thoughts. The hatefulness, the cruelty...It was not him. Not her Liam.

"If we are to be allies," said Volkran leaning forward, his knuckles pressing into the table, "we need assurances."

Silence filled the small room. Only the sound of the roaring fire echoed through the window. Isolde fought to ignore it, focusing only on their voices.

"Let's just say that His Majesty has found a way to make uncooperative virya not a problem anymore."

"How do you mean?" Volkran demanded, his dark eyes narrowing.

"Exactly what I just said," Gage said with a smirk. "They cease to be a thorn in His Majesty's side."

"You mean," said Volkran, his voice low, "he has found a way to...take their power?"

Gage brought the goblet to his lips with a shrug. "They're no longer a problem but can still be useful."

"Useful...how so?"

Gage's lips, stained with wine, pulled back into a vicious grin. "In more ways than one."

Volkran stroked his chin, his mind traveling into places Isolde dared not guess. "I can think of a few troublemakers."

"That old bastard from Thornwood, Cotheran," Lauram spat. "Or that little bitch of a niece."

Isolde felt the others bristle behind her. A faint hiss echoed through the night. She shook her head at Blyana, whose eyes were glowing in fury. She had seen the tear in Isolde's dress the first night. It had taken a great deal of convincing to keep her from hunting down Lauram...or telling the others.

"The king is not concerned with Thornwood," Gage snapped, his eyes blazing. "They are exactly where he requires them." He took another sip of wine, his smile gruesome.

It felt as if a bucket of ice water had been dumped on Isolde's head. Dread. Cold, undiluted dread coated her skin. Her gaze snapped to Liam. The only change she saw, the only one she knew he would allow, was his white-knuckle grip on his sword.

"Besides," Gage continued, pulling her back to the present nightmare, "His Majesty's method of dealing with troublesome virya is not what I have in mind for Lady Isolde."

Volkran chuckled, his fingers spinning the goblet stem. "We all know exactly what you have planned for her, Lord Gage."

Out of the corner of her eye, Isolde saw movement at Cillian's side. His hand pulled at the blade on his belt. Once more, she shook her head. He paused, meeting her eyes. He nodded once but kept the blade free.

"I hope it's teaching that little bitch some manners," Lauram said, scoffing.

Gage picked up the goblet and observed it as if in deep thought. "Among other things. As my wife, she will learn a great deal about how to behave."

The room fell silent. Only the fluttering of the curtains and wood burning in the fireplace dared make a sound.

"Your wife?" Lauram chuckled. A river of wine spilled out of the corner of his lips as he drank heavily. "And how do you intend to sweep that one off her feet?"

"It's all in the breaking," said Gage, his eyes glistening. "By the time I'm done with her...Isolde won't even think without my leave. She will be perfect. My submissive, obedient pet. Marriage comes with its own learning curve after all, one I'm more than happy to *teach* her."

A wave of furious power coated her skin, pulling her own to the surface. She looked back at Malaki, whose eyes burned with hatred. Bracing a hand on his arm, she squeezed until he looked her way. A slight shake of her head told him they were merely words. That they meant nothing. After a moment, his chest rose and fell as he forced the power back down.

"Once I get around to asking her, that is."

Lauram shoved his hand through his hair, his jaw set. "Why even bother asking? Just take the bitch and be done with it?"

Gage chuckled. "Refused you, did she?" Lauram's cheeks flushed red, his jaw ticking. "Like I said, it's all in the breaking. I want her to think that it's her decision. That she actually has a choice in the matter."

"Tell us what you need, Gage," Volkran said, having grown bored of the subject.

"It's not what I need," said Gage, drawing his eyes from Lauram. "But what the king demands."

"And what does the king demand?"

"Bodies. Human, virya, and whatever mutant spawn lies in between."

"And what exactly," asked Lauram as he poured himself another cup of wine, "does His Majesty want with such an expensive hoard?"

"That's his business," Gage said, his jaw feathering with annoyance. "You are making a terrible habit of asking questions about matters that do not pertain to you, Lauram."

"I'm merely trying to find the best way to serve my king," he said, blood leaking into his cheeks.

"You will best serve him by doing what you are told and not asking questions. As heir of Briarhole you would do well to remember that." Lauram worked his jaw from side to side but kept his mouth shut.

Isolde watched Liam, scanning for any sign he knew they were there. But not a finger was out of place or a single glance thrown in their direction. Instead, his attention was solely on the young lord-to-be, his hand still gripping the pommel of his sword.

"We will be back with further instruction once word has reached me from Elenarta."

"And is this something the king will be extending to other territories?" Volkran asked, a hint of jealousy etched into his words.

"Dagan was our first recruit," Gage said. "His contributions were considerable, to say the least. The king will make offers as he sees fit."

"Well, I hope His Majesty knows the depth of my service to him," Volkran said.

"He is fully aware." Gage sighed setting his cup down. "He has not forgotten your betrayal and slaughter of King Viributhian and his family."

Isolde's hand immediately found Malaki's. Vibrations ran through her hand and up her arm. His body shook with anguish and fury, as did hers. She turned to look at him again but he would not meet her gaze.

"Except for one," Lauram murmured, sipping from his cup.

"That is horse shit," Volkran sneered. "A myth started by those loyal to Viributhian. Desperate conspiracy theorists who claim that one of those rats still lives. It is a farce. A foolish lie made in the hopes of restoring a Viributhian to the throne. That line has fallen. Dead and burned. I made sure of it."

She had heard the same rumors over the years. But it was the look on Gage's face, the smirk that made her second guess if those rumors had indeed resurfaced.

"Perhaps," Gage said setting the glass down. He rose from the chair and sauntered to the open doorway. Isolde pushed Malaki to the edge and leapt from the balcony. Blyana and Cillian followed. Their fingers gripped the underlining shelf. The silent, deserted courtyard was nestled beneath their feet.

"Either way," Gage said, bracing his hands against the doorframe, "you will be hearing from me on how the king wishes to proceed."

"Very well," Volkran said, his chair scraping against the floor as he rose. "Shall we return to the party? I'm sure you will find my selection of entertainment appealing. Even if it isn't Cotheran's niece in your bed just yet, I'm sure you can make do."

Gage chuckled, the sound driving nausea into Isolde's gut. Her fingers ached against the hold as she fought to keep silent.

"Soon enough." Beams of the full moon danced across his face. The light made him all the more handsome…and terrifying. With one last chuckle, the sound like velvet thunder, Gage turned and followed the others back down to the party.

Once they were sure the coast was clear, Isolde and the others hoisted themselves up over the ledge. Collapsing on their backs, they caught their breath and shook out their fingers. "Interesting turn of events," Blyana rasped, clenching then unclenching her hands. The leather of her gloves groaned.

"Not the word I would have used," Cillian said sitting up. "He's going to be a problem." Isolde looked at Malaki, but he wasn't listening. No, he was in the past revisiting the same demons he had worked so hard to kill. The same demons that haunted her as well.

She unsheathed her knives once more and stalked to the balcony's edge. "He already is one." She was about to swing over the ledge when a sound stopped Isolde cold.

"Please, please don't!" A sharp cry of pain shot through the air as the sound of flesh hitting flesh echoed between the stonewalls.

"Quiet, bitch!"

Something moved in the shadows of the courtyard next to the servants' quarters. Without waiting Isolde leapt into the air and drove her knives into the side of the tower.

She didn't stop to see if the others followed as bits of rock broke free from the wall, showering her hood with debris. As her boots slammed into the ground, sending painful waves up her legs and hips, Isolde took off in the direction of the sobs. They weren't hard to find. Huddled in a corner between the buildings stood a man, one she instantly recognized.

"It's because of you I have these marks around my damn neck," he growled pressing her hard into the wall. She tried to speak, her words falling silent as his hand gripped her throat.

"And now, you're going to pay for it." His other hand moved to yank the edge of her dress up. Her cries died as the man squeezed harder. Kicking her feet farther apart he said, "Keep it up, and I'll find that little daughter of yours and see how loud she can scream."

Isolde heard the buckle of his belt echo throughout the night. Her control snapped. But before she could take a single step, a body blurred past her. Its massive form knocked the man to the side, his body smacking against the stone wall with a sickening crack.

Isolde sprinted forward to catch the woman before she could hit the ground and gently pushed air into her lungs as she coughed. Blyana helped pull her dress back into place, making sure she was covered.

Looking over her shoulder, Isolde saw the man lifted off his feet. Malaki's massive, gloved hand was like a vice around his already bruised throat.

"You like hurting women, don't you?" Malaki's voice was even, so calm it sent chills down Isolde's spine. "Why is that I wonder?"

Cillian stood beside him, his back stiff and hands balled into fists. Fury, dangerous and unstoppable fury, rolled off him in waves.

"It doesn't matter," Malaki said, his head tilting to Cillian. "When we arrived, you threatened his mate...and someone I care a great deal about. You said and I quote, 'Then I'll come and find you' after you were done...*teaching* this woman a lesson." Malaki's fingers continued to press into the man's skin. "Big mistake on your part." He glanced over his shoulder at Cillian. "Which part do you want?"

A dark, humorless chuckle blended with the gasp that slipped from Blyana's mouth.

"I want his tongue," said Cillian, taking a step forward. He pulled a small knife from his belt. The blade glistened in the moon light. The edge was so sharp it looked razor thin. The man tried to scream but Malaki's hand merely squeezed tighter. The guard's fist swung out but fell pathetically short of reaching Malaki's face. There was no hope for him, no way of escaping what was coming.

Cillian's gloved fist gripped the man's scalp, forcing his head back. "Threatening my mate," he said, malice pouring into his words, "was very unwise of you."

Blood poured into the man's open mouth as Cillian carved away the man's tongue one piece at a time. He fought against Malaki's impossible grip, but earned a punch in the gut instead. Tears streamed down his face as he gasped for air, choking on his own blood. Once he was finished, Cillian turn to Blyana and offered the dagger to her.

He was offering the choice...the chance to take matters into her own hands...if she wanted it. It was something he always did. Cillian always gave Blyana the opportunity to strike back. An opportunity Isolde knew had never been afforded to her before coming to Thornwood. And Isolde loved him for it.

But Blyana stood in shock, her eyes wide. Isolde could see the tremors running through her body as she stared at the blade before her.

When Blyana didn't move to take it, Malaki looked back at her.

"It's alright," he whispered. She looked up at him, her eyes swimming with the demons of her past. "It's alright." Tears soaked into her mask as she nodded.

Malaki looked once at Isolde. There was fury but also hesitation. He wanted her blessing and she was more than willing to give it. She nodded, and he nodded back. The man's struggles continued as he pulled Secrettaker from his belt. Diamonds shined from the pommel, like a trail of stars in the dead of night. He held the black blade with rivers of living metal up to the man's eyes that were wide with terror.

"Only a coward hurts a woman." He lowered the blade below the belt line and slashed. The guard's belt, sword, and trousers fell to the ground. "I have no use for cowards." Malaki pressed the blade's tip to his bare flesh and began to carve. The man wailed in agony. Inaudible gibberish fell from his blood covered lips as piece after piece of his flesh fell to the ground.

The woman in Isolde's arms pressed her face into her shoulder. Dirty nails dug into her leather jacket as the garbled, wet cries of the guard finally died away. Malaki wiped Secrettaker on the man's discarded pant leg. The one piece of clothing not drenched in blood. Once they had disposed of the body in the pig's pen, Isolde followed the woman to her assigned barrack.

"Is your daughter in here?" Isolde asked.

The woman nodded, having not fully gained her voice back. Isolde pushed the door open for her, allowing light to spill into the filthy barrack. The woman rushed forward and pulled back on the rags covering a small body.

"Nyla," she rasped, her voice hardly louder than whisper.

Isolde watched the girl jerk awake, her large familiar eyes wide.

"Mama!" Nyla cried instantly throwing her arms around her. "Are you alright?" She nodded, her hands stroking Nyla's daughter's dirty, blonde hair.

"What happened?" She pulled away and gasped at the dark bruises blooming on her mother's pale skin. "Mama..."

She shook her head and smiled, her hands cupping Nyla's cheeks. Looking back, Nyla's mother waved Isolde forward and she reluctantly took a knee beside the bed, her eyes down cast.

"Did you help her?" Nyla asked.

"It was my pleasure," Isolde said.

Without warning Nyla threw her arms around Isolde's neck. "Thank you," she whispered, the hint of cry carrying in her small, thankful voice.

Isolde smiled and hugged her back. "It wasn't just me."

"Tell whoever it was I said thank you." She heard Malaki stir at the door, doing well to keep out of sight.

The woman pulled Nyla from Isolde and held her close.

"You are just like Lady Zibiah said."

"Oh, really? And what did the Lady of Briarhole have to say about the Hood?"

"That you are not a monster as the master claims."

"She gives me far too much credit." Isolde rose to her feet. "Take care of your mother, little one." As she turned to leave, a glint of metal caught her eye. Dangling from a strap of leather fastened around Nyla's neck was the ring she had given her the night before.

Isolde plucked the ring from her dress and held it up to the light. "And who gave this to you might I ask?"

Nyla's eyes hardened as she snatched the ring back, pressing it to her chest. "I found it." Her answer was instant and so unnaturally serious.

"I happen to know who owns this ring," said Isolde. "Tried stealing from her once, much to my regret. And she would not like seeing it somewhere out in the open to be found or stolen by others. Or to see a gift of hers getting you into trouble."

Nyla nodded, her teeth biting down on her bottom lip.

"Good." Pausing at the door, Isolde looked back at her. "We will see each other again."

They climbed the wall to the hidden closet next to the library. Most of the guests had long since retired, making it easy to sneak back into their rooms. Once inside, they tossed their masks back into their respective hidden compartments.

"That was a productive evening," Cillian said, snatching a bottle of brandy from the bar. He took a long swing from the bottle before pouring them each two fingers worth and passing around the glasses. Clinks echoed through the room as they drank it down.

"We need to get some of this for Thornwood," Cillian said, going back for a second glass. Isolde looked to Malaki who was staring intently at Blyana. Her gaze was fixed on the now empty glass in her hands.

He licked his lips as if unsure of what to say. Her past was not a secret to them. While they didn't know every facet of the horrors she endured at Madame Vara's hands, they knew enough. Isolde knew Malaki didn't want to make her trauma any worse. "Are you alright?" he asked.

She looked up for a moment before dropping her gaze and nodding. "I just…I don't know why I froze." Strings of blonde hair fell about her face. "Why do I freeze?" Her voice was so quiet…so broken.

Malaki discarded his empty glass on a side table and walked to her. Gently he pulled the glass free from her tiny hands and set it aside as well. Her shoulders shook as he gently pulled her to him and wrapped his massive arms around her.

"It's not your fault, Bly." His voice was so soft, so calming she melted into his embrace. Burying her face in his chest, Blyana sobbed as her hands gripped his arms. He ran a hand down the length of her hair, tucking her head into his chest. "It's not your fault...it's not your fault." All was quiet save for Blyana's muffled cries and Malaki's calm assurances.

Cillian smiled at them. An easy smile that tugged at the corners of his lips and softened his gaze. Isolde knew Cillian and Blyana had moments just like this one. Moments of reassurances that the past was the past. That Madame Vara would never get her hands on Blyana again.

Isolde understood that didn't stop the past from haunting her friend. From the nightmares returning or the moments of hesitation plaguing Blyana. It was her response, a defensive mechanism when faced with a predator like the ones she faced in the House of Pleasures.

Before Thornwood, men only represented pain and devastation for Blyana. Cillian was aware of this and he had accepted it with a love and patience that only a true mate could possess. Yet, Isolde also knew that it was Malaki's understanding, his acceptance, that Blyana sought. Along with his love, and perhaps even his protection as well.

She had had that all along. It had always been there. But as she cried, Isolde believed, Blyana knew it for certain. As Blyana and Malaki held each other, Cillian's eyes showed not one ounce of jealousy or reproach, but pure undiluted joy. A joy that stemmed from knowing that the woman he loved and the man he called a brother had found peace with each other at last.

CHAPTER 13

"**O**ne less prick to deal with later." Isolde said, her heels clicking on the floor. It had been two hours since Zibiah fetched her. Lestahere had ended early in the day, allowing just enough sunlight for them to begin their journey back to Thornwood. In that time, Isolde had filled her in on the previous night's events.

"I see you carry work with you wherever you go," Zibiah said.

"It's not really a job one can take a break from, is it?"

Zibiah smiled. "I suppose not. The bastard is taken care of, I presume? You're not leaving me with a dead body to dispose of, are you?"

"Your hogs have a ferocious appetite."

Zibiah sighed in annoyance. "Thanks for that! Now I can't eat bacon until new hogs are bred."

"I'm sure you'll survive."

"I doubt you would be saying the same," Zibiah retorted, her mood souring, "if you had to do without."

Isolde scoffed, pressing a hand to her chest. "I would be just fine, thank you!"

"Says the girl who tried to stab Cillian for stealing the last piece of bacon from *her* plate this morning."

"I don't share food," Isolde grumbled. "You know that."

Zibiah laughed lightly, her face lifting into an unrestrained grin. Her beauty was something Isolde always envied.

"I did hear you had some lovely things to say about me."

"Oh, really?" Zibiah's brow rising. "Doesn't sound like me. From whom, might I ask?"

"From a little girl who works in the stables. A little girl...who needs to learn what songs should and should not be sung in the open."

"Ah!" said Zibiah. A look of fondness blossomed. "Nyla."

"The very one."

"I will speak with her...*again*. That girl's stubbornness rivals even yours."

They walked along the courtyard as the company of Thornwood continued to pack. Isolde sighed with an air impatience.

"Are you that anxious to leave my side?" her friend asked in mocking sadness.

"Not you," Isolde said with a grin. "This place. It's like a nightmare bred from my own dreams. Like losing a loved one only to have them return not as themselves but something far darker, crueler."

Zibiah's eyes swept the long, darkened hallway, her eyes growing somber and distant. "It was rather beautiful...before."

"It was." Memories of Isolde's time here flooded her mind. Memories that had long since been buried under the tree in the woods along with her heart.

Zibiah cleared her throat, her hand resting on the pommel of the sword that seemed to never leave her hip. "Any idea when we'll meet?"

"As soon as possible," Isolde said, glancing around for anyone trying to eavesdrop. "How soon can you get away?"

"I think I'm overdue for a visit to Thornwood." She grinned. "With Lauram here to distract Volkran, I can slip away more easily."

Isolde nodded. "It doesn't need to be immediately. It might take time for the lords and ladies of Arnoria to come up with their ends of the bounty."

"Some longer than others." Her golden eyes swept to Lord Milt, who lingered by the doorway, talking with one of the servants.

"They'll make it happen," Isolde whispered. "They want the Hood gone. Fear and anger make for wonderful motivators. I'll send Fane a week before we are to meet. That should give you plenty of time to come up with an excuse to leave."

"That should work," Zibiah said. Her casual smile slowly faded, her eyes growing darker. "Just be sure you know what you're doing, Isolde. Gage is now involved." The same hatred that coursed through Isolde burned in her friend's molten eyes. "You know there are no bounds to his depravity."

Isolde's lip lifted into a snarl, her eyes shining. "All too well."

They stood for a moment watching the bustle of the courtyard as the various houses arranged their companies for departure. It had been so long since they had this time together, not talking, just enjoying each other's quiet presence.

Far too soon, the company of Thornwood came into view, their caravan packed and ready. Without a word, Isolde swept Zibiah into her arms. "Be careful," she said, fighting the tears in her eyes.

"And you, my sister. I'll see you soon," Zibiah promised, planting a kiss in Isolde's hair.

Isolde nodded, her mouth turning up into her usual cocky smile. "All or nothing."

Zibiah smiled, her eyes shining with mischief. "All or nothing."

Stealing from the fortress, Isolde walked out to the courtyard. Elithrium iron grates that served as extra protection from the drawbridges were slowly being raised as Lady Circe and the rest of Marsh Hall waited to be set free of Briarhole's stronghold.

"Must you take so long?" Circe demanded, her head poking out of the carriage to yell at the human who was working to attach one of the chains connecting to the cog and wheel meant to lift the gate.

"I do apologize, Lady Circe" he said, sweat gleaming on his brow.

Circe circled back to catch Isolde watching her. She waved her hand through the opening, beckoning her over. "Let me steal you for a moment, Lady Isolde." Unease coated Isolde's skin as she moved across the wide-open courtyard. She felt Malaki's eyes on her, his hands freezing on the reins of his gelding.

"Yes, Lady Circe," Isolde greeted, her head dipping.

The woman looked her up and down, her cool eyes scrutinizing. *She truly was a beautiful woman.* If it weren't for the hideous scars Isolde left on her cheeks…Circe's beauty might rival even her own. "An interesting prospect you brought forth this weekend. I haven't seen this much excitement at Lestahere in decades. Not since the fall of King Viributhian."

"I only wish for Arnoria to be at peace with itself," Isolde said, letting a fraction of the truth slip in.

"Hmm," Circe mused, her lips pursing. "You were bold for your first time in front of the council. Bold is respectable, but it is also damning, my dear." A softness fell over her face, making the scars seem less gruesome. "Be careful how you wield it."

Isolde bowed her head giving herself time to find the right words. "Your advice is greatly appreciated, Lady Circe. I hope to learn more in the years to come."

"You will." A small smile broke across her face. "Powerful men have a way of underestimating intelligent, opinionated women, Lady Isolde," said Circe, her polished, blackened nails tapping against the gilded frame of the carriage. "Much to their own demise."

The drawbridge fell with a bang causing both Isolde and Circe to jump. "Worthless human," she spat before disappearing into the lavish carriage. At last, the iron grate rose enough for her four-team carriage to squeeze under. They took off without a second glance back.

"Some things never change." Ferden sauntered to Isolde's side, the aura of power consuming her senses, causing her power to stir. Not in defense but in curiosity.

"Unfortunately, some are doomed to remain in ignorance," she said.

"That is a sad truth in our world." Ferden's jaw feathered, and his gaze was distant. After a moment, he shook himself free. A not-so-convincing smile stretched across his handsome face, the afternoon sun dancing off the strands of his pale, golden hair. "I never did officially congratulate you on your newly appointed position as heir to Thornwood."

"Thank you," she said, her voice wooden, the words utterly hollow.

Ferden's lips pursed slightly, his eyes probing her face. "Not exactly what you had in mind for yourself is it?"

"Not in the slightest," Isolde said, her gaze meeting his.

A smile that did not reach his eyes played on the corners of his mouth, his gaze falling to the stables. "We all have regrets of what should have been, Lady Isolde, but there is always hope for the future. If happiness is within your grasp, don't hesitate to take it...however you can." Bowing once more, he strode to his mount, a solid black mare who stood abnormally still and waited patiently.

"Lord Ferden," she called.

He turned to look over his shoulder, a single eyebrow cocked in curiosity.

"What was the price? The one the prince paid for help from the gods?"

A mask of ice seemed to fall over Ferden's features. His mouth formed into a thin line, and his eyes hardened for a brief moment. "That is a story for another time, Lady Isolde."

With more grace than even a virya was capable of, Ferden leapt onto the saddle and took off into a gallop through the western gate. His form became a distant glint in the early afternoon sun. No escorts or loyal guards accompanied him. He was a speck of night in a sea of endless green.

Isolde had the feeling any who tried attacking Lord Ferden, would live to regret it…if they lived at all. Irritated, she stuck her tongue out at his shrinking form.

"How very mature of you," Liam said, his voice tickling her ear. His warm breath sent a shiver down her spine. "What did that strange man say to gain such disrespect from a lady?"

Isolde longed to lean against him, to feel him pressing into her. "Strange, yes, but very interesting."

"I hope not too interesting." His voice sharpened with just the hint of an edge.

"Why?" she asked, turning around, her fingers itching to touch him. "Would my champion be jealous?"

His brown eyes hardened in warning. "Furiously so," he said with a vicious smirk.

"Did a sense of entitlement come with winning the Tournament of the Guard?" She grinned, swatting his shoulder, the only contact she would allow herself with so many eyes watching. Even that small contact made her skin burn and core tighten.

The sensation of satin running along her hand and wrist drew her attention down. A hand spun ring of flowers now rested on her wrist. It was just like the bracelets he made for her when they were younger. Their petals were white as snow and stems free from thorns. A small puncture wound stood out from Liam's thumb as it moved over her knuckles. Isolde's heart swelled at the gesture, at his kindness.

"Yes," he said. "And I take what is mine." Isolde bit down on her lip to hide the grin, hoping her cheeks weren't as blazing hot as they felt.

"But the king has his suspicions," Liam said, his hand dropping back to his side as he followed her to the stables where Versa waited, already saddled. Alaric and Milt stood side by side, their backs to them, deep in conversation. Malaki, to Isolde's immense relief, was leaning down from his horse, deep in the conversation as well. It gave them just an ounce of privacy. "Do not be associating with him."

"So bossy," she said over her shoulder, swinging her hips in a way she knew he could not and would not ignore.

"Don't do that," Liam growled.

"Whatever do you mean?" Her voice dripped with mocking innocence.

"You know what," he retorted, catching up, a hand cupping her backside, his fingers pressing into the delicate fabric of her travel dress. "Throwing that ass of yours from side to side for all to see." She bit back a smile, her teeth grazing her lower lip.

"But I do it so well," she said plucking the reins from one of the stable boys. She leapt up into the saddle with ease. "Besides, why would I want to deprive them of such perfection?"

"I hope to get a full view of that perfection soon."

"If you play your cards right," she said absently, loving the look of disdain on his face. "When will you be back?"

"Hopefully soon," Liam said, his hand running down Versa's neck. "Gage has me pretty well occupied at the moment. We are heading to Foxclove to assess the situation."

Isolde's playful mood evaporated at the sound of his name, causing her power to slip. A gust of wind played at her fingers, causing a small plume of sand and dirt to engulf them.

"Easy!" Liam said, shielding his eyes from the assault. Versa reared up and her high-pitched scream of fright jarred Isolde from her anger.

"Sorry, girl," she said, smoothing down her mane. "Sorry." Versa finally settled, her hooves striking the cobblestones in frustration.

"Why does that happen?" Liam asked, his hand returning to Versa's neck. "Every time his name is mentioned it's almost as if you're blinded by rage."

The pain hit hard and fast. She was never prepared for it. Never ready to think of him…of Kamden. Of all the what-ifs…the could-have-beens that never would come true. All she saw was his bloody, broken body in her arms. His beautiful, blue eyes robbed of their light.

Why did he have to ask? He knew what Gage had done, what he had taken from her. Isolde forced the pain into numbness, refusing to acknowledge it. But the blue eyes shined in her mind anyway. Her hands gripped the reins as the pain grew.

"Speaking of *him*," she said, her lip turning. "When were you going to mention that I should be expecting a marriage proposal?"

Liam's hand froze in Versa's mane, his eyes gaining a hint of light as his mouth thinned. "You heard?"

"You sound surprised."

Liam shook his head. "You risked sneaking around doing gods know what here?" His voice cut through the air like a sharp blade. "Are you insane?"

"Occasionally, but that's part of my charm," she snapped. "Now answer the damn question, Liam."

"That was the first time I had ever heard him speak of marrying you." Liam ran a hand through his hair, his head shaking. "He's had his eye on you for a while. I thought it was only because he wanted you in his bed."

"Apparently, it's the marital bed he's aiming for."

"That's why I wanted you to stay away! To stop this, Isolde." Liam's voice rose as the light in his eyes grew. "He already looks at you enough as it is. Why are you undermining my efforts in keeping you safe?" Versa threw her head from side to side, shoving Liam away.

"Isolde?" Malaki rode forward, his eyes turning hard when he saw the pain that was undoubtedly etched in her face. "What did you do?" he demanded, his focus shifting to Liam.

"He didn't do anything," Isolde said, her words a hollow whisper.

Liam and Malaki stared at each other over her. A distrust that had formed into hatred flew through the males, their gazes never wavering.

"I was only talking with Lady Isolde," Liam said, his teeth clenched.

"It's fine, Malaki," said Isolde, her temper finally slowing enough for her to think. "I'll meet you at the bridge."

He held Liam's gaze for a moment longer, the hatred palpable. "Fine," he said and spurred his horse forward.

Liam placed his hands on his hips, his head shaking. "He really doesn't like me, does he?"

Isolde smiled grimly, her shoulders shrugging. "Don't take it personally; he doesn't care for most people." She couldn't find it in her heart to tell him his friend now viewed him as an enemy, a loyal servant to the king. Even if Malaki knew Liam occasionally warmed her bed, it did not persuade his opinion of him in the slightest. It only seemed to make matters worse.

"To answer your question," said Isolde. "I'm not undermining you, Liam. I'm doing what I think is right."

He released a heavy sigh, as if to rid himself of as much tension as possible. Again, he stroked Versa's mane. She fidgeted at his touch, but did not pull away. "Please tell me the rumors of Foxclove are greatly exaggerated. That there aren't dead bodies decorating the entrance."

Liam had never supported her as the Hood or the methods she employed. Even before he was named champion at the Tournament of the Guard, he was a stickler for the law.

"Would a lie make you feel better?"

Before he could answer, Alaric rode forward, his eyes hard. "Captain," Alaric said, his tone cold, matching his stare.

Liam bowed stiffly, his eyes dropping to the ground. "Lord Cotheran, it was wonderful seeing you again, sir."

"Come Isolde," Alaric said with enough authority she knew not to argue with...at the moment. He prodded his stallion toward the caravan that lay waiting just beyond the gate.

She couldn't help the pity swelling in her heart as Liam looked after the Lord of Thornwood. A sense of distrust now existed in Alaric's heart for the boy he had taken in, the one he had raised as his own.

"That's not fair," Isolde said, her eyes narrowing on Alaric's back as he passed under the drawbridge. "He shouldn't treat you like that."

"I understand," murmured Liam, his hands stilling on Versa's neck. "He's still angry I joined the tournament. But what he doesn't understand is that when I entered, there was no chance for one of my friends to be picked out of the lottery. And he didn't have to make a choice on who to send. It was the fairest way to choose, but I wasn't willing to risk it."

"He has to see that," Isolde said, her fingers itching to cup his face.

"I think he half expected me to throw the tournament," said Liam, disdain in his voice. "But that isn't me…That's not how he raised me."

"I know," she said. Yet she could not bring herself to admit how much it had changed him. How in a way she understood Alaric and Malaki's resentment. Every day Liam spent with them, he grew more and more like them. Every day she lost a piece of him, which placed them all at risk.

Alaric jerked his horse to a halt and turned back to the keep, his eyes blazing and lips pulling into a line of impatience. "Isolde!"

"I'll see you soon," she said, a smile that met her eyes lighting her face. Reaching forward, damning the possible consequences, she cupped his face in her hand. The warm stubble tickled her palm. He sighed heavily, leaning into her touch to smell her scent and the bracelet of flowers at her wrist.

"Please." His voice was a whisper. "Be safe."

She could not bring herself to warn him of the carnage that awaited him at Foxclove. The mutilated bodies that had littered the doorstep…the hallways, forever stained in blood. He would know soon enough.

"Always." Dropping her hand, she sped through the gate. Versa's muscles bunched beneath her, itching to be turned loose on the long road home.

CHAPTER 14

Cracking open the library door, Isolde smiled at the faces that stared back. Humans, half-bloods, and virya turned to greet her with cheers as she walked into the throng of hugs and shouts. Once freed of their grasps, Isolde took her usual seat between the window and cold fireplace.

"My, what a crowd we have here today! Do we have any newcomers?"

The crowd as a whole turned around to stare. In the back, two girls and a boy, no older than seven, lingered near the doorway. They fidgeted self-consciously in clean, new clothes and avoided everyone's gaze.

Virya children. Their eyes shined briefly, untrained power surging forward in response to their unease.

"Hello," Isolde said, wearing a warm smile. "We are very happy to have you here, and since this is your first day, why don't you three come up and pick our book for the day?"

All three stared at each other, unsure of what to do. With some prodding and smiles from the others, they walked up and gazed down at the books before her. It was a modest pile, one gifted by Liam. They eventually agreed on one and handed it to her.

"Oh, this is a good one," Isolde said, her fingers grazing the cover. "Excellent choice. Well, go find a seat, and we'll get started." They looked to each other and then back at her.

"Which side do we sit on?" the little girl asked, her golden curls bouncing. "Where do the virya sit?"

"We don't have sides," Isolde said, her voice gaining just an ounce of a chill. "Here, we sit together."

The three appeared dumbfounded, their little eyes bulging. "But we can't sit with the humans." A few of the children's eyes fell to their worn, soiled clothes. Their hands rubbed together, attempting to rid themselves of the dirt and grime caked into their skin.

"You will if you want to come to story hour," she said in an even tone. "They want to hear the story just as much as you do." This wasn't the first time she had dealt with this kind of attitude, nor would it be the last.

They looked out at the crowd of awaiting children then back to each other. As if in silent agreement, they took seats towards the back, next to a human and half-blood. She smiled inwardly, as if she had just won another small victory against bigotry. Nan smiled as well from her comfortable lounger in the back of the room. The wrinkles of her tanned face bunched.

Story hour commenced. Isolde relished in the shocked gasps and chuckles that broke out from the miniature crowd as she read aloud. Once the story was over and the children applauded, she bowed to them and said that there was fresh lemonade and sweets in the kitchen.

Nan ushered them from the room leaving Isolde with a heavy silence in the wake of the children's screams of excitement. It had been a week since leaving Briarhole. A week of planning and replanning for their attack on Foxclove.

A sip of her lavender and honey tea slid over her lips and soothed the ache in her throat. It was always slightly hoarse after story hour. With a satisfied sigh, Isolde picked up her most recent read and leaned back in the chair, desperate for an escape. It was a romance, one that had her revisiting her time in the woods with Liam…the long, hot summer afternoons spent swimming in the river. Isolde bit her lip at the memory of his bare flesh pressed against hers.

A bang shot through the library, causing her to nearly drop the book in her hand. Instinctively, Isolde reached for the concealed blade at her thigh. The doors hit the walls, groaning on their hinges.

"Liam!" Her fingers fell from the hilt with relief. Her momentary irritation gave way to surprised relief. "What are—"

"Please tell me it wasn't all you this time!" he demanded, striding toward her. His massive arms swung at his sides, hands balled into fists. Tall and broad, Liam loomed over her; the dark brown of his eyes shined with anger. He looked like a living shadow in his ebony uniform.

"So, I take it you delivered Gage to Foxclove unscathed?"

"Indeed, and do you know what I found?"

"A greeting committee?" Isolde asked, leaning back into the plush leather chair, her feet resting on the table before her in sarcastic ease.

"Cut the shit, Isolde!" said Liam, nostrils flaring. Her eyes cut to him in warning. "At least twenty men are dead and most of Dagan's gold is gone. Much to Gage's disappointment."

"Well, we most certainly wouldn't want to disappoint *him* now, would we?"

Liam growled, hitting the stack of books he had gifted her off the table. They scattered over the floor, their pages flapping in the breeze. Fury surged forward as Isolde's teeth clenched against a growl bubbling in her chest.

"And nearly all the remaining slaves have disappeared without a trace." He plopped down on the chair next to hers, the weight of the situation crashing down on him. "The Hood did a good job of getting them out undetected, only leaving behind rotting corpses and a pool of virya blood spilled in her wake." Isolde ignored the jab, her attention returning to her book. Liam's face fell into his hands, his fingers widely spaced. "You can't keep doing this, Isolde. The Hood has gone too far this time...killing a lord."

"You didn't see what he was doing to them, Liam," said Isolde. "He's lucky I killed him quickly and didn't take my time." She reached over and grabbed another book from one of the stacks nearby. The mood for reading romance had completely evaporated. "I'll remember to carve out some extra time on my next little outing."

"There can't be a next time, that's what I'm telling you!" He rose once again and paced back and forth, his boots kicking the fallen books.

"Quit kicking my books," she growled.

He ignored her but minded his steps. "The king is furious, Isolde. He thinks there is a new group of rebels forming. Attacking local politicians is one thing but a lord's manor is something else. There have been other incidents of rebellion throughout the kingdom."

A jolt of surprise shot through her. "What other rebellions?"

"It's nothing," Liam said, flinching with regret.

"Tell me right now, Liam! What others?"

He ran a hand roughly through his black curls, forcing them out of his face as he sighed. "Certain humans are taking a stand, along with some virya. Against local authorities all over Arnoria. Demanding fairer treatment."

"Good," Isolde said, returning her eyes back to her book. On the inside, Isolde was screaming with joy and terror. Pride for the people bloomed inside her, but so did fear. What had she brought down on them?

"The king is stirring, Isolde."

"I'm not scared of him," she said, knowing good and well that wouldn't convince him.

"You should be," Liam said, his eyes now back on her. "He is hell-bent on your head swinging from the rafters in Elenarta and I can't protect you from him."

"I'm not asking you to."

"Yes, you are!" he roared, forcing her to look up. He had never raised his voice to her, never acted so angry, so…out of control.

"Every time you do this, you are asking me to look the other way. To not report what I know. Damn it, Isolde! I am a sworn soldier in the guard of this territory. Or have you forgotten that what you do also affects me?"

No, she had not. How could she?

"You know I haven't," Isolde said, the words cold as ice. "But I also remember all those the king's reign has affected. The children who will never grow up. The women who are used and disposed of like rubbish after the men have had their fill. The men who are forced into slavery. Or the innocents who go hungry because their masters won't feed them enough. You remember what it was like to be hungry, don't you, Liam?"

He sighed heavily, his shoulders hunching with the memories of his time before Thornwood. "Yes."

"I've seen plenty who have, and that is who I fight for. For those who are unable to fight for themselves. And if that makes me a criminal, then so be it. I have been called far worse." Her fingers tapped against the cover of the book. "If you say I am asking you to look the other way, then don't. Arrest me."

Shaking his head, Liam slowly sank into the chair beside her, his head falling into his hands once again. The black leather of his uniform strained against the muscles of his back. She knew she was putting him in a difficult position, yet she found herself unapologetic for it.

"Just tell the others to back off some," he said, raising his head to look at her, his hands cupping his mouth. The soft sincerity he had as a boy was there once again. The one she felt deeply for.

"Fine," she said, resting the book she had been clinging to in her lap.

He smiled, the corner of his mouth turning up as he slid a piece of stray hair behind her ear. "There's that fire," he murmured.

"What?"

"You have red in your hair, but only in the sunlight." His gaze shifted into one she recognized, the one she remembered from so long ago. He was carefree then, so full of hope, not an ounce of harshness or anger.

Without thinking, she reached up and held his hand to her cheek. How she missed this, longing for his touch in any kind of capacity.

His thumb gently caressed her jaw. "I miss you, Isolde," he whispered. His familiarity was overwhelming, a constant reminder of simpler times. She turned her lips to his hand and kissed him lightly.

"I miss you," she said, taking in his scent to fill her entirely. "Every day you are gone I miss you and the way things were."

Liam sighed heavily, his forehead coming to rest on hers. "I do too."

"Then come back to me." It was a plea, an open invitation to come home. Even as she spoke she knew the answer and it charred her heart.

"You know I can't." His words were hard with regret. "Even if I wanted to, Alaric wouldn't allow it."

"This is your home, Liam," she said. "And soon, Alaric won't have a say in the matter."

"Ah, yes," he said, smiling proudly. "The future Lady of Thornwood."

"If I asked him," she pushed, "how can he refuse?"

"Because of the choice I made, Isolde. By entering that tournament willingly, I have branded myself a traitor."

"That's not you, Liam," she said, cupping his cheek in her palm. Her fingers gently stroked his jaw. "But neither is this newfound temper of yours."

He sighed heavily, leaning into her touch. "I know," he said, his eyes squeezing shut. "Being around Gage and the others is very taxing. In certain situations, I must follow along. Otherwise, I am labeled an outcast, someone who can't be trusted. There is nothing worse in the Guard."

Isolde dropped her gaze, unsure of what to say. Curiosity had questions brewing in her mind. What had he gone along with?

"You never did tell me," he said, jerking her back to the present. "What did Gage do to earn your wrath?"

Isolde's teeth clamped shut, and her eyes grew hard as the hatred flooded back into her heart. She pulled away from his touch, unable to tolerate it. "Please don't, Liam."

"Don't do that," he said, grabbing her hand, forcing her to look at him. "Don't shut me out. Help me to understand."

Thin silver lines formed in her eyes. She shook her head, swallowing the tears. Refusing to let them fall.

"Tell me," he whispered. "Please. What has he done?"

Isolde looked at him, eyes wide with incredulity. "How can you ask that? You know who he took from me, Liam."

"I know," he said, "but that was nearly forty years ago, Isolde."

"Yes," she said rounding on him. "Forty years I could have had with Kamden. Gage stole my future, my heart…my everything." Isolde licked her lips and thought of him. The sound of his laugh, the sight of his smile haunted her very soul. No matter who tried to fill the hole that he left behind, Kamden would always be a part of her. Always. "And for that I will never forgive and never forget what he did."

Liam seemed to be at a loss for words. There was more he wanted to know; she could see it in his eyes. More details were needed to fill in the picture. But he simply nodded. "Very well," he said at last, his voice choked. "Thank you for telling me."

She sighed, her chest rising and falling with slowness, steeling the beast within. "You're welcome."

Liam pressed a kiss to her lips once…then a second time. "Come let's get you something to eat," he said, rising, his hand held out to her.

"I'm fine, thank you," she said, turning back to the book desperate for solace.

"You can't survive on reading alone, Isolde."

"If armed with the right reading material, enough wine, and left to my own devices, sir, I shall survive just fine."

"I don't think you could survive without those little piles of kindling," Liam said, shaking his head, hand falling back to his side. She knew he hated anytime she disobeyed him, and she relished in her defiance. She stuck her tongue out, her eyes observing him over the rim of the book.

"No, I don't believe I could. Life would be dreadfully boring."

"Yes, as if gobbling up coin and mutilating or killing those who cross you isn't thrilling enough." She could tell he regretted the words as soon as they left his tongue.

Silence, heavy and heated, slowly fell between them. He looked away from her fiery stare.

"You know it isn't about settling a score for myself," Isolde said, her voice edged with lethal quietness, her temper flaring.

"I know it's not. I'm sorry," he said, raising his hands in surrender. "Look, I have a few errands to run before leaving for Foxclove. It's the only reason I was able to slip away for a while." She didn't respond, her eyes pointedly on the page. "I'll see myself out."

She let him leave without so much as a glance in his direction. She tried to read, but the words made less sense the more she tried. Eventually, Tanor and Mary arrived for their reading lessons. Closing the book with a snap, she escorted them through the hidden door.

Malaki hovered in the dark corner, his presence doing little to gain the girl's trust. Still, she was making progress, much the same as Tanor did when he first began. Skepticism still danced in Mary's eyes when Isolde was close, her body angling away. Isolde did her best to ignore it.

Her fight with Liam had awakened her darker side. Cleaving away at the layer of patient control that kept her other self in check. The self that thirsted for blood and death. She had let it go on for far too long. Kept the beast locked up longer than she ever had before. It was something she should have taken care of after the stress of Foxclove. Now it was too late. Now…there was only one way to satisfy it. One way to reel the monster back into its cage.

Familiar icy flames ignited in her veins, burning away her control. Each minute grew longer than the last. The clock above the mantel ticked in mocking slowness.

The air shifted as Malaki stirred from his spot on the wall, his arms coming to hang at his sides. Concern but also caution was etched into the lines of his face. He could sense that she wasn't alright.

Licking her lips, Isolde plastered on the best smile possible and turned to the vulnerable, human children still bent over their lessons. "Lessons will be cut short today, I'm afraid."

Tanor glanced up with a look of worry. Never had she cut his lesson short for any reason. Mary, to Isolde's disappointment, looked relieved.

"I promise we can add some more time onto next week if you wish," she said, her voice strained. Tanor shot her a questioning look as he rose. She waved a dismissive hand and forced a smile she knew wasn't convincing. He paused for a moment but nodded.

"Thank you, Lady Isolde." Mary echoed his gratitude and followed Tanor up the stairs and through the door.

"I know that look," Malaki said, pushing away from the wall, his arms tightly knitted over his chest.

"What look would that be?"

"The same one I get...when it's been too long since I depleted my power."

Isolde continued to rearrange the books, needing something to do with her hands. Already her nails were starting to ache. The talons beneath were itching to punch through the nail beds.

"How long has it been?"

Isolde stilled; the cool fire burned through her veins. Her power leaked around what little remained of the boundaries of her control.

"How long, Isolde?"

Her sigh was sharp, eyes squeezing shut as she fought against the building anger. It wouldn't be long before her resolve shattered completely.

"Too long," Isolde rasped, her teeth clenched.

"I thought so," Malaki said, his voice growing darker.

She braced herself against the table, fingertips digging into the wood that dented under the pressure. Fear, cold and resentful, coated her skin, rolling her stomach into a ball of nauseated self-hatred. She despised this weakness, the inability to hold herself in check.

But what she feared most was the vicious, mindless creature. The one who would take over her mind and body when it was allowed out. Still, it was a necessary evil, one she must endure. The last thing she wanted was to age, to walk willingly into vulnerability.

Despite her hatred for her other self, for the danger it placed the ones she loved in...her power was still a monster. It was a living thing. It too needed to breathe the free air.

"Go get the others," Isolde said, her head bowed between her shoulders. Splinters of wood poked around her fingers, the grain moaning in protest. "Bring the elithrium shackles...and chain linked mail."

"Isolde—" Malaki said, his hand coming to hover over her shoulder.

"Do it," she pleaded, her eyes glowing so brightly they shined in his. "Please, Malaki no risks...no mistakes."

Familiar sorrow filled Malaki's gaze, his jaw feathering as he looked at her in such anguish. "Do not stop," he said. Each word was a command, an order she could not and did not want to disobey. "Take the back way out. We will meet you at the Pit."

Without looking back, he darted up the steps and into the light of the afternoon sun. He knew her power all too well, knew it hated pity as much as she did.

Wrenching her hands from the now ruined tabletop, Isolde grabbed a pair of elithrium blades from the mantel and followed. They were an insurance policy. A means of ending the threat she was about to become if the need arose. Claws raked down her mind, causing her to wince.

"Not yet," Isolde begged, taking every shortcut she could remember, desperate to avoid everyone at all costs. The Pit wasn't far. She just had to get outside...and away. Away from Nan...Tanor...from the children who ate cookies and drank lemonade just down the hallway. Unaware of just how much danger they were in.

The beast within needed to consume her for only a little while. She had to grant it freedom. If only for the briefest of time. Isolde had put this off for far too long. She needed to let the monster out.

CHAPTER 15

The faint sheen of the elithrium shackles and chain linked mail caught the monster's eye. Isolde flapped her impossibly large wings, forcing herself higher into the clear blue sky. Even in this form, the creature recognized that shimmer.

"Isolde," Galaena called from below, her voice calm and inviting.

She could see it broke through the barrier in Isolde's mind. Forcing its way back into her consciousness. Past the aggression and unrelenting blood lust Galaena knew ravaged Isolde's mind.

A piercing cry exploded from her beak. The beast refused to be put back into the cage. Galaena's voice had always been a beacon to call Isolde back to her humanity. It served as an anchor into herself. Now Isolde was tossed in a sea of fury and unstoppable power. The same one that tried to drown Galaena every time she had been forced to transform. A torture she didn't miss in the slightest.

"Alaric," she said, her voice now strained with worry.

"I know." He never looked away from the colossal falcon. He was always terrified of seeing Isolde like this. Even as a child she was nearly impossible to subdue. Massive and savage, she could tear through a town without issue, without reproach if she wished. Her white-and-brown wings, a falcon's wings built for speed and agility, snapped in the air. If she wanted to take off...there would be none to stop her.

"Isolde," Galaena said again, her eyes flickering to Alaric, who struggled to stay upright on his mangled leg. Her hand reached out, beseeching. "Come back."

Recognition ignited in the Isolde's emerald-silver eyes...her mother's eyes. The struggle raged beneath the surface. Isolde wrestled for control, forcing the wings to slow. Anguish ripped through Galaena as Isolde cried out. Galaena was familiar with the pain undoubtedly burning through Isolde's mind, the searing agony as the monster refused to back down. Another cry pierced the Pit, talons slashing in midair. Fane perched on a branch nearby. His eyes wild and wings flapping at his sides.

"She's losing," Cillian said, his eyes finding Blyana. "We need to help bring her down."

"Give her a minute," Blyana said, holding a hand out between them, not meeting his gaze. "It's been a while since she last changed. It takes a bit to regain control."

Galaena didn't miss her gloved fingers tighten on the cuffs. Blyana's eyes glowed, her own power stirring with the danger so close.

Cillian swallowed as he forced a sarcastic smile onto his face. "Come on, Isolde." He took a step forward, moving to block Blyana. The wind from her wings tossed his jacket and hair. "I'm starving and you know Nan doesn't like anyone to be late for dinner."

Galaena could see the bird turn, its anger stirring again as Cillian took another step forward. Isolde lunged for him. Her sharp, unforgiving talons lashed out, their points aiming for his heart.

Cillian's hands worked with the wind, attempting to force her back into the sky. But the first wave never founds its mark. She continued on, diving straight at him. From the belly of the forest, a deep growl rumbled through the trees as a wall of brown fur barreled forward. The trees splintered apart, vines and underbrush scattering as the massive bear tore its way through the thicket.

Isolde had just enough time to turn and face the new threat as Malaki, tackled her to the ground. He stared down at her, his massive paw pressing into her chest.

She shrieked, her beak snapping at his face and neck, looking for anywhere to draw blood. A dangerous anger, one that was not Malaki's, glowed in the bear's eyes. It roared down, teeth only inches from the falcon's neck as she flapped her wings uselessly.

Galaena saw a moment of clarity reach Malaki's eyes. He had remembered himself just enough to not sink his teeth into flesh. Instead, he looked to her and Alaric, who hovered on the edge of the clearing. His hazel eyes ignited.

"Move!" Alaric screamed. Galaena felt the familiar brush of his power. The unmistakable current of raw anger meant only one thing. Her mate was fighting against the will to change to let the scales and powerful jaw tear through his flesh and bones.

They acted as one. Cillian and Blyana secured the set of shackles as Galaena and Alaric hauled a large blanket of chain linked elithrium iron chain mail over the two beasts.

Isolde shrieked in anger. Her beak snapped at any part of them that dared come close. Already, Galaena could feel the bird's power draining, giving her a footing in control. The feathers began to recede, Isolde's form shrinking beneath Malaki who growled, his teeth bared in warning.

"Alright, Malaki," Blyana said taking a cautious step forward. "Easy now." Isolde rested beneath Malaki's paw that could easily force two men on their backs side by side.

Control returned swiftly, the rich, brown fur disappearing beneath Malaki's inked skin almost immediately. He fell to the ground; all of his energy having been spent.

"Isolde," Galaena said, so tenderly it was meant only for a mother and her child. "Come back to me." Isolde struggled beneath the bonds. Her eyes danced wildly. "Isolde!"

"Push it down!" Malaki said, taking her other side, hand resting on her shoulder. "Isolde, push it down."

Squeezing her eyes shut, Isolde looked inside and saw the wildness that was her power. It was a kaleidoscope of lights, each unique and constantly in motion. Some she didn't recognize. Others, like the wind and her falcon…she almost smiled at fondly. They scattered around her mind, avoiding the small cage in the very center.

One piece at a time, she forced it behind the bars. Each one fought against her, weighing her down until they were dragged under her control.

"Good," she heard Malaki say. "Just like that."

She felt the beak recede completely, the bones in her face setting. Her wings shrank back into her arms. At last, the final piece, the most difficult one, her power's consciousness was shoved down and silenced.

All was quiet.

Not even the sound of the others breathing assaulted her ears.

She reached up to feel the cool metal around her neck. Elithrium was doing its work, sapping her of all energy, leaving nothing left to transform with. The touch of grass, warm and soft, ran along the length of her arms and legs. The smell of the forest filled her head, driving away her unease.

A few more minutes. You can endure it for a few more minutes. The elithrium felt heavy against her skin, as if her very life was being pulled away, draining her dry.

"Isolde?" Malaki said kneeling by her head.

She sighed heavily, her eyes fluttering open to the dying light of the day.

"I'm sorry," Isolde said, her voice strained and rough with shame. She hated herself, for forcing Malaki to change as well just to keep her from hurting someone else.

"Don't," he said dismissively. "Do not apologize. It's not your fault. I was past due anyway."

"It was harder this time," Isolde said. For the last few years, each transformation had become harder and harder to return from. Fane drifted from the sky to land on her shoulder. Soft chirps filtered through his beak as he nudged her cheek.

Malaki nodded, strands of his ebony hair falling into his eyes. "We'll have to work on that."

Isolde chuckled, running a finger beneath Fane's chin. "Just add it to the list."

A broad smile broke out on his face, his shoulders relaxing. "Can we take these off?" His finger lifted a side of the chain mail draped over her chest.

Her power was quiet in the confines of its cage. All energy had been bled dry. "I think so."

"Come on, Malaki," said Cillian. "I think that's a good look for her. Elithrium brings out the color in her eyes."

"And blood brings out the color in yours," said Isolde.

"Good thing I'm so ruggedly handsome," Cillian said, working off the wide shackles around her feet. "Women like a man who wears blood well."

"The only thing you wear well is your food," Blyana said tossing the remaining shackle to the side.

"Speaking of which…" Cillian grunted, slinging the shackle away and swiping his hands on his jacket. "You've kept me from my dinner, Lady Isolde. You know that's my favorite meal of the day."

"Every meal is your favorite," Blyana said, her shoulder bumping into his.

"There is one that is a particularly special favorite," he murmured wrapping an arm around her hip, a devious grin dancing on his lips.

"You're both disgusting," said Isolde as she stood up. Her knees buckled and shook beneath her weight, nearly causing her to fall back down. Transforming always left her weak, vulnerable. Malaki moved to catch her but she held up a hand, not wanting to burden him anymore. She could see his exhaustion; his own arms and legs were shaking with fatigue.

"Disgustingly adorable." Cillian grinned, his lips brushing Blyana's temple and she all but purred at the attention.

Isolde rolled her eyes. *Let them have their moment.* She turned to her uncle. Alaric rested on his cane as he looked her over. His eyes were dark, hooded with concern.

As if reading his thoughts Isolde said, "At least I didn't kill anyone." Her tone was light and forcibly optimistic. "I consider that an absolute win."

"I suppose," he said, his mouth twisting in disapproval. Isolde ignored him. She knew he saw her struggle, knew that he wasn't upset with her but with the situation.

"It absolutely is!" her aunt chided, her piercing, gray eyes narrowing on her husband. "It's not easy to master a task when it hardly gets used."

"Especially one that can kill," Cillian said jokingly.

Blyana growled, her elbow digging into his gut. "Shut it!"

He merely looked at Isolde and winked. She returned it with a smile.

"Come on," Galaena said, her arm wrapping around Isolde's shoulders. Her fingers stroked Fane's back, and he cooed happily. "Nan will be waiting."

"Just a moment," Alaric said, his tone causing them all to halt. He leaned against his cane, and his eyes were downcast. "There's something Isolde needs to know. Something you all need to know."

A block of ice fell in Isolde's stomach, her exhausted defenses rallying once more. Whatever the news, it couldn't be good if Alaric waited until after she transformed to tell her.

Galaena bristled at her side. "Not now, Alaric," she said. "She's exhausted."

"All the more reason to tell me now." Her uncle remained still. His gaze was on her-assessing and dreading what must come next. "Spit it out, Alaric," Isolde said through gritted teeth. She hated when he did this. *You would think I could handle bad news after living in nothing else for the past forty-eight years.*

"Gage has asked for your hand in marriage." Heavy silence fell over the Pit.

"Well," said Cillian, his hands bracing on his hips, "we knew this was coming."

Blyana nodded. "Just didn't think it would happen this quickly."

Alaric leaned against his cane, his brow furrowing. "How could you possibly have known?"

Isolde's eyes flickered to Galaena before glancing to Alaric. "We might have taken a slight detour on our way back to our quarters the last night at Briarhole."

Alaric ran a hand down his face. Fine wrinkles pulled at the edge of his eyes and mouth. "Explain...*now*!"

"It was a private meeting between Gage, Volkran, Lauram, and Liam. There, Gage made his intentions known," Malaki said, his lip turning up in disgust, "where Isolde is concerned."

Alaric looked between the four of them. His jaw went slack with disbelief. "And you didn't think to tell me this?" he demanded.

"I was trying to think of a plan," Isolde said, dusting off her shirt. "A way around it—"

"There is no way around this, Isolde!" Alaric's voice rang through the clearing, his eyes glowing. "No other choice!"

"You can't be serious," Malaki said, his voice hardly a whisper. "What do you mean no other choice?"

Isolde stared at her uncle, her anger growing. "What did you do?" He shifted his stance, giving his mangled leg a chance to rest as he stared back in silence. A bit of the light faded from his eyes. "You did tell him no, didn't you?"

"Not in so many words," he admitted.

"Please don't say you gave that bastard your blessing," Cillian snarled. They all looked to him in shock. Never had he shown such aggression to any of them, let alone the Lord of Thornwood.

"Alaric Cotheran…" Galaena warned.

"No," Alaric said through clenched teeth. "I told him that the decision was Isolde's and Isolde's alone. He seemed to like that answer."

"I'm sure he did," Isolde spat, brushing a strand of hair from her face. "Apparently, he wants me broken. Filled with the hope of having a choice in the matter only to have that ripped away from me."

"Bastard," Malaki growled, his fists clenching at his sides.

"With his proximity to Thornwood," said Alaric, his jaw feathering, "I have a feeling he will be calling a lot more often."

Fire seared Isolde's chest. The anger burning at her exhausted control. It slipped, allowing a growl to rumble through. She could feel her bones bend and flex. They all cautiously scooted farther away.

"I'm fine," Isolde said. Violent tremors ran up her arms causing Fane to shift nervously.

Alaric breathed a sigh of relief but kept his distance. "Civility is essential, Isolde. He has great influence in the kingdom."

"You know what he did, Alaric!"

The heavy wrinkles of his forehead deepened. Of course, Alaric remembered; Isolde knew he did.

Her uncle's eyes softened, as did his tone. "I know, Isolde."

"I'm not marrying him!" she growled.

"Of course, you're not," Malaki said, his eyes cutting to Alaric.

"And I'm not suggesting you do," her uncle said, his tone sharp. "What I am saying is for you to tread lightly. Especially since he is the

Right Hand of the king, making him the second most powerful man in Arnoria."

He took a steady breath as he shook his head regretfully. Light from the high afternoon sun glistened off his hair. "This will be no easy task to maneuver. The last thing you need is for Gage to find out that you know of your predicament. He will draw it out, make the situation that much harder on you. Nor does he need to catch wind of your...extracurricular activities."

"Obviously," Isolde grumbled, her arms knotting over her chest. "Killing Dagan was a solution that provided opportunities for more problems to grow."

"That piece of shit deserved far worse than what he was given," said Blyana. Both Malaki and Cillian nodded in agreement, their eyes distant and hard with the memory of the horrors of Foxclove.

Alaric sighed, and his eyes turned thoughtful. "Do you think you did the right thing?"

Isolde's arms tightened over her chest, an irritated sigh of her own leaking through her lips. "A lot of people would have suffered if I hadn't. So maybe." She wished it had been different. "If he had listened, if he had been more like Theort, none of this would have happened."

"Perhaps," Alaric said, his eyes growing somber, aged in sorrow.

"Did Gal tell you what was in Dagan's money bag?" she asked.

He nodded. "Raw elithrium."

"There are such steep restrictions on possessing it. How could he have it?" Blyana asked.

"It was sent to him by the king for a reason," Alaric said, shifting his feet in the flattened grass. He grimaced slightly as weight pressed into his leg. "I'm not entirely sure why. Handling the thing without protection is," his gaze flickered to Isolde's hand. "Well, you know."

Isolde nodded as the pads of her fingers grazed over the newly healed burn. "Dagan had been recruited by the king to provide

Elenarta with bodies: virya, humans, and half-bloods. Another little tidbit we caught while hearing of my intended."

"It wasn't clear if he was paid in elithrium or something else," said Malaki. "But it's a safe bet that was the price. Maybe the king wants his allies better equipped to handle virya."

Alaric nodded, his cane digging into the dirt. "Perhaps you're right."

Days passed without interruption.

No unwanted visitors announced their arrival at Isolde's doorstep. She expected each sound to be Gage's arrival with talk of betrothal on his tongue. She would have to be cautious and in absolute control when the dreaded moment came.

She stayed in their hideout, hidden from sight, deep in the heart of Blackford Forest. They didn't have much time to think of a plan to steal the bounty from underneath the nose of the king's Right Hand.

As Malaki, Blyana, and Cillian lounged by the fire, she paced. Drawings of Foxclove they had created from memory, lay scattered on the table before them. There were far too many exposed points to even guess where Gage would place the bounty.

The sound of a bird chirping echoed along the walls of the cave, interrupting her thoughts. She walked to the entrance of the cave and whistled in return. A second call came, one she knew all too well.

In the archway stood Zibiah, her arms overflowing with food and wine.

"And you come bearing gifts," Isolde said, stepping aside. "The others will be most appreciative."

"Anything I can do to support illegal activity," Zibiah said, tossing the hood of her jacket back. Her mare, Heartthrow, whinnied from the tree line, her white head tossing.

"What excuse did you give Volkran?" Isolde asked, setting the goods on the table, careful to not disturb the drawing.

"I snuck out." She grinned, taking a seat by the fire. "Putting those tricks you taught me to good use."

"Those tricks will get you into trouble," Malaki said, his eyes still closed.

"I believe they've gotten you out of a few scrapes," Isolde said, as Zibiah pulled the heavy iron pot away from the roaring fire to stir the soup Nan had prepared. Large chunks of deer, potatoes, and carrots swam to the top as heavily scented waves of spices filled the warm air.

"Scrapes that you got us into in the first place." He rose and stretched, his bones cracking. A tiny hiss slithered through the air as Blyana lazily leapt from her perch on top of a large boulder to land next to the table. She yawned widely, her arms stretching overhead.

Cillian, who had been sleeping on a cot beneath her, shot up. His dagger slashed through the air as his chest heaved ragged breathes that seeped through his clenched teeth. Fear shined from his dark eyes, as if he was still enduring whatever terrors haunted his dreams.

"Put that away before you cut yourself," Malaki said, taking a seat at the table. Cillian shot him a vulgar gesture but took the seat across from Isolde. His hair was matted, and eyes still heavy and dark from his nightmarish sleep.

"Many thanks, Zib," Malaki said, tearing away a chunk of bread to hand to her.

She nodded with a grin. "Only the finest for Arnoria's mightiest criminal enterprise." Isolde held back a grin as she carefully ladled soup into five wooden bowls. Chairs scooted across the rocky floor as they took their seats. Fane fluttered down from his perch to sit on Isolde's shoulder.

"So," Cillian said, his mouth full of bread and stew. "I hear we have a very lucrative job in the works."

"Quite lucrative," murmured Zibiah, holding a piece of meat to Fane.

"How much are we talking?" Blyana asked.

"Three hundred gold pieces," Isolde said. "Per house."

The table fell silent; only the sound of the fire crackling filled the air. Cillian set his spoon down and laced his fingers together.

"Three hundred each, huh?" he said, as if he had misunderstood.

Isolde could see the calculation in Malaki's head. The difficulty of what was being asked was already at the forefront of his mind. "I know it's a large sum."

"It's an impossible sum," Malaki said, stirring his stew, his eyes not meeting hers. "Not even with twenty men could you get that kind of purse out unseen and in one night."

"Doesn't really help that Gage has decided to leave the gold in his personal quarters," Zibiah said. "He believes the Hood's arrogance will be too much for him to resist such an easy score." She snagged a bottle of aged, vintage wine from one of the well-stocked racks that lined the walls, choosing to forgo the stash she had brought from Briarhole. She pulled the cork loose with her teeth and drank deeply. If there was one thing Isolde kept in stock, it was good wine.

"She's right about that," Cillian said into his stew.

"Where did you hear this?" Isolde asked, ignoring him.

"I overhead Lauram and Volkran talking. Seems that neither my husband nor his future heir have much hope in Gage's plan."

"Isolde," Malaki said, "I understand what this means, what this money can do but—"

"But what?" she demanded.

His eyes were guarded but held a patience that infuriated her. "But is it worth the risk?"

"Volkran also received word that the king has overruled our decision on taxing the humans and half-bloods," Zibiah said, her eyes fixed on the fire. "He has personally overseen increasing the taxes so high most of them won't be able to pay this year."

"We all know what that means," Isolde said her voice even but full of steel. "Instant, lifelong slavery. Either they find a way to miraculously pay the taxes or they are sent to the mines or the coast. This would cover their debts, Malaki."

His lips pulled into a line and looked down in thought as his fingers moved the spoon, pushing around the stew. Blyana had continued to eat, her appetite having not been affected in the slightest.

"Doesn't sound like much of a choice to me," Isolde said, reaching for the last slice of the bread. "Besides, we know Foxclove. How hard could this really be?"

"Hard," Zibiah said, looking away from the fire. "Gage has brought a legion of palace guards with him. Trained in combat and in the ability to shift for extended periods of time. There will be more than what you faced at your last visit to Foxclove."

Malaki sighed, his massive arms crossing as he looked at Isolde. She gazed right back, her own arms coming to cross as well. No one said anything for a long moment.

"You do realize this is a trap, right?" Cillian said at last.

"I would be insulted if it wasn't," said Isolde, her eyes still locked on Malaki.

Malaki tossed his spoon on the table. "And if you are caught?"

She shrugged, taking a sip of wine. "Well, then they deserve the reward."

He sighed sharply, his head shaking, a muscle feathering in his jaw.

"This is crazy," Cillian said, his worried eyes settling on Blyana.

"But necessary," Zibiah said. "I can try to find out roughly how many guards will be there and confirm the gold will be in his private quarters."

"We all know Gage is a prick," Cillian said. "Broadcasting the bounty's location seems right up his alley."

"Agreed," Isolde said. "It's a taunt, a challenge."

"And you're playing right into it," Malaki said.

"I need you on my side," she said, her voice low and pleading.

"How do you plan on dealing with Gage?" Malaki asked.

Isolde relaxed back into her chair, "I have a plan to neutralize the king's Right Hand."

"We can't kill him," Malaki said, his gaze now hard. "Even though I would love nothing more than to rid Arnoria of him, that would bring far more heat down on all the territories and us. Who knows what the king would do if his Right Hand was found dead."

"Malaki, I don't plan on killing him," Isolde said, much to her displeasure. "I have other means of removing him from the equation."

"Such as?"

"Let me worry about that," she said, finishing off her wine. Before he could rebuke, she continued. "The real problem will be getting into Foxclove. I can't imagine it will be as easy as the last time."

"I certainly hope not," Blyana said. "We can't rely on your climbing skills, that's for sure."

Isolde's wrist flicked forward, sending the last hunk of her bread sailing at Blyana who caught it easily and stuffed it into her mouth. Her lips pulled around the half-chewed bread in a mocking smile.

"What did you have in mind?" Cillian asked, his fingers now toying with a butter knife. Isolde laid out the plan pointing to various spots on the blueprints, indicating where and when she needed each of them to be.

Malaki looked up to the ceiling in resignation. He knew he was outnumbered. "There are still too many variables, Isolde."

"Our odds have been unkind before," she said, leaning her head back. Victory was near. "And we still came out on top. If we do not do this, more humans and half-bloods will be enslaved. More innocent people will die."

He couldn't deny it and Isolde knew it. It was what they had all sworn to stop. Malaki's eyes roved the room, meeting stares of expectation and acceptance. Isolde knew, apart from her, they would look to him for the final approval which was why he was her second-in-command. If she were to fall, he would take up the Hood's mantle and continue her work.

His eyes found her once more, and he gave her a final look. Grunting, he rose and held the goblet before him, "All or nothing?"

Isolde smiled. She filled her own before rising with the others.

"All or nothing," they said together, their cups singing into the dead of the night.

Isolde sprinted through the trees. An arrow was notched in her bow.

The target swung into view. She released the arrow and pulled out another before it found its mark.

She continued to move, her eyes searching for the next target. Malaki had placed them along the course earlier that morning before her feet had even hit the floor. Shoving away from the ground, Isolde flew through the air and pulled back on the bowstring.

A spot of red caught her eye and she released. Splintered wood exploded from the target's center. Landing on a boulder, she threw the bow over her shoulder and moved on. She jumped from rock to rock, mindful of her footing.

Move...move faster.

Instinct sunk its hooks into her mind, giving her the freedom to not think but simply feel. Burden after burden lifted from her shoulders. The weight of her existence melted away the harder she ran. Here she wasn't a burden to those she loved. Here she could be herself...here she was home.

Fane flew overhead. His eyes were watchful as he dove in and out of the canopies keeping pace with her along the trail.

The snap of a twig brought her out of the place of peace within her head. Reaching up, she withdrew the two swords strapped to her back. Their blades were blinding in the late afternoon sun. To the right, a large body moved from the shadows. It hurled towards her. Ducking under, she allowed it to pass overhead before driving the blade up. Rocks fell from a gaping hole in its middle of the burlap sack.

Fane screeched from above, pulling back to the path. More figures swung in the shadows, highlighting her way.

With a grin, she took off. Each makeshift dummy Malaki had placed was cut down in a matter of seconds. Isolde's blades sang in her hands as she leapt to the left and right. Every muscle remembered the movements. Malaki had drilled them into her since childhood. It was as easy as breathing. Isolde sliced the last mummy in half.

The familiar thoughts, the ones Isolde worked tirelessly to keep at bay, danced at the corners of her mind. *"You are a burden to them. A constant reminder of failure…a danger to those you love."* Their voices, soft as a caress, quickly sharpened into blades. No matter how hard she ran, no matter how accurately she shot an arrow, no matter how precise she swung the deadly blade…they still came.

Worthless…burden…unimportant…failure…survivor…murderer… monster…

Isolde didn't stop. She forced her legs to move, her arms to swing and chop as rock and burlap littered the forest floor. Self-hatred battered against her skull, demanding control, demanding her sorrow.

They are dead because of you…if only you were good enough…they would be alive.

She landed on one knee. Her blades thrust back and her head bent forward. Air ravaged through her chest. Each breath felt like an inferno, burning her from the inside out. Isolde squeezed her eyes shut as she fought to keep the despair at bay.

Taking a single, shaky breath, Isolde rose and gently slipped the blades back into the scabbards at her back. Just as she thought the episode had passed, and peace had found her once more, the most terrifying thought of all echoed through her head. The one that always gave her pause.

Maybe…just maybe…death wouldn't be so terrible. Perhaps it would better for everyone if I died…

Isolde shook her head from side to side. As if she could shake the words away like they were drops of water. "No," she said out loud. "You can't do that to them." Malaki's face came to her. Then Nan, Blyana, Cillian, Galaena, Alaric, the children at story hour...and Kamden.

No...no...no...

Fane chirped from a nearby tree branch. His call pulled her from the dark pit of shame and despair she was drowning in.

"Break time?" she asked, her breathing heavy.

He stared back and blinked. She smiled and ran the back of her hand across her forehead drenched in sweat. "Good." His light weight landed on her shoulder. A soft feather brushed against her cheek.

"I know," she said, her fingertips stroking his head. Off to the left of the trail, she spotted a small meadow. Wildflowers of every color decorated the wide, open space.

"Will this do, Your Highness?" she asked the hawk who released a chirp, its tone dripping with impatience.

"I take that as a yes."

He stayed rooted to the spot as she plopped down on the ground. Removing her bow and quiver, she lay back onto the soft warm grass.

The smell of flowers filled the air. The sun's heat intensified their scent it felt like she was baking in it. Just as her eyes closed, a feeling of contentment washed over her, the snap of a twig broke the silence. Fane shot into the sky as Isolde pulled a dagger from her belt, her arm coming back to throw.

"Easy! Easy!" Liam stood at the edge of the trees. His hands were raised in surrender as a basket swung from his elbow.

A shaky breath rattled over Isolde's lips. "Liam! I almost killed you!"

"Let me be the first to thank you for not." A crooked, shy smile played on his face. He took a tentative step forward, the sun dancing over his dark curls.

She licked her lips and shoved the dagger back in place. "What are you doing here?" Her voice hard and cold. "Come to berate me some more?"

Stopping before her, Liam held up the basket. "Nan said you were out here somewhere and that you didn't bring anything to eat." Rich smells wafted in the breeze as he dangled it in front of her nose. "Interested?"

Shooting him an annoyed look, she pulled the basket to her lap. He smiled taking the seat beside her. "Thank you," she muttered. She tore off a piece of fresh bread and handed it to him without looking his way.

"Have to keep you fed," he said around the mouthful. "Can't let you go hungry while you run yourself ragged out here."

She bit into a piece of dried meat, the rich, savory flavors washing over her tongue. "Yes, that would be tragic."

He glanced her way, gauging how angry she was. The piece of bread turned and rolled between his fingers. "How are you here?" she asked, as she poked through the rest of the basket's contents. "Doesn't Gage keep a tight leash on you?"

He shrugged. "Errands. I can always find something needing to be done in the surrounding areas."

"How convenient for you."

The piece of bread stilled between his fingers, crumbles sprinkling his pant leg. "I'm sorry."

She continued to chew, her eyes forward.

"Please, Isolde," he said. "I lost my temper...I didn't mean any of the things I said."

"Could have fooled me." A part of her wanted to accept his apology. But the more dominating side, her stubbornness, refused to let the words come forward.

Liam sighed through his nose as he raked a hand through his hair. His fingers tightened at the roots. "I was angry...I lost my temper."

"Hmm." Isolde shook her head. "Seems to be happening a lot these days, doesn't it?"

A muscle ticked in his cheek. "I know."

She looked at him then. Her mouth set into a hard line. "Why?"

"I don't know," he said. "Pressure...stress...fear." Liam's eyes swept to hers for a brief moment before quickly looking away.

"Fear? What are you afraid of?"

"Of losing the one thing I can't live without," he said, returning her stare. "Of losing you."

Silence filled the clearing. Only the occasional gust of wind rattled the trees. "That's not an excuse to be an ass." Her voice was small, not holding near the conviction she had aimed for.

He nodded, curls falling into his eyes. "It's not. And I'm not trying to make an excuse. But the things I have heard, seen, and done…" His voice fell away. "It's a lot sometimes."

Isolde toyed with the piece of dried meat. "I can imagine anyone having to deal with those bastards for any length of time would be on edge as well."

A humorless laugh reverberated through him. "It's certainly not a picnic."

"At least not one you would have picked for yourself if circumstances had been different," said Isolde, her hand covering his. "Thank you."

He looked down at them, his brows bunching. "For what?"

"For making that sacrifice for Alaric. You didn't have to do that...but you did." Her fingers gripped his. "I know it hasn't been easy for you."

A smile hinted at the edge of his lips. "I only wanted to thank him for all he had done for me. To show him that I am worthy of having you."

"A part of him knows that. Despite what he says."

"I hope so."

Isolde smiled. "And thank you for the food. It would indeed be tragic for everyone if I got hungry."

"Very tragic," he said plucking, a piece of meat from the basket. "Hungry Isolde is terrifying."

She smacked his shoulder. He smiled at her in a way she hadn't seen in years. In a way that made it impossible to look anywhere but at him.

"What are you looking at?" he asked. She didn't answer. Instead, she continued to stare. He wore a simple white tunic and pair of brown trousers. A light had returned to his gaze. An easiness that she had not seen in so long. A light that showed his eyes were not truly black, but a rich, deep brown.

His gaze hardened as he turned toward her. "See something you like, Lady Isolde?"

"Maybe." She shrugged in feigned indifference, a lip quirking.

Without pause, he moved the basket aside and covered that smirk with one of his own. Fire surged through her blood, her fingers knitting into his shirt. Falling back into the grass, she pulled him along to cover her.

His hands pinned her wrists to the forest floor as his lips moved to her neck.

"Come back to me," she whispered, her hips moving beneath his.

Liam grinned. His face devoid of duty...of honor...of responsibility. He was simply...Liam. "I like it right here," he said, pressing his hips into her. The winds hid her moans as his mouth found hers once again. "Just us...no kingdom...no Thornwood...no Hood."

"We didn't know how good we had it."

Liam paused. "We could have that again."

"You know we can't," Isolde said, resting her head on the grass. "Not right now at least."

"Why not?" He asked, an edge of heat coating his words.

"Because people still suffer."

Liam rolled his eyes. "The problems of others do not automatically become your own, Isolde."

"They do when it pertains to my people."

"Thornwood is thriving!"

"People still need help, Liam," she shot back, her temper flaring.

He sighed, allowing his weight to push her down. Every inch of him was ablaze, a furnace she felt through her clothes. His head rested in the crook of her neck. "You're right," he said, with a hint of softness. "I don't want to fight. Not now, when I have you exactly where I want you." His voice was deep and feral, and it spurred her forward.

Before she could utter a word, his lips were back on hers. He slid a hand up the side of her hip, tugging her shirt up. Memories of the night at the library returned in delicious, excruciating detail.

"Let me see you," he rasped. His warm, practiced fingers kneaded and teased her breasts. "Take everything off."

Fear quickly spiked in her blood. It chilled the lust burning in her veins. "You know the rules," she said against his lips.

A growl rippled through his chest and into hers. "Piss on the rules." He pressed harder, his hands pushing her shirt up further.

Adrenaline surged forward, propelling Isolde up. Shoving against his grip, she flipped him over and pinned his wrists to the ground. He looked up at her in shock.

"Most of the time I would agree." Her eyes were lit and teeth slightly bared. "But not on this." She took a breath and forced the spike of fear down. "You can't see that part of me. Not yet. I can't…show you all of myself."

Liam's chest rose and fell. His eyes were wide as if assessing a threat he was not expecting. She lowered herself down to the bugle in his pants, drawing a hiss from his clenched teeth.

Forcing his arms over his head, Isolde trapped Liam's wrists in one of her hands. "What we have, is all I can give you right now," she said, running a finger down his face, his torso, and below his belt. Heat flared through her cheeks as she watched his face. His teeth were gritted and head thrown back at her touch.

"Isolde." Her name lifted from his tongue in a frustrated sigh. A thrill shot straight to Isolde's core, turning her desire into molten lava. She loved seeing him at her mercy. Relished in seeing him come undone at her touch.

"Can it be enough?" Isolde worked the worn belt loose, then the buttons...then the zipper. Allowing him to spring free. With a touch feather light, she grazed her fingers around him. His hips bucked, driving him deeper into her grasp.

"Isolde," Liam rasped, his hips thrusting with impatience.

"Can it?" she asked again, her fingers searching...stroking...squeezing.

Isolde watched with delight as the need pulsed through his veins, sending him over the edge. Breaking her grip, Liam flipped back and buried her beneath him. His knees moved her legs apart as he whispered, "Of course it is, you little tease." He kept his strong, callused hands beside her face, giving her the choice to make the next move.

"Good," Isolde said, her voice strained and heated. Working her pants down the rest of the way, she threw them to the side and wrapped her legs around him.

They moved together as if it were their last time. As if this was all fate would grant them-stolen moments in the thicket of Blackford Forest, their own private sanctuary. Before long, the sun's rays dipped beneath the canopy, sending brilliant colors dancing across their sweat slicked skin.

Moans and cries of pleasure echoed through the forest. Isolde momentarily worried one of the others would hear. But Liam gave her every reason to not care. She lost herself in him, pretending, wishing, dreaming...she was happy.

It was the same as it always was with Isolde. Absolutely and terrifyingly perfect. From the first time he had her, Liam knew there was no going back. There would be no one else. As time moved on, Liam lost himself in her.

His mind stayed in a fog of joy, worry, and pleasure. *Nothing could top this.* He reeled at the sound he pulled from her lips with every thrust. Needing to be closer, he nestled his nose in her dark brown hair. Strands of fire danced across the rich brown waves as streams of sunlight filtered through the trees.

He breathed deep, taking in everything that she was. Beautiful...deadly...intoxicating. Wave after wave of the familiar scent of pine and rose filled his head. But something else lingered too. Stray flurries of the sea drifted through her scent, coating his impeccable senses. She was mysterious and absolutely beautiful to behold as if she belonged there, in the fathoms below.

As his lips grazed her skin, a puff of breath dancing across the nape of her neck, another scent struck him. This one froze his muscles and locked every bone into place. Hot and alluring, the faintest smell of ember and night rose. They were scents of a fire, an inferno that would not and could not ever be contained. Traces of a moonless sky, dark and powerful swirled around her.

He could feel her heart race against his chest. Her lips pressed into his, demanding more. The smell of embers combined with the sea, the forest, the wind, the very stars themselves. As they moved together as one, lost in each other's ecstasy, Isolde's scent filled Liam's head, making it impossible to think about anyone or anything else.

She felt so right, so perfect against him, around him. It gave him new hope, a new resolve to fix the mess she had gotten herself into. He could make her see...make her understand.

By any means necessary.

CHAPTER 16

M alaki paused, holding his hammer aloft. "I know that look," he said wiping the sweat from his brow, spreading a streak of soot.

"You know all my looks," Isolde snapped, making her way through the smithy.

"I take it getting Alaric to go along with the plan didn't go as well as you had hoped?" he asked, bringing the hammer down once more on the plate of glowing metal. Fiery sparks rained down to the stone floor at his feet and died in a puff of smoke.

"As well as you would expect," she muttered. "How are we on preparing the box?"

"Coming along," Malaki said. "We should be finished with it in a day or two."

Isolde nodded. "Cill, how are the weapons?"

"Splendid," he said, inspecting a newly forged blade. "Tarvo will have a fresh batch of arrows ready for the big day. Made from the same elithrium you took from Dagan. Thought that would be a nice personal touch."

"Very appropriate," Isolde said, a small grin forming that made his glow all the more. She loved this particular happiness from him. The kind that only shined when he was making something with his own two hands. It was so rarely seen beneath the mask of worry. "Where's Blyana?"

Cillian nodded behind him, gloved hands busy polishing. "Napping. Up in the rafters more than likely. She knows I hate it when she does that."

"Why else do you think she does it?"

Hay crunched beneath Isolde's feet as she made her way through the smithy and into the stables. Sure enough, there she was, perched up in the rafters. Blyana lay sprawled on her side, the beam not even half the width of her body. A small, soft purr echoed through the air.

"Furball!" she called.

"What?" Blyana moaned, effortlessly rolling onto her back. "I was having a good dream."

"I need your help," Isolde said. "It involves payback."

"Do tell," she purred, stretching onto her belly to peer down. A flash of green reflected in her eyes.

"Gage will have undoubtedly been in search of some companionship."

"Undoubtedly," Blyana said, her eyes narrowing, foot twitching.

Isolde licked her lips, knowing she was about to bring up a very dark subject for Blyana. "I need to talk with some of the girls from Madame Vara's." The very air seemed to sizzle. Pure hatred ignited in Blyana's eyes. "I need to see if they have been employed by him and are interested in making some real coin and a chance for freedom."

Her friend's piercing gaze shined down in mocking suspicion. "Are you offering to pay off their debts as you did mine, Isolde? You know I get jealous."

"You are indeed my favorite, Bly," Isolde said with a sarcastic bow of her head. "I merely need her services for one night."

Stretching loudly, Blyana swung from the rafters and landed easily on her toes. She barely reached Isolde's shoulder, and her blonde hair was filled with hay. "Like I would pass up an opportunity to screw over that viperous bitch," she said.

Isolde grinned, her arm wrapping around Blyana's tiny shoulders.

"Where are you two sneaking off to?" Malaki asked, plunging the blazing steel into a pail of water as they strolled by.

"Sneaking?" Blyana said, her hand placed over heart. "How dare you accuse us of such a thing, Malaki!"

"Huh," he grunted. His soot covered eyebrow cocked as he yanked the blade out. "And just what are you up to then?"

Blyana smirked. "*Sneaking.*"

"That's the understatement of the century," said Cillian.

"We're off to solve the Gage problem," Isolde retorted waving her hand in dismissal as she walked past. "Don't wait up for us."

"Don't be out past dark!" yelled Malaki, spurring a smile from them both. "And don't kill anyone!"

They saddled Versa and Felix and rode off through Blackford Forest toward the town of Whisper, just east of Thornwood on the border of Foxclove. Both territories had ownership of the town, each sharing the profits.

The town was far busier than usual. Flags of various houses danced in the afternoon breeze saturated with spices and aromas.

"Preparing for the Tournament of the Guard," said Blyana, her eyes twitching as they watched the flags.

Isolde sighed. "Any chance to make some coin betting on a champion and death." It was an event that occurred only once every four years in the capital, Elenarta. An event that the people of Arnoria took great advantage in celebrating for as long as possible.

They gave their horses to one of the stable hands and paid him handsomely to have them fed, watered, and rubbed down. Walking the streets, careful to not let the hem of her violet dress touch the ground, Isolde made it a point to shop at human stores, overpaying as much as possible.

"My lady," a woman said, her eyes glistening. A mound of silver coins rested in her hand. "The gown was only two silver pieces. You pay too much; I cannot accept."

A little girl stood huddled behind the woman's tattered gown. Her eyes were bright and curious in their sockets. Starvation clung to her like an illness. "You can," Isolde said quietly, pressing the coins into the woman's hand. "For her."

Tears fell from the woman's eyes, and her head bowed over the sum that would feed the two of them for months. Isolde began to walk away, but a tug at her gown stopped her. She turned to see the little girl. Her black hair was braided and falling across her shoulder. A large scar, the shape of a crescent moon snaked down the corner of her right eye and kissed the tip of her chin. Mutilation was another way of ensuring taxes were paid on time.

In her hand, she held a single flower.

"For you," she said with a grin, highlighting her missing front two teeth.

Isolde bowed her head and curtsied to the little girl, ignoring the knife in her heart as she took the gift. "How did you know roses are my favorite? Thank you, my lady." The girl giggled and ran back to her mother who was still crying, a homemade doll clutched to her chest.

They continued through the square until they reached one of their favorite bakeries. "Good afternoon, ladies," Freda greeted from behind the counter. "Children, look who's here." A stampede of tiny bodies, all covered in flour and cinnamon raced around the corner and threw their arms around Isolde and Blyana.

They were regulars at her story hour, all virya. Their tiny faces beamed up at her, as did their eyes. "What have you made for me today?" Isolde asked.

"Cinnamon rolls!" they said in unison. The sound of tissue paper echoed over their voices as Freda removed a baker's dozen from the display.

"For you both," she said, handing over the package. Wisps of blonde hair brushed her flour-kissed cheeks as she smiled. "Anything for the ones who get these heathens out from under my feet for a little bit."

"Thank you, Freda," Isolde said with a nod. She began pulling her purse loose but Freda shook her head. "That is unnecessary," she said. "No one who protects our children pays here."

Isolde nodded in thanks, her throat tightening. "Then at least let me buy out what you have on the shelves today." Freda's eyes widened as they glanced around the shop. Every surface was covered in some kind of bread or sweet.

"Lady Isolde—"

"Just promise me you will pass it out to those who can't afford such things." Freda knew what she meant. To whom she wanted the food given to: humans and half-bloods. They were not welcome in most shops in Whisper, leaving them to the mercy of others and whatever they could provide on their own.

Freda looked to the coins, then to Isolde. While she was never openly aggressive to those less fortunate, she had never been one to make them feel welcomed in her bakery. But a sad, knowing smile spread across her beautiful, young face as she nodded.

"You're very kind," Freda said, taking the coins from Isolde's outstretched hand. "I'll see that it goes to those who need it."

The children threw their arms around Isolde and Blyana once more, leaving behind tiny deposits of flour and cinnamon on their dresses. Freda corralled them back to her and waved in farewell as Isolde followed Blyana through the door. After depositing their purchases back at the stables, Isolde and Blyana continued through the throng of bodies lining the streets.

The brothel resided just off the square, not two doors down from one of the virya schoolhouses. A pub sat in the shadows of the great house to the right. Men and women filtered in and out, their minds set on one of three things. Sex, alcohol, or money.

While Vara held no claim on the bar, she sent her *little flowers* into its clutches, looking for anyone who might want a taste of what she offered. The guards Madame Vara hired had free reign of the pub's fine selections of spirits, making it a hot spot to find just the person they needed.

Blyana gripped Isolde's arm just before reaching the doors of the bar known for hosting Vara's thugs. "Unless you want a brawl, I suggest you let me handle this. I'll find the girl we need and meet you out back."

Isolde pouted sarcastically. "What if I want a brawl?"

"Stop pouting," Blyana said, flicking Isolde's nose. "You'll get that soon enough. Besides, I have a far better relationship with Vara's guards than you do. If she hears you were snooping around, she might think you're here to steal another one of her *little flowers*."

"I didn't steal you," Isolde mumbled. "But fine, I'll meet you out back then."

"Good, Lady Isolde," Blyana chided, patting her on the head before prancing up the front steps.

Isolde sighed heavily and moved back to the shadows of the large green building. She kept her eyes averted from the windows, having no desire to see stolen moments of pleasure in the bathrooms.

Nostalgia swept over her as she took a seat on one of the empty liquor carts. It had been raining the day she found Blyana. Wild-eyed and angry, she was beaten, covered in whelps and bruises, as she fought against the restraints keeping her to the whipping post.

Blyana had killed a customer who wouldn't take no for an answer. Madame Vara had been in the process of delivering her punishment when Isolde heard her feral cries.

Isolde remembered thinking how small Blyana looked, how the fury burned in her eyes. A silver, elithrium bracelet, beautiful and terrible, dug into her wrist. A wild animal caged in her own skin. Isolde offered to pay for Blyana on the spot, completely wiping her debts away.

Madame Vara chuckled at the offer. "I still can use her," she said, the cane snapping against Blyana's back. "She can work just as well on her stomach as her back." Madame Vara lashed her again, and a small bead of blood painted her swollen, bruised flesh.

"And what would the king say to you not being entirely forthcoming with your profits, Vara?" Isolde had asked, her posture at ease on top of Versa. The reins swung between her fingers as a wicked smile pulled at her lips. "I hear that tax evasion is one of his sore spots. And I doubt being his cousin would save you from his wrath."

"You dare!" The brothel owner seethed, pointing the cane at Isolde.

"No, Madame," Isolde said, her voice laced with malice. "You are the one who dares beat a girl for defending herself. Now, here is half of what I'm guessing she owes you." Isolde tossed a coin purse at the stunned mistress, whose eyes had morphed into viperous slits. "You're lucky to get that much."

"You little bitch!"

"I don't know about little, but a bitch, I most certainly am," Isolde said with a smile, her teeth flashing. "I suggest you slither back into whatever hole you came from, before I show you just how much of one I can be, Vara."

Madame Vara strode past Isolde, her sharp fangs glistening. "Be careful who you make your enemy, Lady Isolde." Her guards followed behind, leaving Blyana to drop into the blood tinged mud.

"I suppose you think you own me now," Blyana had said, barely able to stand. Her wild eyes were hard and guarded with distrust.

"Hardly," Isolde said removing the cloak from her shoulders to drape it carefully over Blyana's maimed back. "Quite the opposite, in fact. I am offering you a home...a family. If you want it."

"I was promised something similar and you see how well that turned out for me." The betrayal in Blyana's voice was so apparent it still made Isolde's heart ache.

"I give you my word that no one will touch you at Thornwood. Not that someone's word means much these days. But it does to me. If someone dares lay a finger on you, deal with them as you see fit. If it is justified, you will have no repercussions from me or Lord Cotheran."

Blyana's gaze swept back to the House of Pleasures, to the place that had only held torture, despair, and shame. Slowly, Blyana turned back to Isolde and her eyes fell to the dagger strapped to her thigh. "Will you teach me to use one of those?"

A devilish grin had spread across Isolde's face. "Absolutely, I will."

She carefully helped Blyana onto Versa's back, which left her to walk the long trek back to Thornwood, leaving her hair soaked and outfit ruined. Isolde had not cared at all. It was well worth it.

And the rest was history.

Isolde's smile faded, and her mind was ripped from the past as her friend, who had faced hell and survived, trudged through the alley. A girl, hardly old enough to be called a woman, followed. Her eyes were a brilliant pale gray, large and terrified. While she was incredibly skinny, she filled out the exposing dress in all the ways that mattered in a place like Madame Vara's.

"Lady Isolde, Cinta," Blyana greeted, her hand sweeping between them. "Cinta meet Lady Isolde."

Cinta bowed, her light blonde hair falling into her face. "My lady."

"It's a pleasure to meet you, Cinta," said Isolde, smiling. "How long do we have you?"

"One hour," Cinta murmured. It was hardly noticeable. To the untrained eye, it would have been missed completely. But Isolde caught the slight cringe in Cinta's shoulders. The flicker of fear that shone in her eyes. Anger and sadness rolled through Isolde like an avalanche. This poor girl was terrified of them...of what they might make her do. And she would have no say in the matter.

Pushing the thought away, Isolde asked, "Are you hungry by chance? I, for one, am famished." Cinta looked to Blyana as if seeking permission to answer. Perhaps that was required in the brothel.

"You can speak freely," Blyana said, her voice so gentle and reassuring. Isolde could only imagine what Blyana saw in the girl before her.

"That would be nice," Cinta said, a small smile forming.

They walked to a local café and secured a table in the back per Isolde's request. "We have much nicer tables elsewhere, Lady Isolde," the manager insisted.

"This will do, thank you, Armand," Isolde said, her eyes already on the menu. He bowed and moved on.

"Please, help yourself," she said to Cinta.

"I know I will," Blyana mumbled, her eyes scanning the various desserts on display.

Cinta's eyes danced over the menu, a bead of sweat forming at her temple.

"What kind of sweets do you like?" Isolde asked, toying with the ring on her finger.

"I-I don't know," Cinta murmured, her eyes moving from Isolde to Blyana to the menu and back again. Realization dawned on Isolde and the smile fell from her face.

"Can you read, Cinta?"

Tears formed at the corner of Cinta's eyes. She continued to stare at the menu as if willing herself to understand it. After a moment, she shook her head from side to side, causing a tear to fall down her reddening cheek.

"It's alright," Isolde said, and her fingers reached to hold Cinta's hand, but resisted. She remembered, in this girl's world, being touched was something she didn't have a say in.

"My parents didn't see the need in it, nor did they have the money for someone to teach us. Even though we are virya, we were poor." Cinta licked her lips, her eyes down cast. "Besides, being able to read isn't a requirement for laying on my back, according to the mistress."

I'll kill that woman one day. Isolde bit back a growl. *Very.... very slowly.*

"She's a bitch," Blyana snarled.

Isolde tossed the menu aside. "The worst kind."

When the water and coffee arrived, to Armand's surprise and delight, Isolde ordered one of everything off the menu. She wanted Cinta to try as much as she could stomach.

After Armand made his leave, Cinta looked to Isolde. "I appreciate all of this, Lady Isolde," she said. "But what is it that you want from me?"

"Let me ask you a question first," she said, taking a sip of her peppermint and chocolate flavored coffee. "If you don't mind my asking, how is it that you came into Madame Vara's employment?"

Cinta toyed with the handle of her teacup, the fresh, rich coffee swaying. "Well, like I said, my family was very poor." Her eyes were down as she spoke. "I was the oldest of my siblings. Our mother had died of fever, and we had no way of paying the debts. So, I went out looking for a job, hoping to find work as a seamstress. But Madame Vara spotted me in the work line." Her breath shook. Blyana's knuckles whitened as her hands balled into fists on either side of her coffee mug.

"She promised me fair wages, a safe place to live, a way to help my family." Cinta swallowed, her eyes glassing over as tears fell. "She didn't tell me that I would be charged for the clothes, food, or board. Charged so extravagantly, paying her back would be impossible. I tried," she said her fingers pressing to her quivering lips. "I tried to send money to my family, but I learned they had caught the same illness that took my mother."

Cinta clutched at Blyana's offered hand. They both bore the mark of the House of Madame Vara: a small tattoo, a green viper, on top of the left thumb, just below the first knuckle.

"Do you want to be free of that life, Cinta?" Isolde asked.

She looked up, her eyes filled with blatant mistrust. The food arrived, and all conversation stopped momentarily. Once prying ears had dispersed, Cinta said, "I have learned when things sound too good to be true, my lady, that means they usually are."

Blyana chuckled as she took a big bite of the fruit tart. "I thought so too." A strawberry fell from her open mouth and rolled onto Isolde's plate.

"You pig," Isolde said, stuffing her own face with a big spoonful of rich, dark chocolate mousse.

"Her word is true, Cinta. Except the pig comment. She can eat far more than I can." Isolde stuck out her tongue, a half-chewed glob of chocolate mousse dangling on the tip.

Still unsure, Cinta picked at the croissant before her, "I do want to be free, but that is impossible."

"Not if you work with me," said Isolde, reaching for one of the cinnamon rolls. "I can give you the chance of a new life. Far away from Madame Vara and her *clients'* reaches."

"How?"

Isolde glanced around once, making sure no one was watching. "Is one of your new regulars Gage, the Right Hand of the King?"

Instant terror flashed in Cinta's eyes as she lurched from the chair. Her long legs bumped the table and spilled coffee onto the pristine, tiled floor. A small whimper ghosted from Cinta's lips as her wide, frantic eyes looked around in a haste as if terrified Gage or Madame Vara herself were eavesdropping. Blyana grabbed her wrist and pulled her back down.

"We are not with him," she rasped, patting up the mess.

"I don't understand," Cinta said, her voice shaking.

"How often are you taken to him at Foxclove?" asked Isolde, her hands busy working to rearrange the table.

She shrugged, her eyes still searching the room. "He has requested I be there every week, for two nights."

Bile burned in Isolde's throat. *She's just a child.* Swallowing her fury, she said, "Do you want to continue that?"

Fresh tears sprang in the girl's eyes, her head shaking. "No," Cinta whispered, her lips trembling.

"Good, because we have a plan to get you out of there."

"How?"

"We are friends with someone who has a need for Gage to be indisposed for a certain amount of time."

"Oh, I see," said Cinta, her lip curling with distrust. "You want me to do what he is already paying me for." Fire burned in her voice. Isolde smiled slightly, relieved to see Vara hadn't completely broken her spirit.

"No," said Isolde. "We want you to drug him."

Cinta looked taken aback. "Drug him?"

"When he takes you up to his room-which is key, make sure you are in his private quarters-offer him some wine and add the drug into his cup," said Blyana

"I don't understand," she said. "Why not just have your friend kill him?"

"It would cause far more problems than it would solve, I'm afraid," Isolde said, her voice heavy with disappointment. "We just need him incapacitated long enough for our friend to do their job."

"Which is?"

"It's best if you don't know for now."

Cinta stared at Isolde. Her eyes were bright with mistrust and curiosity. The pads of fingers traced the delicate patterns of the napkin draped across her lap.

"If you do this, Cinta," Blyana said, already having read the doubt in her face, "you will never have to take another order again. No one will touch you without your say. I know you remember what that kind of freedom was like. Don't you want it back?"

Cinta's chest seemed to cave in. The weight of hope and doubt visibly crushing her.

"We will also pay you handsomely. Give you a chance for a fresh start," Isolde said.

Releasing a shaky breath, Cinta's eyes rose to Isolde's once more. Grey held emerald and silver in their embrace. "Tell me what to do."

"Do you think she'll go through with it?" Isolde asked as she and Blyana made their way back to Thornwood. The forest was alive, rich in golden afternoon sunlight.

It was Blyana's favorite time of day. The sun warmed the fur that lay beneath her skin. "You didn't give her much of an option. Either work with us or stay in Gage's bed. Doesn't really seem like that difficult of a decision."

"It shouldn't be, but fear has a mind of its own. We'll know when I try to get out of the box, I suppose."

Blyana chewed on her lip, her fingers absently running over the serpent on her thumb. Even after all these years, it still felt like a brand. A stamp of ownership, a constant reminder of the past. "You won't have any kind of backup," she said, her voice hard.

Isolde shrugged. "I can handle it."

"I know you can handle yourself, Isolde, or at least you think you can," she said, hoisting her leg up to drape across the saddle horn.

"You doubt me too?" A fragment of anger laced Isolde's words.

"No," Blyana said after a moment. "I do not doubt your abilities, Isolde. It's your lack of self-preservation and stubborn ass that concerns me."

Isolde's jaw tightened. "I would rather put my life at risk than yours or any of the others. It is my burden to bear."

"Stop being so damn self-righteous; it isn't becoming!" Blyana's said, her words full of impatience. "If Cinta doesn't follow through, you will be stuck in that box without aid. And if you are found, there's no telling what he will do to you. How do you suppose that makes the rest of us feel?"

"He won't kill me immediately," Isolde argued. "He'll want to humiliate me first, drag me before the king."

"Bull shit," Blyana said sarcastically. "So, you are banking on time for Gage to torture you...then transport what remains of you to Elenarta for us to intercept if you are caught."

Isolde remained silent. Blyana shook her head, teeth grinding. *Of course, that was her plan.*

They rode in silence for a while. The sound of their hooves crunching the fallen leaves only seemed to make that silence worse. "I can't ask you all to take the risk, Bly. I am one person in a much bigger scheme."

"You underestimate your importance, Isolde," she whispered. *What do I have to do to make you see? What do we have to do to make you understand?*

"I have faith that Cinta will do her part."

Blyana sighed, her breath sharp as she straightened up in the saddle. "Stubborn ass."

"I do believe that is the pot calling the kettle black...yet again."

She smirked and nudged Felix into Versa. The mare neighed in frustration and pushed back, her teeth snapping at Felix's nose. They continued in silence for a few miles. Before long, memories of the past began running through Blyana's mind. Faces...pain...and memories...She felt the rising panic, the terror of being back in Vara's clutches, constricting around her neck.

"Are you alright?" Isolde asked, pulling her from the edge of the abyss.

She felt her power prowl, its sharp, unforgiving claws racking across her resolve. But thanks to Cillian, Isolde, and Malaki's training, her control remained. It had not been easy for her to be around Madame Vara's House of Pleasures. Let alone speak to another one of its victims. Blyana could not bring herself to answer. It would never be an easy task. Every time she went into town, she avoided the building like the death trap it was.

Isolde pushed. "I know it couldn't have been easy for you today."

Blyana bit her lip. Her fingers tightened on the reins. "No, it wasn't."

Isolde was silent for a moment, letting her think. "You know you can talk to me, right? There's no need for you to keep your memories to yourself."

How wrong you are. Blyana's sharpened teeth ground. The clouded leopard continued to push against its cage, sensing her unease. It waited patiently at the gate in her mind. Its tail twitched, ready to spring forward should there be a need for it.

Should I tell her? Blyana pondered, her mind inevitably falling into the past she wished so desperately to forget. After a moment, she cleared her throat and threw her shoulders back.

"My family was very poor, much like Cinta's," she said. "The lowest class of virya. While the taxes weren't nearly as strenuous on our kind as the humans, there was still gold due. Gold…my father did not have." She kept her eyes forward, wide. As if looking into the past.

"It had been a particularly hard year for crops, a wide spread drought having hit the land. I had come into Whisper to sell anything I could from the beautiful lace work my sisters and I made to the only potatoes we had managed to grow."

Blyana paused, the muscles in her jaw set. Isolde remained quiet.

"Unbeknownst to me, Madame Vara had been keeping an eye on our family, her sights set on me." She had seen men leering at her and her little sisters: Aurelia, Kaliska, and Phontine. All young, all completely ignorant to the world and the cruelties it harbored. Particularly the youngest, Phontine. She saw only the good in the people around her, never the wolves laying beneath the surface.

Obscene gestures were a common occurrence. Every now and then one would try to grab them, but Blyana would always fight back, letting just enough of her power through to scare them away. Still, she had no idea that the true predator lurked in the shadows of her comfortable snake hole.

"One morning, we were woken by a messenger from town. A tax collector. He had informed us of our outrageous sum that was due. My father had told the man we just needed more time. He was given one week. It wasn't an hour later another carriage arrived. Two of the most beautiful virya I had ever seen stood in our doorway. I can remember the shame of it. To have such beauty in a place of such filth. They did not seem to mind though."

Not a sound penetrated their conversation, as if the forest had stopped to listen. But Blyana could not force her lips to work anymore. Her mind was lost to the worst day of her life as it mercilessly played out in her head.

"We come with the opportunity of employment," the female had said, her rich golden locks falling over her shoulder. "For your daughter." She pointed one long, polished finger at Blyana. Her family looked to her, their eyes pleading.

"She will accept," Blyana's father answered. Not a care in the world as to what the work would entail.

The man stared at her, his cold, dark eyes assessing. A small grin formed on his full red lips. "Very well. Come with us."

Blyana took nothing with her, except the memories of those she loved. Kissing her sisters goodbye, she strolled out into the sunlight. Her mother shed tears but did not reach for her as their brute of a father averted his gaze, his hands on his hips.

Laying a firm hand on her shoulder, the handsome male escorted her to the lavish carriage that waited by the road. "Your debts have been taken care of," he said over his shoulder to her father before climbing inside after the female and Blyana.

"Who is it that has employed me?" Blyana asked, her eyes wide.

The two ignored her, their gaze focused out the windows.

"Please," she said, her fear rising. "Where are you taking me?"

"Shut your mouth," he hissed, his gaze piercing and cruel. "You will find out soon enough."

Blyana kept quiet, her hands wringing together on her lap. It wasn't until they pulled up to Madame Vara's that she understood, and the fear nearly choked her.

"No," she said, her hands frantically reaching for the door. But the male was far quicker. Gripping her wrist, he forced a bracelet into place, and Blyana instantly felt an overwhelming sense of emptiness. It's beautiful, intricate design made her hate it even more.

"Elithrium," the female said her mouth twisting into a wicked grin. "Wouldn't want you to wander off, now would we?"

They drug her up the stairs. Their impossibly strong arms pulled her with ease. She called out to her power in desperation, begging it to come forth. But the cat that lingered in her mind was caged, silenced into submission. She was defenseless…. utterly powerless against what was to come.

As they worked their way through the house and mass of bodies, Blyana couldn't help but marvel at the beauty within. Both the architecture and the people.

Velvet and silk lined every seat-able surface. Chandeliers hung from the ceilings. Their light danced merrily across the gilded walls and the bare skin of the women and men entertaining the guests.

She was taken to the back, and a door set in deep red was swung open to reveal an office. A wide desk, large enough to serve as a bed if need be, stood in the middle. Her heart raced at the sight of who sat behind it.

The dark hair, neatly arranged on top of her head in an intricate bun, contrasted so strikingly with the creamy skin of her face and chest. Diamonds and rubies decorated her throat, plunging beneath her neckline, hinting at the cleavage below. But it was her eyes that had captured Blyana. The dark green that struck her soul. They were so cold, yet impossible to resist.

"Well, well." Madame Vara grinned, her voice was so warm and alluring. Standing, she was slightly taller than the female who gripped her arm. Blyana felt the tremor run through both of them as Madame Vara slithered around the desk to stand before her. Everything about the woman was beguiling. She was attractive to any and all who had the misfortunate to look upon her. Which made Madame Vara of the House of Pleasures incredibly dangerous.

Vara's eyes probed and assessed, not missing a single detail. Blyana could practically feel their gaze. They landed on the bracelet on her wrist. A single, well-manicured eyebrow arched. "I see elithrium was necessary."

The male bowed, his grip tightening. "Yes, Madame. She was quite reluctant."

"How ungrateful," Madame Vara said, her full red lips puckering. "You will learn gratitude, my dear."

Blyana's eyes narrowed at the threat.

Madame smiled in return. "Defiant, aren't you?"

The growl was lost in Blyana's throat. She wasn't a threat to them now, no better than a human.

"As I am sure these two have explained, the debt against your family has been paid off. However, you can't get something for

nothing. I am many things but a philanthropist is not one of them."
The ghost of a laugh followed her words. "Which means you belong
to me."

She couldn't control the shaking that racked her body. Nor could
she fight the fear that lingered there. "I am not your property," she
said, her voice so thin and frail.

Madame chuckled; a hiss mingled with the melody. "Oh, but you
are. Until the debt is paid. According to the contract your father
signed." She gripped Blyana's chin, her nails digging into her skin.

Small slits of a viper replaced the pupils in Madame Vara's eyes as
she stared her down. "You are mine," she hissed. "Mine to do with as
I please, to give to whomever I see fit. Or would you rather one of
your little sisters take your place? Little Phontine, perhaps? I know a
few patrons whose tastes lie with the much, much younger crowd...the
sweet, innocent ones."

Fear and anger roared inside her. "Leave them out of this," Blyana
snarled. Vara's fingers tightened on her face, the perfect nails piercing
her flesh.

"Then I suggest you do as you're told. Now..." her hand thrusting
Blyana's head back, "Let's see what the debt a filthy farmer has bought
me. Take off your clothes."

A new fear grew in the pit of Blyana's stomach. When she hesitated,
her new mistress' hand shot out and collided with her cheek. The
impact was so precise, so practiced to extract the right amount of pain
with only minimal damage. She couldn't fight the cry that escaped her
lips. Her two captors dropped her arms.

"You will learn there are consequences to not doing as you are
told," Vara said evenly. "Take off your clothes *now*." Still, she hesitated,
unable to fight the fear and shame that coursed through her.

Without warning, the male came up behind her and ripped the
worn dress her mother had hand stitched herself into shreds. Blyana
quickly covered herself as best she could but the male held her still
forcing her arms to her sides. A single tear cascaded from her cheek.

"None of that," Madame Vara hissed, her icy finger flicking the tear away. "You will find that tears only result in punishment. Tell me, have you ever been with a man? A woman?" She did not respond; could not move. Her body shook beneath the grasp of the man's massive, unsympathetic palms.

"A virgin?" Vara mused, a cruel smile forming on her lips, her eyes roving. "That is a nice little treat. It's been a long time since we had an auction."

Vara continued her assessment, noting the size of Blyana's breasts and tiny hip bones. "She will need to eat more," Madame said, her fingers grazing her breasts. "No one wants to fuck a skeleton." Blyana shrunk away from the touch, another tear falling.

Vara struck again, her fist colliding with Blyana's exposed abdomen. She gasped in pain trying to curl into herself but the male held her firm. "You are a slow learner, my dear."

Blyana fought back the wave of nausea, refusing to vomiting in front of her. She stood as best she could, finding any way to not show the pain. Madame saw her resolve and smiled once again. "Your power is a clouded leopard, am I right?" Blyana held her tongue, her teeth grinding.

The female struck next. Delicate fingers twisted around Blyana's pinky finger and snapped. Pain exploded up her hand into her arm, forcing a cry of pain to burst from Blyana's lips.

"You will answer her," she sneered, her lovely face twisting with disgust.

When Blyana refused to answer again, the girl grabbed another finger and twisted until the bone snapped.

"Yes!" Blyana cried, her eyes swimming.

"Very good," Vara said, a satisfied grin forming. "After you have cleaned her up, take her to the Snow Room. A healer will meet you there."

They both bowed and shoved Blyana to one of the side doors, but stopped at the sound of their mistress' voice. "No, no," Madame Vara said, now positioned behind the desk once again. "By way of the parlor."

Blyana's mouth dropped in horror. Her hands once again tried to hide herself from the eyes that had yet to see her.

"If there is to be an auction," Vara smiled. "Shouldn't they have a little preview of what they will be bidding for?"

Without question or hesitation, the two moved her back to the main door. Blyana fought against them, her anger growing. "Welcome home, my dear Blyana," Vara said as the door closed behind them.

She fought back the fear, forcing numbness through her veins as they pushed her into the parlor. An endless sea of eyes found her. Laughs assaulted her ears. Obscene comments and gestures were slung her way. Blyana did her best to ignore them, only thinking of keeping one foot in front of the other.

Hands, besides those of her captors, found her body. She flinched from their touch, their pinching and poking. New tears swelled in her eyes, but she refused to let them fall. Relying on the hands of her captors to keep her up right, Blyana pushed forward and tried to ignore the hell her father had so blindly delivered her into.

Blyana blinked and shook away her thoughts of the past, bringing her back to Blackford Forest. "I was only seventeen," she finally said, turning to Isolde. "It's been over ten years and sometimes it still feels like only yesterday."

She sighed, refusing to let the sting of betrayal progress further. How she wished desperately for the memories to fade into oblivion. To not remember...She was desperate for it.

Scars still decorated her skin from her time in Madame Vara's employment, but the physical wounds could never compare to the emotional damage done. She could still feel them. Their hands...their breath...their weight pressing her down. No matter how many times Cillian kissed them, made love to her, as if to try and take the pain away-they remained.

"It is far better you don't have those memories in your head, Isolde," Blyana said, clearing her throat of the lump threatening to suffocate her. "You have enough nightmares of your own." Driving her heels into Felix's sides, she shot into the forest without a glance back.

Isolde watched her ride until the path turned left. "That I do," she said. Versa danced beneath her as she pawed at the soft earth.

Isolde twisted in the saddle, looking back to Whisper. To the path that led to justice….to revenge. The weight of her blades bore down on her hips, as if they too longed to spill Blyana's tormenter's blood. Forcing out a sharp breath, she willed herself to face forward.

"Not my life to take," Isolde said to herself. "Not mine." Vara's life was entirely Blyana's to end. It would be her choice on her own time. And Vara's position as the king's cousin, didn't help the situation.

No. That monster's death would have to wait. With the click of her tongue Isolde unleashed Versa. The horse's powerful hooves dug into the soft, warm dirt as she tore through the forest like a bolt of lightning.

CHAPTER 17

Isolde ground her teeth as Malaki drove the carriage into another hole in the road. "I'm going to kill you," she growled as the hard floor of the hidden compartment bit into her shoulder blades.

Hundreds of pounds of gold jostled above her head. The floor of the main compartment bowed and flexed, inching closer and closer to her chest and face.

"Not in there you won't. Besides," Malaki said innocently, his knuckles rapping against the side. "It was an accident." Isolde could hear the smile stretching across his face.

"The first few times were an accident," she ground out. "The following twenty were anything but!" Her head knocked painfully against the hidden panel. A string of swears flowed from the small holes drilled into the planks of wood.

"It couldn't hurt that bad," Malaki said. "Not with a head like yours."

"This was your plan, Isolde," Alaric said. His voice was muffled and not nearly as enthusiastic as Malaki's. "Surely you didn't think it was going to be comfortable."

"No," Isolde said, eyes narrowing at the ceiling. "But I hadn't planned on my second giving me a concussion before the plan actually played out."

"Again," Malaki said, his knuckles banging obnoxiously on the box, "not with a head like that."

A few miles back, just south of Foxclove, Isolde had stuffed herself into the tiny compartment. She now wished Malaki and Cillian had thought to put more holes along the lining of the box for ventilation. While the ones they had strategically placed would keep her from suffocating to death, they did little to make the ride easier. The air was stale and hot inside her mask, making each breath more stifling than the last.

"I didn't think this through," Isolde said bitterly to herself. If she was stuck in here, for more than a day or two, she would suffocate or leave with her head turned permanently to the right. She shifted her weight as much as possible to find a better position.

Sweat pooled at the back of her neck, saturating the fabric. Why did Gage have to arrange this bounty in the dead of summer?

Malaki's voice rumbled over the wheels, his tone far from playful. "Do not do anything stupid, Isolde."

"Whose definition of stupid are you referring to, Malaki?" she said, a slight smile forming on her lips. "I'm going to need you to be more specific. There are many different ways for me to take that."

A growl rolled through the wood. "Anything that you know will make me worry."

Isolde answered his growl with a chuckle. "Making you worry is what I do best."

"Please." The sound of his voice cut her laugh short. "Please don't be reckless, Isolde. I'm begging you. Please, be careful."

She licked her lips and nodded. Malaki had never let her do something like this alone. She knew he would worry, constantly. Until he saw her again, in one piece, he would be a mess. A twinge of regret echoed through her heart. Not only for him but for those she left in the forest and at Thornwood.

"Promise us, Isolde," Alaric said, his voice thick with emotion.

"I promise." She sighed, shifting her hips just an inch to get some relief on her backside. "I promise not to do anything that would make either of you worry."

"At least that's something," Malaki retorted, banging against the compartment one final time.

Isolde bared her teeth, her hand working into an obscene gesture against her chest. "I can always change my mind."

"Hush," Alaric said, his voice barely breaching the thick walls. "We're almost there."

A deadly focus draped over Isolde's mind, forcing every discomfort and irritation into irrelevance. She shifted once more, allowing her right hand, which was closer to the trap door, to slide along the handle of a blade at her hip while the other clutched at her bow draped across her chest. *If they find me, at least I'll take a few out before they catch me.*

"Halt!"

The wagon came to a stop, and Isolde sighed with relief.

"I wish to speak with Lord Gage," Alaric said, his voice leaking through the layers of wood and gold.

"And who might you be?" the guard demanded, his voice deep and suspicious.

"Lord Alaric Cotheran of Thornwood."

"And what business do you have with him?" the man asked, his voice dripping with suspicion.

"My own," Alaric said, his voice rung with authority.

"What's in these crates?" A loud thud exploded around Isolde's head. Her teeth jarred.

"Also, my business. Now be a good lad and fetch your master."

Isolde heard his retreating steps. Alaric and Malaki fell silent, their breaths even and relaxed. After a while, they were instructed to pull forward into what Isolde assumed was the courtyard.

"Alaric! I was beginning to wonder if you were going to make it." Isolde froze at the sound of Gage's voice, her fingers gripping the handle of her elithrium blade tightening.

The wagon shifted as Malaki and Alaric descended. "Three hundred gold pieces isn't an easy sum to come up with on short notice."

"For some I suppose," Gage said, his voice heavy with sarcasm.

She felt the wagon sway and then the sensation of floating hit her as the crate was lifted off the wagon. They deposited her on the ground, jostling the gold above. Isolde dared not breathe as Gage opened the lid.

The jingle of coins echoed from over head as he ran his fingers over the purse. "I will assume it is all there and accounted for. I would hate to be the one who was short on their part of the bounty."

"It's all there," Alaric said, his voice disinterested. "Feel free to count if you are so inclined."

Gage chuckled, dropping the remaining coins back into the box and slamming the lid shut. "I'll take your word for it. You're an honest man, Alaric." His tone was anything but complimentary. "Besides, what would people think if I didn't trust my future in-laws?"

A beat of silence thickened between them. "So, Isolde has agreed to your proposal then?" Alaric asked, his voice mildly interested.

"No yet," Gage admitted, "but soon enough. Once I get around to asking her."

"Bit foolish to claim victory when the battle hasn't even begun, isn't it?" Malaki asked. She could practically see the shit-eating grin on his face and she smiled in turn.

"It's only a matter of time," Gage said, his words sharp. "She is a smart woman. It's a union she can't walk away from. Quite beautiful too. She will look lovely on my mantel...and in my bed." She felt the earth stir beneath her, the coins above her head bouncing in protest. Malaki's anger shifted the bedrock below.

"As I said before," Alaric said, stepping back up on the wagon, "it is her decision."

"Indeed, it is." Each word rolled from Gage's lips in wicked delight.

"Best of luck on your hunt." The wheels crunched beneath the gravel as her uncle and best friend drove away. They eventually faded, leaving her behind, trapped in a den of wolves.

"The day I marry Isolde is the day you die, cripple," Gage growled. "Get this into my chambers."

Isolde felt herself being hoisted up. She braced her hands and feet against the side of the small compartment, not wanting to shift her weight or make any movements.

They ascended flight after flight of stairs, the men groaning under the weight. At last, her bearers reached Gage's chambers and dropped the trunk with a bang. Pain shot through her neck and back. *Bastards.* The men moaned and stretched their muscles before leaving her and a mountain of treasure in peace.

Now it was a waiting game. The hours passed with only a few interruptions. Hurried feet, followed by shouts, echoed from the courtyard below. Pushing the hidden door out just a little, Isolde saw that night had fallen. *Won't be long now.* She took a deep breath of cool night air and slid the piece back into place.

An hour later, a voice she recognized echoed from the doorway. Cinta's laughter filled the chambers as the door creaked open. Her voice was so light and carefree it gave Isolde pause.

"What do you think of the improvements?" Gage asked, closing the door. The familiar click of a lock sliding into place found her ears. Isolde's heart galloped in her chest.

"Your wealth certainly has grown, my lord," Cinta said, her footsteps vibrating over the wooden floor beside Isolde's head. "Is this all for the Hood?"

"It is," Gage said, his footsteps coming closer to where Cinta stood. "Soon I will have his head on a spike and my place back in the palace. Wouldn't you like to see me in Elenarta?"

"Yes," Cinta said. "But aren't you worried that the Hood will come and steal this away?"

"Do you doubt my plans, little doe?" Gage asked, his voice laced with malice. Isolde instinctively pulled the blade free. She had promised not to kill him, but if it meant saving Cinta then so be it.

"Not at all," Cinta said, her voice muffled as if he was gripping her face. "I was merely curious. You are quite brave and smart to leave such a trap. You will surely catch him."

Gage chuckled. "Indeed, I will."

"A toast then," Cinta said, her feet moving away from Isolde's head. She breathed a sigh of relief. "To your capture of the Hood."

Metal clinked, and the sound of guzzling filled the night air. Gage sighed with satisfaction. "Take off your clothes."

Isolde squeezed her eyes shut. She had promised that this would never happen to Cinta again. Unclenching her teeth to take a silent breath, Isolde placed her hand on the trap door, readying herself to launch at Gage whether he was drugged or not.

Cinta giggled, walking back across the room. "Do have one more cup with me, my lord. I have never had such delicious wine before."

"I suppose one more wouldn't hurt," he said, following her to the bar. He never made it. Isolde heard a large thud as Gage fell to the floor. A beat of roaring silence filled the chamber.

"Hello?" Cinta said, her voice now heavy with fear and uncertainty.

Working quickly, Isolde checked her mask and forced the trap door open to slid out. Each muscle felt like stone, unyielding and stiff. She groaned as she stood, the ache of having laid for so long settling into her bones.

"Oh, my gods," Cinta said, her eyes wide. Her hands gripped the small vial of poison to her chest. Isolde had taken extra care to ensure it had arrived to Cinta in secret the night before.

"The Hood," Isolde said, her voice muffled. As she took a deep bow, the back of her gloved hand grazed the floor. "At your service."

Reaching back into the hole, Isolde removed several large cloth bags and tossed them to Cinta. "Fill these with gold," she instructed.

"I'll take care of the rest." She glanced once more at the unconscious Gage and set to filling the bags without delay.

Gazing out into the courtyard, Isolde lit a candle and waved her hand in front of it three times. Off in the distance, near the rows of deserted barracks, she saw a flame burst from the darkness. It winked back three times.

Her eyes scanned the walls, searching. There, stationed exactly as they had planned were Malaki and Cillian, dressed in royal uniforms, their backs to her. They faced toward the barracks. Bows clutched in their hands.

Isolde plucked an arrow from her quiver and attached a lightweight rope to the end. Taking great care with her aim, she launched it into the darkened alleyway between two barracks, aiming just above the small flame. It vanished as the arrow found its mark, the trail of rope disappearing over the sleeping courtyard.

Still gripping the end, she stepped away from the window and told Cinta to get down. A moment later the arrow returned, embedding into the rock wall on the other end of the room.

As Cinta continued to fill the bags, Isolde fashioned the rope around one of the arms of the extravagant chandelier, recreating a pulley system. She took one of the already filled bags and fastened it to the rope and began to pull. The bag quietly disappeared out the window and into the night.

No sound broke through the darkness. No alarm announced their presence. After a few agonizing minutes, the bag returned empty.

Working quickly, Isolde added bag after bag, being careful to not overload the rope. As they returned, Cinta unfastened and refilled them. She never asked any questions, for which Isolde was grateful. A smug smile broke beneath the mask as each bag disappeared and reappeared once more.

"Nearly done," Cinta said, her voice oddly loud in the quiet chamber.

Isolde's arms were shaking with exhaustion, her breathing heavy. After attaching the last bag, Isolde pinned an empty one right behind it. Their signal that all the gold had been removed. "Excellent." Isolde reached once again into the compartment and slid it shut, making the box whole once again. She took the bags from Cinta and placed them into the satchel, before slinging it over her shoulder.

"Are you not going to send those as well?" Cinta asked, pointing to the two remaining bags of gold.

"These are for you," Isolde said adjusting the strap. "You risked your life for this; you should be paid handsomely for it."

Cinta's eyes filled with tears, her teeth biting her lower lip.

A dark shadow bled from the inner corner of Cinta's right eye down to her cheekbone. Cold fire ignited instantly in Isolde's eyes.

"Did he do that?" Isolde asked, her voice dangerously calm.

Cinta dropped her eyes. Her fingers gingerly tapped the bruise, and she nodded. As she looked the girl over, Isolde saw more shadows painting Cinta's porcelain skin. Some of them in the shape of a hand.

Others...

Cintas quickly moved a hand to her low neckline, to cover the bite mark that peeked over the lace trim at her cleavage.

But the Hood had seen.

A cruel chuckle ghosted through the mask as Isolde turned back to Gage. His eyelids fluttered briefly as she roughly hauled him to the chair she had occupied on her last trip to Foxclove. Its wooden frame groaned against his weight as she slammed him into the velvet cushions.

"Your friend said you couldn't kill him," Cinta whispered, her voice so full of hope Isolde nearly reconsidered her decision.

"She was right," she said over her shoulder, her eyes glowing. "I'm giving him something far worse than death."

"What could be worse than that?"

Isolde slowly pulled a knife from her belt, turning it in her hand. "Humiliation."

Gage's eyes finally opened and focused just minutes after Isolde had bound his hands, feet, and chest with the whips that hung beside the door. Strips of clothing littered the floor about him. Light flickered across every inch of his bare skin. Every inch was carved from stone. A monster disguised as a knight in shiny, handsome armor.

Gage's cruel blue eyes finally landed on the Hood, who lounged on the lavish bed. One boot was crossed over the other, arms extended behind her head.

He bared his teeth in fury against the gag tied around his mouth and head. A string of incomprehensible swears seeped around the bit. His shoulders and hips bucked against the chair. Isolde chuckled at the sight.

"Do save your strength, Lord of Foxclove. You'll need it to survive the night."

He looked down at his bonds and froze. Isolde had placed an elithrium shackle on each of his wrists and ankles, robbing him of every ounce of his power apart from the sheer strength that lied within his muscles. If she was going down this path, there could be no mistakes, no chances of him escaping.

His knees bunched together, trying to hide all that lay bare to the world.

"Yes." The Hood laughed, her eyes dropping. "I'd try to hide myself as well…if that's all I had to offer."

Gage growled at her, his teeth snapping against the cloth as if to chew through it. She could only guess at his words, but still they brought a smile to her face. Gage looked around the room, searching for the one that resided directly behind him, safe from his penetrating stare.

"Are you looking for your little *pet*?" Isolde asked. "Yes well, I do hope the money was worth it. Because her death is going to cost you so much more where Madame Vara is concerned." A smile spread across Cinta's face. Far better to be dead than with one eye constantly glancing over her shoulder for the rest of her life.

"Don't look so concerned," Isolde continued enjoying the fear in Gage's eyes. "I ensured it was a quick death- if that's your concern. However, I have a feeling it's not. Although I doubt she minded, after the disappointment, I have no doubt she experienced in your..." her eyes dropping again in disdain to Gage's crotch, "*company*."

Gage yanked at his chains. Malice burned in his gaze. But something else...Isolde could see he was thinking, concentrating on her voice. Trying to pick it apart, to figure out if he had heard it anywhere else before. Her smile only grew. Using a certain blend of fabrics she made herself, Nan had hand sewn each of their masks. Thick but breathable, the blend muffled their voices, making it impossible to discern if she was a man or woman. Let alone give away her true identity. Not even Cinta could distinguish who was really lounging on the lord's bed.

"It has come to my attention, Gage, that you have been wanting an audience with me for some time. Went to such extravagant lengths, even pulling on the hopes and needs of those I help. Wrong move." His wrists jerked right and left, and his bare feet yanked against the restraints causing his chair to scoot across the stone floor.

Gage's eyes flicked to Estetul that lingered by the door.

"Is this what you want?" Isolde asked hopping up from the bed in one fluid motion. Gage's eyes tracked her every move as she brought the sword up to her hooded eyes. The handle rested oddly in her hand. Another's callus marks embedded the polished wood.

Lord Theort. She felt a moment of nostalgic sadness. Isolde knew the blade couldn't remain. As with the rest of the houses, whoever resided as lord or lady would be nothing without the sword of their house resting at their side. Theort would not want it here, not in the hands of someone so unworthy of it.

"This room is most unfortunate for High Lords and Ladies of Foxclove," said the Hood slowly sauntering over to Gage. She grazed a hand down his shoulder, feeling the heat radiating from his skin.

"So many have died here, so much nobility...gone. I killed Dagan right there," she said, pointing to the spot on the ground Dagan bled to death. A dark stain still lingered like a bruise.

"His was a quick death, something he did not deserve. It's not something you deserve either." Gage's shoulders shook, his broad chest heaving as a battle raged between fear and anger.

"Don't look so worried. I won't kill you now," she whispered, the side of her cheek coming to brush against his. "No, we'll have our time soon. And trust me, it's not something you should be looking forward to. You owe me a life."

Gage stopped fighting. His brow bunched on his forehead.

"When you are brought before the king to answer for this utter disaster," said the Hood, interrupting his thoughts, "I want you to deliver a message. Tell him, I send my thanks for payment for my efforts in undermining his every move. That if he wants a war, he's got one."

Before Gage could make a sound, Isolde brought the pommel down on his head. A sickening thud vibrated through the room, sending Gage into unconsciousness. Isolde walked over to the desk and plucked a feather pen from its holder. She dipped the tip into the well of ink and scrawled a note across a piece of parchment:

In memory of your failure, Your Majesty.
- The Hood

Isolde plucked a spare hood from within the confines of the box and hammered it, along with the note, into the wall above the mantel with a spare dagger at her side. As she walked past Gage, her hands twitched in longing for the blades that hung at her back. With great effort, she forced the bloodlust away. His shame would have to be enough for now.

Reaching up, she grabbed the rope and turned to Cinta. "Put your arms around my neck."

Terrified, the girl walked closer, her eyes glued to the three-story fall below. "I can't," she mumbled.

Isolde turned the full weight of her gaze. "My friend claimed you were brave," she said. "Are you making her a liar?" The fear in Cinta's eyes grew with each passing second, her fingers twisting into knots at her chest. "It's either hold on or wait for Gage to wake up. The choice is yours."

Isolde secured Estetul at her hip and waited until she felt Cinta's tiny arms constrict around her. Isolde choked against her hold, her windpipe crushed. "Cinta," she said, gasping, "not so tight."

Cinta relinquished a little bit of her grip. "I'm sorry," she mumbled. Taking a breath, Isolde swung from the safety of the ledge out into the open air. Her arms began screaming in pain as she moved one hand in front of the other. The downward slope of the rope made it that much more difficult to keep her grip.

Isolde could feel Cinta bury her face into her back. The handle of the bow dug into her spine. Refusing to look down, she constricted her tiny arms again. Isolde's hands began to sweat inside the leather gloves, causing one hand to slip from the rope.

Cinta stifled a cry in Isolde's cloak, her body shaking.

They dangled over the center of the courtyard. A few coins fell from a small opening in the bag. A metallic ring pierced the silent courtyard. Cinta's hand flew to the hole, cupping the rest of the purse.

A few of the guards stirred at the noise. Their heads turned and eyes searched the still, sleeping courtyard. Carefully drawing on her power, Isolde forced her strength into her hand, arm, and back willing them to be still. The guards returned their gazes forward, having dismissed the sound entirely. Relief spiked as she fought to regain her grip on the rope.

At last, she secured her fingers around the rope and continued the climb down. They passed by Malaki and Cillian, who were both still facing out into the barracks. Light from the full moon danced across the quivers on their backs. Once full of arrows, now remained half-empty. A wolf howled off into the distance, sending a chill down Isolde's spine.

She saw Malaki's eyes slide to her as they passed. His face was set in stone. Cillian nodded, a smirk stretched across his lips. "Almost there," she whispered to Cinta.

At last they reached a point low and deep enough into the shadows of the barracks for Isolde to drop. They landed with a thud, the coins jostling beneath their weight.

The shock of the impact and weight on her back, drove Isolde's knees into the ground. Forcing down a grunt of pain, she held a finger up to Cinta, telling her to keep quiet. Isolde looked around the corner of the barrack. A trail of small, bloody footprints and dead guards littered the ground. Blyana's path for retrieving the gold and returning the bags led them to the southern border of Foxclove.

Isolde glanced over her shoulder to Malaki and Cillian. An arrow was notched into each of their bows, ready to give cover if needed. Working as quietly as possible, Isolde cut the rope from the arrow embedded in the wooden pole and pulled. It gave way easily to coil into a mass at her feet. "Think you can carry this?" Isolde asked, holding the rope to Cinta.

She nodded, her hands already looping her arm through the links to rest them on her shoulder. They worked their way through the barracks following Blyana's bloody breadcrumbs. Upon reaching the edge of the forest, Isolde dropped to one knee, her chest heaving under the weight of the gold.

"Are you alright?" Cinta asked, her body shaking.

"Never better," Isolde lied, forcing her voice to be cheerful. In truth, her body ached terribly. Every muscle in her back groaned in protest as she adjusted the bow and quiver.

Blyana emerged from the brush astride Felix, dressed in her usual dark, purple hood. She nodded to Isolde, her eyes reflecting in the moon's beams. She took the burden of rope from Cinta's shoulders, much to her relief. Isolde tossed the mass to the side and retrieved a pair of metal clippers from Blyana's saddle bags.

"Hold out your arm," she ordered. Without delay, Cinta offered the Hood her wrist. A bracelet of finely woven elithrium-laced silver gleamed against her porcelain skin. Isolde wanted to know how long she had been forced to wear this but thought better of it. Her temper as far as Madame Vara went was not something she wanted to test.

Blyana stirred in her saddle but Isolde refused to meet her gaze. So many years had passed since Isolde removed her imprisoning elithrium jewelry. She had them fashioned into the blades strapped to Blyana's side.

The metal strings broke away easily under the pressure of the blades. They fell to the forest floor, silent in the gusts of wind that swept through the small clearing. Cinta gasped as her power returned. Her fingers curved and wove through the streams of air that encompassed her body.

"An air wielder," Isolde said with a smile.

"Yes," Cinta said. Her voice was so different from the hollow shell of a person they found at Madame Vara's. Her skin all but glowed with the power that coursed through her veins. Isolde could feel it humming through the air. It was an outrageous amount, one that could only be possible if blessed by the goddess of air herself.

After placing the shears and ruined bracelet in the bag, Isolde shrugged the remaining gold off her back and held it out. "Lady Isolde mentioned payment," she said. "I believe this should cover whatever she might have promised."

"This is too much," Cinta said. "I cannot accept." Her hand shook at her side, as if longing to reach for the bag that swung between them.

"Use it to find a better life, Cinta" Isolde said. "To help others have a better life."

Hesitating for just a moment longer, Cinta reached forward as if unsure and gripped the satchel, pulling it to her chest. "Where should

I go?" she asked, hardly able to lift the bag to her shoulder. "I have never been outside of Whisper before."

"If you wish to leave Arnoria, I can take you to one of our outposts," Blyana said. "It might take a week or two to get there but we have safe connections."

Cinta nodded, there was nothing left here for her now except Gage's wrath. "How do I thank you?" she asked Isolde, who kept her face down. Her eyes were hidden in the shadow of her hood.

"By helping make the world better than it is now."

Cinta sighed, her eyes filling with tears. Reaching up, she took Blyana's outstretched hand and pulled up into the saddle.

"They say you are a murderer and an outlaw," Cinta said, looking down at Isolde.

"They aren't wrong," the Hood murmured, her eyes downcast as she stroked Felix's neck.

"Perhaps not," Cinta said, her voice soft. "But you are so much more than that. If they call you anything, let them call you a thief of sorrows. That is what you are. You steal away pain and give something far greater in return."

"And what might that be?" The Hood asked.

Cinta smiled, a single tear falling from her cheek. "Hope."

Isolde fought against the lump in her throat, against Cinta's gratitude she could not and would not ever deserve. Instead, she bowed her head, her arms flowing out away from her body. "Always at your service." Her gaze shifted to Blyana, and she gave one firm nod. Without delay, Blyana took off into the night with a hope of a new future riding on her back.

Versa kicked at the dirt in impatience a few yards into the forest. Isolde slid to the ground beside her. She couldn't fight the smile on her face or the rush of vengeance that saturated her blood.

The thought of Gage's face when he awoke in the morning would be worth it all. A little less than 21,000 gold pieces rested in wine barrels just on the other side of Versa, waiting in a wagon bound for their hideout.

Eventually, Malaki and Cillian found their way to her.

"Are you alright?" Malaki asked, his eyes searching for any injury. She smiled back, rising to her feet.

"You worry far too much, Malaki."

"And you don't' worry enough," he said, reaching up over his head to tuck an arrow back into the quiver.

"Worrying leads to wrinkles," she said, pulling herself up onto Versa, who stirred happily. "I would rather not age before my time."

Malaki sighed with frustration but smiled all the same.

"Where's Bly?" asked Cillian, his eyes glancing around.

"Taking Cinta to Yvek," said Isolde, nodding to the path Blyana had disappeared down. "We can meet her on the road."

"Let's get going then," Cillian said, climbing up into the wagon. The coins jingled in their barrels. The team of four large work horses pushed into their harnesses as he pulled the reins free. "I don't want to be anywhere near here when Gage wakes up."

CHAPTER 18

Chaos erupted over Arnoria.

"This will not end well," Liam whispered in Isolde's ear. Her eyes roved Thornwood as the king's men tore apart the manor, searching for the gold and any evidence of the Hood.

Good luck with that.

All of their contraband was safely stashed at the hideout. The trap door in the cellar leading to the underground tunnels had been resealed with fresh stone by Malaki and covered with several barrels of wine for good measure. Bags of sweets Liam had brought for the children at story hour were clutched in her hands.

Liam sighed heavily, his muscles straining as a gloved hand ran through the mess of ebony curls. "Gage is humiliated, Isolde, and people are suffering because of it."

An ounce of shame pierced her heart, causing her steps to falter...but only for a moment. The bite mark on Cinta's breast sung in her mind. Bruises that covered her delicate skin were burned in her memory.

"People have already suffered because of him," she said, her eyes cutting. "More people than you know and in more terrible ways you can imagine."

"You speak of this as if you know firsthand."

"Because I do."

Liam's hand gently wrapped around Isolde's elbow, bringing her to a stop. He opened his mouth to say something but stopped. His eyes glanced around, cautious of prying ears. Jerking his head to the left, he led them to one of the side rooms currently unoccupied.

She wanted to jerk away from him but could not bring herself to do it. Despite her anger, she wanted to be close…wanted that connection with him. *How much longer? How much longer before the mating bond takes hold?* She had hoped all the time they had spent together recently would push it forward, awakening that lost connection within herself. But it only remained silent, dormant.

Not even a tether bloomed from her chest as Liam turned his eyes to her. Nothing beyond what she had forced her heart to forge around the vast emptiness she knew no one would ever fill.

"This can't go on, Isolde," Liam said. "Gage told me what he will do to the Hood if he catches you." His eyes were now hard on hers, begging. "You must stop this."

"You know I can't do that," she said, leaning against one of the heavy tables lined with scattered books discarded by uncaring guards. She dropped the bags of sweets to the side.

"The thing is, you can." A humorless smile playing on his lips. "You just won't."

"That's right, I won't."

"You're impossible," he growled, his hands resting on his hips. "I can maybe understand stealing the gold…but did you have to do that to Gage?"

The same cruel smile she wore for Gage a few nights before played out on her face. "He deserved it."

"He might have," said Liam, his eyes flashing. "But do the people of Arnoria deserve his wrath? Does it make you feel better?"

"Considerably," Isolde said, her voice low and lethal.

Liam shook his head, his hand rubbing the back of his neck as his eyes probed her. "I love you, Isolde. And because of that I can't let you keep doing this. I won't let you keep going down this path."

"Let me?" Isolde pushed away from the table, her eyes narrowing. Standing before him, she locked her eyes onto his. Every word was full of challenge and dark intrigue. "And just how do you plan on stopping me, Liam?"

Resolve mellowed his gaze. A muscle feathered in his cheek as his hand cupped her cheek. The worn leather felt ice cold against her skin. "Don't make me have to figure it out."

"Liam!"

Gage's towering form hovered in the sunlit hallway. Ray after ray danced across the silken chestnut strands pulled back into a messy tail at the nape of his neck. A new sword hung at his side, one far less grand than the one that rested in the hideout. "Did I not instruct you to search the slave quarters?"

"Yes, you did, sir," Liam said, tearing his hand away. He looked down once more, his gaze full of promise to finish the conversation later.

"Lady Isolde," Gage greeted, his voice forcibly cheerful. "Might I steal you away for a moment?" He held his arm out to her expectantly.

"I'm rather busy, Gage," she said dismissively, turning her back to him. "As you can see, your men have left Thornwood in quite a state. Thank you so much for that. Perhaps another time."

His cool, firm hand gripped her arm, stirring her toward the sunlight. "Oh, it won't take long, I assure you."

Her teeth ground but she didn't fight his grip. Killing him now, with so many of the king's guards present, would not end well for her or Thornwood. They passed into the direct sunlight, the heat of the day bearing down on her.

Taking a right, Gage led her to the stables. His grip grew tighter with every passing second. The blade sung at her thigh, begging for his blood. Inside the stables, the smell of hay and horses was strong, almost stifling. Not a soul greeted them, save for the few horses in their stalls.

"What do you want, Gage?" Isolde demanded, yanking her arm free. He smiled down at her. His cruel eyes shadowed from lack of sleep, made him all the more terrifying.

"You and Liam appear to be awfully...*close*," he said, the lines of his jaw tightening.

"We've known each other for years," she said, knotting her arms across her chest. "We grew up together. We're childhood friends."

"Childhood friends?" Gage mused, his fingers toying with the pommel of his sword. Each sweep of his eyes burned into her skin. "I don't seem to remember acting like that with any of my childhood friends."

"Your loss."

"Perhaps," he said, the hay crunching beneath his feet as he walked slowly, circling her. "So, he was a burden of Thornwood...a charity case?"

"He was and still is a welcomed addition to my house." Poorly concealed fury charred her insides, lapping at the control of her power.

"And has he laid claim to your hand?"

"What if he has? What business is it of yours?"

"Oh, Isolde," Gage said, his voice wickedly light. "It very much is my business."

"It's amusing you think so."

"Well...has he?"

"No." More regret than Isolde imagined possible lingered in the word. A fear of this exposure…this vulnerability coated her skin. This conversation was coming. She knew it was inevitable.

"That's most pleasing to hear." He hooked a finger around a strand of her hair, the dark brown wave flowing effortlessly over the leather glove she wished was Liam's. "Since the young captain of the guard has not stepped up to the task, I will." Gage's voice was a whisper at her ear. "Marry me, Lady Isolde."

She snorted, pulling away from his reach. A smile of incredulity formed on her lips. "Marry *you*? I couldn't think of anything I would rather do less."

"Come now Isolde, I'm sure I can think of a thing or two that would be less pleasant for you to experience or…witness."

"Is that a threat I hear, Gage?" Isolde asked, her tone level and full of subdued warning. She let a fraction of her power through, igniting the beast in her eyes.

A wide smile formed on Gage's face, his teeth growing white and far too sharp. Gage's power had never been made public knowledge. But Isolde knew he had to be powerful to have earned the position he was in. "I don't deal in threats…only promises."

The faces of those she loved most ran through her mind, each one adding a layer of fear onto her heart. Still, she couldn't back down from him, not now. "You really expect me to accept?" Isolde laughed, the back of her hand gently covering her mouth as if to hide her humor.

"Yes." His tone darkened at the sound of her amusement. "You are a lady of a great house, heir to its lands and fortunes. And I am the Right Hand of the King and now ruler of a territory of my own. What a powerful couple we would make. Second only to the king and his future bride, whoever she might be."

"For now," Isolde said. Gage stopped before her, his clear, blue eyes narrowing.

"What?"

"For now," Isolde repeated. "You are the Right Hand of the King…for now. How long do you plan to keep that position once he discovers you failed to capture the Hood yet again? All while managing to lose thousands of gold pieces?"

Gage burned with rage, his nostrils flaring. A shade of red painted his high cheekbones. There was something else there as well. Isolde knew it all too well: fear.

"And rumor has it," she continued, "the Hood left you in quite a…*delicate* position. Rumors have spread that he left you with your pants down and cock and balls hanging out…what little there was to begin with. I'm sure a few things were exaggerated of course. How embarrassing would it be if they were actually true." A subtle glow erupted in Gage's eyes. Blue hardened into sapphires as his anger rose. His massive hands curled then uncurled, his power stirring just beneath the surface.

"But you know how rumors are. Still, I suppose you should be thankful he didn't leave you in a more awkward situation." She was pushing the line. A very dangerous, deadly line. Yet she couldn't be bothered to care. Not after what he did to Cinta and Kamden. Isolde relished in his humiliation, his failure…so did the beast within.

"I'm afraid," she said backing away. "I will have to decline. No woman wants a husband who can't live up to his…*duties*."

Isolde turned to leave, a smile of smug delight ghosting on her lips. But she was stopped short as a biting pain erupted in her shoulders. Gage's fingers dug into her skin, wringing out a small yelp of pain from her lips as he hurled her against the stable doors. The wood groaned in protest, as did her wrists as he pinned them to the door beside her head. "You will be my wife," he rasped, his fingers squeezing.

"The answer is no," she said, pushing uselessly against him. Her power stirred. The beast scratched and bit at her control, at the dam that held it back.

"You're a smart girl, Isolde," Gage said, his body pressing her into the stable door, leaving no room between them. "I'm sure you're well aware of what kind of power I wield over you and your family." The same menacing, vulgar smile slowly formed over his lips. "How easy it would be to make this shithole you call home far less pleasant."

Furious fear coursed through Isolde, draining her of every ounce of fight. As if reading the fear in her eyes, Gage quickly forced her hands overhead and held them in place with his left. He rested the other on the side of her neck, forcing her jaw up.

"The Hood will be caught, and the king will thank me for it. Then you and I…"

His thumb and forefinger pinched her bottom lip. Pain ripped through the sensitive skin forcing a growl from her throat. She yanked one of her hands free and swung. But Gage was ready, waiting for her attack. He caught her hand just before it collided with his cheek.

"I love a woman with spirit. But tell me, do you like pain, Isolde?" Gage cooed, his fingers squeezing around her wrist, the bones popping. She fought back the cry bubbling in her chest, willing herself to not break. To keep quiet. "I can tell you do," he said, eyes dropping to her lips. "And if not…well—" a cruel smile spreading across his face— "you'll learn to like it."

As if sensing her anger, the ring on Isolde's hand warmed against her skin. A gust of wind, controlled by the hand he held captive against the door, rushed into Gage's face, sending hay, manure, and filth along with it. He dropped her instantly, shielding himself from the filthy assault. Isolde shoved his chest, sending him flying to the opposite door. It cracked in half from the impact, and wood littered the stable floor.

Rushing to the door, Isolde burst from the side of the stables and headed for the manor. Gage's echoing growl called after her, "This isn't over, Isolde!" His voice chased her across the courtyard, each word laced with malice. "Far from it."

Isolde all but ran to her room where Nan was mending the laundry. Isolde had wanted her safe and away from Gage and his men while they searched. The smile faded from Nan's face when she took in Isolde.

"My rose," she said, her gentle hands resting on Isolde's cheeks. Her eyes fell to Isolde's lip and wrists, where small bruises had begun to form. "What happened?"

Isolde laughed humorlessly. "Gage finally proposed."

Nan's face went utterly blank only to be filled with a rage Isolde had not seen since she was a child. "Have you told Alaric?"

"Gage asked Alaric for my hand," Isolde said taking a seat on the bed. "He told him it was up to me. A much safer choice than flat out refusing the Right Hand of the King."

"But it puts all the blame on you," Nan said, her voice hard.

"He didn't have very many options, Nan," she said, her hands wringing together. "Besides, I can take it."

"You shouldn't have to!"

The door swung open and banged against the unyielding stone wall. "What is going on?" Galaena asked but froze when she saw Nan's anger and Isolde's bruised skin.

"Nothing," Isolde said. "It will heal by tomorrow."

"Do not down play this, Isolde!" Nan said, pointing a finger at Galaena. "You tell your husband to keep that brute's hands off of her, Gal!"

Galaena raised an eyebrow at Isolde, demanding an explanation, completely at a loss for Nan's outburst.

"She means Gage," Isolde said, reading her aunt's confusion. "He proposed and did not like my answer."

A faint sheen ignited in Galaena's stormy eyes. "Alaric!" she roared, her footsteps thundering down the hallway.

"Poor Alaric." She leaned against the headboard and gave way to the exhaustion that burned through the adrenaline.

Nan grabbed one of the soothing balms from the washroom and generously applied it to her lip. "This will help with the soreness," she said, her feather light touch cooling.

"There's a blessing." The balm immediately eased the pain.

Nan dabbed a small amount onto her neck, her normally warm blue eyes were hard. "This isn't right."

"None of this is, Nan," said Isolde.

"We'll have to come up with something. He won't stop at one refusal."

"No," Isolde said, despair and fear settling into her heart. "No, he won't." She had too many weaknesses. Too many pressure points that Gage could use to force her hand. The only question that remained was…which one would he use first?

Zibiah smiled from the back of the library. Briarhole's youth was amongst those in attendance for the weekly story hour. It was a rare treat for the children of the territory. One Isolde knew could cost her friend greatly.

"I wish I could have a story hour of my own," Zibiah said as the children filed out to get their treats. "But Volkran has forbidden it."

"I wish you would let the Hood pay him a visit," Isolde murmured. "Give him a warning to look at every morning he woke and every night before he slept."

Zibiah shook her head, causing the trinkets decorating her braids to jingle. "It would only make things worse for them and for me. It is my job to keep him safe. And it would be a shame to kill my best friend."

"Oh, yes," said Isolde, her hands clasped behind her back. "That would be tragic. I would be devastated for days to come."

"You think you would win?"

"Of course, I would," Isolde said, her fingers smoothing out the front of her dress. "Why would you think otherwise?"

Zibiah laughed, her wide smile spreading across her face to ignite a sea of golden stars in her eyes. "Nothing ever changes. Overly confident and impossibly stubborn."

"The best there ever was…and exceptionally gorgeous. Don't forget that part."

Zibiah rolled her eyes. "Do you ride for Harrow Hall tonight then?"

"Yes," Isolde said, placing a book back on the shelf. "Half will go back to the houses, and the rest will be distributed to the people. Malaki believes it'll instill some level of good will with the lords and ladies. Show them that the Hood is not about destruction, but fairness."

"It is a good plan," she said. "I wish I could ride with you."

"As do I."

The children laughed and played in the courtyard, their minds filled with stories and their imaginations rejuvenated.

"Any word of how the Hood managed it?" Zibiah asked, a small smile forming on her face.

"There is plenty of speculation but nothing close to the truth. Apparently, the Hood is a ghost."

"Partly true," Zibiah said. Isolde bumped her hip and laughed. "What of Liam?"

"What of him?" Isolde's mouth pulled into a tight line. They had yet to finish their conversation from the day before.

"Last I remember, you two were stealing away to the library for a little…extracurricular activity. Or were you two actually reading?"

"Oh, there was plenty of activity." Isolde giggled. "And yes, there were books involved."

Zibiah scowled. "Please tell me you didn't ruin any of my favorites."

"No books were harmed," Isolde assured her. Memories of her backside pressing against the leather covers surfaced. "Not that I'm aware of anyway."

They walked on for a moment, stepping to the side to allow a few children to race past.

"He's angry with me," Isolde continued, taking a seat under one of the large oaks lingering at the side of the manor. Leaves rustled in the early afternoon breeze. The faint scent of wildflowers and freshly baked bread traveled with them.

"I'm not surprised," Zibiah sighed, taking the seat beside her. "He has been forced to listen to Gage's rants on the Hood for a while now. It's bound to rub off on him."

"This was different."

"How so?"

Isolde's fingers knitted in her lap, her eyes distant. "He said because he loves me...he can't let me keep doing this. That he would stop me."

Her friend sat still, her muscles locking. "So...he threatened you."

"I don't know what it was," Isolde confessed, her fingers pressing into her temple. "But it wasn't the Liam I know."

"Well, best of luck to him if he thinks he can stop you from doing something once your mind is made up. He might as well try to stop the winds from blowing or the tide itself."

Her humorless laugh curved her lips. "Gage also proposed."

A chorus of swears followed as Isolde relayed her encounter with the Right Hand of the King. Zibiah's golden eyes flickered to Isolde's mouth and wrists.

"That's one bastard I wouldn't mind running through," she snarled, her eyes turning into molten gold. "What do you plan to do?"

"Tread lightly," Isolde said, repeating Alaric's advice. "For my family and friends...I can't provoke him any more than necessary."

"How unfortunate," Zibiah said, a fraction of her anger dissipating.

"Yes, most unfortunate."

They sat in easy silence as the children played in the courtyard. Versa stood patiently to the side, her head dipping, as little hands stroked her forehead and decorated her mane with braids and flowers. It was a peace Isolde rarely enjoyed. A brief pause from the death and sorrow. *Will this ever be normal?*

"I am sorry, my friend," Zibiah said rising. Her hand rested on Isolde's shoulder. "But we better be off."

"So soon?"

"Volkran and Lauram are due back at Briarhole in a week's time. I want to get back with plenty of time to spare." Isolde knew Zibiah's punishment for taking the children from Briarhole if her husband ever found out. It screamed down her back in three long, angry scars.

"Hurry back to us," Isolde said wrapping her arms around her friend's shoulders. They held each other tightly, neither wanting to be the first to let go. It had been months since Zibiah had graced Thornwood. Isolde feared it would be many more before she could again.

After a long moment, each dropped their arms allowing their hands to rest on the other's shoulders. "All or nothing," Isolde said, her forehead resting on Zibiah's.

"All or nothing."

They loaded up the wagon. Each child carried a basket for their family filled with cakes, coffee, jams, and a small purse of silver coins hidden in the bottom. Isolde stood at the gate waving until their small convoy was out of sight.

Malaki, Cillian, and Blyana appeared beside her, their eyes following the procession. "Tonight then?" Blyana asked, her hand still waving as the dot disappeared beyond the horizon.

Isolde nodded, her power stirring with anticipation.

"Tonight."

CHAPTER 19

As the sun fell below the tree line of Blackford Forest, the Hood and her cadre, rode for Harrow Hall.

Four shadows sped through the trees. Each one carried a portion of the gold meant to be returned to Lord Milt. Malaki led the pack, using his power to bend the branches and brush away from their path, quickening their journey. Weapons gleamed from their backs and sides.

The proud manor sat on top of a hill that looked out onto the plains of the south, toward the next territory and the sea. Thousands of Arnoria's finest horses lingered in the fields. Their heads bent to the grass, and their tails swished back and forth. Isolde remembered where the weaknesses were in the defenses laying along the fence and the guard.

Harrow Hall had little to fear from the Hood. Milt had never needed correction in his treatment of the humans or half-bloods. A fact Isolde was truly grateful for.

Carrying his share of the gold, she slid into the lord's private offices and waited. Blyana, Cillian, and Malaki waited in the shadows of the balcony, all having deposited their load of the treasure on the table. Isolde relished in the theatrics. *Let him think I carried hundreds of pounds of gold in on my own.*

Before long, the lord strode into his office, the door clicking closed behind him. It wasn't until he reached the desk that Milt noticed her. The familiar outrage shined in his eyes as he reached for the house sword that hung at his side.

"No need for that," Isolde said, her legs crossed comfortably. "How do I find the great horse lord tonight?"

Milt sighed, his eyes glancing around the room for anyone else. "I was doing quite well," he snarled. "Until now."

"Don't let my presence be in the way of your happiness." Her hands were held up before her in surrender.

"Hard for it not to," he retorted. "What business do you have here?"

Isolde waved a casual hand at the piles of coin on the floor. "I'm merely returning these to you."

He went still, his eyes growing wide. "Is that…?"

"It is," Isolde said. "It's half your share of the bounty over my perfect, very expensive head."

"Let me guess," Milt said, teeth bared. "You kept the other half for yourself."

"No." She paused to pluck a coin from the stack. "The rest went into the pockets of your people. I didn't think you would mind. Especially since the king has raised taxes…yet again."

A fraction of his anger chipped away, leaving behind a small beacon of gratitude.

After a moment, Milt offered her a stiff bow of his head. "You have my thanks, Hood. This will mean a great deal to my people."

"I know what it will mean to them, Lord Milt," she said, her voice much softer than intended. "Which is why you have it. Because I know how you will use it."

His lips pressed into a line, but an edge had fallen from his gaze. "How many other houses are being afforded the same treatment?"

"You are in the minority." There was skeptical hesitance in his eyes that irritated Isolde. "We are not enemies, Lord Milt. Far from it. In fact, we are very much the same."

"Except for being a murderer," he said, the same hardness finding its way back. "I would say we are quite different."

She shrugged. "If you say so."

He surveyed her casual presence as if trying to solve a riddle. "Why do you do this?" he asked.

The Hood rested her hands before the mask, knotting her gloved fingers together. "Because I believe in a free Arnoria. I believe in what it once was. What it can be again. Surely you remember a time before our...*good king.*"

Milt nodded, and his eyes, a lovely shade of greenish brown, warmed. While he was now the youngest lord, thanks to Dagan's demise, she knew he still remembered the time before the current king. A time of peace...of prosperity.

Flames danced in Milt's gaze as he moved from the gold to observe her. "If that is why you truly do this," he said, "then this will interest you."

Moving to one of the bookshelves on the far wall, he extracted a single book. Her fingers lingered on the hilt of the dagger, once stained with another lord's blood. But he merely set the volume down in front of her and stepped back. Pulling the book forward, she realized it wasn't a book at all, but a false compartment.

Flipping the lid, Isolde sat back with a jerk, her lip curling behind her mask. Nestled in fine black satin was a piece of raw elithrium. She looked up at him, her eyes wide.

"I believe Lord Dagan had a piece similar to this, did he not?"

She neither confirmed nor denied it. "Did the king send you this?"

Milt nodded, taking a seat across from her. "Along with a letter demanding that I send some of my virya, humans, and half-bloods to the capitol. He wanted various talents, birds, predators, reptiles, etc. And any kind of wielder. The humans, I assume, will be sent to the mines."

"The mines? Of Helecdol?"

Milt nodded. A muscle ticked in his jaw. His beard, normally so well-kept and manicured had grown wild. Stray sprigs of rich brown hair stuck out at random points along his still impressive jawline.

Isolde relaxed back into her seat, her mind reeling. "Those mines were shut down decades ago. They're a death sentence. When did they become operational?"

He shrugged. "A while ago. It's not information most have the privilege of knowing." He shot her a look.

Isolde twisted her fingers over her lips, and threw the invisible key behind her. "And did you send them?" she asked.

He nodded, his eyes falling to the floor. "They have not returned."

"How long ago?"

"Six months."

Isolde's blood went cold. They were either dead or far worse in Elenarta and the mines. "Why virya?"

"I don't know," he said, his large forearms resting on his knees. "But I'm sure it has something to do with the currency in which he paid for them." His finger pointed to the elithrium.

"Why would you say that?"

"There have been rumors circulating," he said, his voice dropping into a whisper, "of the king experimenting on virya. For what purpose, I don't know…but it can't be good."

Isolde's teeth clamped down. Gage had said the king had found a way to take care of troublesome virya. But how? "Was there anything else in the letter?"

He shook his head. "Only that more would be required in due time, and that this would all be discussed at the Tournament of the Guard in three months."

"Do you know of this happening anywhere else?" she asked.

"Two other houses, Lady Circe and Lady Yvaine, mentioned it to me at Lestahere. I'm sure others have but aren't talking about it."

Alaric hadn't mentioned such a gift or request from the king. She would have to find out for sure when she got home. She looked into Milt's eyes and held his stare. "Don't send anymore or at least hold off for as long as you can."

His wide shoulders rose in a sigh. "I'll do my best."

She leaned forward, matching his stance. "As I said before, I am not your enemy."

Milt nodded. "I'm starting to believe that." He opened his mouth to say something else but snapped it shut.

"Ask away, Lord Milt," Isolde said. "In my line of work, there is no promise of tomorrow."

Milt released a chuckle that quickly turned into a heavy sigh pushing past his lips. Running a hand down his face, he found her eyes once again. "Why do you do this?" he asked, his head shaking. "What is it that you want in the end?"

For a moment, all Isolde could do was stare. Stare into the eyes of someone who was a man after her own heart. "I want the same things you do." Her voice sounded gravely to her, as if pulling each word from her chest was a struggle.

"You serve your people the best you can by being a beacon of hope in your territory. I'm trying to do the same." She waved a hand at her hood in sarcastic flair, doing her best to hide the shame in her eyes. "This is all I can give Arnoria and her people. Because sometimes the only thing a monster fears...is another monster. There will be a time when Arnoria will need a hero. One not soaked in blood, dressed as a nightmare, and stained with death. But not now. Now...it needs a villain."

She licked her lips and turned to look out the window, where she knew her family waited...where they listened. "In the end, I want a place where my existence is no longer necessary." Her voice dropped as the truth of what lived in her heart was laid bare. "A place...where I can be at peace."

Milt watched her, his lips parting slightly. She had never seen that look before, one of awe and...perhaps regret. After a moment, he cleared his throat and nodded to the returned bounty scrawled across his table. "Thank you."

She nodded and rose, a finger pointing to the elithrium. "I will look into this matter." She walked to the window and hovered on the frame. "For Arnoria."

And with that she disappeared into the cool night air.

Isolde's muscles froze as they always did in his presence. A subtle power lingered beneath his skin, one she knew to be weary of.

"I was wondering when you would turn up," Ferden said, plucking two golden goblets and pitcher of wine from the cabinet. Turning back, he eyed her with only a fraction of caution. "I hope you didn't keep the rest of the purse all to yourself. You must be very well off at this point, Hood."

"My dear Ferden," Isolde said, easing into their little game. "What kind of friend do you take me for? The rest of your purse lines the pockets of your people."

A small smile played on his face, his golden mustache twitching as he poured the wine. "I suppose giving it all back to me would have been too much to ask."

"It would not do for the Hood to play favorites," she said taking the goblet from his offered hand. "Others might get jealous and believe you to be in bed with the enemy."

Ferden's scent wafted about her, mixing in with the scent of the rich, earthy wine. It always perplexed her, confused her senses. It was as if it could not decide what it was exactly, but a mixture of the sea and the earth, rich and vast but ever changing.

She swirled the wine, an old vintage. Smiling regretfully, she set the goblet aside. Her mask must stay where it was, preventing her from partaking-another sadistic, little game he liked to play. Ferden's curiosity for her identity was ferocious but never overbearing or forceful.

He grinned at the gesture, taking his seat by the fireplace. "I see you have learned a thing or two."

"I was rather new to this life when you first caught me," Isolde said, a bit of steel cutting into her words. "Does it make you happy to know you are the only one to have done so?"

He shrugged, his pale blue eyes searching her own. She couldn't help but find him beautiful. Aged and full of memory, he gazed at her almost lazily. Ferden was old, much older than any other virya she had met. The courage had not found her to ask him just how vast his years ran. Compared to Alaric, Ferden could pass as his son, meaning he had not stopped transforming into whatever beast lurked below the surface.

"Why is it you did not unmask me that night?"

"Where would the fun be in that?" he said, taking a sip. "We have an entertaining relationship and as long as that remains true, there is no need to bring to light who you are. After all, who doesn't love a good mystery?"

She didn't miss the hidden threat in his answer. Their relationship was entertaining for both sides. Isolde wasn't lost on the notion that might one day change. If so, there would be no choice. She would slit his throat and not think twice about it.

"Tell me," she said at last, the silence having grown heavy. "What news have you heard?"

"Only rumors, titters of tales of the crown buying up human and half-blood stock and bringing them to Helecdol. Word has it the mines are in mass production once again."

Ice fell in the pit of Isolde's stomach. "I've heard the same. I thought the mines were empty, that all of the elithrium had been unearthed years ago."

"I suppose they found more-a new pocket of the finest elithrium Arnoria has to offer, this one being far closer to Elenarta," said Ferden. "The king is a rather...ambitious man."

"Have you received anything from the king?" she asked.

They held each other's stare. Ferden's eyes grew guarded. "Why do you ask?"

Isolde shrugged and threw a leg up on the ottoman before her. "A little lord or two told me of a gift they had received from His Majesty. A gift with the understanding that humans and virya would be sent to him with more of the same gift to follow."

Ferden sighed heavily, his jaw flexing.

"Don't grit your teeth at me," she chided, narrowing her eyes. "It makes your jaw look far broader than it already is."

"Most people find that attractive," Ferden retorted, his voice deep and full of meaning.

"Most people are fools."

His golden head fell back in laughter, his eyes sparkling once more. "I cannot argue with that point." Rising, Ferden crossed the small study and pulled out a leather satchel from one of the cabinets lining the walls. An eerie green glow spilled from the edges, causing Isolde's hair to raise in alarm. The animal within snarled, a small bit escaping her clenched teeth.

Ferden ignored the sound and offered it to her. Carefully, Isolde wrapped her gloved fingers around the roughly cut mineral. She had never held raw elithrium before intentionally and could not help the shudder that rolled through her bones.

"This is only a fraction of what was sent," Ferden said, extending the bag to her. She dropped it in willingly.

"And what does he expect in return?"

Ferden was quiet for a moment as he replaced the small weapon on the shelf. "The same as the other houses," he said. Pain coated his words, and anger. "My people."

"How many?"

"Does it matter?" he snapped. Ferden tossed the bag back into the cupboard and slammed the door. He walked past the cold fire place and stopped. Reaching up, his hand hovered over the flint and stone. Isolde shifted in her seat as the wave of panic struck. Ferden sighed and let his hand drop to his side. "Virya and human alike," he continued, leaving the fireplace cold. "At least he has spared the children. This time."

A small mercy. Isolde breathed a sigh of relief both for the children and the fireless fireplace.

"We do not have very many of them here," he said, retaking his seat. "As you know, virya children are so hard to conceive, they are a treasure. As are the human children."

"Yes, they are," Isolde said, her mind finding its way back to the little ones in Thornwood. *Why has the king not sent such a gifted request to Thornwood?* Surely it was only a matter of time.

A knock at the door interrupted the silence. "Enter," Ferden said over his shoulder. Isolde moved instantly, her body a mere blur in the dark as she hid in the safety of one of the curtains that swayed over the windows.

A child, no older than ten, walked between their two chairs. In his little hands was a tray laid with food and more drink.

"Your supper, Master Ferden," the little one chimed, his face bright with having successfully completed his task.

"Thank you very much, Boe," Ferden said, with a genuine, unrestrained smile. "Tell your aunt it looks delicious and to give you a little sweet."

"Thank you, sir," the boy said, bounding from the room.

Warmth spread through Isolde's cold heart, breaking off just a facet of ice that coated it. Sauntering back into view, she regained her seat. "You once asked me why I did not mar your face like I did the others."

"Because you wouldn't want to ruin such perfection?" he asked, a mouth full of roasted chicken.

"Hardly," Isolde said, her stomach growling. "It's because you love them and treat them as such."

"I am alone here," he said leaning back, licking his long fingers. "Why would I want to surround myself with melancholy?"

"True, but I think there is more to it than that," she said, her eyes cutting slightly.

A playful grin formed on his lips, his eyes piercing, "Are you asking for my secrets, Hood?"

"Are you offering them?"

Ferden watched her over the goblet's rim as he drank, the golden metal reflecting in his eyes. A cocky grin pulled at the corners of his lips. "I'll trade you, a secret for a secret. Take off the mask and I'll tell you whatever you want to know." His elbows rested on his knees, eager for her answer.

Isolde merely smiled beneath the mask. Her eyes rolled as she stood. "You should know a thief never reveals their secrets, Lord Ferden."

He chuckled, leaning back once more, "Neither does a lady."

Fear spiked through her veins, but she forced herself to ignore it. "Besides, I would hate to ruin your definition of beauty. One look at me," she said, her hand waving before her face, "and I am all that you will think of until your last day."

"Rather presumptuous of you, Hood." Ferden grinned.

"I'm simply stating the facts. I am rather irresistible." She grinned beneath the mask and she could have sworn Ferden saw right through it.

"Beauty is in the eye of the beholder," he said, taking a sip of wine. "But I have a feeling most who beheld you would share that opinion."

"This is true. I do believe it is past your bedtime, my friend. I will not impede on your beauty sleep any longer."

The Hood walked to the window, the heels of her boots clicking against the wooden floor. Her cloak bellowed around her as a gust of warm, night air snaked through the gossamer curtains.

"Hood."

Isolde froze on the ledge, her hand bracing against the frame.

"Be wary of those in your circle," Ferden said, over his shoulder, his chin turned slightly towards her. She could see a muscle tense in his cheek, as if attempting to control his anger. "If one gives you cause for doubt, listen to your instincts."

"Do not speak in riddles, Ferden," Isolde said, her irritation spiking along with her fear. "It does not become you."

"It is part of my charm, my darling thief. Just a word to the wise: be cautious of who you trust."

Isolde rolled her eyes. "Always a pleasure to hear your insufferable words of wisdom." Her hand swept into a bow of sarcasm that had him chuckling before she plunged into the night.

"Until we meet again," he said, his pale eyes shining with anticipation.

CHAPTER 20

"Please stop."

A light, feminine chuckle echoed down the hallway as Isolde made her way through Blackwater Manor.

"Come now, Eli," Yvaine purred. "I know that's not what you really want."

Isolde glanced around the corner to see Yvaine crawl across a bed of gold to straddle a man chained to the headboard. His naked body quivered in disgust as the Lady of Blackwater ran her perfectly polished fingernails along the ridges of his abdomen.

"I'm betrothed, Lady Helm," Eli said, his teeth clenched as he fought against his body's response and the chains that held him in place.

"That's a matter easily dealt with," Yvaine said leaning forward. Her lips curved as she dipped her face to his. Eli shoved his face to the side, toward the wall on the opposite side of the doorway where Isolde lurked.

Yvaine's unforgiving fingers grip his jaw and pulled his face forward once more. In her other hand was a small, beautiful blade. Its surface held an elithrium sheen that seemed to fight against the gold it had been forced to bind with.

"Play hard to get all you want," she said. "But you know I own every inch of you. You don't get to say no to me. And if you try..." Yvaine slid the blade's razor-sharp edge across his chest, drawing out a grunt of pain from Eli's tightly sealed lips. "Then this will seem like foreplay compared to what I will do to your little betrothed when it's her turn in my gilded cage."

Isolde's eyes locked on Yvaine's hand gripping Eli's jaw. The memory of another's hand pressed against her mind. She could practically feel Gage's fingers pressing against her skin. A faint sheen of sweat coated her palms as another memory came to mind. Of that same hand assaulting Malaki.

Revulsion and anger spiked in her blood, bringing her power roaring to life. Isolde felt herself move as instinct and fury seized control. Reaching up, she plucked an arrow from the quiver, slid it into place, and drew back.

The bow string hummed as Isolde let the arrow fly. She felt the wind rush past the skin on her face. The only exposed part of her felt the kiss of the nightly breeze from the sea as the arrow sailed past.

A cry of surprise and pain pierced the gilded chambers. The arrow's tip embedded itself into the pristine golden wall directly over the headboard and into the mistress of the manor's hand.

Blood cascaded down Yvaine's arm and around the smooth shaft of the arrow sticking out from the center of her palm. The knife clattered to the floor and slid under the bed and out of sight.

"No means no, Lady Yvaine," Isolde said, stepping into the light. "I believe someone has already told you that once before. Or at least that's the rumor sweeping Arnoria. That and the heir of Thornwood laid you on your ass."

Yvaine snarled as she narrowed her eyes to where Isolde lingered in the doorway. "Bastard!"

Isolde rolled her eyes as she drew out another arrow and fixed it in place. The string groaned beneath her gloved fingers as she pulled back. "You people really should come up with a new name for me."

Isolde looked at the man trapped beneath Yvaine. She could see he was handsome, beautiful even. But he was not there willingly. His voice had carried through the halls, begging Lady of Blackwater to stop. Briarhole returned to Isolde in full force. The memory of her assaulting Malaki, refusing to accept no…boiled in Isolde's mind like acid.

Cuts decorated Eli's sculpted chest, marring the once perfect, sun kissed skin one only obtained from working at sea. He looked at Isolde with both fear and longing. The pools of turquoise green shot to his captor hovering over him. A hint of light shined in the depths of his eyes. Isolde noticed then that the chains holding him in place held the same greenish tint Yvaine's knife did.

He's virya…or at the very least a half-blood.

Without a second thought, Isolde released the arrow into the golden chambers. Its elithrium tip cut through the golden chains holding his wrist. The heavily laced arrow cut through the gold like butter. Isolde sent another to the opposite hand. The arrow's edge kissed Yvaine's arm. Her teeth baring in a snarl as a small stream of blood tricked down her elbow and onto the bed.

"I'm sure you have far more entertaining things to do than bed this," Isolde's finger flicking at Yvaine who was seething, "*thing.*"

Eli moved just as Yvaine sliced her claws through the air, aiming at his face. His thick thighs jerked Yvaine to the side yanking her hand free of the arrow. Shrieks of anguish and fury filled the room as he moved to the doorway.

"Thank you," he said. Isolde nodded and turned back to the room but was stopped short. A warm, callused hand rested on her shoulder. She looked up into Eli's eyes. They were filled with an anger…and a shame she had seen in many others before him. One in particular. She pushed Blyana's eyes out of her head as he said "Make her pay." His voice was heavy as river rocks and hard as steel.

"That's one thing you don't have to worry about," Isolde promised, her power flowing and filling her eyes with light. "I intend to."

Eli's jaw tightened and his eyes grew bright for a fraction of a second before he cast one last look at his abuser and sprinted out the door.

"You cost me my best slave!" Yvaine rasped as she rose from the floor. Drops of blood fell upon the gilded sheets crumbled at her feet like discarded rubies.

"Oh, I'm sure I saved him from a night of disappointment," said Isolde crossing her arms and leaning against the doorframe. "A little bit of force can be fun. But only if both people enjoy it. And him," Isolde said nodding behind her. "I can't say he looked too enthusiastic about the prospect. Forget to brush your teeth tonight, Lady Yvaine?"

"Guards!" Yvaine roared her lips peeling back over her teeth. "Guards!"

"Oh, they won't be coming," Isolde said, resting her chin in the palm of her hand. She used it to look bored but really it was a way to check the mask's placement. Even the smallest detail could expose her. "They're occupied at the moment."

Blood pooled at the hem of Yvaine's dress as she balled her hands into a fist at her side. "You little shit."

"It's been years since I've been called that," Isolde chuckled. "By one of your late husbands in fact. But I'm not here to run down memory lane. I have brought you a little something, Yvaine."

"I want nothing from you, parasite."

"Really?" Isolde said, looking back with a shrug. "Fine, I'll take it back then. I did work awfully hard to steal it. I think I've earned a little something." Isolde backed up down the hallway, keeping her eyes trained on Yvaine as she followed.

Yvaine turned her glowing eyes down the hallway past Isolde's leather clad shoulder. They dilated at the sight of the mounds of gold littering the table. Flames from the roaring fireplace danced across their shimmering surfaces.

"You're welcome," Isolde said. Her eyes crinkled as a sarcastic smile formed on her face.

"You think returning some of my coin is going to save you?" Yvaine screeched. Her face twisted with rage.

"Oh, I have no doubt the coin will do little as far as my life is concerned," Isolde said, her eyes never leaving the creature before her.

Isolde could feel the subtle shift as a blanket of unease fell over her skin. Power pulsed from Yvaine as her fingers curled into claws. The threat was there, burning in Yvaine's eyes. Isolde had to be careful. She had come into the manor without the others. Looking back now, that might have been an incredibly stupid, fatal mistake.

"Then you're rather foolish coming here alone," Yvaine said, as if reading Isolde's mind. The train of her peony-pink dress, stained with drops of blood, flowed behind her as she circled the room. Isolde kept pace, not allowing her to get an inch closer.

"I have another matter to attend to," said Isolde, her hand waving casually through the air as the other gripped the bow tighter. "Why not kill two birds with one stone? I would hate to burden you with my company twice."

"What other business could you have with me, thief?"

"It has come to my attention that your treatment of the humans and half-bloods leaves much to be desired," she said, her anger rolling on the last words.

"Oh." Yvaine chuckled darkly, her eyes shining with wicked delight. "Is that what gets your feathers all ruffled? That I discipline my property as I see fit?"

"If you call torturing, raping, and nearly drowning them as discipline, then yes."

"And what exactly do you plan on doing about that?" The light in Yvaine's eyes grew.

Isolde felt Yvaine's power stir, the threat growing. It set her teeth on edge and caused her own power to growl back in return. "I will offer you the same choice I offered the others. Either learn to be a real leader or…" Her hand rested on the pommel of dagger strapped to her hip. "Well…you get the idea."

"My late husbands tried that same tactic. Behave or be forced into submission," Yvaine said, her sharp eyes narrowing. "It didn't end well for them."

"I can see that. Three dead husbands, all of them brothers…and at last you are the ruler of Blackwater. You must be so proud."

"Nothing will change, Hood. Except perhaps their punishments…they can thank you for that. No one will dare utter the name *Hood* in my territory for fear of losing their tongues…their eyes…and hands. And the little brats? Well," she said, a wicked smile pulled at her bright red lips, "I'll make sure to pay extra attention to them."

Yvaine struck so fast Isolde could hardly track it.

A streak of gold blazed past Isolde's face, forcing her to take a step back. Pricks of pain radiated over her right thigh as a small streak of blood ran down the length of her pant leg. Shock and fury pulsed through Isolde's muscles as she yanked an arrow from the quiver.

How did I miss that damn sword?

But Yvaine kept coming, the golden blade clutched in her hands. Each step Isolde took was perfectly matched, if not out maneuvered as Yvaine continued to strike. Each swipe of the blade accurate and frighteningly well trained.

"I wasn't aware that sword fighting was a part of a lady's education," Isolde grunted as her hip collided with one of the tables stationed around the room.

"A woman is forced to learn what she must," Yvaine said, twirling the bloody blade in a figure eight, "when faced with a life destined to be ruled by a man."

Isolde notched an arrow and fired. The tip barely missed Yvaine's shoulder as she shifted to the right and came at her again. They moved through their dance. Isolde firing an arrow and Yvaine dodging or severing the arrow before it could find purchase.

She's good. Isolde felt a sense of unease begin to form as she bled through her arrows one at a time. *Really good.*

Reaching back, Isolde felt the shafts of only two more arrows. Her head tilted to the side, her hand grasping air. It caused her eyes to drift off Yvaine for only just a moment. But it was enough.

Yvaine slammed the pommel of the sword into Isolde's face. A grunt slipped through her lips as she landed on one of the tables. It shattered beneath her, burying her and the bow in a pile of gold, wood, and glass.

Pain ripped through Isolde's back as Yvaine drew the elithrium laced blade down her back. It tore through the leather and her ruined flesh with ease, setting her skin on fire.

"You think you helped him," Yvaine said, her voice dripping with humorless malice. "But all you did was make things far worse for him...for his betrothed...and for the human filth of Blackwater."

Isolde reached for the handle of her bow as Yvaine stalked forward. The tip of the golden blade scrapped across the marble floor, leaving an ugly scar behind. Isolde fought the fear, the terror as the sound of the sword carving into stone hammered against her head. The bow was just out of reach, buried beneath debris.

"They will suffer because of you, Hood." Yvaine's voice held a ring of promise. A vow of retribution and pain. Isolde pulled herself forward. Her body slid over the sharp points of the ruined table as her back screamed in pain. "The king will welcome me with open arms when I drop your head in his lap."

Isolde's gloved fingers gripped the familiar wood as her other hand rose up and latched onto her remaining arrows.

"And in case you were wondering," Yvaine said, her voice soft as a caress. "I am going to make this hurt." Isolde watched as a slender shadow rose along the golden wall. The tip of the bloody sword pausing overhead.

In one fluid motion, Isolde yanked the two final arrows from the quiver and rolled to the side. The whistle of the blade kissed the side of her hood as she notched the final two arrows, pulled back on the string, took aim, and fired.

Victory turned to fear as the arrows' poisoned tips sliced through the skin of Yvaine's perfect, porcelain cheeks.

A shriek of fury and pain erupted as the sword clattered to the ground. Her blood-stained hands clutched her face. Crimson waterfalls that matched her lips ran down her chin and onto her chest. She fell to her knees.

"My face!" she shrieked. "What have you done to my face?" Yvaine crawled to the large dining table, her blood-soaked hands sent gold coins flying as she searched for the mirror residing at the edge.

"I simply made you what you are on the inside," Isolde said, pushing up off the floor. "A hideous beast."

Yvaine stared at herself, her eyes wide as if to see past the gaping wounds. The golden mirror shattered in her hands, bits of metal and glass falling around her. Slowly, her eyes turned to Isolde, her gaze full of unchecked, unfathomable madness.

The mounds of coins scattered across the tiled floor as Yvaine's arms thrashed out. Her body bent and curved, bone after bone snapping. Slowly, the fresh slashes on her face began to stretch. Large black feathers bloomed from every inch of her skin.

Terror kept Isolde rooted in place. Her own power stirred in response. The hunger for a fight growing was almost intolerable.

Yvaine was no more. Now stood a vulture, whose eyes gleamed with hatred. Its head slammed into the ceiling. Bits of plaster peppered into her massive wings. Flakes of gold dusted the ebony feathers. Identical red cuts stood out against the black skin of her newly formed face; even in transformation they remained.

"I'll never hear the end of this," Isolde said, making for the window. A wall of colossal black feathers flew out in front of her, and the heels of her boots skidded across the blood-slicked floor. A loud shriek pierced the lavish chamber. Isolde clutched her head, her ears ringing.

"It isn't polite for a lady to raise her voice!" she yelled. The vulture screamed, her large beak snapping for Isolde's head. Ducking beneath the deadly vice, Isolde sprinted for the door. She slid across the floor, narrowly missing the gnarled, bony beak.

In the doorway, she felt the searing pain of torn flesh cascading down her back once again. She cried in agony but kept moving. Looking back, she saw one of Yvaine's talons clawing at the empty space. Her blood dripped from its tip.

Isolde tried to force her legs to work, to move faster. But they simply would not obey. Each step was an effort, strained as if she were walking through molasses.

"That was rude," she said through clenched teeth. Turning for the far window, ignoring the pain, Isolde pushed the air around her into the glass. It shattered effortlessly and she leapt into the vast, empty night.

Nothing but open air resided between Isolde and the churning water below. Waves crashed against the side of Blackwater. Their white caps hugging the jagged rocks came closer and closer. Isolde tried pushing air beneath her, doing anything she could think to slow herself down. But each gust of wind she sent merely grazed the water's surface, scattering over the waves. Her power pushed forward, the need to let the monster out roaring to life. Just as she reached for that part of herself, the thunderous beat of wings reached her.

Black as the night sky, the same blood-covered talon wrapped around Isolde's arm. Its tips dug in, cutting her to the bones of her shoulder. Isolde cried out as fire raged through her back and arm. The bird merely laughed.

"Those rocks won't take the pleasure of killing you from me, Hood," it rasped, the voice barely resembling Yvaine's. Never had a transformed virya communicated with her. Its voice scrapped and clawed at her sanity. Isolde shot beats of air at her wings, hoping to throttle her flight and crash them into the water below. In the water, she had a chance, but in the air…

The creature chuckled darkly. *"Your little tricks won't work this time."* She squeezed on Isolde's arm once more, which forced a muffled cry from her lips.

She scrambled for her blades at her back, her fingertips grazing the polished silver handles. The talon squeezed tighter, refusing to let her to do little more than hang. Yvaine circled back around to the manor.

"Do thieves break?" Yvaine asked. *"We're about to find out."* She banked left. Coming closer to shore, her massive wings straightened. The windows of Blackwater manor glowed in the night sky. Their lights danced off the unforgiving waves that broke against its base.

An impenetrable rock wall ran the perimeter of the fortress, hugging along its side to end in the sand dunes that resided just off shore. Isolde knew instantly what Yvaine intended. Her heart hammered in her chest. *She's going to slam me into that damn wall!*

Frantically, she groped for the blade again, hoping to cut the talon loose. The joints in her shoulder began to slip and tear. A cry of fear echoed in the shriek of pain that erupted from her throat.

Like a great shadow, a colossal form leapt from the edge of the monstrous dunes. Claws sharp as the finest daggers gleamed in the full moonlight as they sank into the vulture's back. Yvaine had no time to react before the full weight of the massive clouded leopard slammed into her. They fell like a stone into the churning waves. Water coated Yvaine's feathers as the cat's weight dragged them below the surface.

Isolde felt the talon's release, and her bones and flesh shifted in one blinding moment of pain. The water was pitch black and murky, making it impossible to see the dangers that lurked below. The salt water stung her eyes and wounds covering her body. Struggling to use her only good arm, Isolde swam to the surface. Air filled Isolde's lungs in desperate gasps, her throat and nose burning. She looked around for the leopard, suddenly afraid of what lurked in the depths.

Giving way to fear, Isolde swam to shore, her left arm still dangling uselessly at her side. When her feet found the gentle slope of soft sand she turned back to the horizon and watched in horror. A hundred yards off shore, the vulture fought desperately to get away from the ferocious leopard that held Yvaine's neck in its teeth.

The shriek of the bird was so human, Isolde trembled.

"Bly!" Isolde screamed. "Bly, stop!"

The cat ignored her; its only focus was killing the creature struggling beneath her. Billowing white waves erupted around the colossal virya as they battled, each trying to land a fatal blow. Yvaine jabbed at Blyana with her beak, the sharp point piercing her snout. It sent a river of blood down her face, saturating her fur. Blyana snarled in response, the sound piercing Isolde with fear.

Fifty feet down the shoreline, Cillian emerged from the tall grass. His eyes were wild with panic.

"Blyana!" he screamed, his hands cupping his mouth. Terror like Isolde had never seen before shined in Cillian's eyes. "Bly!"

The sound of his voice carried across the waves. It forced her to stop. Blyana's large, terrifying teeth dug into one of Yvaine's wings. She stared back at him in furious confusion. Her gray, intelligent eyes watched as he extended a hand to her.

"Come back to me, love," he called, every word coated in love and desperation. Isolde knew even in her current form...she would hear her mate. Hear him calling her back to her humanity. The cat growled in warning. Her lip pulled back further over her teeth buried in a mound of feathers and flesh. Blyana was struggling, fighting for control of herself.

"Please, love," Cillian begged, stepping into the surf. Water broke over his knees as he moved toward her. "Come back to me."

With one final pull, Blyana turned and dove, leaving nothing for Yvaine to do but cry in terror and follow.

"No!" Cillian's wide, panicked eyes scanned the water's stilling surface. "Blyana!"

The water splashed gently against Isolde's legs that were barely holding her up. Ripple after ripple followed but Blyana nor Yvaine emerged.

Without waiting a second longer, Cillian charged through the water. His feet hurtled over the snowcapped waves intent on keeping him away. But gusts of wind rushed from his hands, severing the waves in half, making a path for him.

"Cillian!" Isolde cried. But he did not turn; she knew he wouldn't. Not with his mate, his life, his everything...still beneath the waves. With one final thrust of power, Cillian cut a wave in half with a blade of wind and dove head first into the abyss. He disappeared beneath the shimmering moonlight. Not even a ripple disturbed the surface as Isolde looked on in terror. "Blyana!" she screamed, forcing her lips to move. "Cillian!"

"Isolde!"

Malaki sprinted down the dunes, sand spraying behind him. His form had grown so large she could tell he was on the verge of transforming himself.

"Blyana," she cried, pointing to the water that had gone so still, save for the tide. "She...she...Cillian."

"You're hurt, Isolde," Malaki said almost to himself, his horror filled gaze focused solely on her.

"Blyana," she repeated, stumbling back through the water, fighting Malaki. "Help them!" She saw the pain in his eyes as he looked back out to sea. The fear and the anger that could tear a world apart.

Without a word, Malaki scooped her up into his arms. Her left one dangled uselessly, a cry of pain cutting into the night, forcing him to turn from the horizon. They walked just out of sight of Blackwater Manor. "Malaki, leave me and help them!" she begged, feebly pushing against his chest.

Malaki gently lowered her to the earth. The cool sand was utter bliss on her cheek. She felt him tear away her black jacket, exposing her back. His hands went still.

"Oh my gods, Isolde," Malaki said, his voice an agonized whisper. "Your spine."

Then she felt it. The pain that ripped through the freshly torn skin. She screamed into the sand, fighting to claw at the paste he was spreading across the wound.

"You have to be still," Malaki ordered, words grating through his teeth. "She cut you with an elithrium blade. You need the antidote." She refused to listen as she tried again and again to throw him off. "Be still, Isolde!"

"Bly...Cill!"

"Fine," he snarled, shifting his weight to sit on her legs. "Have it your way."

Isolde growled as Malaki forced her wrists above her head. Pain ripped through her shoulder and down her back as he poured his magic into her. After a few minutes, the pain and itching gave way to soreness then a dull ache. He wiped away what remained of the antidote.

"There," Malaki said, his hand resting on her bare back, his fingers pressing and reassessing his work. They moved up to her mutilated shoulder, and the same painful sensation burned into her joint as muscles and tendons fused back together. She stifled a scream as he pressed. Malaki sighed heavily. His hands moved to her other shoulder and squeezed reassuringly. "It's over."

Isolde nodded into the sand, but the relief was short lived as he took hold of her nearly healed shoulder. Before she could get a breath to protest, he snapped it back into place. Light flashed in her eyes, the pain so blinding it nearly sent her into oblivion. The agony finally lifted enough for her to turn her eyes to the horizon.

"Cill...Bly." Their names burned through Isolde's throat as she shoved away from the ground, sand coating her cheeks and neck. Every step was heavy, an effort as she stumbled down the dunes. "Where are they?" She searched the horizon, her eyes scouring for any sign, any hint of movement. Only the waves answered back. The sound was hollow and final.

"Where are they, Malaki?' Her voice carried over the sand. "Blyana! Cillian!" Tears sprang from Isolde's eyes as true fear began to poison her heart. "Damn you, both!" she screamed, terror driving her knees to the sand. "Answer me!"

"No need to shout."

A gasp escaped her lips that carried a cry of joy as Isolde spotted two figures slowly working their way through the surf a few yards down the beach. Scrambling to her feet, Isolde sprinted, sand kicking up behind her with every step she took. Cillian smiled as she tore through the water, his arm held securely around Blyana's waist.

Without thinking, Isolde threw her arms around their necks and pulled them close. *They're safe.* Tears streamed down her sand covered cheeks. *They're here...they're alive...they're safe.*

Blyana let out a grunt. "Easy," she said, her free arm wrapping around Isolde. "I can't heal like you."

Isolde instantly dropped her arms and looked her over. There were deep scratches and puncture wounds that bled freely from her cheek and forehead. Yvaine's beak had found its mark.

Tremors ran through Blyana's frame. From pain or exhaustion, Isolde didn't know, nor did she care to. Stepping to her free side, Isolde, along with Cillian, helped her wade through the water and up the gentle slope of the beach. Malaki met them halfway and gently carried Blyana past the dunes and up into the tree line.

As they walked, Isolde heard Malaki's unmistakable growl. "Don't ever do that again, Bly."

Blyana chuckled as she wrapped her arms around his massive shoulders. "Whatever you say, Papa Bear."

Cillian stepped forward, placing a hand on Malaki's shoulder. Cillian's eyes swept Blyana's face, noting every scratch, every drop of blood. A line in his jaw feathered. It was the first time he had gotten a good look at her, at the mess Yvaine had made.

She smiled softly, her palms pressing into his hands that now rested on her neck.

"I'm alright." The words were hardly a whisper, but they drew him back to her.

Carefully, he cupped her face and brought his lips to hers. It was just a graze, a promise. After a moment, he sighed and stepped aside, allowing Malaki to begin his work.

"I knew we should have gone in there with you for this one," Blyana said. Her teeth ground as Malaki began to heal her face. The wounds wove together slowly, each piece carefully placed. He once explained faces were far more difficult, required more concentration due to the attention to detail and the delicate tissues.

"Yvaine is incredibly vain, Bly," Isolde said. "I took her beauty tonight. There isn't enough gold in the world to fix that. Only my very slow, very painful death would have satisfied her."

"Another lord...or lady rather," Blyana sighed. "I wonder how Gage will respond to this. Or Liam, for that matter."

Isolde cringed, already dreading the look of anger in his eyes.

"That's one meeting I am not looking forward to," she mumbled, trying to move her arm. Pain sliced through the wound on her thigh. "Malaki—"

"Not tonight," he said, his attention focused on Blyana. "We still have to get back to Thornwood, and gods know what we might run into. Besides, a little bit of pain will do you some good."

She growled at him. His eyes, still holding a hint of light, flickered to hers momentarily but reverted back to the task at hand.

Blyana's face looked as it always had, only her eyes had lost some of their luster. Only two fine scars remained. Visible only at the right angle and in the correct light. "It has been so long," she said as Malaki tied a piece of cloth around the wound at Isolde's thigh. "I haven't lost control since…"

Cillian wrapped his arms around her, pulling her into his chest. "I almost didn't hear you," Blyana cried, her face pressing into his chest, tremors racking her limbs.

"But you did, love," he whispered, his lips pressing into the top of her head. "You came back to me." Cillian's eyes closed as a shaky sigh escaped his lips. Pulling her closer, he tucked her soaking wet head under his chin.

"Always," Blyana said, her fingers pressing into his back like claws. "Always."

Isolde dropped her gaze, suddenly feeling like she was impeding on a precious moment. She watched Malaki's hands as they secured the bandage into place. Looking up, she saw a knowing grin tugging on the corner of his lips. After a moment, as if sensing she was watching, he looked up at her.

She had known Malaki her entire life. He had trained her, taught her how to survive and over the years they had developed a way of speaking by a simple glance. They had always suspected a mating bond would form between Blyana and Cillian. And now, as they stood on the beach of Blackwater, their bond was more palpable than ever.

Malaki smiled, broad and unrestrained. Happiness swelled in Isolde's chest. A smile of her own shining through the mixture of bloody sand caked on her face and in her hair. She glanced at them again, her heart growing impossibly larger at the sister that had found happiness in a world that had only shown her despair and pain.

The ride back was jarring. Isolde bit against the pain as Versa raced home. She could tell the horse was trying to be gentle, as if she could sense her discomfort. Fane flew overhead, his eyes watchful on the road ahead.

"At least that was the last one," Cillian said, the familiar path to Thornwood winding through the trees. Circe's delivery had been uneventful. They had all agreed that leaving the gold with a note was the best option. Isolde had no desire to face that particular monster again. As for Foxclove and Briarhole, the cadre had distributed their entire contribution to the people.

"Hopefully, that's the last job for a while," said Malaki, his voice thick with exhaustion.

They dropped the horses off at the stables. Each took their time in wiping down their steed. Isolde gave Versa a few extra sugar cubes before closing the stable door. As she walked to the gate, Malaki pulled her aside.

His warm hazel eyes looked at her thigh, and he pressed his hand to the bandage. "I really just needed some time to rest," he said. "I'm sorry if you were in a lot of pain."

"It was rather excruciating," Isolde said, her eyes sarcastically sad.

He chuckled. A small light from his hands warmed her skin as he pulled from the earth, forcing the torn skin and muscles together. She bit down hard and forced herself to be still and not flinch.

At last, he released her and she sighed in satisfaction and exhaustion. "Thank you," Isolde said, bending her leg, now free of pain.

Malaki bowed and began walking to the house but stopped dead in his tracks. "All the lights are on," he said, a slight edge to his voice.

Blyana and Cillian turned from their horses, their eyes narrowing. Unease filled the air, anticipated dread poisoning every breath Isolde took. It was hours before dawn…not a single light should be on at this time of night. Scenario after scenario raced through her mind, each one more horrific than the last. Without waiting, Isolde took off into a sprint, terror slicing through her heart.

"Isolde, wait!" Malaki bellowed.

She ignored him. Her heart raced in panic as she reached the front door and yanked it open. The warm air of the house hit her exposed back as she ran down the hallway.

After a few frantic moments, she found Alaric, Galaena, and Nan in the library. Alaric's face was grim as he sat by the fire. Her aunt paced the floor, her body tense and shaking with rage. And Nan…her wrinkled, tanned cheeks were wet with tears.

"What's happened?" Isolde asked. The others filed in behind her.

Alaric looked up, his lips stretched into a tight line. She had seen that look before...only once, many years ago. It was one she had prayed to never see again.

"Damn it, Alaric!" she screamed. "What's happened?"

"Liam was just here," he said, his voice so strained it hardly sounded like his at all. "He reported that children from Whisper and the homes of Thornwood and Foxclove...are gone. Virya...half-blood...and human children."

Shock immediately gave way to numbness. Isolde took a step forward, her hands balling into fists. "What the hell do you mean, they're gone?"

Galaena met her stare. Her own eyes were shining with a dangerous, powerful fury, and irrevocable sorrow. "They were taken, Isolde."

She wasn't sure if it was anger or fear that kept her tongue still. Only the stir of her power came forth. The cold fire roared to life in her conscious mind. It spread, lurking within the cracks of her control, looking for a way out.

"How many?" She heard Malaki ask.

Nan sniffed as a fresh wave of tears fell. "All of them."

CHAPTER 21

I solde crumbled to the floor. Her knees struck the unforgiving stone with a crack, splitting the skin open. But she couldn't find it in herself to care. Numbness melted into despair as her face fell into her bloodstained hands.

Thoughts raced and stumbled over one another, too rapid for her to fully comprehend. The children's faces were so bright in her mind. They were smiling, and eyes wide with wonder as she spun them stories of a world far different than their own.

"Was it punishment?" Isolde asked, her voice hardly a whisper. She wasn't sure they heard it.

"We don't know," Alaric said. "No word has come of children being taken from other territories. It is possible. We take a great risk with reading to the human and half-blood children. You never know who might take offense to mixing their children." Isolde's nails dug into her scalp.

"So, you're thinking its related to that and not the Hood?" Cillian asked.

"It could be both," Galaena said, her voice laced with anger. "Punish the House of Thornwood and the Hood in one move."

"Did Liam have any idea where they might have been taken?" Malaki asked.

Alaric shook his head. "No. Our only guess would be Elenarta or somewhere rather close to it. Still, there is no way of knowing. No one is speaking of this."

Tremors rolled through Isolde's body in violent, uncontrollable waves. They had been gone for over two weeks. Too long, she had left them for far too long. Plenty of time to get the children to Elenarta and out of her reach. She felt the brush of Malaki's pant leg at her shoulder.

"What of their families?" he asked. "Were they harmed?"

"Only those who fought back," Galaena said, a bit of her anger cooling. "The others were left to grieve, to be tormented."

"The king has been recruiting others to send slaves and virya to the capitol," Isolde said, forcing her feet beneath her. "At Lesterste, Gage informed Volkran and Lauram the king had found a way to deal with virya who don't toe the line."

Galaena steps paused. Her eyes gray and hard as steel. "What way?"

"I'm not sure." Isolde sighed. "But if I had to guess, it has something to do with elithrium. It's the only substance we are susceptible to." Galaena exchanged a looked with Alaric, and his jaw tightened.

"Do you know something of this?" Blyana asked.

"When we still lived in Elenarta," said Alaric, "there were rumors of experiments. Mad men trying to find a way to neutralize a virya's power." He shot a glance at Galaena, who had turned her gaze to the fire. Her hands balled into fists, knuckles white. "Your aunt led the team responsible for investigating the rumors."

"We thought the problem had been dealt with." Galaena spoke as if she were looking into the past. Her voice and eyes were hollow. "We thought we had squashed every sick attempt, but we were wrong it seems." She looked now at Isolde. Her lips pulled into a tight line. "If that is what's happening...if those children were taken for this *research*...We can't let this happen again."

Isolde nodded. "Milt said he sent a group but have not seen or heard of them since their departure six months ago. They were paid in pure elithrium."

"He told you this?" Alaric asked.

"As did Ferden. I saw it for myself. It looked exactly like the one at Dagan's."

"And you trust them?" Galaena asked.

"They're different," Isolde said. "There are others that have received this gift and a set of requests as well."

Alaric leaned against his cane, his mind deep in thought.

"There has to be a connection," Malaki said, his eyes finding Alaric's.

"Possibly," Alaric said.

"Have you received one?" Isolde demanded, her voice far harsher than she intended. Galaena's eyes narrowed, but Isolde ignored her aunt's stare. Alaric's reaction was the only one she cared about right now. "Have you?" she pressed.

"Do you honestly think I would keep something like that from you?" The hurt shined so brightly in his eyes she recoiled from it. She raked a hand through her hair, sending bits of sand and blood to the polished floor.

"No," Isolde said, letting out a shaky breath. "No, of course I don't, Alaric."

Her uncle sighed, his hand scrubbing at the beard that lined his jaw. "I'm surprised we haven't though. It's the sort of torment the king would relish in."

"He got Thornwood for cheap," Isolde said. "Why pay when you can just steal?" The hood groaned in her fists, the leather straining in protest. "I'll leave for Whisper tomorrow. Can we spare some food and supplies for the families, Gal?"

"Of course," she said. "Take what you need. We'll go as well."

Alaric began to protest but she cut him off. "These are our people," Galaena said, her voice stern. "It is our duty to help them."

"We'll all go," said Blyana. Her hand threaded through Cillian's, and he nodded in agreement.

Exhaustion rolled down Isolde in waves. Having used her power, even for that small a time and blood loss, had taken its toll. She began to sway on her feet, her eyes drooping.

"Come, my rose," Nan said, her wrinkled cheeks still glistening with tears, "Let's get you to bed." She felt Nan pause, her warm hand resting on her bare back. "Isolde…"

"I'm fine, Nan," she whispered, keeping her feet moving. It took every ounce of her strength to make it to her room. As she left, she felt everyone's eyes on her back. Where long, gruesome marks cascaded down her spine, finding a home amongst the others that resided in her ruined, tortured flesh.

As if death had come and gone, leaving absolution in its wake, Whisper stood in silence. It had taken two days to gather supplies needed and still she didn't think it was enough. Moving past the main square, they saw faces disappearing into the doors and windows of the surrounding buildings. Doors and windows slammed shut, echoing throughout the deserted town.

"This might have been a wasted trip," Alaric said, his eyes constantly watching. Turgon, his family sword, hung at his side. The impressive ruby adorned in gold shined from the pommel. It had been the one thing, besides his life and family, not taken when Briarhole was ripped from his grasp.

Knives similar to the ones that hugged Isolde's waist shined from Galaena's belt. "People still need to eat, Alaric," she said. Isolde heard the strain in her aunt's voice. They were all on edge. Word had reached Thornwood of where the people laid blame.

Isolde dismounted Versa and tied her to one of the posts near the main stables. "We'll start this way," she said, pointing down the side road that was meant to be the residential area. Malaki was at her back, Cillian and Blyana to her sides, each armed to the teeth.

"Be careful," Alaric said, before he and Galaena headed in the opposite direction for the magistrate's headquarters.

Isolde knew this was in response to one of two things. Either the crown was seeking retribution for the Hood's actions, or someone had reported her dealings with the humans and this was the price. Either way, a threat was present.

They turned down one of the alleys that led to the neighborhood she visited often. A small doll lay in the street, covered in filth. She picked it up gently, the soft fabric nearly tore away as hay spilled out on the ground. Despair savaged Isolde's chest. She knew this doll…remembered the little girl who bore the crescent moon scar on her cheek, her two front teeth missing. She carefully tucked the precious jewel into her bag with the hopes of returning it to the rightful owner.

Malaki placed a hand on her back, urging her forward. She saw the same despair echo in his eyes. Emerging between the two houses she spotted another large caravan. Zibiah stood apart from it, next to one of the smaller houses that resided in the neighborhood. Her back was to them, but Isolde could see the tension in her friend's arms and shoulders.

Isolde instinctively fingered the pommel of her elithrium dagger. Zibiah was arguing with a woman whose arms were swinging wildly in a fit of madness. As Isolde approached, she started to catch the snippets of the conversation.

"Of course, it is," the woman said, who she now recognized as Freda. The baker's eyes burned with tears, and her teeth were set in anguish. "Why else would they take them?"

"It is not by her doing," Zibiah said, taking a cautious step forward her arms wide as if imploring. "She is only trying to make things better for us all."

"Better," Freda rasped, turning away. Her eyes landed on Isolde, widening for a moment in surprise. "You!" she screamed, pointing a finger, freezing Isolde in her tracks. The others halted as well, their hands on their weapons. "This is your doing!"

"Freda," Isolde said, watching the woman she had known for years who never hurt anyone stalk towards her, that accusatory finger still raised.

"They took my babies," she rasped, shoving Isolde back, hard. Malaki stepped forward. Isolde threw a hand out to stop him. She could see the changes, the glowing eyes and shifting of bone in Freda's face. The animal within was barely caged, a virya's fury needing a hearty meal and Isolde was willing to be the sacrifice to it.

"They took them because of *you* and your association with the humans!" she cried. "I knew I should have never let my babies go to mingle with those filthy children. Nothing good has come of it!"

Zibiah had placed a cautious arm around Freda's trembling shoulders, creating a barrier between the grieving mother and Isolde. She knew if Freda changed, there would be no going back, no stopping her. The anger would be too much for her to control, and Isolde would be forced to kill her before she could hurt anyone else.

"I'm sorry, Freda," Isolde said, her eyes cast down in shame and self-loathing. "I never intended any of this to happen."

"Of course, you didn't," Freda said, pushing against Zibiah. Her golden eyes lit with warning. "You are just a child. A spoiled child playing with the lives of others, not heeding the consequences."

"Do you know who took them?" Isolde asked, ignoring the unrelenting waves of crushing self-hatred.

"A note was left." She laughed bitterly. "It said to ask the story teller where your children are." Freda shoved a piece of paper into Isolde's stomach.

Isolde held it up. The letters were made by an elegant, practiced hand. In the top right corner was the royal seal: a ruby snake eye with a golden slit pupil set in a triangle.

"I'll fix this, Freda," Isolde said, the words sticking in her throat. Even she could hear the doubt, the uncertainty that coated her words.

"Haven't you done enough already?" Fresh tears fell down Freda's face. "We still have a few children left. Leave well enough alone before you get them killed too." Freda pursed her lips and spat in Isolde's face.

"Enough Freda," Zibiah growled, blocking Malaki, who stepped around Isolde. She pulled Freda back to the silent bakery, leaving behind the sound of her anguished cries in their wake. Only when she was out of sight did Isolde clean herself with the back of her sleeve.

Blyana put a hand on Isolde's shoulder, but she shrugged it off. She didn't deserve their sympathy or comfort. This was her burden to bear.

"There are children left?" Isolde asked Zibiah when she returned.

Her braids, which were tied back with a single strand of worn leather, bobbed as she nodded. "A few. They were off playing in the woods when the soldiers came to take the others."

A small mercy.

"When did you arrive?" Malaki asked.

"Just this morning." A streak of white and red shot from the sky and landed on Isolde's shoulder.

"Hello you," she said. Fane nuzzled against her cheek, his amber eyes closing as she stroked his chin.

"That's a needy one," Zibiah said, her finger pointing at Fane. "Ever since he arrived at Briarhole with the news, he has been nothing but demanding. Constantly needing attention."

"You're not wrong there," Malaki said, his forefinger stroking Fane's chin, his eyes hard.

Fane snapped his beak at Zibiah. Irritated, he leaned against Isolde and sulked.

"But you are still very handsome," Zibiah said. He peeked around a wave of Isolde's hair and chirped in satisfaction, allowing her to stroke his chest.

The rest of the day went much the same. As Isolde attempted to console the families of the stolen children, she was met with contempt. Only a handful opened their doors to her.

"I'm sorry," Isolde said, unable to hold back the tears as she sat before Tarvo. "I should have been here. I should have protected Tanor."

Tarvo forced a smile onto his withering face. While she saw hints of Tarvo in his son, mainly his jaw and nose, Isolde saw another in Tanor. The warm, soft eyes, gentle set of his mouth, and the sandy blond hair all belonged to his mother.

"I do not blame you, Lady Isolde," Tarvo said, his voice raspy from sorrow. He gripped Isolde's hand. "Tanor loved—" He paused and stilled his shaky breath. "He loves story hour, and he looks forward to studying with you every week. It gives him hope that the world is not so full of dark places, with evil people. So, for that I thank you."

Isolde couldn't fight the overwhelming sense of guilt she felt. An hour a week of hearing her lecture him on reading was what this poor boy had to look forward to. New tears fell, landing noiselessly on the broken table.

"He is a brave boy who dreams of a world like the one you created at story hour. One where no one cared if you were human, virya, or a mix of the two. One of equality."

"What of the girl?" she asked. "Mary?"

Wiping away the tears, he shrugged. "She was taken too."

Isolde knew Tanor would not budge. She had no doubt in his ability to keep their secret, but the girl…There was no way of knowing what would happen if Mary was in the hands of the king with the possible threat she now possessed. She felt Malaki stir behind her as if he was thinking the same thing.

"You both are my family," Isolde said, her hand resting on Tarvo's. "A member of Thornwood. I will get him back. I will get them all back. I promise."

Tarvo bowed his head. His other hand came to fold over her own, and tears of gratitude and sorrow fell freely. His skin was hardened by scars and burns from years of work as a smithy. "Thank you, Isolde."

As the day wore on, they walked down to the center of the square, Malaki and Cillian broke off to check in with Alaric and Galaena. Heaviness had fallen over them as they moved, their eyes always searching, until they came upon a familiar street, one she and Blyana had walked not too long ago. The woman she had purchased the gown from was sitting out on the front porch. She was rocking back and forth, her hands clutching a tiny dress and a single flower.

"Isolde," Zibiah said reaching for her. She shrugged from her hand, looking for the little girl praying that she had been among the few that managed to escaped.

"Hello," Isolde said kneeling before the woman. Her eyes slowly came into focus and new tears fell from her eyes.

"Lady Isolde." The woman wept as her arms wrapped around Isolde without warning. "Why did they take her?" she cried. "Why did they take my little Insil?"

Isolde could do nothing but hug her back, being careful to not crush her. She ignored the smell of the woman's unwashed body.

"I don't know," Isolde said, tremors of guilt rolling through her.

"They told me to forget her," she cried. "That a gutter rat human like me could lie on my back and have another litter if I wished."

She remembered the little girl. Her loving warm face, deformed by the hideous scar. Isolde's eyes roved the shack that was barely standing. A basket of sewing supplies rested by the small, kitchen table.

Isolde pulled away but kept her hands on the woman's far too thin shoulders. "What is your name?"

"Asha," she said, sniffing.

"I can't give you your child back right now, Asha," Isolde said. "But I can give you a different life if you wish it."

"I don't understand," Asha said, her head shaking.

"I can offer you a place at Thornwood. Not of enslavement, but employment."

There was light in her eyes, but it was quickly cast in shadow. "What if she returns and I am not here? What if my Insil comes home?"

"Then I will see to it that she comes as well," Isolde said. "You both will have a home with us, Asha, if you want it. The choice is yours."

Asha looked around at her surroundings. At the home, she had worked so hard to make and keep for her family. At last, she turned, biting her lower lip and nodded.

"Good. And as your first project…" Reaching into the bag she pulled out the nearly destroyed doll. "I think Insil would be very happy to have this when she comes home."

Asha sobbed as she clutched the doll to her chest. "Thank you, Lady Isolde."

They left Asha to pack what little belongings she had, with instructions to meet them at the caravan when she was ready.

They walked farther into town, until they reached the main square. Each was lost in their own thoughts when a voice rang through the air. It stopped Isolde cold in her tracks at the mouth of an alley just off the main square.

"Lady Isolde!"

Perched on a beam that ran the span of the alley, connecting one building to the other, stood Freda. A necklace of rope hung from her throat. It wound around the beam she stood on, a good forty feet from the cobblestone streets below. "Freda." The name echoed through the deserted square. Isolde's voice was a horrified whisper.

An icy smile tugged at the corner of Freda's lips. "You did this," she said, a cold, humorless laugh coating her words. Tears fell down her face, rivers cutting through the faint film of dirt on her cheeks. "I want you to remember...to always remember...you killed my children...just as you have killed me."

"Freda, please," Blyana said, her hand reaching out.

Tears formed in Isolde's eyes as she took a step forward. "Don't, Freda," she said, her words gritted against the horror raging inside her chest. "I'm begging you, please don't! I can fix this!"

Freda merely laughed again. Her voice was mad, devoid of all joy...of all logic and hope. The sound was filled with such frigid hatred, Isolde felt her blood freeze. "That's exactly what I said, when they took my children."

Isolde looked around, desperate for help...for anything to stop what was coming. She could have easily shot the rope in half with a single arrow. But her bow was safely stowed away in her bedroom at Thornwood. Making it and herself...utterly useless.

Isolde turned back to the woman she had known for years, had visited at every trip to Whisper. The memory of Freda's cinnamon rolls coated her tongue. Their eyes locked, and Isolde saw nothing but hopeless malice. "May the gods damn you." She took one final step forward.

"NO!"

Isolde's cry wasn't enough to stop the sound of Freda's neck snapping from reaching her ears. It ricocheted through her mind, her heart, hammering down into her very soul. Isolde's knees struck the cobblestones, and blood saturated her pant legs. Burying her face in her hands, a cry of anguish exploded from her chest. It echoed through the silent streets. Only the sound of the straining rope above answered back.

Guilt ravaged her. Sawed at her sanity. Freda's face joined those of her children in Isolde's mind. Their eyes shining with accusation...with blame.

She could feel Blyana and Zibiah nearby. Their hands hovered over her, as if to reach out in case she lost control. Looking up, Isolde gazed at Freda. Her limp body swayed in the warm afternoon wind. Strands of dirty blonde hair brushed against her cheeks. Eyes devoid of life and streaked with red were open and staring. As if, even in death, Freda was damning her.

"Isolde." Zibiah's hand gripped her quivering shoulder. Blyana knelt to her right, her head bowed, and hands clinched in her lap. "I'm sorry."

Isolde cupped her hand to her mouth as nauseous guilt rolled through her gut. "What have I done?"

"Well, well..."

Fury pulsed through Isolde's blood. Lurching from the ground, she let out a growl that rolled easily through her teeth as Madame Vara descended the steps of her House of Pleasures. The dark green dress that showed off every bit of curve billowed in the wind.

Her bright green eyes took them in, a wicked gleam shining from their depths. "It seems the mere sight of you is enough to kill, Lady Isolde." Vara smiled. "What brings the mighty house of Briarhole and Thornwood into our midst today?"

"Nothing that concerns you, Vara," Isolde said, her fingers itching for her blade.

"Oh, I believe it does," she said, stopping before them. "Word around the block is that many of the children have miraculously disappeared."

"Again, not your concern," Zibiah said, her tone biting.

Madame Vara's eyes roved them until they at last landed on Blyana. A cruel, beautiful smile formed on her bright red lips. Blyana was stock still; Isolde wondered if she was even breathing at all.

"My, my," Vara said, her eyes running up and down her frame. "How time away from my house has changed you, my Blyana."

The clouded leopard remained frozen, her eyes shining with what Isolde guessed was either fear or anger. She prayed for the latter. "What do you want, Vara," Isolde growled.

The viper's eyes slid to her and narrowed. "I should be asking you the same the thing. From what my little flowers tell me, it is your fault the children were taken in the first place. And judging by this little demonstration—" her bony, polished finger waved to Freda, "I'd say they weren't singing lies."

Blyana growled, her fury finally breaking through. Vara ignored her as she tucked a piece of shiny ebony hair behind her ear. Leaning in close, she whispered. "I can't imagine what that kind of guilt would do to a person." Her tongue clicked, and her red lips pursed. "I'm surprised the good people haven't drawn and quartered you yet."

"I think if they let filth like you still exist in their midst, they can stand my presence for a little longer," Isolde said with a wide sarcastic smile. She refused to let the pain in Vara's words show.

"On the contrary," the viper said, her lips turning up viciously. "My clientele has only grown. Not as many mouths to feed means extra coin for a few hours of pleasure. So, thank you for that. My little flowers are *exhausted*."

Bile rose in Isolde's throat. The ring warmed on her hand as ribbons of wind curled through her fingers, longing to drive down the bitch's throat.

"Although, we have been slightly understaffed," Madame Vara mused, her perfectly polished nails toying with the large ruby that hung at her neck. "One of my little flowers has gone missing. She never returned from Foxclove."

"Much to your dismay, I'm sure," Isolde smirked, feeling a flutter of joy. At least Cinta had escaped.

"Not at all." She waved her ring-clad hand in dismissal. "In fact, it has put me in a rather unique position with the new Lord of Foxclove."

"Gage?" Isolde said.

"Why, yes. She did, after all go missing on his watch, which leads me to believe there is foul play. You know how men can be. Their tastes are so unpredictable...so feral. I'm sure our sweet Blyana can tell you all about that."

Her wicked eyes cut past Isolde. Blyana remained still. Isolde could only imagine the nightmares revisiting her in vivid, horrific detail.

"Anyway, his purse continues to pay rather handsomely for her absence and my silence. Displeasing the cousin of the king is just as dangerous and displeasing the king himself."

"Hazards of the job?" Zibiah sneered.

"It can be I suppose, but it gives me the chance to offer employment to those who need it," Vara said, her head bobbing as she fixed her eyes on Blyana. "How about it, dear? Care to come back home? I know of a few patrons who would love to have you back."

Blyana's shoulders began to tremble, but she kept her lips tightly sealed. Madame Vara brushed a piece of hair from Blyana's face. "Perhaps not quite worth the price you once would have fetched, but still…"

A snarl ripped through Isolde's teeth as her hand flew through the air, knocking Vara's fingers away. She and Zibiah forced their way between Blyana and her former mistress. Isolde gripped the dagger at her side as Zibiah palmed her sword. A hiss leaked through the viper's teeth. Her eyes turned to slits and fangs descended as she clutched the now bruised hand to her stomach.

"She is not yours to torment anymore," Isolde rasped, her own teeth bared and eyes glowing. "That is my job now."

Vara hissed once more, but grinned. "Now you, Lady Isolde." The slits roving, stopping to assess every one of Isolde's assets. "You would be quite the prize. Not as slender as our Blyana here, but most men like that. A full body. They also like a little bit of spirit." Vara took a step closer, her voice dropping. "Someone with fire, someone who will…put up a fight."

Isolde chuckled, the sound dark and full of deadly promise. "Others have tried that before. I can't say your retention would benefit."

"There's a cure for that." Heat rose in Vara's gaze. "And I'd love to give it to you." Her lips curled to expose the deadly fangs. "As I've said before, you can work just as well on your stomach…as on your back."

Her eyes moved to Zibiah. "Most of my patrons have never seen a virya from beyond Arnoria's borders," she mused. "Let alone fucked one. I'm sure they would pay handsomely for the experience."

Vara's eyes fell to the sword at Zibiah's side. A dark chuckle ghosted from Vara's lips as she slowly pulled the blade free, the metal screeching. "Another spirited one...even better." Vara's gazed moved back to Isolde once more.

"Things are stirring in Arnoria. I would take great care about who you threaten." She retreated to the steps of her establishment. "When things get hard, remember Madame Vara's door is always open."

Chuckling once more, the snake slid back into her hole. Music and laughter bleeding out into the street as the door closed behind her.

"I can't wait to run that bitch through," Isolde growled, her hands trembling.

Without a word, Blyana turned and walked back down to the center of town. Isolde and Zibiah followed, not exchanging a word. By the time they rounded the corner, Blyana had disappeared into the trees, her horse was still tied to one of the posts.

Zibiah looked to Isolde, who shook her head. "There is a lot of history there. History that she hasn't shared, even with me." Isolde softly stroked Versa's neck. "This is the most I have seen you in a year, my friend."

"It's a shame catastrophe must strike before friends can visit each other." Zibiah's fingers twirled in Versa's mane. "And I'm afraid Briarhole might be next."

"What do you mean?"

"Volkran's temper is getting worse, believe it or not. He's harsher with the humans than usual."

"And?"

Zibiah sighed. Her eyes were watchful, almost assessing if Isolde could handle it.

"Spit it out, Zib," said Isolde.

"Volkran received a package from the king a few days ago. I stumbled upon him looking at it in his study. It contained pure, uncut elithrium."

"You're sure?"

"Absolutely," Zibiah said, her eyes flickering to her own impregnated blade, a parting gift from her father on her wedding day. "I remember my time in the mines of Helecdol. It is a sight one does not forget easily."

Isolde had never been to the elithrium mines that resided in the Helecdol Mountains, separating the kingdom of Arnoria and the wild, frozen lands of the north. But stories had circulated. Horrible tales of slaves who were sent deep underground to extract the element. A long time ago, it was once a slave camp, meant to be a final resting place for criminals.

"Ferden and Milt showed me a piece as well. Payment for them sending humans and Virya to the Elenarta. It's probably safe to assume Circe and Yvaine received some as well."

"Has Alaric received anything?" she asked.

"No. Not yet anyway. But this all has to be connected," Isolde said biting her thumbnail.

"What do you think it means?"

Isolde stopped, an edge of tension and concern having formed in her gut. "I'm not sure. Do you think you could get your hands on that elithrium?"

"He keeps it pretty well guarded," Zibiah said, a crease forming on her brow. "But it shouldn't be an issue. Why though?"

"I want it out of his hands," Isolde said. "That kind of weapon shouldn't be anywhere near someone like him."

CHAPTER 22

N ews of the children's disappearances spread through the territory.

As did many parents' fear of allowing the remaining children to come to Thornwood for story hour. Galaena, Nan, and Isolde assured them that it was safe. That no harm would come to their children.

Yet skepticism was their main response, along with false promises of thinking about coming. When the day arrived, not a single child graced Thornwood's door. Isolde sat at the window in her usual plush chair. The book she had chosen rested unopened on her lap. The silence was suffocating. It was quiet. Far too quiet.

Drops of rain danced over the stained-glass windows, each drop racing down the glass into the seal. *Perhaps it is the rain that keeps them.* She sighed heavily to herself, knowing the truth.

They're frightened of me. The thought stung her more than she thought it would. It hurt, to know her people didn't feel safe to be around her, as if she couldn't protect them if she needed to. Doubt wormed its way into her mind, causing the hurt to sting all the more.

The familiar, suffocating guilt wrapped itself around her neck and squeezed. *"Your fault, your fault!"* Freda's voice echoed in her mind as the pain morphed into a crushing weight. It pushed down on her chest, the pressure growing until she wished for death itself. *"Your fault!"*

"Ah, Isolde Cotheran," a familiar voice chimed, wrenching her from her thoughts. "Still beautiful as ever."

Gage sauntered forward, his thumbs digging into his belt. A fuming hatred hardly hidden beneath a mask of forced civility raged at her unannounced guest.

"You do know you are banned from Thornwood, right?" She knew it wouldn't stop him. Still, Isolde had hoped that formally banishing him from the territory would provide them an ounce of reprieve from his insufferable presence.

"Oh, Alaric can try. So can your aunt, Lady Cotheran," Gage said, in disdain. "But I have authority in all territories, Lady Isolde, not just Foxclove...and now Blackwater."

Shock mixed with a hint of horror blossomed across Isolde's face. *How in the hell...*

Gage chuckled. "I see you haven't heard the news. Lady Yvaine unfortunately finds herself unable to perform her duties as Lady of Blackwater for the moment."

"For the moment?" *So, the birdy bitch survived?*

Gage grinned. "She is in an unfit state to run a territory and has asked for my aid."

"By your own hand, I assume," Isolde said.

"Hardly. An unfortunate run-in with that bastard, Hood." His lip turned up into a sneer. "Forced her to lose control, and she transformed. They say a massive beast dragged her to the bottom of the sea. It's a miracle she survived at all. For now, she is recovering in Elenarta."

"Most unfortunate," Isolde mumbled, her thoughts of that night returning. She could still feel Yvaine's talons digging into her flesh. Isolde had assumed the horrid bitch had perished beneath the waves.

"Yes, indeed." Gage inspected a book on the nearby table only to toss it back into the pile with disinterest.

"To what do I owe this visit then?" Isolde asked as she rose, her words biting and not at all welcoming.

Gage smiled ruefully, the bronze skin of his cheeks stretching. "Do I need a reason to visit the citizens of my great kingdom, especially those whose beauty has no rival?"

Isolde gripped the book in her hands, needing anything to cling to besides Gage's throat. "You are wasting your flattery, Gage," she said, turning her back to him to return the book to the shelf. "Speak your piece then be gone."

"I come bearing an invitation to this year's Tournament of the Guard." His hand disappeared inside the lining of his lapel and extracted a black envelope with a single line of red down the middle. "Your whole house is invited, of course." He held the envelope out between them.

"Why would I want to go to Elenarta?" Isolde asked, pointedly ignoring the invitation. "I've seen it. Witnessed the games in all their glory. Why should I go again?"

"Because it is by my personal invitation." Gage said, his hand dropping to his side. "As good as any official order. You are expected to attend."

"I have far better things to do with my time," she said, slamming the book into place.

"Such as teaching filthy little rats to read?"

Isolde froze, her hand half raised to place the next book back on the top shelf. Fear chilled her veins. Had Mary or Tanor betrayed her? Forcing a sarcastic smile, Isolde turned and said, "What lies you tell, Gage."

"So, you deny children being in this room, sitting in those chairs, reading?" he asked as his hand swept over the empty library. "Seems pretty hard to deny." He took two casual steps forward.

Isolde turned back to jam the book into its rightful place. "Reading to human and half-blood children is not a crime, nor is having them in my house. Unless the king, in all of his infinite wisdom, has stripped that privilege as well."

She whipped around, another remark on her tongue but was stopped short. Gage stood so closely it forced her back against the shelf.

"I would be very careful with what I say about His Majesty, Isolde," he chided, coming closer. She pressed further into the bookshelf, the wood digging into her sore back. "He is not a forgiving man. Especially when one's loyalty is in question."

"My loyalty is where it has always been. With the people of Arnoria."

"How adorably noble of you," Gage said, his thumb and forefinger toying with a strand of hair that had escaped her braid. Isolde's mind raced back to the barn, and the same fear his touch invoked surged forward.

"There could be other rumors," Gage mused, his eyes rising to meet hers. "Rumors of far worse crimes than teaching worthless human and mutt spawn to read. Rumors that could reach the king's ear. Of course, if there was someone who could turn the king's gaze to someone else…that might be quite the benefit."

"How many times must you ask the same question only to have the same response?"

"You saw what your last response earned you," he said. "Or what it earned those children, I should say."

Isolde stilled, her hands slowly forming into claws. "You…you took those children?"

A lazy smile spread across Gage's face as he stared into her horror-struck eyes. "I did warn you that your actions affect more than just yourself, did I not?"

"Are they dead?" Isolde demanded. The words fell from her mouth before she could stop them. "Tell me right now, did you kill them?"

"Not yet," Gage said with a shrug. "But that can change very quickly."

"You…deplorable bastard."

Anger swept over Gage's face as his hand clamped around Isolde's jaw. Her skin stung with pain as pressure built around his fingertips. "You will mind your tongue, darling." Isolde fought back a cry, her fingers digging at Gage's hard, unforgiving grip. "I will not have my wife speaking to me in such a way."

"I will never be your wife," she spat, her jaw working around his grip.

"How many times must you learn the same lesson before you finally understand?"

"You can't force me to marry you!"

"Oh, but I can. Things are changing in Arnoria. You don't want to be on the wrong side once it is unleashed," he said forcing her chin up. "As my wife…I can protect you from that."

"I don't need or want your help," she snarled. Light from her eyes danced in Gage's. His teeth raked over his bottom lip.

"You have no idea what you need…but I'd be more than happy to show you."

"Fuck you," Isolde growled.

"What a filthy mouth you have, Lady Isolde," Gage said, wetting his lips, his eyes dropping to her mouth. "Let's find out what else you can do with it." He took a step forward. The darkness of his eyes grew wild with intent.

Fiery rage burned through Isolde as her fingers wrapped around the dagger she kept at her thigh. Flicking her wrist, she pulled the blade free and Gage halted. A mixture of outrage and terror etched into his face at the touch of her blade on his crotch.

"You bitch," he said, not daring to move a muscle.

"My, how quickly your tune changes," she said, shoving his hand away. "Isn't it rather pathetic you have to use children to force a woman into matrimony? If you had any real proof of my wrongdoing, I would be in elithrium chains heading to Elenarta by now. But alas," her wrist twisted slightly, "I see you came up short again, leaving everyone…unsatisfied." Gage's face began to redden as his eyes bore into her with such hatred Isolde felt a flicker of fear. From behind him a small figure shifted and something crashed to the floor.

Nan stood in the doorway. A tray, bearing their afternoon tea, had slid from her hands into the floor. "I'm so sorry for interrupting," she said. A puddle of steaming tea, shattered glass, and cookies littered the floor around her.

Gage snarled, his teeth bared at Nan as she slowly, painfully dropped to the floor. "Worthless human!" he roared. "Aren't you capable of doing anything right? Perhaps I should teach you a lesson." His hand moved to the whip that hung at his side.

Red flooded Isolde's vision as her power came forth in an uncontainable wave, obliterating her control. Grabbing Gage by the collar, she hurled him across the library. He crashed onto a table, snapping it in two. Before he could recover, Isolde was crouched over him, the blade pressed to his throat.

"I would think twice before threatening another member of my house again, Gage." Her lips pulled back into snarl. "You might lose more than you care to." Isolde's eyes darted to his crotch. "And if the rumors are true, I doubt there is much there to work with anyway." Hatred poured from him, the animalistic need to kill filling his gaze.

The sound of Nan cleaning brought her back to herself and Isolde moved away to stand in front of her. The blade was still held tightly in her shaking fingers. Standing up swiftly, Gage brushed the dust from his uniform. It was nearly identical to Liam's save for the thin red strip that ran from his right shoulder down to his hip.

"Be careful, Isolde." Gage turned back to the hallway. "You never know who will pay the price for your foolishness."

He walked past her. A faint light still shined from his eyes. "By the way…" he said, turning around. A small, evil grin was on his face. "Your attendance is expected at the tournament. I look forward to seeing you there." He walked out without another word, only a small strut.

Once the sound of his steps faded, Isolde bent down to lift the ruined the tea set. "Are you alright?" Nan asked, her hands gently probing Isolde's face. Lines of concern joined those that already resided on her brow as she saw the new bruises.

"I'm fine," said Isolde. "I'm fine." But truly, she was not. What trouble had she just caused?

"I worry, my rose," Nan said. "One day, he will not take no for an answer."

"But not today," Isolde said. "And that's not what's important right now. He took them, Nan."

Her hands stilled. The broken pieces of the fine, ruined tea set dangled in her hands. "The children?"

Isolde's teeth ground together. "Yes. Gage took them to punish me. Because I refused him."

The remaining piece of glass clattered from Nan's withered, sure hands. They shook, her own rage forming. "Where were they taken?"

"Elenarta."

"Isolde!" Liam crashed through the library doors. "Are you alright?" His eyes swept over the mess. "What happened to you?" He dropped to his knees, his callused hands moved gingerly over her still sore jaw.

"Gage did not take well to me calling him a deplorable bastard," Isolde said.

Surprise flickered through his deep brown eyes, but also an ounce of pride, "Why did you call him a deplorable bastard?"

"Besides the obvious?" She laughed.

"Your commander," Nan snapped. "He's the one who took those children, Liam."

The smile fell from his face only to be replaced with guilt, making every beautiful angle of his face harsher, less like Liam.

Isolde rose to her feet, her knees weak. The terror of what she was seeing solidified. "Did you know?" she asked, her voice hardly a whisper.

Liam looked between her and Nan, his head shaking. "I was only just told this morning," he said. "That's why I'm here. Gage kept it very hushed around me because of our friendship. He doesn't trust me when it comes to the affairs of Thornwood…or you." A hand pushed through his hair. "The only information he tells me are the plans he has for you after you two are married. Like he's rubbing it in my face."

Isolde pinched the bridge of her nose.

"I'm sorry," he said. "Had I known I—"

"Would you have helped him?" Isolde demanded, cutting him off. "Would you have helped load those children onto the carts bound for Elenarta?"

He rubbed his face. The black stubble had grown since the last time she saw him. *How tired he looked.*

"I don't know, Isolde. I wouldn't have had a choice; he is my commander."

"You always have a choice," she said, her tone lethal.

"I would have warned you," he said. "I would have given the Hood time to help."

"Well, there's something, I suppose."

"Which is why I'm here," Liam said his hands busy collecting the broken pieces of porcelain. She could see the strain, the burden on his shoulders.

"Spit it out then, Liam," Nan said, her anger still simmering.

"Nan," Isolde murmured. Nan bent down again and began cleaning the tray, her eyes still hard.

"Gage has heard of other people who have begun reading to the humans, other sympathizers, and he plans to act."

A breath caught in Isolde's throat. More children, more suffering. There was only one other place she knew of that was actively attempting such a thing. "Briarhole," she said.

He nodded, his dark curls fell over his eyes. "Briarhole."

"But Zibiah wouldn't risk that," Isolde said, her hands before her pleading. "She knows that Volkran would punish not only her but them as well."

"She must have taken the risk and gotten caught," Liam said. "By taking the children, Gage is not only punishing them, but he is hurting you too. She's your close friend, another weapon he can use against you. To force you to agree."

"You think he means to take her as well?" Isolde asked, her heart suddenly racing.

"Possibly. Volkran is cruel and unforgiving. He won't stand for his wife to blatantly disregard his command. Especially now that Lauram has been named his heir. He needs to show force, to show him how he thinks Briarhole should be run. No tolerance for human sympathizers, no disobedience."

You did this. You brought this on them all. She wanted to take off, to unleash the monster within, and fly to Briarhole. The lust for Volkran and Gage's blood was so palpable she could hardly stand it.

"When does Gage plan on doing this?" Isolde asked, her fear burying itself in the wall of hatred that kept her power in check.

"In two weeks…maybe sooner."

"And do you plan on being there?" she asked.

Liam's eyes met hers. "I am expected, yes."

"Good." The familiar throb of healing tickled at Isolde's jaw as she spoke.

"Good?" Liam said, his brow rising. "How is that good?"

"Because you are going to help them get out," Nan said. Isolde reached over and took the rest of the shattered tea set as Nan rose. A small grunt echoed from her lips, causing Liam to jump up and help her to her feet. Nan looked at him for a moment but eventually took his arm, her hand squeezing lightly.

"You are going to help the Hood," said Nan, her tone ringing with an authority Isolde knew Liam remembered well.

He swallowed, the conflict between duty and honor clearly raging in his eyes. "How am I going to do that?"

"We'll think of something," Isolde said. "Is there any reason for you to go to Briarhole right now?"

"Yes, Gage has a meeting with Volkran the day after tomorrow. I am due there that morning."

"Perfect," Isolde said, setting aside the heap of mangled glass to pull out a piece of fresh parchment. "Because I need for you to deliver a message."

CHAPTER 23

Volkran's crushing weight finally lifted off and Zibiah breathed a sigh of relief.

"Don't sound so satisfied," Volkran sneered, pulling on the velvet black robe strung across the back of the leather chair. "That wasn't for your pleasure. With your womb barren, you're worthless. Except for one thing."

The sting of his words had long since left her. The scars of each uttered phrase had hardened her heart against him. It amazed Zibiah to this day that she had ever held out hope of finding love at Briarhole. Hope that Volkran was not the monster rumors had claimed him to be. How wrong she had been. It was his doing, along with the king's, that she was barren. The time she had been forced to serve in the mines of Helecdol had destroyed her ability to ever pass on her bloodline. Starved, beaten, and worked to the brink of death, those mines had changed her.

Alas, Zibiah rose to sit at the side of the bed she visited only to perform her wifely duties and felt the hollow soreness echo through her body. She knew it had been the hope of a fool. Never had he shown her an ounce of kindness. A twinkling of love a husband should show his wife. Her slender, graceful finger traced the lines of the bruises that marred her arms.

The day before, she had done as Isolde had asked. Zibiah had gotten rid of the elithrium Volkran had received from the king. He had thought his hiding place was clever. But little did he know that she knew of every single one that existed on the property. Whether it was by Isolde and Malaki or her discoveries, Zibiah knew Briarhole like she did her own home.

How he had raged last night. A poor human boy, who happened to be walking down the hallway at the wrong time, would have taken the brunt of Volkran's anger if she had not stepped in. He had been angry. So, so angry. And she was always the main outlet for his terrifying temper. Whether it was with his fists…or by other means, Zibiah always paid the price. But it was one she was more than willing to pay. A small smile pulled at the corners of her lips as she thought of her husband's fury for the loss of his precious elithrium that now rested at the bottom of the Lenda River.

"I am meeting with Gage and his lap dog this morning," Volkran said, disappearing into the closet. The wooden door banged against the stone wall and the sound of ruffled clothes filled the hot, heavy air. "You are to find my elithrium, Zibiah. I do not want to see you again today unless you have it. Nor do I want my colleagues to be subjected to your embarrassing presence."

"Are you sure, my lord?" Zibiah asked, her eyes shooting to the doorway to the closet. "It is my duty to guard—"

"Do not question me!" he roared. "I do not need you constantly following behind me like a bitch in heat. Besides, if Gage wants a fight, he will not be the one to walk away."

"Very well, my lord," Zibiah said. The words fell from her mouth, as they always did-with subdued detachment. A hint of mocking anger hung in the air with the way she said, "my lord." Over the years, Zibiah had learned to play her part well. An obedient wife, filled with fear of her husband. That was what Volkran wanted. A beaten, submissive woman. But the fire that burned in Zibiah's soul was anything but fear.

A savage hatred, hidden behind a mask of submission, dwelled in every fiber of her being.

His dismissal caught her off guard. Never had he not wanted her, or her sword rather, by his side in a meeting with another lord. Those who came to power by spilling blood always feared to lose it by the same means. Volkran was no exception. Which made his behavior odd, suspiciously so.

There was nowhere she would rather be less than at his side. Still, there was clearly something that Volkran did not want her to know. Something that he did not trust her with. Especially after what happened at Foxclove and Thornwood, it was imperative she be there. Grabbing her own robe from one of the nearby chairs, Zibiah slipped her arms through. The silk felt wonderful against her skin. Reminding her of the waves of the Sea of Calca. Her home.

Pain bit into Zibiah's heart as she plucked Airendia from the corner. The pommel, lined with pearl and silver, felt warm to her touch as if it too recognized her. The glorious weapon never left her side. It had been a parting gift from her father. Given to her the night she wed and tied herself to the monster preparing himself in the other room.

"For you," her father had said, handing the beautiful blade over. His face, once so warm and unrestrained with happiness, was cast in shadow. He too had been forced to serve in the mines. A punishment for standing with the Viributhians. Perhaps the sword had been an apology. A penance for what his daughter was about to endure. Either way, his warm hands closed around hers that held the glorious piece of work out before her.

The handle shined against the white of a wedding dress that was far too big for her emaciated body. A beautiful glow that not even the elithrium could outdo. It fit her hand perfectly. Pulling the blade free from the scabbard that was covered in waves of metal, Zibiah ran her eyes over the blade. Along the rivers of living metal, whoever had forged this sword, had inscribed a message. A message her mother had repeated countless times.

Love knows no depth.

"It's beautiful, Papa," Zibiah had said as her fingers grazed the words. The sound of her mother's voice, light and full of love, filled her head. "Love knows no depth, my sweet girl." Zibiah's heart was both full and broken. "I shall name her…Airendia. The heart of the sea."

"A fitting name." Zibiah's father looked at the sword, his golden eyes, her eyes, swimming. "I'm so sorry, my child."

"It must be done, Papa" Zibiah had said, pushing the blade back into the scabbard. "If this is what our people need, for some form of freedom, then I won't fight them."

"You could kill him, minnow." The sound of her father's voice was so hollow. Laced with a hatred she had not thought him capable of.

"No," Zibiah had said looking to the doors that led to a future she was terrified to enter into. "Only our kingdom would suffer. And our people have been through enough. If this is the price, it is one I am more than willing to pay."

She could still feel his arms as they wrapped around her shoulders. Zibiah felt a shudder roll through his body. "My little girl," her father, the ruler of the depths had said, forcing himself to meet her gaze. "I love you." His golden stare was full of pride and love. But also, something else. Respect. "For our queen," he whispered. "For Arnoria."

Zibiah sighed heavily and walked to the door. "Do not let me catch you down with those filthy creatures again," Volkran barked from the closet. "It's shameful for my wife to spend so much time with humans."

"As you wish, my lord." Zibiah ground her teeth as her hand closed around the handle of the door and pulled. Desperate to wash the smell of Volkran from her skin, she made for her own chambers just down the hallway. The sound of footsteps caught her attention as she reached her door. The pit in her stomach soured as Lauram rounded the corner, coming from the direction of his own quarters.

A knowing smirk played on his annoying face as he looked her up and down. "Performing your wifely duties, Zibiah?" Lauram asked. "I do hope you put him in a good mood."

"Lauram," Zibiah said, her lips curling with disdain. "He is preparing for your meeting with Lord Gage in the library."

Lauram stopped at her door, the light from the morning sun danced across the curls of his unkempt, red hair. "And he did not request your presence there as well? Highly unusual for him. Normally he likes to show off his prized wife and guardian."

"He wishes for me not to attend."

A dark chuckle ghosted over Lauram's lips. "My lord really is a bastard for keeping you all to himself, isn't he?"

Zibiah's gaze shot to Lauram, her lips thinning. "Awfully brave of you to speak of your benefactor in such a manner, Lauram. Or very foolish."

A wicked smile pulled at the corners of his lips. "Volkran is nearly three hundred and fifty years old. We are not immortal, Zibiah. No matter how much we wish it. It won't be long before I am the lord of Briarhole...And where will that leave you?" His forefinger and thumb pinched one of her braids. The tiny golden trinket clinked together as he tugged. "Where, oh where...I wonder."

He gave her braid one final tug before sauntering off down the hallway. Once the sound of his retreating footsteps died away, Zibiah took a deep breath. Shoving all thoughts of Lauram seizing power out of mind, she stole into her rooms. Closing the door and clicking the lock into place, she leaned back and let herself melt into the sturdy wood.

The same nauseated hatred she felt every time she walked into her chambers, rolled in Zibiah's belly. Volkran would have left her a cot to sleep on if he had had his way. But rumors would spread of his wife living in such conditions. So, he saw fit to lavish her apartments with every comfort imaginable. A massive bed rested to the right, covered in pelts of fur from animals Volkran had killed himself. Ones he had forced her to watch him kill in cruel, vicious ways. A large wardrobe sat near the window. It was crammed with pieces that left very little to the imagination. All hand-picked by her husband. Other bits of useless furniture were scattered about the room, making it feel like a glorified prison.

After scrubbing her skin rare, in the bathroom that was the size of a small house, making sure to erase every bit of Volkran, Zibiah threw on the most practical dress she had in her possession.

A soft, cotton piece the color of midnight that gently hugged around her curves. The loose fabric allowed her to move, to fight, to run if the occasion called for it. She cast a mournful look at the hidden compartment where her hood and cloak resided within the confines of her wardrobe.

Fastening her braids with a strip of leather to the back of her head, Zibiah plucked Airendia from the bed and strapped it around her waist. If things went badly today, there would be no other choice but to fight her way out. If she was caught, everything would be undone.

The halls of Briarhole were filled with a tension that seemed to hang in the air. It covered Zibiah's skin like a film, causing her heart to race. The servants, virya, human, and half-blood alike, all kept their eyes down. She assumed it had something to do with Gage's presence. Any time he was at the manor, a shadow of dread seemed to follow him like stench upon a corpse.

With her hand resting on the pommel of her sword, she took the stairs up to the tower that led to the library. As she rounded the corner, intending to use the secret passage by means of the broom closet, Zibiah stopped dead in her tracks. A pair of guards lingered by the doors. Their armor was shining in the light of the early morning sun. Swords hung at the sides while elithrium laced spears rested in their grasp.

"The library is occupied at the moment I'm afraid, my lady," one of them said. His voice was gentle and one she recognized.

Ceron. He was one of the few men in her husband's service who still possessed a heart. Not once had she seen him strike a human or half-blood. Never had he shown any cruelty.

"I apologize, Ceron," said Zibiah, taking a casual step forward. She clasped her hands in front her, a gesture of submission, of meekness that had been beaten into her at Helecdol. "I merely wanted to ensure my lord made it to the meeting intact."

A kind, knowing smile formed on Ceron's face. "He is well, my lady. Thank you for coming to check for yourself."

"He is lucky to have someone so concerned for his well-being." The guard to Ceron's left bowed his head to her. His voice was a deep baritone. One that sent a thrill shooting through Zibiah. Comforting and warm, almost like slipping into a hot bath at the end of the day.

"I don't believe I have had the pleasure of making your acquaintance," Zibiah said, keeping her voice low. The last thing she wanted was for Volkran to overhear her.

"Apologies, my lady," said the guard, bowing once more. "My name is Eryx. I'm new to Briarhole. A recent recruit from Elenarta." Zibiah's back stiffened, that thrill instantly dying away. If he was from Elenarta, he was the king's soldier. Someone to not be trusted.

A knowing, sad smile pulled at Eryx's lips, as if reading her thoughts. "The capital is not my homeland, my lady."

"And where exactly is that?" she asked, trying to hide the tightness in her voice.

"Endurmure."

The name hung in the air like a mist at dawn. It was one Zibiah had not heard in a long time. "The Forgotten Lands?" She could see it now. Beautiful, flawless caramel colored skin covered his face and neck. His shoulders were broad, making the armor that clung to his form appear even larger. Dark locks of ebony fell about his shoulders like curtains of purest night. And his eyes...she had seen them somewhere before...They were black as obsidian stone.

"Indeed," Eryx said, a full smile now forming, as if the name of his home brought him joy. "Not so forgotten, I suppose."

A smile spread across Zibiah's face. "I suppose not."

Ceron looked nervously between her and Eryx, then back to the doors behind him. "The library should be vacant soon, my lady." Zibiah knew what he was implying. Ceron had laid witness to Volkran's treatment of her on more than one occasion. A blush of red that covered his pale cheeks told her he remembered. "If you wish to wait downstairs, we will be happy to escort you—"

"That's not necessary," she said already taking a step back. "I wouldn't want my husband displeased with you for leaving your posts. A pleasure making your acquaintance, Eryx."

"The honor is mine, Lady Volkran." He bowed again, this time bending at the hip.

Zibiah offered him a single nod and Ceron a smile. Turning to leave, the smile fell from her face. She took the stairs at a calm, normal pace. Once reaching the landing, Zibiah took off into a sprint. She looked down at her dress as she ran, thankful for having worn a darker shade. There was one other avenue into the library.

Slipping into one of the many unoccupied chambers within Briarhole, Zibiah shoved the window open and glanced around. Thirty feet above her head, stood the balcony to the library. All she had to do was reach the landing. She looked to the ground below until she found what she was looking for. A trough of water pushed up against the side of the tower winked up at her.

Zibiah took a deep breath and calmed her mind. A wave of familiar power slammed into her with a force she had grown accustomed to. A sea of strength that flowed like the waves of the Sea of Calca moved through her body with ease. "Be mindful," her father had said. "You are in control. Do not allow your power let you think otherwise."

Reaching out into the air, Zibiah called to the water. She felt every drop as it lifted from the trough soar through the air to her open palm. The rush of the cool, silken water felt like glorious victory. She opened her eyes and smiled. A ball of murky water rested in her palm, waiting for her orders. A picture formed in her mind. The ball broke away into tiny pieces and flattened into platforms. Zibiah pushed her will out, forcing them away and up the wall.

Each one followed her command. They formed a path that hugged the stone wall, leading up to the balcony. An ounce of exhaustion flittered through Zibiah's muscles as she stepped over the lip of the window sill and placed a tentative foot on the first patch of levitating water. A flicker of fear entered her mind as the will of her power faltered. She felt the surface begin to break and shift beneath her.

"You must trust your power," her father had reminded her. At the time, she held the weight of the ocean itself above her head. Sweat poured down her face as she forced the water away from her, creating a sphere of air. "It is your control to keep and to give away."

Zibiah let the confidence in her father's voice fill her. Steeling her resolve, she shoved her power into the steps and began to climb. Each flattened, watery surface was unwavering. She had nearly reached the landing when she spotted the tips of two spears jutting out above the railing of the balcony. Freezing mid-step, Zibiah realized with exhausted irritation that Volkran had placed guards around the entire library.

Looking to the pale, blue sky above, Zibiah saw the outline of a chimney. A smile formed on her lips as she pulled the remaining disks down and around the side of the tower. Being careful to stay out of the soldiers' line of sight, she made her way to the opposite side. The courtyard below was busy with the usual business of Briarhole. But none looked her way. Very few dared look up for fear of catching the wrong person's eye.

Once on the other side, Zibiah forced the water up. Every step grew heavier than the last. The soles of her shoes began to slowly sink into the floating puddles. She could feel the cold, invasive tendrils of panic begin to creep around the corners of her mind. Only ten more steps remained, but Zibiah knew it wouldn't be enough.

Without thinking, she took off into a sprint. With every step, Zibiah forced herself not to think, to not heed the exhaustion that was pouring from her lips in bucketfulls. As she reached the last step, her power gave way and she jumped.

The tips of her fingers caught the edge of a tile that lined the roof. The water fell to the ground below. Shouts of anger filled the manor's courtyard. Without waiting, Zibiah pulled herself up. Every muscle twitched in pain and overuse. She lay on her back, her chest heaving. It had been too long since she had used power in that manner. On land, she relied on her sheer strength and agility. If she was still in the depths of Calca, this little adventure would have been nothing. Tricks a child would know. Living on land had made her soft.

Taking a deep breath, Zibiah tiptoed to the chimney that was, by the damned gods' mercy, smokeless. Voices echoed from below but nothing she could make out clearly. Pulling _____ around to her front, Zibiah climbed over the lip and dropped down into the abyss.

Soot covered her hands instantly as she braced them against the wall. The air was heavy with ash and smoke, making it hard to breath. The bottom of her shoes braced against the sides, allowing her to slowly move down at a reasonably safe pace. Zibiah couldn't help but think of Isolde and wonder if she had snuck into a place in this manner as the Hood. It wouldn't have shocked her. In fact, Zibiah wouldn't have been surprised if her dear friend had not made her entrance in such a way, at some point in time.

Just as she reached the lip of the fireplace, Gage's voice rang out with absolute clarity.

"His Majesty knows of Foxclove," Gage growled. "And believe me, he will not take kindly to being disobeyed by the Lord of Briarhole lightly. As for Isolde…let's just say he approves of me getting between her legs, Volkran."

A soot filled breath caught in Zibiah's lungs. *The king approves of Gage and Isolde's union?* Fear spiked in her blood. The king had approved, demanded even of her marriage to Volkran. She couldn't let that happen to Isolde. The pad of her palms pressed into the chimney's belly.

"So, I ask you again," said Gage, pulling Zibiah back into the moment. "Is that the response you wish me to take back to Elenarta?"

The room fell silent as they waited for the lord of Briarhole's response. "Not at all," Volkran said at last relinquishing with a growl. "What of the humans and half-bloods?"

"Do you honestly care?"

"They were an expensive investment," said Lauram, his voice not holding even an ounce of the smug confidence it had in the hallway.

"For which you will be handsomely compensated," Liam assured him. Zibiah reeled at the sound. It was so unlike him. Zibiah had her reservations about Liam as much as the rest of the cadre. But one facet that stood her apart was that she tried to love him. Tried...because of what he meant to Isolde. He was a light in a world that had only shown her darkness.

If Isolde could love Liam despite his choice in joining the king, then any of them could.

The sound of someone snapping their fingers ricocheted up the chimney. The door to the library opened and echoes of shuffling feet filled the air. The smell of body odor and blood filled Zibiah's nose. *Humans.*

Their pants of exhaustion ceased as they set something heavy down right at the mouth of the cold fireplace, not three feet from Zibiah. Free of their burden, the poor souls hastened from the room.

A faint glow bloomed along the ashes beneath Zibiah feet. A hollow horror filled her shaking limbs. She found herself begging the gods to not let it be what she thought it was. But her prayers went unanswered as the lid was thrown open.

A mound of raw elithirum shone from within the depths. Zibiah had to fight to keep her hands from balling into fists, to stay absolutely still as Gage sauntered forward. "We will take all of your humans," he said. "They are to be used in the mines."

Old fear, potent and unstoppable, clogged at the back of Zibiah's throat. Memories of her time in the horrible mines of Helecdol slammed into her like a hurricane. The cries for mercy, the pain, the darkness…it all came back to her in one massive, unstoppable merciless wave.

"The mines," Volkran murmured, as if lost in a trance.

"Yes, the mines," Gage said slamming the lid shut. Zibiah felt relief instantly.

"Seems like His Majesty is overpaying," said Volkran. She had to agree. This kind of gift had the ability to destroy any virya force.

"Can't the king be generous?" Gage asked.

A dark chuckle ghosted through the room, a sound that sent a chill down Zibiah's aching spine. "He wouldn't be king if he was. What else does he require?"

"Your cooperation," said Liam. A twinge of sorrow pierced Zibiah's heart at the sound of his voice. He sounded…like one of them. "He requests you send virya to Elenarta. Powerful ones of your choosing."

"I can send you five changelings, all predators. And water yielders."

"Ten," Gage countered. "Of each."

"Each!" Volkran said. The sound of fists hitting the wooden table shot through the room. "I need my people to work Briarhole, Gage! To make money and goods for his majesty. No workers mean no profit."

"Fine," Gage said at last. "Nine of each."

"Six."

"Eight," said Gage.

Volkran roared, his voice echoing like a thundering boom. "Seven!"

"Eight, it is then," Gage beamed. His hands clapped together, sealing the deal. "And with His Majesty's thanks."

Sweat had begun to form on Zibiah's brow. Every muscle ached as she forced her feet to press harder into the wall, taking the burden from her hands. Careful to not make a sound, she squeezed her hands into fists then stretched her fingers out, sending a dull ache up her arms.

A growl rippled through the room, Volkran's way of begrudgingly agreeing. Lauram remained silent.

"Surely, that isn't all the king wants," Volkran said. "That amount of elithrium could buy all of Briarhole twice over. What else does he require?"

Gage paused for moment as if in thought. "Nothing you wouldn't be too upset to part with, I'm sure."

The room grew silent. Tension spilled into the air like vapor. *What else could the king possibly want?*

"We will be back in two weeks to retrieve our purchase," Gage said, the sound of his retreating footsteps sent a wave of relief through Zibiah. "Oh, and do be careful if you decide to play with the elithrium, Lauram. It has a nasty bite." The scrapping of chairs over the stone floor hardly covered the growl that ripped from Lauram's throat.

The door swung open and Volkran's voice pierced the space once more. "Make yourselves useful and carry that to the armory."

Ceron and Eryx answered in unison. "Yes, my lord."

The plates of their armor caught the hue of elithrium as they lifted the chest. When the final footstep faded into the hallway, Zibiah breathed a sigh of relief. Pressing her hands once more to the sides of the chimney, she slowly lowered one foot at a time down into the pile of ashes waiting at the bottom.

Careful to hold her breath, Zibiah ducked underneath the lip of the chimney and stepped out into the library. She pulled her filthy shoes free to stand on a clean spot on the hearth and looked to the door. Not a soul stood guard now. But she couldn't simply walk out. No, she needed to wait. After placing her soiled shoes back into the ashes, Zibiah walked the length of the library as her mind raced through what she had heard.

Isolde had told her of Gage's intentions. Of his sadistic attempts at forcing her into marriage. But did she know the king had given his stamp of approval? She highly doubted it. Isolde nor Malaki wouldn't have let Gage live long enough for that nightmare to become a reality.

Zibiah bit her thumbnail as she paced. How she wished Isolde were there. She needed to know! A ray of sunlight caught her eye, stopping her mindless wondering. The sun was nearly overhead, causing the tips of the trees that made Blackford shine like the sea. *Was she out there masquerading as the Hood again? Where the others with her?* Anxiety, the kind that only rose where Isolde was concerned poisoned her blood.

It was not the life she would have chosen for her friend. Far from it. The subject of her giving up this life as an outlaw and becoming something far greater had not been broached in decades. Not since their friendship had nearly been shattered into unrepairable pieces. Isolde had made Zibiah promise. Swearing on their friendship itself, their very lives to never bring up the topic again.

Zibiah shook her head at the memory. At the anger in Isolde's impossibly beautiful emerald silver eyes. "Swear it, Zibiah," Isolde had said, tears of fury and chaos swimming in her eyes. "Never mention it again."

Zibiah had bowed her head, her eyes falling to the ground as the weight of Isolde's words and the power they held, descended upon her very soul. "I swear it, my dearest friend. But only if you make one to me in return."

"What is it?"

Zibiah stood to fullest height. "Promise you will never ask me questions about my marriage to Volkran. Or how it came to pass."

Isolde had looked dumbfounded, completely at a loss for words at her request. "Why would you—"

"Do not ask me to explain," Zibiah had said, fighting her own anger. "It was my choice. That is all you need to know." It had been her choice. That wasn't a lie. But it also wasn't the whole truth either. The king had forced her father to give her over to Volkran. A piece of his heart that could be held over him, a way of forcing the king from under the sea to comply. No one could know. Not even Isolde. For if her best friend knew that her imprisonment was not by choice…there would be no stopping the tidal wave of blood Isolde would unleash on Briarhole in order to save her.

No, Zibiah had walked willingly into the life she now led. With sword in hand, she married Volkran and became the Lady of Briarhole. But little did her husband or the king know, that she was feeding her father information about the kingdom. Every opportunity fate afforded her, Zibiah would slip down to the river with glass bottles in hand. There was always a silme seal or two lurking near the docks. Always on standby in case she needed to send a message. The creatures were small, no bigger than an infant and pale as moonlight. Travelling only under the cover of darkness, they would carry her messages the length of the Lenda River and out into the open sea.

Dusting her backside, Zibiah took a seat by the window. Mindful of staying behind the current, she pulled a book into her lap. The edges of the pages tickled her fingers as they ran along the edges.

The sun had risen to mid-day. Rays of light danced over the pine woods of the forest. If Zibiah tried hard enough, she could almost pretend it was the Sea of Calca. How she longed to be there; to feel the salt on her skin, the water running through her hair…to see her father and brother.

The pain in her heart only grew, the homesickness practically squeezing her heart so tight she knew it would burst. Licking her lips, Zibiah turned to the only solace she had been given. Books. This one was a personal favorite. A fantasy with an undertone of romance that tugged at her heart strings. Leaning back into the comforting nook, Zibiah lost herself in a world that was not her own.

Lost in the words that spilled from the page, she wasn't sure how much time had passed when the sound of someone clearing their throat cut through the haze of her imagination. Her hand immediately fell to the pommel of her sword, her heart racing. A figure stood near the door, his handsome face smiling sheepishly.

"You two really are two peas in a pod," Liam said, taking a cautious step forward. "Nose always stuck in a book."

A sigh of irritation pushed through Zibiah tight lips as her hand fell from Airendia's handle. "You really shouldn't sneak up on me like that, Liam. Did Gage give you the day off from his insufferable presence?"

"Not entirely," Liam scowled. "I have something for you." Reaching into the lining of his leather jacket, Liam pulled out a single envelope. Zibiah set the book down and walked over to him to pluck the letter from between his gloved fingers.

"She recognized the handwriting instantly. "Isolde?" Her eyes flew over the words, her panic risking with each pass.

Once finished, Zibiah looked up to Liam. He was standing by the bookshelves his eyes lost in thought…or memory. "She is coming here?"

He nodded, stray strands of black curls falling into his eyes. "In two weeks. Gage is taking all the humans, half-bloods, the children, some virya, and…you in a two weeks' time."

"Why me?"

Shock wrecked through Zibiah, causing her to go absolutely still. She stared at Liam, her golden eyes widening. "For many reasons," he said. "You're a known human sympathizer, who reads to the children—"

"That was one time!" she said, her voice rising.

"Shh!" Liam hissed. "All it takes is one time to be labeled a traitor. You know that." Hatred filled Zibiah's mind. The muscle in her cheek rippled with anger. "And there is another reason."

"Which is?" she asked.

"It will force Isolde's hand."

Zibiah stilled, her eyes searching his. "Isolde?"

"Yes," he said. "Gage believes if he uses you as leverage, he can force Isolde into marriage."

The gold flared in Zibiah's eyes as fury rolled off her in waves. The protective kind that sent her nostrils flaring and teeth bared. "And she would do it, wouldn't she?"

Liam sighed, his eyes looking away, out the window. "Without a second thought."

Zibiah closed her eyes, forcing herself to breath in through her nose and out her mouth to calm herself. To control the terrifying power lurking beneath her skin. "Two weeks then?"

Liam nodded.

"Where do they intend to take us?"

Liam braced his hands on his hips. Rays of the morning sun reflected off the black leather of his uniform. "Elenarta and the mines of Helecdol."

Zibiah could feel the blood drain from her face. Her skin paled as dread doused her burning fury. She remembered the mines and the capitol and the horrors that awaited them. "Why the virya? Surely they wouldn't put them into the mines."

"I don't know. It's possible. Gage just informed me they've found a few places in the mountains that is riddled with elithrium. They might need more hands."

Phantom pains bit into Zibiah's stomach. Memories of her time under the mountains, lost in the dark threatened to overtake her. A brush of her power pushed against her mind. A soothing wave that kept the panic at bay. Zibiah ground her teeth and forced herself to stand taller.

"What does Isolde need me to do?" Zibiah asked, her resolve found at last. The resolve that might give her a fighting chance.

Liam placed a comforting hand on her shoulder. The hint of a confident, warm smile shined in his eyes. It was a look that fought her fear and gave Zibiah something she had not felt in a long time. Hope.

"Be ready."

CHAPTER 24

Voices refracted off the high rock walls of the hideout.

"I shouldn't be here," Liam murmured. He glanced around nervously. A strap of leather, securing a package of guard uniforms, twirled between his fingers. Eyes returned his gaze, eyes of hatred and distrust.

"Perhaps coming in your uniform wasn't the best of choices," Isolde said, her lip curling at the black jacket and pants.

"A change of attire isn't going to make things any better, Isolde."

A smile quickly replaced the look of distaste. "Probably not." She chuckled, pressing her lips to his neck.

Galaena and Alaric rested by the massive fireplace that had been carved from the wall by Malaki's magic. The simmering strands of gray in their hair seemed to glow in the fire, highlighting their vulnerability and increasing fragility.

Blyana lounged upon one of the boulders. Her arm dangled over the ledge as she looked down on them. Cillian leaned against the wall below her. His feet rested on a small table as a knife danced from one finger to the next.

Malaki was who she looked to now. His arms were crossed as he leaned against the wall near the entrance. Beams of moonlight crept around the corner, hiding him in shadow. She couldn't help but feel safe, secure in knowing he was there.

Delicious smells filled the air as Nan pulled a massive pot from deep within the fireplace's belly. Her eyes were down, but Isolde knew she was listening. Isolde pulled her quiver between her knees and plucked an arrow free.

"Briarhole," Alaric finally said. His eyes remained forward, lost in the flames.

Isolde nodded. The arrow danced in her fingers, her muscles smiling at its touch. "In a week and a half."

He sighed, his eyes closing slightly.

"That doesn't really give us much time," Cillian said, his jaw tightening.

"I apologize if the timing isn't convenient for you," Isolde retorted. "I'll be sure to tell Gage he needs to clear it with your schedule next time."

Cillian held his hands up in surrender, "I only meant—"

She shook her head. "I know what you meant," Isolde said, running a hand through her hair. "It isn't much time."

"It's a two-day trip one way," her aunt said. Her honey braid fell over her broad shoulder as her eyes swept to Liam, who remained as far from the group as possible.

"Not if we travel through the night." Isolde could already feel the exhaustion creeping into her bones.

"We'll need rest," Blyana said. "Especially if we're taking on something like Briarhole."

"Fine." Isolde sighed. "Then we'll leave a little earlier and take the night before to recuperate."

"And a two-day trip to the nearest crossing for the river outposts," Malaki said. "They will need warning."

"Already taken care of," said Isolde.

"When did you—"

"The moment after Liam told us, I had Fane fly a message to the outposts." The hawk rested near the opening of the ceiling, his large amber eyes sweeping the room.

Malaki looked to Liam, who held his stare. "Is that so?"

"It got to the right people, Malaki," Nan said over her shoulder, her hands still busy kneading dough.

"They have stationed patrols along every possible spot near Briarhole," Isolde continued. "Wherever we decide to meet, they will be there."

Malaki's muscles bunched and flexed beneath the lining of his thin, worn shirt. He still wasn't content. His eyes slid back to Isolde as a sigh heaved from his chest.

"What?" Isolde demanded, her hands now resting on her hips.

"This isn't Foxclove," Malaki said, teeth on edge. "This isn't Dagan, an unchallenged, weak lord you will face. This is Briarhole, the Wall of the North. The most well-armed and guarded territory in Arnoria." He stared at her as if willing her to understand. "And it is Volkran."

"I am well aware of that." Her temper roared to life.

"This isn't going to be like any mission we have ever done. The heist will seem like a cake walk compared to this."

"I do wish you would come to the point, Malaki."

His face flushed as his hands curled into fists. "Is it even possible?"

"You act as if it matters, like we even have a choice," she bit back. "This is Zibiah, Malaki!"

"I know."

"She is one of us!"

"I wasn't implying that we not go, Isolde."

"Yes, you were!" Anger and power surged through her blood, her eyes glowing in warning. They stared at each other, a heat rising in the room that was not of the fire's doing. A deep rumble vibrated through the air, hitting Isolde in the chest.

"You can't save everyone," Malaki said, a fraction of light igniting in his eyes. His voice was like grated steel.

"I can damn well try," she growled back. Her own power leapt forward to challenge his.

Malaki balked slightly, his eyes dropping for only a fraction of a second. Alaric moved his body in front of Galaena, ready to shield her if necessary. Cillian's feet were on the floor, and his eyes looked up to Blyana, who was now crouching on the ledge, her eyes wide and dilated.

Liam stepped forward, a faint light igniting in his eyes.

"She wouldn't abandon us," Isolde continued. "We are not leaving her or the others to be turned over into the king's hands."

The mention of the king seemed to rouse Malaki, jerking him back into his right mind. He breathed deeply, his eyes never leaving her but she could see the power recede as the warm, familiar hazel returned.

"What do you have in mind?" Alaric said, easing back down, a hand still on Galaena's thigh.

Isolde tore her attention from Malaki and looked to Liam. He swallowed once and squared his jaw before turning to the others. "Gage will be there," he said. "Along with at least a hundred of the king's hand-picked guards."

No one spoke. Only the crackling of the fire and the sound of Nan's work invaded the night air. Liam looked to Isolde, whose eyes smiled in encouragement.

"They are to accompany the caravan," he continued, "and make sure the exchange goes smoothly. From what I have been told, he will bring those who can transform for considerable periods of time."

"And we are to just trust you?" Blyana asked, her bell-like voice cutting through the air.

Liam turned toward her. His jaw, which held a five o'clock shadow, was set as he nodded. "That is the information I have to offer."

"What an offering," Blyana said, her catlike eyes widening.

"His word is good, Bly," said Isolde. A wave of pity swept through her. "He is one of us."

Alaric straightened in his chair, his eyes cold as ice. "He might have been…at one point in time." Galaena's hand fell to his shoulder, her eyes hard with disapproval.

"I have never betrayed you, Alaric," Liam said, taking a step closer to where the Lord of Thornwood lounged. "I would never betray you."

Malaki shoved off the wall, his arms unfolding to hang at his sides like two mountains of iron. "And what do you call willingly joining with the enemy?" A humorless grin pulled at his lips. "Face it, Liam," Malaki said, his eyes running up and down his uniform. "You're one of them now."

A growl ripped from Liam's throat, his eyes glowing in fury. "I volunteered so he," his finger jabbing at Alaric, "wouldn't have to make that choice! To save him the heartache of sending another one of his people into the slaughter."

"And look at you now," Malaki said, his arms still relaxed at his side. "Look at what your sacrifice has mounted to. A captain of the guard…for that murderous coward."

"Enough of this," Isolde said moving between them. They stared over her in hatred. Liam's teeth were bared as Malaki grinned, the thorns and vines covering his skin swayed as his muscles tensed.

"Stand down!" They ignored her, the lights in their eyes surging forward.

A clash of metal and glass erupted from off to the side. "You heard her!" Nan said, her voice ringing. Fire blazed from her eyes as her weak hands shoved against Malaki's chest. "You know who orders you, Malaki." Her voice was so low, so fierce, the man before her dropped his gaze, his eyes softening.

He bowed his head to Nan who nodded once. She then turned her fury on Liam. "You might be a captain of the guard Liam, but you will heed Isolde's orders if you wish to stay."

Her voice had softened. A flicker of kindness had worked its way back into her gaze as Liam bowed. "My apologies, Nan." Her warm, withered hand cupped his cheek before turning back to her work.

Isolde shot Nan a thankful glance.

"Well," Blyana chimed in, her legs swinging above their heads. "Seems to me the most logical course of action would be a distraction." Her eyes still held a coldness, a look of distrust Isolde knew would never thaw.

Isolde nodded. "A damn good one."

"Will they bring wielders, Liam?" Cillian asked, leaning forward with his elbows on his knees.

"Gage did not mention them but I doubt it. They want muscle, intimidation. Still, it's something we need to be prepared for."

"How many bodies are we thinking?" Malaki asked.

"At least fifty in total." His fingers drummed against his thigh. "The virya from Briarhole might still hold loyalties to Volkran but I'm sure it will dwindle when they learn they have been sold to the king."

"Children too, I assume," Galaena said, her mouth set with disdain.

"Unfortunately, yes," Liam answered. A look of sadness ghosted into his dark eyes. "Gage would not pass up the opportunity to take them to force Isolde's hand."

A low growl vibrated through Galaena's chest as she turned back to the fire, her teeth grinding.

"One advantage is the proximity to the river," Blyana said. "If we can get them on the river, Gal, you could use the water to push the boats?"

"If there aren't water wielders in their company, it might work. Not that they would stand a chance against her," Cillian said. A crooked grin broke across his face.

Galaena winked, her lips pulling up into a cocky smile.

"Could you use the water as a distraction?" Isolde asked.

"Depends," her aunt said, her eyes thoughtful. "If I had the help of someone else—" her gaze turned to Alaric, "then we could put on quite a show."

Alaric bristled, his lips pulling into a tight line. "I'm way out of practice."

"Good thing you have a week and a half then," Cillian said, his knife dancing between his fingers. "I'm sure it's tough getting back into shape...especially for someone of advanced years such as yourself."

"I could start with drowning you," Alaric snarled.

"I'm pretty fast, old man. Think you could keep up?"

Alaric's eyes shone with anger but Gal simply smiled. "I wouldn't push him, Cillian," she said, her fingers running over her husband's shoulder, "He was the most powerful water wielder in the kingdom once upon a time."

Cillian's smile only grew, the blade dancing between his fingers. "Oh, the good ole days."

Alaric growled, his teeth growing sharp.

"Wait," Isolde said, holding up her hand. "What about your decision? Won't using your power make you start over?"

"It will hinder us some," Galaena admitted, her fingers trailing through Alaric's hair. "But not enough to truly matter. A few years perhaps. No, it would take us using the full force of our power to revert back."

Alaric nodded, his hand resting on Galaena's thigh. "We would need to transform."

"Would that be so bad?" Cillian asked. "I mean you are looking rather wrinkly, Alaric."

Isolde shot Cillian a warning glance. "Do you think you can do it?" she asked.

"Probably," said Alaric, drawing his eyes away from Cillian. "You will need to aid in the getaway, wind wielder."

Isolde nodded, a small knot forming in her stomach. *You don't have a choice. If they can do it, so can you.* Still, the thought of pulling any part of her power sent a chill down her spine. A force in and of itself sent a wave of unease over her muscles.

"It might not be a bad idea to have another distraction," Galaena said, her eyes still on Alaric. "One that doesn't require us using all of our powers."

A flicker of shame swept over Alaric's face. Isolde nodded. After being out of the game for so many years, she knew they needed to conserve their energy. "Right. Cillian, Liam…think you can come up with something?"

Liam cast a nervous glance behind him. Cillian looked him up and down in appraisal before a wide, mischievous grin spread across his face. "We'll think of something. Your boss won't know what hit him, Liam."

Liam returned the smile, but the light did not reach his eyes. Isolde saw the flicker of bitterness as he turned back. She caught Malaki watching him as well, and she could tell by the deep look of distrust that he had not missed it either.

"There is something else," said Isolde, drawing all eyes to her. "Or someone, rather."

Blyana perked up, her elbows snug beneath her chest. "Who?"

"A little girl who likes to sing, is good with horses," her gaze moving to Malaki. "And who has very nice taste in jewelry."

Confusion gave way to realization. "The daughter of the woman we helped at Lestahere…Nyla."

Isolde smiled. "The very one."

"How is she going to help?" Cillian asked. "She can't be more than five years old."

"Six," Isolde corrected. "And she works in the stables. Can't imagine anything more disorienting than a stampede racing through Briarhole. Along with whatever you two geniuses can cook up."

Cillian winked at Liam who returned the look with a sheepish smile.

"So, absolute chaos then?" her aunt asked, as a smirk spread across her face.

Isolde returned the smile. "Glorious chaos."

"Once we get them outside," Malaki said, "and have extracted the targets, we will need something to lure them back into the keep and away from the river."

Isolde smiled, the same one that let them know she was up to something.

"No," Malaki said, a tone of finality ringing in his voice. Galaena looked between them, the smile falling from her face.

She chuckled. "I don't believe I asked for permission. Besides, what else is going to draw every single one of those soldiers back into the keep besides the Hood?"

"Isolde," Alaric said, his face falling into his hands. As a child, he would always tell her the stress she invoked on him would be his death. "The only way you can get out of that is if you transform, and you can't—"

"I won't need to," she said, fear and anger lacing her words. "I can handle myself." She didn't want to face her own failures, her own short comings. Not now. "The Hood has gotten out of plenty of scrapes before."

"But not like this," Malaki said, his massive hands resting on a chair before him. The wood groaned beneath his grip. "You have never faced a hundred of the king's men on your own."

"If I plan things correctly, I won't have to."

"Isolde, if they catch you…" Cillian began, his voice so soft, Isolde couldn't stand his sincerity.

"They won't."

"But if they do—" Blyana murmured.

"They will do far worse than kill you," Liam rasped, a hand raking through his hair. "Not only will they torture you, but they will come for Thornwood as well."

Alaric sighed, his eyes squeezing shut as Galaena touched his shoulder. Her own worry, that was normally so well hidden, burned in the light of the fire.

"They won't catch me," Isolde said. "And if by some slight chance they luck out, I'll transform, and they can have my carcass."

"My rose," Nan said, her hands having finally gone still. She leaned against the dining room table, her eyes shut. "I've already buried my son; please don't make me bury you too."

Isolde's eyes flickered to the cave's opening, toward the grave that lay not a hundred yards away. Memories flooded her, making breathing nearly impossible. She walked to the shaking woman that had in more ways than one made her who she was. Carefully, she placed a hand on her shoulders, feeling the tremors pass into her.

Tears flooded Nan's face, the streams falling into the many wrinkles that lined her cheeks and eyes. Isolde folded her arms around her. "You will never lose me, Nan," she said. Blue eyes flashed before her, but she shoved them away, forcing them into a place she would face later. "But I cannot leave Zibiah and the others to face Elenarta. They need the Hood, Nan."

Quiet as the monster within, Blyana dropped from the ceiling next to Cillian and perched on his lap. His arms wrapped around her tiny waist, forming her to his body. "They need us," she said, her arm resting around his shoulder, the tips of her fingers pulling through his hair. "We have to help them."

Isolde watched Cillian's eyes shine, mesmerized by the woman he held onto. Blyana too wore a smile, one Isolde had not thought possible for her after her time at Madame Vara's. After a moment, a heavy sigh pushed through Cillian's chest and he nodded in agreement.

"For Zibiah," Galaena said rising. Her hand rested on Alaric's shoulder. She wore a mischievous grin, one that promised violence. The smile of a fighter.

Sighing, Alaric rose as well, pushing his hands into his knees. His right hand clasped onto his cane. "For Zib," he said, taking his mate's hand, his thumb running down her own.

All eyes turned to Malaki, who was still braced against the chair, his head having now fallen between his shoulders. "I still think this is a bad idea," he said, straightening. His eyes were stone, his lips pulled into a tight line. "But I will follow you, Isolde. As I always have and always will."

She opened her mouth to argue but thought better of it and simply nodded. An uneasy feeling descended over her confidence, a sense of dread that had never been there before. Malaki had never fought her this hard. They were going into the most dangerous job they had ever faced on opposites sides of the board. Doubt festered, infecting her mind.

"All or nothing," Blyana said, her eyes only on the man she loved, who smiled back.

"All or nothing," they said together--even Nan who held an arm around Isolde's waist. Liam stood apart from them. The words left his tongue, but there was no conviction behind them.

Malaki's gaze swiftly moved to Liam and narrowed. He felt Isolde's attention like a heavy blanket. As he turned to leave, he caught sight of Blyana. She nodded to him once, her eyes burning with a hatred he shared before turning to bore that fury into Liam's back.

Without another word, Malaki stormed from the cave to wait in the shadows of Blackford Forest.

The warm summer breeze rattled the leaves that littered the forest floor. Malaki felt the pull of the earth. It called to his nature, the bear that lurked within. Centuries of practice had stilled his resolve, nearly solidifying his hold on the beast he had come to rely on.

It stirred now, the rise of his anger. The beast within...wanted out.

He merely shook his head and leaned against a large oak that lined the path.

This plan is insane. Thornwood lay not five miles south. Even now he didn't like being this far from her. It set his teeth on edge.

But this was something he couldn't avoid. It had to be done.

The sound of hooves broke the silence, and his guard was instantly up. Shoving against the tree, Malaki walked into the road. Leaves covered the well-laid path that snaked through the forest.

Before long the steed charged into view. Five feet from where Malaki waited, the horse bearing Liam skidded to a stop. The beast's hooves punched the air as a whine pierced the night. Liam tumbled backwards, a stream of vulgarity flowing from his mouth. The horse bolted into the shadows as Liam regained his footing. His sword glowed faintly in the night.

"Malaki!" Liam roared, the lights of his eyes shining in the dark. "What are you playing at? Is it a new habit for you to stand in the middle of the road and scare people off their horses?"

"Our conversation isn't over," Malaki said stepping forward. The black uniform made Liam appear nearly invisible, the light of the elithrium cast a faint green hue across his heaving chest.

"What more is there to talk about?" Liam demanded, the sword still raised. "I've told you everything I know!" A flicker of fear shone in his eyes as one of Blyana's small daggers rested lightly against his neck.

"You might have fooled Isolde," she said, from behind him. "But you don't fool us."

"I'm not trying to fool anyone," Liam rasped, his eyes darting from the blade to Malaki.

"There was a time I would have believed you." His tone was calm as he walked to the right, being mindful of the blade Liam still held forward. "How do we know that you aren't selling a tale of shit?"

"You seriously believe I would do that to her?" Liam demanded, his eyes wide.

"I think you would do anything to get what you want," said Malaki, coming to a stop, light from the moon glistened in his dark hair. "Just as you always have."

Liam licked his lips. "I love her, Malaki."

A blade pressed farther into his skin. He dared not breathe. A hiss escaped from Blyana's teeth as she said, "You love the idea of her and the position she holds as Thornwood's heir."

"That's not true," he pressed, the tip of his sword falling to the ground. Malaki watched with hooded eyes as Blyana reluctantly pulled the dagger away. She shoved him forward to the ground.

"You have always wanted power," she said, her eyes burning. "The control, the luxury to never suffer. Always thinking you are owed something."

Liam rose, his free hand dusting the dirt from his knees as his other held the sword limply in his grasp. "I only want to make a start for us!"

A humorless, harsh laugh sang from Blyana's lips. "You think she wants the start you offer to be drenched in the blood of innocent people? Or a start with someone who betrayed her friend for a job?"

Liam froze, his eyes dropping to the ground. "I…I…couldn't…"

"You took vengeance from me, Liam." Her voice was so calm, so full of quiet hatred that a shiver ran down Malaki's spine.

"It…it was…my job," Liam said, his eyes still glued to the forest floor.

"She killed them!" Blyana shrieked. "All of them! The week after Isolde brought me to Thornwood, that viper bitch sent her men to take my sisters. To replace me!"

A thin line of silver lined Blyana's bright, piercing eyes. "But my father," she continued, the word laced with hatred, "finally decided to be a man and refused to let those monsters take them. You remember what they did…don't you Liam?"

Malaki turned his attention back to Liam. He couldn't bear to look at his friend…his sister anymore.

Tremors rolled through Liam's frame, his dark eyes refusing to meet her gaze. Memories of that night flooded his mind. Malaki heard the soft crunch of leaves as she slowly stalked forward.

"They burned them alive…but not before the men had their way with my mother and sisters. The neighbors said they could hear the screams, the cries for mercy that weren't answered."

She stopped in front of him. "Once Isolde and I found out, we went to Whisper. Isolde let me have them, fed them to my wrath. But you…" She pointed the dagger at him. "Look at me."

Still, he refused, his hand clutching the sword as if it were a life line.

"Look at me!" she said again.

Malaki took a step forward. He felt the chains of his power begin to pull at his resolve. If it came to it, he would slaughter Liam in a moment. The thought pained him because of Isolde. It would break her heart. A heart she had finally learned to use again after so many decades.

Liam's eyes squeezed shut as he sighed heavily before finally lifting his eyes to her. Fresh tears fell down her face, a sight that broke something in Malaki.

"You stopped me from killing her," she said, her lips curling up into a snarl. "The one person responsible for my family's death and torture…for my years and years of torture and abuse. After I killed her men, Vara knew I was coming. And she has since taken the proper precautions. Because of you, I missed my chance at vengeance. And all for what? What was it you said to me?"

"I said…" Liam's voice was shaking, but his eyes…his eyes had hardened into a resolve that Malaki recognized. It was the look of regret, of a shame that could never be rectified. "I said it was my duty to protect the royal family, to prevent more death. That the ones responsible for your family's murder had paid the price."

"And for that," she stepped so close she was forced to look up at him, "I will never trust or forgive you. You, Liam, are my enemy."

Liam's eyes fluttered ever so slightly but did not waver from hers. The kind, cheerful virya had been replaced by a creature Malaki did not recognize. He stepped forward to rest a hand on her shoulder.

"If you love her like you claim to," Malaki said, "you will help her."

"That's all I want," murmured Liam. His gaze was still fixed on Blyana.

"I make you this promise, Liam." Malaki stepped forward to block Blyana from Liam's eyes. He wanted the captain of the guard only focused on him. Slowly, Liam's gaze moved to his.

"If you betray Isolde, I will kill you." His tone left no room for doubt. "That is, if she doesn't kill you first."

Liam's throat bobbed as he nodded. Regret filled his eyes. It was a look that made Malaki want more than anything to forgive him. To forgive the boy he knew once. The one he saw so much of himself in. They shared the same power. But he was now a sworn soldier of his enemy, a willing participant. And for that…there was no forgiveness.

"I would expect nothing less," Liam said, his voice thick.

Malaki looked him up and down before stepping away. "Good," he said, his tone clipped. "Glad we have an understanding."

"As am I."

Blyana sheathed the small dagger, her face grim. "I believe you have a horse to catch. Don't want to keep your handler waiting."

Keeping his eyes locked on Malaki, Liam began retreating. His hand still clutched the sword, the tip covered in dry earth. Before turning, he shifted his attention to Blyana.

"I truly am sorry, Bly." Without waiting for her reply, he sped off into the night, his horse long forgotten.

They remained silent for a moment as the sounds of the night filled the air in comfortable quietness.

"What do you think?" she asked, her arms crossing her chest.

Malaki sighed, his fingers running absently over the fine axe at his side. "I don't know," he said. "I just hope the mating bond doesn't form."

"How do you know it hasn't already?"

A knowing smile formed over his face. "Because Isolde wouldn't have taken you, Alaric, and me threatening Liam as lightly as she did. Blood would have been spilled if they were mated. I'm sure you know the feeling."

A smile spread easily across Blyana's face. One that told him she knew exactly what he meant. "What about you?" She asked.

"What about me?"

A coy smile bloomed across her face. "You and Isolde."

A deep chuckle erupted from his chest. "I don't think Arnoria would be able to survive that."

"Still, you two—"

"Argue like we are mated?" he asked. Blyana nodded. "Every chance we get." His smile slowly fell away. He loved Isolde, their bond, while never physical, ran far deeper than friendship.

"No, Bly," he whispered. "I lost the love of my life a long time ago."

Her face flashed in his mind like a blade. Long blonde hair fell about her cream-colored shoulders. Eyes of the warmest brown stared back at him. If love had a face, Aurora's would have been it. He forced the image away, burying Aurora deep within himself, along with the pain. Turning around, he placed a hand on Blyana's shoulder and squeezed.

"Isolde…might have lost hers too." Kamden's death still pained her. He could see it in her face. Some days were better than others. But that was a wound not easily healed…if ever. An ache that would never be relieved. And if it was real…it was a bond that could never be replaced.

"The thought of a mating bond developing between those two is nauseating." Blyana turned and began walking back. She was clearly desperate to think of anything other than the pain of losing a mate. "Wouldn't it have formed by now if it was going to?" she asked.

"Not necessarily," said Malaki, following beside her. "Sometimes it can take years…decades to take hold." He sighed heavily, his eyes following the path Liam took. The forest floor was undisturbed. "Let's hope it doesn't come to that."

CHAPTER 25

"Just let me—"Galaena fiddled with Alaric's hood and cloak. Tugging...pulling…only to tug and pull again, ensuring no part of him would become exposed. They each wore a standard issue guard's uniform. They were entirely uncomfortable and unflattering. Isolde was the only exception. She would need her usual attire to lure the king's cronies back into the fortress. The bait had to be set.

Isolde leaned against a nearby tree, her head pressing into the smooth, cool bark. A hint of a smile ghosted her face.

"Darling," Alaric said, catching his mate's hand to bring it to his lips. "Stop fussing."

"I'm not fussing," Galaena said. "I'm merely…being careful." Her fingers tugged at the sleeve of his jacket, pulling it down to ensure every bit of his skin was covered.

A bright smile pulled at Alaric's lips, a whisper of his youthful self coming forth. Alaric gripped her chin gently between his thumb and forefinger. "My lovely, thoughtful lady," he said.

She allowed him to pull her face to his. "My stubborn, kind lord."

Giving them privacy, Isolde walked out of the clearing and towards the forest with Fane perched on her shoulder. They resided ten miles from the outskirts of Briarhole. Already the sun was beginning to set, the evening shadows playing across the fallen leaves of the forest floor. Her steps were near silent but she knew Malaki heard them.

He remained unmoving, his eyes scanning the trees for any sign of movement.

"I do not wish to talk," he said, his back to her.

She shrugged, pulling her mask and hood away. The scent of the forest filled her lungs as a breeze swept her cheeks. "Too bad."

He sighed sharply, his shoulders bunching. "What if Liam was wrong about the numbers?" he demanded. "What if Gage has been feeding him the wrong information?"

"Then we have a far bigger problem on our hands," she said, resting her elbows on the limb beside him. "If Liam is being fed false information, then that could only mean one thing: Gage suspects us of being the Hood. Either one of us...or Zibiah."

Malaki shook his head, his shoulders tensing. "Isolde."

"I trust him, Malaki," she said. "Even if we are suspected, Zibiah still needs help. That hasn't changed."

"I know you trust your gut. But I trust my own just as much, and I am telling you something is wrong."

"We don't have a choice. She is family. We would do the same for you."

He laughed humorlessly. "I pray you wouldn't."

"Would you think differently if one of those humans was Aurora?"

Pain erupted across Malaki's face. A deep pain that caused Isolde to regret speaking her name. "That is who we are trying to help—humans just like her."

"Why would you mention her?" he asked, his voice thick as if it took all his strength to speak. Anger quickly replaced pain and his eyes glowed. "How dare you, Isolde."

"I just want you to understand that there are several Auroras in the world...and Kamdens."

He whipped his head to her, eyes wide with concern. It had been decades since she said his name out loud. The name lifted off her tongue like a blade from flesh, cleaving her heart in two. Memories flooded in…drowning her. The kind, blue eyes flickered to her over the spine of a book in her mind. His loving, unrestrained smile-Nan's smile-spread across his face.

Malaki reached for her, but she shied away. He hadn't heard that name in so long it stunned him.

"I'm sorry," she said, her eyes stinging. "I would never intentionally hurt you, Malaki. Especially not where she is concerned."

His eyes were hazy and filled with memory. "I will always love her," he said finally. "But my love cannot outweigh my common sense and duty. Especially to you."

"The plan will work," Isolde said against the lump in her throat. She ignored the small prickle of fear and doubt that came forth to swallow her torturous thoughts.

Malaki sighed once again, the limb groaning under his grasp. "I need you to promise me something," he said. She looked up at him. Her cheek rested on her arm, as she waited for him to speak.

"If things go wrong, you must promise to leave." At last, his eyes met her. They shined in fear and pleading. "No matter who is left behind, no matter what you may see or hear, you must promise to save yourself. That is the only way I can get through this."

She stared at him, her own battle waging within herself. Images of him and the others being captured flashed through her mind. She knew it would be impossible, that leaving anyone wasn't an option. Still, she would do what was needed to keep him calm.

"Fine," Isolde said, turning her gaze back to the forest. He would see the lie, the false promise.

"I want your word, Isolde," he said, his lips thinning. "On Kamden's grave. I want your word that you'll leave if things take a turn."

Isolde's teeth ground. The leather of her gloves groaned as her hands balled into fists. *Damn him!* He waited in silence, his breathing irregular. She could hear his heart racing, the power within him saturating the air.

"I will give you my word that I will try, Malaki. That is the best I can do."

He shook his head as a heavy sigh lifted from his chest. A beat later, he said, "I suppose that's better than nothing." He turned to leave but halted at the touch of her hand on his arm.

"I am sorry, Malaki." A lump lodged itself in Isolde's own throat. "I should have never mentioned..." She knew the pain it caused him to think of Aurora and their unborn child. Indescribable pain that Isolde knew all too well. "You know I would never intentionally hurt you like that. I'd rather die than be the cause of your pain."

New tears formed on the corners of Malaki's eyes. His gaze, while sharp with sadness, shined with love. Without hesitation, he took her in his arms. Fane flew away, nearly missing the embrace. Razor-like agony carved at Isolde's chest. How could she have brought up Aurora? Self-hatred racked down Isolde's mind, her chest burning. He would never have done that to her.

Father, brother, friend, confidant, protector.

All were roles Malaki played in her life. When Isolde looked to the future, she knew he was an absolute certainty. Their paths had been woven together since the day she was born and would remain so until their last breaths. She had wondered why the mating bond had not formed between them. They were both incredibly powerful virya. It only made sense.

But Isolde had never seen him as anything other than her watchful shadow. Her constant, faithful friend. And she knew he saw the same in her. Perhaps that kind of love was not possible. There simply wasn't enough room for that kind of love in either of their hearts for each other.

Kissing the top of her head, Malaki pulled away. "We'll get through this," he said, a half-smile at last forming on his lips. And for just a moment, like a star shooting across the night sky, she believed him. For a moment, she wasn't afraid.

Night had fallen at last.

Fane soared overhead as Isolde led them through the forest, keeping to the shadows as much as possible. Their procession was nearly soundless save for the occasional extra step from Alaric, his bad leg dragging.

A mile in, he and Galaena stirred left toward the river, to the boats Liam had placed upstream earlier in the week.

A hundred yards away, they leapt into the trees, their steps careful as they jumped from branch to branch. Malaki led the way, weaving footholds among branches, making the process much faster. Isolde picked off the few guards that lingered on the ground, dropping down to only retrieve her arrows and toss the bodies aside.

They reached the edge of the forest and fell silent. The last line of trees hugged the northern most point of the territory where no barrack was stationed. The peaks of the Oronilma mountain range rose at their backs. A towering mass of snow-capped, jagged rock faces ran northwest to collide with the Helecdol mountains and southwest to fall into the Thurin Sea. To the east, Oronilma held Elenarta in their infinite beauty. Their peaks were so high and vast they seemed to touch the stars. They were the only line of defense against the wild, forgotten kingdom that lay to the north.

Briarhole was indeed a fortress. Forty-foot walls of solid black stone surrounded the heart of the keep. Two massive drawbridges, one placed at the southern and western ends were drawn tight.

Every twenty feet a guard stood at their post along the top of the wall. Flames from the torches that ran along the top of the wall danced upon the elithrium spears clutched in their hands. Unease swept through Isolde as her sharp eyes fell to the ground. Below a pair of hyenas, the size of horses prowled the gates. Their broken, sharp teeth were a glistening yellow.

"Volkran still favors showing off, doesn't he," said Cillian. To his right Blyana rested comfortably on a narrow limb, her cat eyes ever watchful and piercing.

"Some things never change," Malaki said, his shoulder nudging Isolde on the left. "Looks to be a bit more than what Liam led us to believe."

Isolde couldn't help but agree. "He might not have known," she countered, refusing to believe what Malaki was insinuating. Blyana scoffed at her side, her eyes flashing.

Isolde ignored her.

"Should be any second now." Cillian said, his eyes glued to the hyenas.

And just like that, a crash pierced the night, causing all of them to jump. The hyenas were instantly on alert. A deep, menacing growl rumbled over the barracks. In a shot, they took off to the west. The guards perched on top of the wall followed suit as orders rang out from within the keep.

"Does that answer your question?" Isolde said as she leapt from the tree. They darted across the overly exposed stretch of land, their hands ready to grasp their weapons. No secondary alarm sounded. All eyes were on whatever was happening in the west.

Isolde plucked the pair of climbing knives from her belt and drove them into cracks that ran up the obsidian rock wall and climbed. The others followed effortlessly, keeping to the shadows as much as possible. They hung high in the sky, unfiltered by a single cloud. Puffs of ragged breath escaped Cillian's lips the higher they climbed. Isolde turned back to see Blyana moving along with him. Each step she took, he followed suit. Every thrust of the knife, his was there to match hers.

As they breached the tip, Isolde stowed away the knives and withdrew her bow. Notching an arrow, she surveyed the surroundings. It wouldn't take long for Liam's distraction to play out; soon the guards would return. They had to move quickly.

Once they were all up and armed, they moved along the wall, their backs crouched keeping below the ledge. Isolde glanced over the railing. Her heart stuttered momentarily. Liam stood in the middle of the courtyard, Gage at his side.

Their backs were to them. Their focus was on whatever he had concocted as a distraction in the west. As they neared the first set of stairs leading down into the level below, Isolde caught Liam looking back ever so slightly in their direction, letting her know he knew she was there.

The faint smell of smoke wafted through the night. A flicker of light caught her eye and she smiled. A massive blaze had erupted from one of the numerous storage buildings that housed the grain and lumber Briarhole was so well known for.

Liam had promised a distraction. A cry to call them in and a blaze to keep their attention-that ought to keep them busy. Isolde led them through the maze of alleyways. Her bow was notched and ready.

Twice she unleashed an arrow, effectively silencing anyone that came into their path. They hid the bodies in whatever nook they could find and moved on.

At last, they reached the slaves quarters. The lock on the door was elithrium. "Beg your pardon, ladies," Cillian said, pushing past Malaki. Cillian's hands began working with the picks. "Where would you be without me?"

"Less talky, more picky," Isolde said, her fingers twitching on the bow.

"You know I work better when I talk," he said his eyes shifting to Blyana. The only visible part of her face flushed a deep red, and a smile crinkled at the corners of her eyes.

"I could have lived centuries without needing to know that," Malaki said, his voice even deeper with the mask. His large crossbow was aimed forward, his finger resting on the trigger. The large battle axe was slung across his back, a faint hint of a greenish hue shined against his uniform.

"Such hostility," Cillian said, the sound of the lock finally giving way. He opened the door with a sarcastic bow. "Criminals first."

Isolde smiled and punched his shoulder as she passed. "Don't get cocky. We still have the shackles to contend with." The smell was just as overwhelming as Foxclove. The stench of waste, body odor, and blood filled the air, nearly suffocating her. Even with the mask, she nearly gagged.

Reaching the landing, Isolde gazed at the amount of people within. Their eyes lit with terror at the sight of her and the others, but they soon melted into an expression of hope.

"Hood?" An older man whose hair, if clean, would have been snow white rose from the ground. His voice was strained, as if his throat was bone dry. Isolde nodded, her eyes searching the group for one in particular. She sighed with relief as Zibiah came forward. Her braids were pulled back, and the elithrium sword hung at her side.

"Took you long enough." Zibiah said as her arm wrapped around Isolde's shoulders. Malaki and Blyana began working on the shackles on the wrists and ankles of the prisoners. Iron fell easily from their bodies, decorating the floor with bent metal.

"And why aren't you chained up like the rest?" Isolde asked, her eyes running over the obsidian leather that covered her from head to toe. It was nearly identical to Isolde's. She was night incarnate.

"I might have hidden away for a day or two," Zibiah said, tightening the straps at her wrists.

Isolde smiled. "You could have at least let them try. Given them a sporting chance."

Zibiah's golden eyes rolled. "Not all the guards here are ruthless. It'd be a shame to kill any of the few I actually like."

"Yes, that would be tragic," Isolde said. "Where are the virya?"

She turned and led them to the back. Her hand never left the pommel of her sword. In the back, away from the humans, stood a small group. Their clothes were finer, bodies fuller than the rest. A faint shine lifted from their shackles.

Isolde stood before them, taking in their skeptical, frightened glances. "I'm sure Lady Zibiah has told you why you are here." A few nodded, the others remained motionless.

"Do you wish to go to the Elenarta?"

"Of course not," a woman, retorted, her eyes boring into Isolde's. "Nor do we want to go with you, a criminal."

"Paraca," Zibiah hissed. It was clear this was not the first objection she had made about the Hood.

"Well, you are more than welcome to stay and see if Volkran will keep you," Isolde said, shrugging with an air of indifference. "I rather doubt it considering the king has already paid for you handsomely. Once we have you out of Briarhole, you are free to go wherever your heart desires."

"How do we know you will keep your word and let us go?"

"I have given you my word," said Zibiah.

Paraca stepped forward, her eyes shining faintly despite the shackle. "And what does that mean from the wife of the one who keeps us here?" she demanded. "I want to hear it from him!" Her bony, gnarled finger jabbed to Isolde.

"Would you rather take the word of the one who hurt you? From Volkran?" Isolde asked. "Because the way I see it, you can either trust Volkran who has treated you so well," Isolde said, her gloved hand sweeping around the room. "Or you can trust the people who are risking more than just their lives so you can have a chance for freedom."

Paraca's teeth ground, clearly not happy being spoken to in such a way by a criminal. She looked to the others, who were staring at her with imploring eyes. At last, she sighed and waved her hand through the air. "Fine," she said.

"Smart move," Isolde said, jutting her chin to Cillian. "Go ahead."

He began working on the locks, his eyes not wavering from his work.

Zibiah came up beside Isolde, her eyes scanning the eight virya. "Those four are water wielders," she said, nodding to the group on the end. "And this one is an earth." Her head nodding to Paraca. "And the rest are air manipulators."

"Good," Isolde said. "We'll need them."

"They will do their part," Zibiah said loudly enough for them to hear as well, her eyes boring into theirs. Paraca merely narrowed her gaze, her teeth pulling up into a snarl.

"I thought there would be more," said Isolde.

"There will be," said Zibiah. "This was all Gage could manage to take in one trip."

"We're all set," Blyana said behind Isolde. The humans stood huddled together, their eyes ever watchful. Little children hid behind their parents' legs. Only a few dared peek around to gape at her.

"Did Gage bring any water wielders?" she asked.

Zibiah shook her head, the golden clasps nestled in her braids clinked together. In her hand was a dark hood and mask, identical to the one Isolde wore. "Not that I am aware of. They plan on taking the road to the capitol in a large caravan."

"Alright," Isolde said, releasing sigh of relief. "There is one other person I need."

"Nyla." Zibiah nodded, jerking her head to the left. They walked to the back of the holding cells. The sound of muttering filled the air.

"Hood!" The word punched the air as a pair of arms wrapped around her middle. Isolde froze but quickly thawed.

"There's my horse expert," she said, giving Nyla's thin shoulders a squeeze.

"I knew you would come." The child smiled. One of her eyes was swollen shut. Black painted the left side of her face.

"Always for you." Isolde squatted downed. "Who did that?"

Nyla covered her eye with her hand. A look of unease reached her face. "I broke a rule."

"Which one?"

She licked her dirty, cracked lips. "I was singing."

"Singing?" Isolde snuck a glance at Zibiah, who shook her head. Burning gold shined from her eyes.

"Yes." Her eyes flickered up to Zibiah.

"And what were you singing?"

"Something a friend told me not to sing." Her voice was so small, so incredibly broken. Isolde reached forward and plucked a small chain from beneath her soiled gown.

"Was it the same someone who gave you this?" Her finger jostling the chain, causing the ring Isolde had given her to dance.

Nyla nodded, her eyes dropping. "Do you really know her?"

"I do, in fact," said Isolde, holding the ring before her hooded eyes. "She has exceptional taste." A chorus of sighs ghosted through the chamber. "In fact," Isolde continued. "I would say her taste is impeccable. She must be quite extraordinary."

Cillian coughed, his fingers slipping on one of the remaining shackles.

"Wouldn't you agree, Lady Zibiah?"

Zibiah rolled her eyes, fighting the smirk on her lips. "She has her moments."

A grunt sounded through Malaki's towering form, his eyes narrowing in annoyance. Nyla looked at him in fear.

"Don't worry about him," Isolde said tucking the ring back in place. "His sense of style ends at a pair of trousers and a tunic."

The girl laughed nervously, still keeping an unsure watch on Malaki. Isolde placed her hands on the girl's shoulders. "Nyla, I need your help."

She looked briefly at Zibiah, who winked back. "What can I do?"

"How many horses are in the stables right now?"

Nyla thought for a moment. "Thirty in the stalls...and at least forty more in the corral."

"Excellent," said Isolde. "Do you think you can sneak into the stables and let the horses out for a midnight run?"

Her eyes grew big. "I...I would get into trouble."

"We need cover," Zibiah said. "Something to keep the guards occupied while we sneak everyone out."

Uncertainty coated Nyla's face. Her tiny teeth biting down on her lip. "We won't leave you," Malaki said, reading her fear. His voice was so soft and reassuring. "We would never leave you."

A flicker of relief eased the worry in the one eye that could open. Her shoulder relaxed under Isolde's palms. "Is now a bad time?" Isolde asked with a wink.

"Not for you."

"You're a very brave girl," Isolde said, replacing the ring beneath her dress. "Where is your mother?" she asked, looking around. "We'll make sure she is one of the first ones out."

Nyla's eye dropped to her hands. Dirt and filth lined her fingernails. "She's gone."

Isolde paused, her eyes turning forward in time to see silent tears falling down her cheeks. Looking up, Isolde saw Zibiah's furious gaze land on the row of whips that lined the walls.

Ripples of fury coated Isolde's skin. Heavy, harsh breaths found their way to her and Zibiah. Malaki stood at the entrance, his hands clenching and unclenching in waves of anger.

Sighing, Isolde gently cupped the uninjured side of the girl's face. "I'll make them pay," she said. Isolde knew the girl understood when a small light of vengeful anger shined in her uninjured eye. But still she nodded, her throat bobbing as she fought back tears of righteous fury.

Isolde rose and turned back to the group. "It is essential you keep absolutely quiet. Two boats are waiting on the river to take you out of Briarhole and to a better future. But you must do as we say. Is that clear?"

They nodded, their eyes intent as if awaiting orders. The Hood moved her steely gaze back to Paraca, who nodded once. "Good."

"I need the virya and Nyla first. We'll use your power to help steer the boats," Malaki announced, moving to the side. The eight prisoners shuffled forward, their eyes wary.

Cautiously, Nyla reached up and gripped one of Malaki's fingers. He stared down at her as if trying to decide what to do. She continued to watch until he at last swept her into his arms. "I'll get you to the stables." Her tiny fingers gripped the leather straps of his uniform.

"Follow along and do as he says. Four in each boat. Two water wielders in each," Blyana instructed.

Isolde went first, her bow loaded and ready. The ground floor was deserted; all focus was spent on putting out the inferno quickly moving north. Wordlessly, Isolde waved them forward. Zibiah slipped the hood and mask into place, securing her braids underneath. With the hood in place, she might as well have been Isolde's twin.

Malaki slunk to the right. Nyla held tightly to his neck as he sprinted to the stable doors.

Cillian led the way, his daggers drawn and glistening in the light of the fire.

The virya followed suit. Their glowing eyes were wide and mouths firmly closed. Both drawbridges had been lowered. Men ran back and forth, racing to throw buckets of sand and water on the flames. All focus was on the fire. None noticed the small group that hid in the shadows and slipped into the night over the bridge.

Pulling on her power, Isolde saw through a falcon's vision two boats waiting patiently along the docks. Two hooded figures lurked in the dark nearby.

Movement to the right caught her attention. Whirling around, she aimed the tip of her arrow at an impressive black stallion. He pranced into the courtyard. Drifts of smoke hung about his frame. After a moment, more and more bodies emerged from the darkened stables.

"Blyana," Isolde whispered, allowing the rest of the horses to fill the space. "Eight more."

She took the same route, her daggers out and waiting for blood. She kept the humans moving easily.

Malaki returned with Nyla in tow. He placed her next to Isolde and plunged back down into the dungeons. "Excellent job," Isolde said.

Nyla beamed up at her. The pride of having done her job glistened in her good eye. "What else can I do?" Isolde pulled her closer, deeper into the shadows. "You've done more than enough."

Malaki was next to emerge with ten humans.

Her eyes narrowed at the number.

"It will be fewer for you and Zibiah to handle," he said, his eyes twinkling. She shook her head at him. Two small children, not old enough to run yet, were cradled in his arms. His crossbow hung over his shoulders.

"Go with him," Isolde nodded to Nyla. She followed without hesitation. Her little finger hooked through one of the many loops in his belt. A small crease formed at the corners of Malaki's face, his eyes softened. The ghost of a smile on his lips. He led them down the same path Blyana had taken, disappearing into the night.

"Alright Zib," Isolde said at last.

Zibiah emerged with the last of the bunch, mostly children. Her arms were full. A child no older than three, clinging to its mother's skirts, made up the end. Isolde let Zibiah lead the way. She took up the end, her bow at the ready. The small children made their procession far slower than the others.

They were halfway to the bridge when a lone guard looked up just at the wrong time. A gap had formed in the herd as a breeze swept through the courtyard, taking the cover of smoke along with it. Isolde saw confusion then alarm blossom onto his soot-covered face. Fear iced her veins as she took aim and fired.

The tip of the arrow found its mark at the back of his throat, silencing him. His lifeless body fell backwards into a pile of scrap metal. The clang echoed off the horseflesh and stone walls of the massive courtyard. Cries and whines from the wall of horses erupted in the night.

Isolde rasped to Zibiah, "Run!"

They took off for the gate. Isolde kept to the right of the group, using gusts of air to startle the horses from their path. Voices from the guards and snarls from hyenas grew closer.

"Hurry!" Isolde said, shoving another gust of wind into a terrified stallion, forcing it from Zibiah's path. Just as they breached the looming arch of the drawbridge, the mother in front of Isolde stopped dead.

"My baby!" she cried hysterically, pushing against Isolde's outstretched arm. Her hand stretched back to the dungeons. "Stop, my baby!"

Terror seized Isolde as she turned to see a little boy slowly running after them. Tears were streaming down his face as he tripped, falling forward into the dirt. Hooves of the frightened horses danced around him, barely missing his tiny body.

"Intruders!" one of the guards screamed from behind the wall of horses and smoke. "We have intruders!"

"Go!" Isolde growled at Zibiah. She shoved the mother to her, preventing her from following. Without waiting, Isolde took off into a sprint. Her fingers groped for an arrow as she ran. Notching the arrow into place, Isolde fired between the necks of the horses. The guard's voice was garbled as blood filled his mouth. Snarls ripped through the night as the hyenas returned, their eyes glowing in the light of the fire.

A divot of dirt erupted from the ground as Isolde's boot sliced into the earth and slid to a stop. She snagged the child from the ground, just before two arrows pierced the dirt where he sat seconds before.

He was like a block of muscle, frozen in terror in her arms. After turning back to the drawbridge, Isolde took off, willing every ounce of power and energy she could muster into her legs. She felt the terror, the icy dread leaking into her blood, making it harder to move.

Five feet before crossing under the archway, the massive grate dropped with a bang. Her shoulder slammed into the metal, her ears ringing.

Trapped. She was trapped inside Briarhole-with the king's men, Volkran, Gage,...and a child. Zibiah was on the other side, her golden eyes wide with horror as she looked for a way back in. *No...no...no...*

"Hood!"

She knew that voice and growled in response. The boy wailed in fear at the sound, his hands cupping his tiny ears. Isolde searched for an opening, anything for them to slip through. Her eyes fell to the gate itself. The holes were just large enough for her to fit him through.

"Just go," Isolde said, working the squirming child through the gap, mindful of his head as he fell into Zibiah's awaiting arms.

"I'm not leaving you!" she growled, struggling to hold the child still with one hand while maintaining the grip on her blade with the other.

"I'll be right behind you. Don't worry about me," Isolde said, forcing the fear down. Zibiah still lingered, her head shaking as she cradled the child to her chest. "Damn it, Zibiah, go!"

A growl ripped through her friend's teeth as she tore away from the gate, her eyes mournful and furious. Off to the side, Isolde saw the two hyenas round the corner and fix their sights on Zibiah. Without hesitation, she fired through the gate, killing them instantly just a foot away from Zibiah's retreating shadow.

She felt the wind of a blade before she saw it. The edge panged off the grate in a deathly echo just above her head. Forcing the bow over her back, she turned to face the attacker. Anger and fear seized her at once.

Liam stood before her, his eyes ablaze. "Hit me," he growled. Without a second thought, she launched into the fight. After exchanging a few blows, she disarmed him with what she hoped for his sake was a convincing show.

Twenty more guards pushed through the doorway and charged. Without waiting, Isolde worked her boot into the grate of the drawbridge and climbed. Spears and arrows ricocheted inches from her hands and back as she rose.

Once up, she hauled herself onto the railing of the wall of the fortress and prepared to make the forty-foot drop. But a great roar of water stilled her. To the south, the banks of the Lenda River, crawled with guards.

There shouldn't be this many. Malaki's words of distrust echoed in her mind. *Not this many...*

Sharp terror pierced Isolde as massive pillars of water exploded from the river. They crashed down on the figures running along the bank. Her aunt and uncle worked to keep the boats clear.

Ribbons of air danced in her fingers. The build-up of power tore through every muscle and nerve ending as it surged forward.

She sent a gust of wind their way, hoping to push the sails forward, unleashing the dam a fraction of an inch. It came at her all at once. Her control slipped as the animal prowled forward. Gritting her teeth,

Isolde shoved more of her power into the air. The powerful gust caught the sails of the boats. They lurched forward, cutting through the water like a knife to flesh.

Isolde prepared to send another wave as two guards appeared on the wall, caging her in. The tips of their spears aimed at her heart. Afraid she couldn't control it and her movements, Isolde forced the power down and ran for the weaker of the two guards. Her hands found the twin blades on her back and pulled them free. The young guard was dead in the same moment it took her to steal his spear and send it flying into the chest of the other.

She looked back to the river. The boats had begun to move...but not fast enough. Columns of water pounded away at the shoreline. Each wave that rose grew smaller and smaller, its force becoming nothing more than a nuisance.

A cry of horror lodged in her throat as an impossibly large hyena leapt over the water's edge. Its teeth, cracked and sharp, shined in the light of the moon as they snapped at Galaena's neck.

Isolde gripped the wall, ready to launch herself into the air as another figure emerged. Its massive jaws, set with rows of deadly teeth, caught the creature mid-air and clamped down. A cry of sorrow ripped through the night as the colossal crocodile charged. A terrifying hiss filled the night as its jaws clamped down on the snarling hyena and rolled to the edge. The boat rocked back and forth with the weight of the creature. Its port side dropped beneath the surface of the water.

Haunted cries filled the night air as the crocodile moved along the bow, its body nearly capsizing the vessel of humans, half-bloods, and virya. It's scaled head dragged the yelping creature along with it. The cries died as their heads disappeared beneath the surface of the river.

A wail of sorrow pierced the night and carried over the turbulent waters as her aunt's body gave way to the monster beneath. Isolde watched as her beloved aunt's body bent and twisted. Galaena's horrible cries gave way to another sound. The fierce snarl of a large cat replaced her cries of anguish. It was a sound she had not heard in years and one that made Isolde tremble in fear. With one final growl, a massive cat launched from the boat's side and unleashed itself on the soldiers that lined the river's bank.

Fresh blood appeared black against the mountain lion's golden fur that appeared almost silver in the light of the moon. She tore through them with ease, not a single blade finding its mark. Tearing herself away from the pile of bodies that now lied along the Lenda River, Galaena leapt into the trees. A few seconds later, a chorus of screams filled the night and continued to follow the boat as it moved down stream.

Tears of disbelief fell from Isolde's eyes. It had been too long...they hadn't transformed in decades...The horror of what had happened settled into her bones like lead.

"Alaric...Galaena."

CHAPTER 26

Chaos continued to unfold. But the river's surface remained calm.

What have I done? Isolde's gaze moved over the boats in panicked sweeps. *Where are they? Where are they?* The only disturbance from the water was the unorganized rowing of those aboard the boats. Screams followed the boats as Galaena mauled the soldiers lying in wait along the riverbank.

They had not used their power in so long. Isolde knew if they had transformed, it would be nearly impossible for them to remember who they were once that power had taken hold. Not to mention the pain...

She was about to leap over the edge but was stopped by a pack of four hyenas and ten other guards rushing forward. Their arrows were aimed at her head.

Swearing, Isolde broke from the wall and ran along its edge. Replacing her blades, she extracted her climbing daggers and launched into the air. The knives drove into the wall of the most central tower of Briarhole. Spears and arrows continued to bounce off the stone on either side of her. A few came close to meeting their mark.

At last, she reached the balcony of the library and climbed up and over. By some small miracle, it was empty. She made her way to the main door and yanked them open and stopped dead in her tracks.

Gage and a posse of ten royal guards stood before her. A look of surprise and a beat of silence passed between them. Before he could utter a single word, Isolde slammed the doors shut and fastened the elithrium lock in place. Volkran was a bastard, but he was careful about keeping locks on all the doors, even the interior ones.

"Hood!" Gage screamed, his fists beating the door. "Face me you son of a bitch!"

Isolde looked around, her eyes searching for another exit as she used all her strength to brace against the door. She reconsidered the balcony, or the secret passage through the broom closet but that was out. They had seen her come in this way, and they would be waiting.

Did they have a virya who could transform into a damn ram? Her teeth rattled as the bastard continued to slam into the door. Wave after wave assaulted her head and back. There was no way out. The feeling of being caged descended on her, forcing the monster to prowl forward. There was no other choice; she had to fight them.

Closing her eyes, Isolde took a deep breath and leapt to the landing that held the lifeless fireplace. She extracted her bow and notched two arrows…and waited.

The door broke free with a bang. Wood and metal spilled over the cold, stone floor. The first two soldiers were dead instantly, an arrow protruding from their skulls. She felt nothing as she dropped two more. These were the king's soldiers, sworn to protect His Majesty and his interests. They knew which side they chose.

She fired two more, dodging an overly zealous soldier, his blade swinging wide. Isolde dropped to her knees and fired. Two more fell. Pressing her chest to the ground, she moved just in time to avoid another fatal blow from the young soldier looking to make a name for himself.

Without pause, she drew the dagger from her hip and leapt to her feet. He wasn't terrible, matching each of her blows. He kept his feet moving, striking hard, putting her on the defense. But Isolde was better. She saw the fatal flaw immediately. He raised his arms to deliver a powerful blow, exposing his ribcage. She struck so fast he only felt the sting of the blade as she yanked it free from his side.

He fell to the floor, blood trickling from his mouth as she shoved him to the side. A moment later, a searing pain exploded in Isolde's calf. She fell to one knee, clutching the arrow shaft that was buried deep within her lower leg. Gage grinned back from the doorway, already notching another arrow.

"Well," he said, bringing the bow up, the string groaning. "He does bleed after all."

Isolde quickly placed an arrow and fired as Gage did. Their arrows met midair and fell to the stone floor in a pile of splintered wood and poisoned steel. Before he could react, Isolde loaded her final arrow and shot.

He moved just in time for the bow's handle to catch the arrow instead of his heart. It fell to the ground in a pile of ruined wood and string.

"Just as well," Gage said, unsheathing his sword, metal screeching. "I'll enjoy killing you the old-fashioned way."

A small pool of blood had begun to form around her boot as Isolde rose to her feet. Sharp stabs of pain radiated up her leg, making it hard to stand.

Ignoring the inferno in her leg, the Hood stepped forward. Twin blades shined in each of her hands. Emeralds and sapphires glistened, the elithrium steel humming with the need for blood. She twirled the blades, "I do hope your fighting makes up for your talking."

Gage smiled with anticipation, air gathering in his chest as if to speak. Before a word passed his lips, Isolde gathered a gust of wind and shoved it forward. It struck him in the chest like a punch, sending him flying through the corridor.

He somehow managed to keep a firm grasp on the elithrium sword as his back slammed into the far wall. Bits of rock fell about his slumped form, his chestnut hair speckled in debris.

Icy flames pushed Isolde forward. The cold, mindless anger chilled her blood as he rose, using his sword as a prop. The light of his eyes burned into her, and his teeth were bared. She could feel his power stirring, a chill pulsing through the air. The light in his eyes grew as Isolde felt the temperature drop and the very shadows seemed to shutter.

"I thought you were going to kill me the old-fashioned way," she said, her swords extended to either side, their blades scraping against the stone as sparks flew off the razor-sharp edges. "Or is that too much ask?"

Shoving against the wall, Gage met her halfway, their swords colliding in mid-air.

She shoved him back, a smile creeping onto her face as she advanced. Each strike was precise, a familiar step in a dance she had been performing her whole life. His blade sang to hers as they met again and again.

Isolde drove him back down the corridor, forcing him to turn left where she knew a wider room resided. Each step she took left a trail of blood in her wake. Drifts of smoke filled the corridor.

"For the Right Hand of the King," she grunted, blocking his strike. "I expected a lot more than this."

Gage, in a blind fury, charged forward, the tip of his sword aimed at her throat. She shoved the blade up and moved farther into the corridor, allowing him to take the offense. The pain in her calf was growing, causing her to limp. She needed this to end soon.

"You talk an awful lot for the ghost of Blackford Forest," Gage sneered, continuing to strike.

Isolde's fist collided with his jaw. The sound of cracked bone echoed down the hall. "I am known for my riveting conversations."

"We'll see how well you talk after I'm done with you," Gage said, as blood dripped from his lips.

"You have to catch me first." Isolde retreated a step or two forcing him to follow. "And what a disappointment you've been thus far."

Gage rushed forward. His hands strained against the handle. The sword swung right into Isolde's awaiting blade, its unforgiving edge inches from her face. Jarring vibrations wrecked her hands and wrists.

He shoved her back, and her wound barked in pain. Excitement ignited across Gage's face, the smell of blood and weakness drove his blade harder, faster as Isolde lured him into the meeting room they had used at Lestahere. Light from the chandelier danced on their blades.

Isolde flipped onto the table's black, glistening surface only to land gingerly on her leg. The pain sent a wave of nausea hurling into her stomach. She needed a second to breath…just a second…

The door at the back of the room opened, its light flooding the room. "Stand down!" Gage roared, his power surging forward. "This one is mine!" A dark chuckle followed the faint sound of screeching metal that echoed from the doorway.

"This is my house, Gage," Volkran said, his black eyes wide. "The pleasure is all mine." The gigantic sword meant for hacking more than sparing radiated a greenish hue. Isolde felt a small flicker of that icy fury die. Whoever had forged that sword used far more elithrium than any she had seen before. Rivers of the living metal snaked across the flawless blade.

Liam stood a foot behind the Lord of Briarhole. The mask of the captain was in place. A look of hatred that did not meet his eyes stared back at her. They flickered momentarily to the small pool of blood forming around the heel of her boot.

"What is the order, sir?" Liam asked. "Capture…or kill?"

Gage's breaths came in quick angry puffs, his eyes never leaving Isolde. "I don't care one way or the other."

Isolde's mind raced. She could already feel her strength to hold the beast at bay fading. Its claws scraped at her resolve. The ring on her finger hummed with power. It called to the elemental part of her, willing her to use that side of her nature as if it too didn't care for the odds.

Her eyes moved back to Liam for a just a second. A slight narrowing of his eyes was his only response. Act now, they seemed to say. Act now…or die.

Isolde shoved the fear and pain down deep and allowed the hatred to come forth once more. Its frozen blaze charred her heart…numbed it. Isolde brought the pommels of the swords together. Their intricate groves lined up perfectly in front of her eyes. A few twists and the blades locked together, creating a single weapon, each end fixed with a double-edged sword.

She felt the power surge. The desire to unleash a hurricane throttled her mind. "Let's see if you gentleman can entertain me a little more than this one has," she said and pointed the end of the blade at Gage. "It's been nothing but a disappointment. Something I'm sure he's familiar with."

Volkran and Gage launched themselves at once, Liam a few seconds behind them.

As Gage cleared the table, Isolde sent a gust of wind into one of the chairs and hurled it. The wood shattered against Gage's side, throwing him into the far wall. He crashed to the floor and did not stir.

Spinning around, she caught Volkran's sword with a broad side of her own. The impact forced a grunt from her clenched teeth.

"I have waited a long time for this," Volkran said. Two massive canines had descended over his lips, the black panther clawing its way to the surface. He threw her back with enough force to knock her off the table.

Searing hot agony shot through Isolde's leg as she caught herself. A fresh stream of blood fell down into her boot.

"My, what patience you have," Isolde rasped, twirling the handle between her hands. "All this fuss over me. I'm flattered."

He charged again, the blunt force of his merciless strikes hitting her again and again. Air played at the tips of her fingers and shot forward. A chair was lifted, carried by the currents flowing over Isolde's hand, and was sent flying into the back of Volkran's head. It cracked on impact. Splinters of wood littered the room.

Isolde's arms slumped to her sides. Most of her strength was now gone, swept away by the wind.

Volkran fell to one knee his hand clutching at the wound to the back of his head. Her reprieve was short-lived as Liam launched himself into the attack. Their blades sang a song of beautiful death.

It was a game they had played so many times before. Neither delivered a blow the other could not block. They both knew this had to look convincing. Their blades locked together, forcing them into a standstill. He stared at her, his serious eyes narrowing sharply as he shook his head. She knew he was holding back; she could feel it in each blow. She felt the air stir behind her.

Twisting back, she gripped Liam's wrists, swinging him to the right as she tilted the free side of her blade to block Volkran's silent attack. The weight crushed her beneath them, causing her right knee to strike the stone floor hard.

Before Volkran could move, Isolde swept her left leg out, catching Liam in the ankles. He fell to the floor in a heap, allowing her blade to swing back on Volkran. The lord drove his sword down, blocking her jabs, each time his anger growing. Rolling to his back, Liam threw his legs forward and jumped to his feet. His blade danced in his hand, the light from the fire catching its sharp edge. There was a man to her left and the other her right.

Kicking out, she slammed the heel of her boot into Liam's chin. He flew backwards, his head striking the wall with a sickening crack. He crumbled to the floor, his blade dangled in his limp hand. It tumbled to the stone floor as his eyes fluttered shut.

Volkran pressed forward. Each of his strikes grew more powerful. She could feel her energy being drained, her muscles straining against every attack. She had to end this now!

Volkran struck again. The sword collided with the beautiful handle of her joined blades, severing her beloved weapon in half. Before Isolde could move, Volkran's foot slammed into her chest.

The air left her lungs as she crashed to the floor. Pain radiated through her chest and back, taking every ounce of air with it. Stars shone before her eyes as a foot connected with her ribcage, flipping her onto her stomach. Air refused to fill her now bruised lungs. Pain, agony, and fear coursed through Isolde, pounding at her mind until she could think of nothing else. One side of her chest wouldn't move.

Giving her no reprieve, Volkran latched onto the collar of her jacket and yanked her back. Blinding pain radiated through Isolde's spine as she collided with the table's unforgiving edge. Every ounce of her strength faded, causing her knees to collapse.

Before she could fall, Volkran's massive claw caught her by the front of the jacket, and the leather groaned. His pitiless eyes stared into hers, which were half closed. Without warning, the fist clutching the sword slammed into her cheek and did not stop.

Her vision went black as he continued to unleash thirty years of rage. His knuckles found her face…her stomach…her broken ribs…over and over again. She clutched at the hand holding her up, needing to hold on to something…anything. Her breaths came in short, uneven wheezes, blood saturating her mask.

After it felt like every bone in her face was shattered, Volkran stilled his hands. Her blood painted his skin, hiding the bruises forming on his knuckles. "The great Hood of Blackford Forest," he sneered. Spit flew from his mouth, landing on her mask. She was in too much agony to care. "What a disappointment you are."

A memory surged forward. It pierced through the haze of her pain and fear. She was just a child but she still remembered Volkran's voice. It was the night he killed her father. The night he helped murder her mother and brothers. His voice echoed in her mind. They were the same words he had said to her father. *"What a disappointment you are."*

Her power called to her once more. Its pulse pushed past her pain, into a realm of power she had never experienced before. One that at first glance appeared…endless. A well of untapped energy. It terrified her, the vast ruthlessness that dwelled in the deepest part of herself.

Isolde felt the wind stir around her fingers that gripped Volkran's wrist. The animal beneath purred with delight. Ribbons of silken air snaked over her skin, the ring humming against its current. Their cool, deadly touch slithered up the leather guards of his arm and on to the Lord of Briarhole's bulging neck.

A look of confusion was etched in Volkran's face. But as the air tightened its grip, his confusion melted into terror.

His fingers immediately withdrew, causing her to crumble to the floor. Through the fog of pain, Isolde lay on her back, watching as Volkran clawed furiously at the invisible bond that continued to squeeze. She felt it, the power...the need to kill coursing between her and the ring.

It wanted him dead...This part of her craved death. Volkran's large black eyes bulged as his fingers dug into his flesh, beads of blood running down into his shirt.

There was no escaping this. Her hands twisted at her sides, forcing the band to tighten even more. Blood continued to flow from her mouth and leg, but she didn't care. She wanted him dead, for more reasons than just Zibiah...Isolde knew he deserved to die. The faces of her family flashed in her mind. Her father's handsome, kind face...her mother's fierce, courageous eyes...her loving brothers' protective, cocky smiles...all gone...all dead.

"Don't," Liam murmured, his eyes slowly opening. Reluctantly, Isolde pulled herself from the trance and forced her head to look over. Pain radiated through her back and neck but she hardly noticed. "You are better than this," he said.

But she wasn't better than this. Isolde knew she wasn't. Every part of who she was, wanted Volkran dead. *He deserves it!* the power growled in her mind. Its voice while ancient and beautiful...was utterly terrifying.

But for him...for Liam, she had to be better. Isolde grit her teeth, causing more blood to run down the corners of her mouth. The need for retribution was so potent she couldn't ignore it. She turned back to Volkran who was gasping for air. Wide, bruised bands blossomed across his neck. Streaks of red painted the whites of his eyes that bulged from his skull.

"For me," Liam whispered before once again slipping into oblivion.

Isolde felt the power begin to drain her. After another ten seconds, Lord Volkran's hands fell to his sides, his eyes fluttering shut.

Unforgiving fury burned her heart as Volkran was launched through the air. His body slammed into one of the doors that lined the wall. It broke from the hinges, and a mound of splinters covered the lord's still form. A shriek of fury burst through from her mouth. Taking a deep breath, Isolde rolled onto her stomach and forced her hands beneath her chest. Pain, hot and unforgettable, radiated through her body as she forced her knees beneath her stomach. Tiny shards of bone scrapped beneath the skin on her chest. *It's broken. That bastard broke my sternum.* Catching herself on the side of the table, Isolde used what little strength she had left to stand.

Glancing at Liam, Isolde ran her eyes over his chest to make sure he was still alive. It rose and fell in a steady rhythm. She had given up revenge for him and she prayed he would remember that. Bending down, she picked up the ruined swords, their handles bent and broken.

Taking a few unsteady steps, she looked around for Gage and stopped cold. Only a smear of blood covered the wall where she had left him unconscious. Dread laced through her veins as her instincts rushed forward. Her fingers gripped around the ruined pommels that felt foreign in her grasp.

The destroyed room was quiet, save for the cries of the men below as they worked to stop the fire that had spread to the fortress. Limping, Isolde moved around the table, her swords at the ready. Turning the final corner, Isolde felt the slightest change of the air at her back.

She turned just in time to catch Gage's blade before it delivered a fatal blow. Weakness and pain fought against her will to shove against him. Instead, she brought her knee up, catching him in the groin.

He fell to the floor, gasping for air, his hands cupping his crotch. She was on him in an instant, her knees digging into his arms.

The edges of her blades crisscrossed against his throat. His breath reeked of sweet licorice and whiskey. "Any final words?" Isolde asked, aware of just how much she was going to enjoy watching him die.

Gage's eyes darted between her and the blades. "Go to hell," he said. Hatred and fear filled his face, which gleamed with sweat and blood.

Isolde chuckled and pressed the blades further. A small river of blood snaked down his neck. "By all means...you first."

A scream broke through the night, stilling her hand. Then another...and another. Until a chorus of children screaming in terror filtered through the windows from the courtyard below.

The distraction gave Gage just enough time to throw her off and reach for his sword. She was on her feet again, but not in time to miss the blade that split her side down to the ribs. She cried in pain but kept her swords held tightly. Blood poured from her side, as she moved to gain what little distance she could which wasn't far. The pain in her side drove Isolde to one knee, her hand clutching at the open wound. Blood spilled between her fingers, drenching her gloves.

Gage sauntered toward her, savoring the victory. His dark laugh pierced the night. "The king will be awfully upset about this," he said, her blood trickling down his blade, painting his hand. "But he will have to be content with just your head." He loomed over her, the tip of his sword pressing against her chin. "Now, let's see who's behind the mask."

As Gage reached forward, his balance shifted forward. She knew he would make that particular mistake. It was the moment she had been waiting for. Knocking the blade to the side, Isolde sprang forward and brought the edges of her blades down on his cheeks.

Waterfalls of hot blood cascaded down his cheeks and splashed over the fine, polished wood of the table...then into his gaping mouth. "You bastard!" he screamed, clutching his face. "You bastard!"

Isolde slumped against the wall, her shirt and breeches sticking to her skin. For a moment, she considered killing him then and there...but only for a moment. Kamden's eyes flashed in her mind and the rage, the need for absolution drowned out the thought.

The blades seemed to sing in her hands. Their edges pleaded for Gage's life, begged for more of his blood. But her grip only tightened.

Nothing would have given her greater pleasure than to watch the light drain from Gage's eyes. To be there for his final breath. But the pain that rolled through her in waves told her there wasn't enough time to extract the revenge she wanted. To pull, clip, burn, carve, shred, and tear every ounce of agony from him she could.

The day Kamden was stolen from her was the day she vowed to not grant Gage a quick exit from this world. Reluctantly, Isolde stowed away her swords. Limping down the hall, she said over her shoulder, "You should be grateful for the improvements."

One final gust of wind shot over her shoulder. It collided with Gage's head, forcing it into the side of the table. He fell to the floor in a heap of bloodied muscle and did not move again.

Forcing herself to move, Isolde ripped a piece of unsoiled cloak from her back and pressed it against her side. She made for the now deserted hallway.

No other guards crossed her path as she stumbled through the fortress. Whatever excitement was going on outside had their full attention. Fear and exhaustion coated Isolde's nerves, trying to freeze her in place. Grunting, she shoved against them and continued to move.

As she descended the last flight of stairs, a sense of lightheadedness slowly crept upon her. The edges of her vision blurred; her steps weak and uncoordinated. *Too much blood.* She pressed her hand to her side, biting back a scream. *I've lost too much blood.*

Isolde knew her time was running thin. Every drop of blood that painted Briarhole's halls, was a little bit of her life slipping away. As she reached the final step, her vision swam, and her strength evaporated. Falling forward, she braced for the impact but felt a pair of strong arms envelope her. Instinct had her fighting their grasp, grabbing for her blades at her back, at the bow she clung to her chest.

"It's me," Malaki said, stopping her. "It's me." His bare hand pressed to her cheek, and his eyes stared into hers. "I'm here," he said, his hand cupping the back of her head. "I'm here."

The relief was almost overwhelming. Her eyes stung as she wrapped her arms around him and sighed. "Malaki!" His name faded into her mask. She attempted to take a step but could not make herself move. She slumped into his arms, unable to hold herself up a second longer.

"Isolde?" Malaki said pulling back to look at her. Her eyes fluttered, and the piece of cloak fell from her side to land with a sickening, wet smack on the floor. Streaks of blood painted Malaki's boots and the stones at his feet. "Isolde!" Without waiting, Malaki hoisted her up into his arms and ran.

He crept along the wall, making his way to one of the nearby doors that led to the outskirts of Briarhole. Holding her to his chest, he ducked behind a set of barrels and waited for a trove of soldiers to pass. Once in the clear, he continued.

She breathed a small sigh of relief as they slipped under and through the gate, but the relief was short-lived.

The full moon hung high in the night, its beams casting a light on the dreadful scene before them. All the children from Zibiah's group were being thrown into the caravan. A steel cage far too small for so many bodies was attached to a team of massive horses. Each child received a lash of a whip as they were roughly tossed into the cage. Their cries stirred Isolde awake, piercing her heart.

One stood out from the rest. Her bare back, scarred and mangled, was split open before she was thrown into the cage. A tiny glint of gold shone from around her neck, hidden beneath her dress. "Nyla," Isolde cried. She looked to her, fighting in Malaki's arms. He turned left, away from the river, but he was too late.

She had seen.

One body was lying on the ground before the caravan. They were surrounded by twenty guards, each aiming an arrow at their unmoving chest. A beautiful mass of braids tumbled down their shoulders as the hood was ripped free.

Zibiah.

"No," Isolde mumbled. "Malaki, stop."

He ignored her and continued moving to the wall that led into the forest. Just before they reached the shadowed border of oak and cedar, Isolde saw Zibiah roughly shackled by the wrists and ankles.

"Malaki, stop!" Isolde begged, pushing against him. "We have to help her." Tears fell down her face to join the blood that saturated her mask and hood. "Please stop, Malaki! Please!"

He remained silent, his own breathing labored.

Just as they slipped through the trees and she fell into oblivion, Isolde watched her friend be thrown into an empty cage. One made entirely of elithrium-laced steel. Impenetrable and inescapable. Zibiah's head slammed against the frame. A small line of blood flowing over her sleeping face.

Zibiah rose slowly into a sitting position, her head throbbing. She could feel her power leaving her, the cage and shackles sapping every bit of energy.

Liam stood to the side, his eyes heavy with pain but unyielding. A streak of dried blood fell down the back of his head, over his neck, and across his throat.

"Where are we taking this lot?" one of the guards asked, shoving a thumb at her.

"Elenarta," Liam said, his eyes not meeting Zibiah, whose eyes shone with murderous anger. "No stops." She lunged at him through the cage, her fingers curled into claws and teeth bared.

"Bastard!" she screamed.

"Quiet!" the guard snarled, hitting her exposed fingers with the back of his sword. The bones cracked instantly. She snarled in pain but relented.

"You son of a bitch."

"How very unladylike," a voice said from behind her.

Bile and fury filled her throat as she turned to see her husband and his heir. A wide, swollen band ran around Volkran's neck. His eyes were bloodshot and teary.

"Darling wife," Volkran sneered. "I do hope you enjoy your time in Elenarta. I won't be too far behind you." He rapped the cage with the edge of his blade and chuckled, causing her to jump. "All this time," he said, his eyes raking over her in hatred, "it's been you."

Zibiah stared back at him, but was careful to not show an ounce of the confusion racking her mind. "The Hood...in my house...in my bed. I'm looking forward to seeing you in the capital," her husband said before walking off.

Lauram gazed up at her, his face infuriatingly unreadable. His eyes shifted to Liam but only for a moment. Without a word, he followed after his master and benefactor.

When they were left alone, Zibiah sat against the wall of her temporary prison. Her back to Liam. "I didn't have a choice," Liam said, his voice low.

She wiped at the cut on her head, the wind stinging her torn flesh. "The words of a true coward."

"I'm sorry, Zib." Regret hung in every word he spoke but that meant little. Zibiah knew Liam could do nothing. If he was to tell the truth, he would be doing nothing more than revealing Isolde as the Hood, thereby, killing Thornwood and all who lived there. She knew he wouldn't do it. Nothing would cause him to give up Isolde, not even his own conscious.

Zibiah squeezed her eyes shut and sighed heavily. "Well, at least one good thing came from tonight."

Liam rounded the corner of the cage, directly in her line of sight. His shadowed, tortured gaze ran over the caravan of crying, beaten children. He was unable to hide the shame in his voice. "What good could have possibly come from this?"

"They think they won." Zibiah grinned, eyeing her mask that was tucked in the loop of Liam's belt. "They think they sacked the Hood."

CHAPTER 27

No matter how hard Malaki tried, every punch, every cut, every shattered bone sang Isolde awake as they rode for Thornwood. Versa's feet hammered beneath them. Her legs were moving so fast he knew she felt the danger too. That she knew just as well as he did…Isolde was dying.

"Hold on," Malaki rasped, searing pain radiating down his back as the ripped skin pulled farther apart. It had been a lucky blow from a young soldier as Malaki had snuck back into the fortress. A blow that cut his young life very short. "You have to hold on, Isolde."

"Zibiah!" Isolde cried, and her head bobbed against his chest. "Nyla!" The smell of her blood and tears drifted past him. His heels dug into Versa's sides, pushing her faster into the night.

Blood still trickled from the wound at Isolde's side, spilling out onto Versa's flank. Panic set in as her body went limp in his arms. "No, Isolde!" Malaki roared. "Not now!"

The bear clawed at his restraint as he sent small waves of his healing power into the wound, sealing the vessels that still leaked what little life she had left. It was all he could do, the only healing he could manage until they reached Thornwood. The elithrium in her blood fought his power, neutralized its potency. But enough slipped past to staunch the flow…for now.

Weakness threatened to overtake him as they entered into Thornwood territory. Foam billowed around Versa's mouth, and sweat soaked her now dark gray coat. A small stream of blood flowed from her nose as she pressed on.

"You can't leave me," Malaki growled into Isolde's ear. But she didn't respond; her hands had gone limp around his. Her breathing was shallow and uneven. "Isolde!" he cried, tears falling around his face as his hand gripped the wound at her side.

Gritting his teeth, he pushed his strength into her, willing the wound to close. *She can't die, She can't…she can't!* The familiar taste of fear brushed his mind. The protective numbness that guarded his heart was falling into place. His mind and soul were protecting themselves…preparing him for the blow that would surely kill him.

Malaki refused to think, refused to do anything but keep his hand planted firmly at her side. The hours ticked by, each one more torturous than the last. Familiarity registered as he turned left at the fork in the road. "We're close," he said. "We're almost home, Isolde." But she had been silent for far too long.

Each squeeze of her heart kept his sanity in place. Kept the beast from breaking forward, ending him entirely. The opening of the cave came into view; a small cart and mule lingered just off to the side.

Nan!

Jerking Versa's reins back, he threw himself and Isolde off her back without waiting for her to stop. Versa collapsed onto the ground, her sides heaving with each breath. Isolde's head fell back. Her eyes were shut. A small, uneven breath forced her chest to rise and fall.

"Nan!" Malaki screamed, his voice banging against the walls as he sprinted through the tunnel of rock.

The cave was warm and filled with the scent of freshly baked bread. She had been here preparing for their arrival. The frail woman rose from the table. Her warm blue eyes were wide with terror as she beheld Isolde clutched in his arms. She was nothing but a doll, a plaything torn into pieces and bleeding all over the floor.

"On the bed," she ordered, a steely determination settling into her withered features.

Malaki rushed to the far side of the wide cave where a monstrous four-poster bed resided. He hardly noticed the ridiculous lavishness of it. A sapphire velvet duvet crinkled beneath Isolde's weight as he gently set her down. The canopy above cast a shadow over them, hiding the blood that seeped into the extravagant bedding.

"Remove the jacket," Nan ordered, her hands full of remedies, herbs, and bandages. A faint silver sheen lined her eyes.

Malaki's hands tore at the ruined, wet leather. The material ripped easily, a sick wet sound peeling through the cave. He had been there for her birth. Her nakedness was nothing new to him. But this…he had never seen her body so beaten…so broken.

Black and purple bruises spread from her collarbone, over her sternum, between her breasts and along her ribcages. The bones beneath pressed against the damaged, frail skin. Each breath Isolde took pushed the jagged points further and further. One side of her chest refused to move at all.

Malaki's eyes traveled farther down to her side. A growl escaped his otherwise disciplined lips. It was far worse than he thought. Stark white ribs shined in the light of the fire. Layers of frayed muscle pushed and pulled as she struggled for every breath. The wound ran from the tip of her rib cage and hugged around to the side of her back.

"Nan," he said, his voice a strangled gasp as his hands moved to her without a thought.

She swatted him away, her eyes focused on the small stream of blood pooling at Isolde's side. "I can see it," she rasped. "Do something useful and pull that damn mask off her face. She needs air."

Vulgarity spilled from his lips as the fabric lifted from Isolde's face. One of them had beaten her. A dangerous inferno raged through his chest at the sight of a face he didn't recognize.

Blood and saliva bubbled from her slightly parted lips. A hideous deformity ran along her cheekbones and jawline. Her nose curved in a vicious, nauseating angle. Dried blood ran around her mouth and down onto her chin and neck.

Nan's experienced hands mixed a concoction of herbs in the bowl. "She doesn't need your anger right now, Malaki," she said, her voice far calmer than before. Her eyes were glued to Isolde's mangled face.

He nodded once, his teeth grinding in effort as he forced that white-hot fury down. It burned and charred his heart as he cupped his hands around her face. She gave a small whimper of protest as he probed her cheeks, feeling for the breaks.

"It'll be fine," he whispered. "We'll have you looking like your annoyingly good-looking self in no time."

Malaki closed his eyes, his mind and body reaching out into the world beyond the cave. Into the sleeping forest beyond, life stirred all around him. Bands of energy beamed at his power, urging him to take what he wished.

He had to be careful. If he did not stay focused, he could lose control and take from Nan by mistake. A buck wandered into his path, its life force brimming with power. He pulled at it, sucking the energy from its beating heart and shoving it into Isolde's.

It died instantly. Its carcass fell to the forest floor as Isolde's cheekbones slide back into place. She moaned in protest, pulling away from his gentle fingers.

"Do what you can with her chest," Nan ordered. The mixture in the bowl was now resembling a paste. Thick and pink, it slopped against the sides as Nan stirred furiously. "I can fix the gash but the bones around her heart are yours to mend."

Leaning over, Malaki gently slid his hand under Isolde's back. His palm rested just below her neckline.

"This may hurt, Isolde," he said, his lips brushing her ear. A slight tremor rippled through her body as his free hands rested over the crack in her sternum. Pushing farther into the forest, Malaki searched frantically for anything that held life.

A massive wave of power slammed into him. It rippled from one of the trees just beyond the cave's opening. A tree that served as a grave…a tree…he could not bring himself to pull from. *It would be like killing him all over again.* He moved away from the nearly endless source of power.

After another moment, Malaki stiffened at the creature lurking in the dark. Its massive paws scraped against the earth, the snout rooting through the dirt scavenging for anything it could find. The bear lingered a hundred yards away.

Malaki latched on to the bear's life force and yanked. A moan echoed through the night as the creature fell to the ground dead. Pulling the power forward, Malaki gently pressed it into Isolde's chest and the shattered bones beneath.

Her back arched in protest, a hiss seeping through her clenched teeth. "Easy," he whispered. The bones beneath his fingers forged anew, the strong bond forming once again. "Nearly done." She rested back into his hand. He probed her chest, searching for any more fractures. A few fissures still remained. They would have to wait until the elithrium was out of her system.

Nan tossed the stone utensil aside, "It's ready."

He moved to Isolde's left side, his hand already in place. Dipping her fingers into the paste, Nan spread a heaping mound onto Isolde's side. A cry of pain exploded from her gaping mouth. Her back arched in protest, hands fighting to grab at Nan.

"Isolde," Malaki said, holding her hands in his. The pad of his thumb ran up and down her wrist. "Isolde, it's okay…it's okay."

"Make it stop!" she begged. "It burns! Nan, stop, please!"

"I can't, my rose," Nan said, her fingers working up the length of the cut. Tears fell down her cheeks as she worked. "We have to get the elithrium out of you."

"I don't care!" Isolde cried, another piercing scream echoing into the night.

"I'm sorry," Nan said as she applied another dose into the wound. "I'm so sorry."

"Her calf too," Malaki said, eyes locked on Isolde's that were staring at the ceiling. Tears stained her blazing cheeks. A glow beamed from their depths. He couldn't imagine the war that raged in her mind, the struggle to keep her nature under control in such immense pain.

"Done," Nan said at last. "Roll her to the side."

Carefully, Malaki rolled Isolde over, keeping clear of the gash on her side. The substance once pink and light, had begun to darken, pulling the poison from her system. Nan pulled a knife from her pocket and cut the soaking pant leg free. A gaping hole smiled back at them. Keeping a hand on Isolde's ankles, Nan slathered another helping of the pink mixture into the wound. Isolde screamed again, thrashing against their holds.

"Please…please stop!" she begged, her fingers clawing at Malaki's arms.

"We're almost done," he promised. "Almost." His hands cupped her cheek as tears fell from her open bright eyes.

"How did this happen?" Nan demanded, wrapping a clean bandage around Isolde's calf before signaling for him to lay her back down. The ruined velvet duvet billowed around her broken body.

"She went back," Malaki said, his hand still pressed to her face. "For a child."

"Of course, she did," Nan murmured, her lips pulled tightly.

Malaki looked up. "Would you have expected anything different?"

Wrinkles of her warm, tear-stained cheeks deepened as a loving smile pulled at her lips. "No," she said, her gaze falling to Isolde, "I would have expected nothing less."

The paste at Isolde's side and calf darkened into a sickening black. Nan gently wiped it away from the edges, inspecting the progress. Malaki continued to slowly heal her body, weaving his power into the broken parts.

The bleeding had finally stopped, bringing a sigh of relief to Nan's lips. "Not long," she said. "Where are the others?"

"On their way to the first drop off." Malaki's gaze dropped to floor. Utter failure and self-hatred radiated through him like a brand.

"All of them?"

Malaki shook his head. Strands of blood and sweat soaked ebony hair fell over his brow. He collapsed into a chair beside Isolde's bed, the weight of the night hitting him at last. Pain burned through his back as the wound opened up once again.

Nan's hands stilled, her lips pressing into a thin line. "Who?"

The night rolled by in agonizing flashes of pain and memory.

Pain unlike any Isolde had ever felt burned at her side and leg, as if a red-hot poker had been jammed into her chest and calf.

She begged them to stop, unable to understand why they wouldn't. Faint voices broke through the veils of torture. Soft voices and easy, familiar hands kept the beast at bay. She forced herself away from the pain, to ignore the inferno that savaged her body. Instead, she turned inward to the torture that lay there.

Zibiah and Nyla's faces flashed in her mind. Bloody...broken...*No*. She willed her limbs to move. *I have to reach them!* She fought against the invisible restraints at her wrists and shoulders.

"Isolde," a voice said through the haze. "You must be still."

"I have to get to Zib," she said, her fingers stretching towards the cages bound for Elenarta as they rode off into the night. "We have to save her!"

"We will," another voice said. It was one she recognized. One she would know anywhere.

"Nan?" Isolde's eyes fluttered open. A bead of sweat stung her eyes as she looked up at the canopy of a four-poster bed. Light from the fire danced across a new silken duvet.

"I'm here, my rose," Nan said at her right. A wet cloth dabbed lightly at her brow as Nan smiled down at her.

"Where's Malaki?" she asked trying to push up. "I need to see him. I need to know..." Pain shot through her body like lightening, refusing to let her move an inch more. A small cry leaked through her lips as she tried again.

Nan's fingers pushed her back into the bed with gentle firmness. "He's fine," she said, her head nodding to the other side of the bed. Malaki's massive form was sprawled across one of the large loungers that had been moved to her bedside. A white bandage ran down his right shoulder blade, covering up half the ink of his tattooed back. Thorn-covered veins, etched with names ran underneath the bandages. His hand rested palm up on the bed, next to where hers had been. She sighed, so overcome with relief that fresh tears fell down her now burning cheeks.

Isolde licked her lips and turned back to Nan, who was smiling down at her. "Zib...Nyla."

"I know." Nan gently brushed bloody strands of hair from Isolde's forehead.

"I have to get to them," Isolde said trying again to sit up, only to be pushed down once more.

"Do you want Malaki to tie you down?" Nan threatened, her tone hard.

Isolde scoffed, her temper flaring. "As if he could," she muttered resting back down into the soft goose down bed.

"I'll do it," Malaki said, his voice rumbling through the cave. "Gladly."

"You think ropes can hold me?" Isolde demanded, shooting him a hateful look.

A smirk pulled at the corners of his lips. "I think even Nan could take you right now."

Isolde rolled her eyes in frustration but settled back down in to the bed. "Are the others back?" she asked.

Malaki sighed, his eyes opening as his legs swung around to rest on the floor. "No. But that's not too concerning. It might have taken a little longer to get to the checkpoint."

Isolde forced herself to look at him. "What happened?"

He didn't have to ask what she meant. "We thought most of Gage and Volkran's guards were too busy fighting the fires. The last thing we anticipated was a second battalion to be waiting along the riverbanks." A sharp edge formed onto his features. "Something *Liam* did not mention."

Isolde continued to stare at him. "There were too many," he murmured. "Alaric…Alaric did the only thing he could. He transformed."

Isolde's mouth went dry, dread coating her skin. "As did Galaena," he said, his voice hollow. The mountain lion's fierce growl ripped through Isolde's mind. A flash of claws and teeth burned in her memory. Even then, when she was fully in control, Galaena was terrifying. But now…

Isolde knew the risk, the danger that existed without transforming for so long. To suddenly unleashing that power...It was nearly impossible to rein in, to remember the humanity...Years of raw power were unleashed in the blink of an eye. And nearly thirty years had passed since they last gave themselves over to their animalistic sides.

"Did ...did they transform back?" Nan asked.

Malaki held Isolde's petrified gaze. Her second-in-command, her oldest friend and confidant shook his head. "I don't know."

Isolde shook her head, the stiffness in her neck radiating down her back. "What about Nyla? I thought you put her on the boat."

"I did," Malaki said, his voice raw. "But when she saw you on the wall, being chased by the guards, she jumped overboard, trying to get back to shore...to help." He rested his head in his hands. "I went in after her, tried to get to her...to pull her back. But I couldn't find her." His shoulders sagged as a shaky breath rolled through his chest. "I promised we wouldn't leave her. I promised!"

The next few days were utter hell.

Isolde prowled the confines of the cave when Malaki would allow it and only with his assistance. While she hated having to rely on him to move about...she was grateful for his presence.

"They should be here by now," Isolde said, her fingers clutching at the back of a chair next to the dining table. Weakness still wrecked her body. Nan had applied another layer of the antidote to her wounds. Nearly all of the elithrium had been sapped from her blood, allowing the wounds to slowly heal with Malaki's help. Already, she could feel her body mending itself, making her all the more tired.

"It's a long way to some of those outposts," Malaki said, pulling another chair closer. "And they might have been forced to take a different route."

He motioned for her to sit. The nearly closed wounds of her side and leg barked in protest as she slowly lowered herself down. A hissing sigh ripped through her teeth.

"His blade must have been coated with ground elithrium," Malaki mused. "A new trick for him."

She had been reluctant to tell him what happened, especially her newfound seemingly endless well of power. It scared her. Even now, as the stone shined in the light of the fire, Isolde could feel the potential...the deadly power that lurked within it. And within herself.

"We can't stay here for much longer," she said, shoving the thought away. "Nan can't keep making excuses for our absence. Especially if someone from Elenarta shows up on Thornwood's doorstep."

He ran a finger down the stack of books that littered the table. Nan had brought her favorites from the library. But not even that could distract her.

"One more day," he said. "At least until the wounds close and you can walk without assistance." His eyes roved her face, searching for any defect he had not mended. "At least your face is somewhat presentable again."

She snorted. "My face is always presentable," she said, her wicked emerald eyes flashing. "Even when beaten to a pulp."

A snarl rippled through his teeth. "Volkran will pay for that."

"We can take turns," she offered. The ghost of a smile crept on his face. Reaching over, she took his hand in hers and squeezed. "Thank you."

Malaki bowed his head over their hands, strands of now clean silken hair falling over his eyes. "Always."

Shadows crept along the sides of the walls that led to the outside. Malaki was on his feet in a second, his massive body blocking Isolde. A growl ripped through his teeth.

"We just escaped death, Malaki," the deep, familiar voice said. "Let's not try our luck again."

Isolde forced herself up, her hand cradling the wound at her side. Stepping into the light, she saw the ghosts from her past.

Locks of gold fell from their heads like crowns shining in the sun. Gone were the strands of gray. Smooth, polished skin of radiant youth stretched across their faces. But familiar lines of worry remained, their youthful eyes glued to the bandages at Isolde's side.

"Alaric?" Isolde breathed, a tear falling down her cheek. "Galaena?" Without a word, they rushed past Malaki and gently wrapped her in their arms. Alaric's hand stroked her hair, his forehead resting against her temple. Galaena rested hers on the other side, her flawless cheeks wet.

"Isolde." She sighed, her bell like voice cracking. "Oh, my Isolde."

"I'm sorry," Isolde said, sorrow and shame lacing her words. "I'm so sorry. It's all my fault."

"No, no," said Alaric, pulling back only to cradle her face in his hands. His thumbs brushed the tears from her cheeks. "It was our choice," he said. "You made us see that our time here is not yet done." He kissed her forehead and smiled. "You have nothing to be sorry for."

Guilt still ravaged Isolde's heart; not even his words could serve as a balm. But the joy of seeing them both alive was enough to shove the guilt away to deal with at a later time.

"What happened?" Galaena asked, her eyes still looking over Isolde. She turned to Malaki who had retreated to the mantel. She explained what had happened in the courtyard and the events that followed.

Malaki interjected every so often to explain a point Isolde had purposefully downplayed. "If nearly bleeding to death," he said, his eyes glued to the fire, "or being beaten beyond recognition is nothing…then yes."

She needed to change the subject. "Where are the others?"

As if by magic, they appeared. The tiny, hooded figure lingered in the archway of the cave. Another emerged behind her. Their eyes ran over the scene, eventually finding hers.

"About time," Isolde said, her hand bracing against the table.

Without saying a word, Blyana rushed to Isolde and threw her arms around her neck. She stifled a grunt of pain as Blyana squeezed. "You're alive."

"I won't be if you keep squeezing me like that," Isolde squeaked. Blyana's arms dropped away instantly.

Cillian stepped up, a tired smile sweeping across his face. "It'll take more than that to kill the Hood."

Isolde winked and matched his smile. "Far more." She wrapped her arms around him, and he carefully engulfed her in a hug of his own.

Blyana looked around. "Where are Zibiah and Nyla?" Sorrow and fear drenched Isolde's skin, chilling her to the bone.

"They took them," Malaki said, his hands bracing against the table.

Alaric and Galaena, who stood by the fire both turned. "Where?" Alaric asked.

Malaki met his gaze and Isolde saw a look pass between them. "Elenarta." The name echoed through the cave, sending shivers down Isolde's spine.

Blyana froze, her eyes wide with undiluted fear and rage. A small bit of light began to glow in their depths. "How?" she demanded.

"Gage had a second battalion waiting downriver," Malaki said. "They seized control of the gate as Isolde turned back for a child that had been left behind."

The sound of a carriage approaching stopped them all. Tension swelled in the air as they turned to the cave's opening. The sound of soft footsteps was soon followed by Nan. Isolde's anxiety dissolved, at least for a moment.

Nan's face was grave, her lips pulled into a tight line. "What is it, Nan?" Isolde asked. Her warm eyes glistened, making them all the more beautiful against her copper skin.

"The King's courier was just here," Nan said, handing Isolde an envelope. "I was ordered by penalty of severe punishment, to give you that." It was beautiful. Her callused fingers grazing the elegant thick ebony paper.

Isolde turned the letter over and her blood ran ice cold. The royal seal of the House Tenebriath stared back at her. The eye of a snake set in ruby and gold seemed to look straight through her. "How special I am to receive a letter from the king himself."

Ripping the thick envelope open, Isolde unfolded the letter and angled it towards the light to read the solid gold lettering sprawled across the page.

Lady Isolde Cotheran of Thornwood,

On behalf of His Majesty, King Erebus Tenebriath, it is with great pleasure we extend a personal invitation to this year's Tournament of the Guard at Elenarta. This year marks a great triumph for the kingdom of Arnoria with the capture of thief and rebel sympatizer, The Hood of Blackford Forest and will be celebrated as such.

This invitation is extended not only to you but to your entire household. The king expects your arrival the night before the Tournament begins.

Not a day later.

Until your arrival,

Your faithful king,

His Majesty protector of Arnoria,

Erebus Tenebriath

Isolde's hands were shaking so badly she nearly missed the small side note at the bottom. Its handwriting clearly was different from that of the one above. She knew immediately from the elegant and practiced hand this was a personal note from Erebus himself.

This is not a request, Isolde. I would suggest you not treat it as such.

She read it through three times, refusing to believe what was on the page. Reluctantly, she looked up at Nan, whose eyes were wide and glued to hers. Wordlessly, Isolde handed the note over to Nan, who read it out loud.

When she finished, Nan's lips tightened and her were eyes hard with resolve.

"So, they believe Zibiah is the Hood," Galaena said. "Well, that was unexpected."

"Not entirely," Isolde said, biting her thumbnail. "They need a success where the Hood is concerned. Neither Gage nor Volkran can survive another failure. She is their scape goat. Also, Gage extended his personal invitation as well, but in a more aggressive manner. At least this was more civil."

"When was this?" Malaki demanded, his eyes flashing. "Why did you not tell us?"

"I've been a little busy," Isolde murmured. He scoffed, clearly angry. Isolde ignored him. "We can use this to our advantage. It might look strange if I took Gage up on his offer to attend after Briarhole and my repeated rejections. But, now I have no choice. I have a legitimate excuse."

"A way in," Blyana said.

Her friend slowly met her gaze. For a breath, they stared at each other. A flicker of understanding and hope shined in Blyana's eyes.

Isolde nodded. "A way in."

They all stood in silence as realization rose with the dawn of the day. Fear Isolde had not faced in so long resurfaced. Its cold, familiar fingers gripped her heart in an unforgiving vice. She was attending the Tournament of the Guard…and the king, in all his wretched, traitorous glory would be there.

Her power rose up in response, igniting an old hatred. It snuffed out that fear in an instant. A resolve set into Isolde's bones as she lifted her gaze to the others. They stared back with the same determination, the same craving for retribution.

They were heading into the capitol, into Elenarta. Once standing as the crowning jewel of Arnoria, Elenarta now stood as a beacon of debauchery, corruption, and death. It was a place that bred nightmares and shadows.

Isolde felt the monster stir beneath her skin. That endless well of savage power opened up into a terrifying chasm. Faces of so many flashed in her mind. Faces of those long since turned to ash…faces of those she failed at Briarhole…at Foxclove…and all the others that came before them.

The creature within stood at attention. Its teeth bared in a vicious smile. It too remembered.

"Erebus believes he's won," Isolde said, the hint of a vengeful, cruel grin playing on her lips. "Let's show him the game has only just begun."

ACKNOWLEDGMENTS

This story has been in my heart since I was eighteen years old. At the time, I had the idea for the story but not the heart. That heart wouldn't come along for several years and it came in the form of a tragedy. A young life was cut far too short for very selfish, horrible reasons. As nurses, we tend to blame ourselves when we can't save someone. This little one was no exception for me. I still carry that guilt with me, every single day. This book has been a way for me to cope with those feelings that at times feel too much to bear. At least through this series, that he will get to live on in some way. So, this is for him. For the boy, I will never forget. Who deserved so much more.

There are so many people I have to thank for helping bring this book into reality.

My parents- I can't thank you both enough for letting me strive for my dream of being an author. Thank you for always supporting me and encouraging me to do what I love. I love you more than I can possibly say.

Dr. Michael Burduck- You are still one of the funniest professors I have met but also one of the scariest. Thank you for pushing us to see the beauty and importance of literature.

Trevor Barrett at Barrett Knives-Your weapons are pieces of art and I am so happy to have found your page when I did. They helped inspire so many weapons in this book. Never stop doing what you love.

Megan Walker- Thank you for always supporting me. You are a beautiful friend that I am so blessed and thankful to have in my life.

My amazing beta readers- you guys are the jam to my PB&J sandwich. Thank you for taking the time to read Thief of Sorrows in its infant stage.

Alice Powers- You have created an absolute stunning piece of artwork that I will cherish forever. I am so blessed to have you as my cover artist.

Katie Wolf- Thank you for your encouragement and wisdom. This book would not be what is today without you.

A special thank you to Halestorm, Breaking Benjamin, Howard Shore, John Williams, and Lindsey Stirling for creating music that inspired Thief of Sorrows series.

And to you, my dear reader. Thank you for going on this journey with Isolde and the cadre. I hope you enjoy where the road leads you throughout the series. However, I would like to take this opportunity to apologize for what is to come. It's okay to cry. Believe me, I did.

ABOUT THE AUTHOR

Kristen (Kris) Long is the author of the Thief of Sorrows series. She is a graduate of Tennessee Tech University with a degree in Biology and Nursing. When Covid hit, Kris left her home to become an Emergency Room travel nurse. It is her dream to one day leave her stethoscope behind and become a full-time author. She is happiest sitting on the front porch reading and looking up at the mountains in her home town of Whitwell, TN. Her favorite books include: A Court of Mist and Fury by Sarah J. Maas, Dracula by Bram Stoker, Jane Eyre by Charlotte Bronte, and The Book Thief by Markus **Zusak**

CPSIA information can be obtained
at www.ICGtesting.com
Printed in the USA
BVHW040850100223
658270BV00006B/305

9 781570 754715